PRAISE FOR

SONATA IN WAX

"*Sonata in Wax* is a masterful tale of art and ambition, war and illness, desire and discovery. Exquisitely crafted and vividly attuned to the intricacies of its fascinating characters, Hamlin's novel sweeps across a century, unfurling the secrets of a sonata that becomes at once a totem of genius and the forbidden. I've rarely read a novel where music is such an astounding life force of its construction. This is a beautiful book, symphonic in scale, immersive in its depths, and morally complex in vision."

—STEVEN SCHWARTZ, author of *The Tenderest of Strings*

"With the beauty and build of great classical music, *Sonata in Wax* interweaves a modern-day mystery with a World War I–era drama to create a novel unlike any I've read. Hamlin's characters resonate with vitality, their struggles with poignancy and danger. When the threads finally entwine and the crescendo arrives, it does so with symphonic force. *Sonata in Wax* is a bravura performance from a writer at the top of his game."

—PAUL COHEN, author of *The Glumshack*

"In Edward Hamlin's brilliant novel, past and present merge when a lost sonata's restored beauty sheds light on the ravages of war and intergenerational trauma. Both epic and intimate, *Sonata in Wax* is a triumph of storytelling."

—BRENDAN NEIL CASEY, author of *She That Lay Silent-like upon Our Shore*

"*Sonata in Wax* is pitch perfect. Like the mysterious musical composition at its heart, the novel twists and plumbs towards a tumultuous and satisfying finish. Part homage and part elegy, *Sonata in Wax* celebrates musical heritage, and honors the unsung heroes whose ingenuity and sacrifice help art and humanity survive."

—Rachel Swearingen, author of *How to Walk on Water*

"What a feast! Edward Hamlin's *Sonata in Wax* features what I love best in a novel—theft, lies, betrayal, music, and a time-defying mystery—all written in Hamlin's lyrical and captivating style. A gorgeous book, and not to be missed."

—Erika Krouse, author of *Tell Me Everything: The Story of a Private Investigation*

"Sometimes you want a single movement, a slip of a novel that won't weigh you down for long. And sometimes you want to stay and indulge in the novelist's richly imagined world. *Sonata in Wax* offers the latter experience, driving the reader toward an inevitable end she dreads reaching . . . Hamlin pays for and earns the ending to this exquisite novel, full of drama and humanity and tragedy and rescue and truth and lies and heritage and . . . music, glorious music."

—Kathryn Eastburn, *The Rocky Mountain Reader*

Writer and composer Hamlin (*Night in Erg Chebbi and Other Stories*) unspools an intriguing epic about a mysterious century-old sonata . . . Hamlin holds the reader's attention with his impassioned depictions of Ben's and Elisabeth's mutual love for music. Musicologists and lay readers alike will find much to enjoy.

—*Publishers Weekly*

Sonata in Wax

A NOVEL BY

Edward Hamlin

Sonata in Wax

GREEN CITY BOOKS
Bend, OR

First Edition
Designed by Isaac Peterson
Cover photograph by Edward Hamlin
Back cover photograph and author photo by Adam Dooley

Library of Congress Cataloging-in-Publication Data has been applied for.
Paperback ISBN: 978-196310119-5
Hardcover ISBN: 978-196310100-3
Epub ISBN: 978-196310103-4

23 24 LSC 10 9 8 7 6 5 4 3 2 1

SONATA IN WAX

A NOVEL BY
EDWARD HAMLIN

Since I was able to enjoy everything this sonata had to give me only in a succession of hearings, I never possessed it in its entirety: it was like life itself. But, less disappointing than life, great works of art do not begin by giving us the best of themselves.

— Marcel Proust, *Within a Budding Grove*

THE SONATA

Prélude

Andante

Allegro

Adagio

Appassionato

PRÉLUDE

THE MUSIC is a fold in time. Given just a few piano notes—the quiet opening phrase, say, hovering like smoke—Ben is transported straight back to the moment of discovery, every detail of time and place intact. The muted, undersea lighting of the Studio A control booth where he's sat beside Itzhak Perlman and Daniel Barenboim and so many other brilliant players over the years, listening to breathtaking music recorded only moments before. The companionable glow of his meters and indicator lights. The tang of stale coffee from a mug forgotten atop the microphone safe. The smooth glide of the faders under his expert fingers. And the vague sense of Chicago, somehow, roaring about its business just beyond the soundproof walls, the subsonic rumble of buses and the screech of El trains, the airhorns trumpeting from the ballpark, the snatches of mariachi and hip-hop and rowdy banter along the sidewalks—the city's soundscape felt rather than heard, a raucous shivaree that never lets up.

All this will snap back in an instant whenever Ben hears even the smallest fragment of the lost sonata, blazing through his heart without losing a single watt of its electricity.

THE PIECE HAUNTS HIM LIKE the voice of a missing child. Tender and untouchable, it murmurs in the back of his mind as he wanders home from the studio on rainy evenings, sings to him as he dawdles over his solitary dinners. The unknown pianist churns through darker chords as Ben hurries past the hallway mirror, then listens in bemused silence when he sits down at the piano to unwind with a little jazz. On some mornings he's jolted awake by the breakneck Allegro and springs from bed feeling better than ever, perfectly steady on his feet, almost fully recovered—only to have the music snatch its energy back, and his along with it. But as mercurial as the sonata is, he's grateful for its company when the house fills with stillness, when all is a little too quiet in his life.

I

For weeks now Ben's kept his discovery to himself. He's played the strange piece for no one. In every spare moment, meanwhile, he's hammered away at his amateurish research, trying to identify composer and performer, trying to make musical sense of what he's hearing. He's listened to the crackly recording countless times, by day and by night, at home and at work, on cheap earbuds and on Studio A's thirty-thousand-dollar speaker rig. But the deeper he goes, the more he's aware of his own limitations. It's a job for a scholar, not an enthusiast. More often than not it feels like a lost cause, a problem with no real solution. Pure folly.

He forges ahead nevertheless, because he has to. He can't let it go. Night after night, day after day, he scours the literature on early twentieth-century French piano music, listening to Debussy and Ravel and Satie for hours on end until the fierce ringing in his left ear forces him to stop. Like some befuddled philosopher he fills a notebook with stray facts, wild guesses, tenuous theories that only confuse him more, bringing him no closer to the answers he needs. The only thing that's clear, lately, is that he's badly out of his depth. While it's true that there's an expensive piano in his living room and a piano performance diploma somewhere in a bottom drawer of his life, he's just never done this kind of detective work. Wrung out, he loses heart and gives up. Then begins again.

AT TIMES HE'S WISHED ROBIN WAS THERE to kick around ideas, then reminded himself of all the reasons why it's better she's not. Though everything's changed between them, he certainly hasn't forgotten her profound musical intuition, the way she can go straight to the heart of a piece on the very first hearing. It's one of the many things that make her such a fine musician.

Robin would hear things in the sonata he doesn't. She'd take it apart measure by measure, study its inner workings and reassemble it without missing a beat, quickly grasping the composer's ambitions. He's watched her do it a thousand times. Bartók, Górecki, even Bach—he owes his love for each of them largely to her. The memory of listening to music with his brilliant wife, of hearing her revel in its glories late into the night, is precious to him.

There are other moments Ben misses—so many. The way she'd nestle against his neck, jet-lagged and exhausted, when he'd collect her at O'Hare after a grueling tour, horns blaring in the arrivals lane, her body releasing itself into his like a quiet shift of earth. On summer mornings, the scent of sleep she'd leave on the pillow if she rose before he did. On winter evenings, stretched out on the sofa opposite one another with her feet tucked against his chest, the wriggle of her toes inside socks stolen from his drawer. The tiny tattoo of a sixteenth note on the inside of her thigh, so high up that only a lover or a doctor would ever come across it.

In the back of the bedroom closet there's a grocery bag with a black sweater crumpled inside it, a stray left behind in the chaos of her move-out. A few filaments of fine bronze hair still cling to the cashmere, a fading trace of her Lancôme. At the bottom of the bag is a register slip listing the ingredients for a dinner they must have shared, long ago: lemon risotto with prawns, he's deduced, an arugula salad, the lazy splurge of a store-bought blueberry pie. An ordinary Saturday evening in their long life together. Robin making the salad, he the risotto. A glass of yesterday's wine passed back and forth between them while they cook. Ben's known about the grocery bag and its contents for some time now but leaves it just where it is, wary of its power to harm him. Or perhaps he's holding it in reserve—for what, exactly, he couldn't say.

If she were still in his life they'd listen to the sonata according to their old ritual, lying side by side in darkness on the Moroccan tribal rug in the living room, the music spreading over them like a Saharan sky full of stars. But Robin's not here: in the darkness it's only him, alone with the starry mystery of a piece of music he may never fully understand.

GENIUS IS THE ONLY WORD for what Ben hears on that first late-summer afternoon in Studio A. Cueing up the digitized recording, the Counterpoint staff already scattering into the stifling city streets on bikes and buses, he has no inkling of the explosion the sonata's about to set off in his life. He certainly can't imagine how quickly it will turn him into a liar and a fool. Auditioning the

3

century-old track is a last chore to be knocked off before going home, nothing more.

He clicks the Play button. A percussive pop, then a long stretch of dead air . . . though *dead* is hardly the word for the chaos that bursts from the monitors. The sound is more like a sky full of locusts. There's no telling what lies on the other side of it. Ben tilts back in his chair, interrogating the spitting noise with a specialist's ear, already considering ways to neutralize it. He's been at this for three decades now and is among the best in the business, but he's no miracle worker. The hiss and crackle threaten to smother the music the moment it's born. But the noise may be the least of his worries. At four seconds there's a sudden dropout: the needle plunges into a divot on the original recording surface, gouging into the wax like a power tool, an excruciating shriek filling the control booth. The digital track replicates the analog disaster with the grim fidelity of a photographer at a hanging. Ben trims his faders quickly, bringing the gain down so it's bearable. But after a few beats the needle claws its way back out of the rut. Seeing its opening, the static roars back in with a vengeance, loose and feral, back on the warpath. There's no stopping it now.

At last—a relief—the invisible pianist arrives. Four notes pirouette through the control booth, lighter than air. Despite the hiss and crackle, despite the ten long decades that have passed since the player touched the keys, the final note rings like a chime. To Ben's practiced ear it sounds like the performer's in a small, resonant space, maybe a music room or salon, certainly not a hall. Even on the crude recording he can hear the sonic signature of a quality piano—a ballroom grand, if he had to guess, a bit too big for the room. But after the brief arpeggio the music disappears without a trace. The pianist absconds from the scene.

Ben nudges his faders up: nothing but noise. The pianist's gone off the air.

"That's it?" he says, puzzled. "Can't be."

Only after five seconds, far longer than his musical sense tells him is right, is the opening phrase answered by another. The sonata tumbles headlong into a minor key, landing on a moody, complex chord that utterly delights him. He didn't see this coming, after the feather-light, optimistic opening notes. Through the roaring locusts, a darker bell tolls. A conversation begins. Ben shifts in his chair, intrigued.

As the sonata unfolds he listens with rising excitement. He's fascinated by the sly feints and attacks, the daring melodic turns, the thread of dissonance that shuttles through the playing. Jazz chords surface and then vanish without explanation, decades ahead of their time. At a certain point the pianist sprints into double time, then triple time, ripping through a passage so devilishly complex that Ben can't begin to track it. The music is boundlessly curious, eager to trespass and transgress and build anew. Even today it would be considered avant-garde—how could it possibly be a century old? And the unknown player is a virtuoso by any measure. Every second of the recording beguiles.

Ben scrambles to his feet and begins to pace the room with hands shoved in jeans pockets, galvanized by what he's hearing, incapable of sitting still. His legs waver under him, weak and fickle; his head spins with a faint sidereal wobble. When he passes the studio door he has to clutch the handle to keep from falling off his feet. But the invisible pianist has shifted him completely outside of himself. For once his body's failures barely distress him.

The hiss on the old recording no longer matters, either. The ravishing music shakes it off like a dusting of snow. He certainly never expected anything like this. He was expecting—dreading—fifteen or twenty minutes of tedious, homemade parlor music, a bit of shaky Gilbert and Sullivan or Couperin played by some well-meaning amateur a century ago. What's flowing from the monitors on this Chicago afternoon is on another plane entirely. It's the direct transmission of a vision. As the recording comes to a close Ben sees the lost sonata for what it is: a dream of modernity, dazzling and feverish and wild as only the truest dreams are.

FIRST MOVEMENT
Andante

CHICAGO

SEPTEMBER 2018

I.

EDISON COMES HOME

AFTER LOCKING UP THE STUDIO on that first evening Ben walks slowly home through the sweltering city, a bulky package tucked into his messenger bag. MR. BENJAMIN WEIL, CREATIVE DIRECTOR, COUNTERPOINT STUDIOS reads the carefully typed label, CONFIDENTIAL. The return address is for the Wooden Arabian, an antique shop in Belfast, Maine. Inside the package sits a spirited letter from one Willa Blount, a set of five wax recording cylinders in bubble wrap, and a jump drive with the raw audio he's been listening to—a first digital capture of the original recording, etched into the cylinders while the Great War was raging.

The house is quiet and cool, a blessed refuge. Ben's planned on his usual jog along the lakeshore before fixing dinner, but after a long walk home through marshy heat and bus exhaust it's the last thing he cares to do. And there's a question of balance: only yesterday, veering onto the easy gravel path along Montrose Harbor, he'd stumbled over nothing at all and fallen hard, skinning his knees like a boy knocked down in a schoolyard fight. Hardly serious damage—more of an embarrassment, really, when a watery-eyed old man helped him to his feet—but distressing nonetheless. It wasn't the first time he'd fallen for no reason.

"See somebody, for chrissakes," the old man said as Ben picked gravel from the heel of his hand. "A doctor! You fell why? Ask yourself." The man leaned in, crowding him. "Look, I was an oral surgeon for forty-eight years," he rasped before shuffling off in his rubber sandals, his authority on all medical matters thus established. The odd encounter, coming on the heels of a fall that never should have happened, dogged Ben all the way home.

The old man had a point. Between bouts of vertigo and the urgent ringing in his left ear it's become harder to pretend nothing's wrong. He should see a doctor—yes—but the thought of it only makes his head spin faster. The plain truth is that he's been losing control of his body since June and has done nothing to find out why.

Instead he's tried to seize back the wheel, tried to power through. Sometimes a run tamps down the vertigo; sometimes it throws him to the ground. Alcohol deadens the ringing, but a second glass of wine can send him reeling. Long work days take his mind off the situation for a while, then fatigue makes the ceiling spin when he lies down to sleep. Through the endless nights his thoughts stumble down one blind alley after another, colliding with brain tumors, Parkinson's, ALS, maladies he's never heard of, diseases his fear conjures out of thin air.

The final weeks with his mother, paralyzed in her hospice bed by the spinal cord tumor that would kill her, are never far from his thoughts. In the early stages Sylvia Weil stumbled too, reeling around her spotless apartment like a woman on a bender, toppling stools and end tables, terrifying herself. Ben can't help but relive it. It's all too easy to line up his symptoms against hers. Yet in the morning he gets to his unsteady feet and tries to go about his day as if nothing's wrong. Clings to his routines stubbornly, knowing in his heart that he can't outrun whatever's chasing him.

At this moment, though, his head is still and steady. Ben scoops the mail from under the slot and flips quickly through the circulars and *To Resident* clutter, his thoughts elsewhere. The sticky walk home has left him wanting a shower. For fifteen minutes he lets the plashing water settle his mind, the stream not much warmer than the atmosphere outside. After putting on clean clothes he opens a beer and settles himself at the dining room table, unbuckling the messenger bag in his dead-quiet home.

With curatorial care Ben unwraps the package from the Wooden Arabian, sets the envelope aside and undoes the bubble wrap to lay bare the relics, source of his delight.

A bronze sun angles through the windows to set the room aglow. Before him on the table sit five cylindrical boxes a little smaller than soup cans, the old cardboard abraded and tallow colored. Edison Gold Moulded Records, the labels read, Echo All Over the World. On the back of each box is a cameo of the famous inventor, debonair and intense, the deep-set eyes suggesting late nights at the lab bench, the bow tie knotted with an engineer's precision. The signature below the portrait has a look of painstaking penmanship about it, as if the signer were a schoolboy not entirely comfortable with cursive.

The lid of each box is hand-labeled with the word *Sonata*—as if anyone would know exactly which sonata—followed by a sequence number. The piece must have been recorded in sections to overcome the limitations of the medium. In the studio this afternoon, as a first order of business, Ben had spliced the digital files together to get a sense of the whole, planning to smooth the transitions later.

He nudges the cap off one of the boxes. Inside, cosseted in batting, sits a rigid spool, precision-turned like a machine part. Ben plucks it out and stands it on the table, feeling all his breath leave him in a gust. It's a thing of beauty: a perfect cylinder of cobalt blue, lustrous and refined as a hand-blown vase. It is also, unmistakably, a piece of vintage technology, casually elegant in the manner of hand-tooled brass telescopes and tortoiseshell fountain pens. Whoever chose such a blue had something to say to the world, something to sing out. It's hard to imagine it was the magician of Menlo Park.

But what matters is the signal the cylinder carries. Leaning in close, Ben can just make out the faint pattern of grooves etched by a long-ago stylus, interrupted in several places by cruel nicks and a wandering hairline scratch: the wayward path of the sonata, rutted as a back-country trail.

As he studies the cylinder, the sun dips below the house across the street and casts the relics into shadow. At the same moment he becomes aware of the scent of meat on a grill. Somehow it's slipped through the air conditioning and into the house. Incredible that the neighbors would think to barbecue in such punishing weather, but it wouldn't be the first time. Life rattles on regardless. A child's squeal twirls up the gangway and disappears, then reappears somewhere behind the house next door.

The beautiful Farahani kids—gifted with Persian genes on their father's side, Minnesota Swedish genes on their mother's—will be roistering in the backyard, oblivious to the heat, as their father

Behrouz prods at kebabs with the same hellbent zeal he brings to everything. Nothing slows the man down. Lean as a greyhound, he'll be sweating out Coronas now as fast as he can put them away. Meanwhile Eva Farahani will be occupying herself in her cool kitchen. Good people; good neighbors who took care of him when he needed it most, through the bleak winter months after Robin left. The scent of their dinner makes his stomach rumble.

In the dining room's cool twilight Ben slips out Willa Blount's letter and spreads it across the table, the tidy cursive pleasing to the eye. Surely the work of a fountain pen, which seems only fitting for an antiquarian. When he skimmed the letter this morning—his assistant setting up mikes for a session, the frazzled temp cursing at the laser printer, Ben's office ablaze with summer sun whose heat bled right through the industrial-grade windows—he imagined his correspondent to be some starchy New England matron who was selling off family heirlooms to keep herself afloat. But no: Willa's a bona fide antiques dealer, even if she seems to have no interest in selling the antiques sitting before him now. She's entrusted them to him strictly in the name of music. Now that he's heard the sonata, he can understand why.

II.

KINDEST REGARDS

DEAR MR. WEIL, Willa writes,

Thank you for taking on my modest project. I'm told you're
the best in the business, so if anyone can make sense of these
recordings, I'm sure you can.

Enclosed are the original wax cylinders, as well as digitalized
versions made by a client of mine who collects vintage
Graphophones. Peter's extracted the audio to the best of his
abilities, using (he asked me to tell you) a vintage Dog and
Baby stylus purchased from an English specialty supplier. He's
quite passionate about his work, so I assume he's recovered
whatever can be saved, but please feel free to give it a go yourself. I'm sure you can scare up a functioning Graphophone in
Chicago.

I believe the cylinders were part of the original inventory of
my shop, which opened its doors in 1922. The ledger lists the
consigner as simply "Family," with the offer price shown as
"NFS." In our business that means Not for Sale, which is how
the lot wound up in our overflow storage, tucked away who
knows how many years ago in a mislabeled crate.

What will be more interesting to you is the descriptive note in
the ledger. This indicates that the lot consisted of five Edison
Gold Moulded wax cylinders, in fair condition, with contents
identified as follows:

Oct. 1, 1917 home recording, Aigremont, Winchester Mass.,
first of five. American debut of Fr. piano sonata. Performed by
J Garnier for an invited audience.

Sonata recording pt two.
Sonata recording pt three.
Sonata recording pt four.
Sonata recording final pt.

I can add to this that "Aigremont" refers to the mansion of
the Oren Sanborn family in Winchester, Massachusetts,
just outside Boston—Oren was the son of James Solomon
Sanborn, co-founder of Chase and Sanborn Coffee. C&S
was a household name when I was a girl, but it's pretty much
disappeared now. About the only place you'll find their coffee
these days is in office supply stores, in a five-pound can with
the Styrofoam cups and creamer and break room supplies. No
great loss to the world of coffee, I suspect, though being a tea
drinker myself I'm in no position to say.

I mentioned that the ledger identifies the Consigner as simply
"Family." This, too, points to the Sanborns. Why? Because the
original owner of my shop was Oren's daughter Helen, who
grew up at Aigremont. At the time of the recording Helen
would have been an eligible debutante; an heiress, technically,
though the family fortune was being frittered away by a father
with a weakness for show horses and yachts. All that coffee
money spared Oren the need to work, but his pockets weren't
quite as deep as he thought. By the time his wife showed
him the door he didn't have two pennies to rub together.
Aigremont was sold to speculators for a song.

After this unfortunate turn of events the Sanborns stopped
reproducing entirely. Interesting, isn't it? Like something from
the animal kingdom. Only one Sanborn has survived to the
present day, and she's childless—when she's gone, the line will
be extinct.

All of which brings us round to the sonata. Of course the
sound quality of the recording is poor, but I found the music
astonishing, Mr. Weil—although bewildering might be the
better word. I'm not ashamed to say that I didn't understand

a single note. But I'm as certain as certain can be that this sonata deserves to be heard. As does that pianist, J. Garnier, who's every bit as astonishing as the music itself, wouldn't you say?

So, then—while I hope you can improve on the audio quality, the music is what's important to me. That "American debut of Fr. piano sonata" note in the ledger certainly suggests it may be of historical interest. With your background and contacts in the classical music world, I'm hopeful you can identify it. It may be a known piece, nothing notable about it. Maybe you'll recognize it right out of the gate. But perhaps it's something far more precious. At this point I'd just like to know.

Enclosed is a check to get you launched. I hope it's enough. If so, please begin work. I'll anxiously await your report.

Kindest regards,

Willa S. Blount

BEN FOLDS THE LETTER and slips it back in the envelope, considering how to proceed. The first step, obviously, is to do what he can to restore the audio, work that will have to be squeezed in between recording sessions and studio business. It happens to be a particularly busy time at Counterpoint. The pianist Ana Clara Matta has several more Debussy préludes to record for her new CD, having fallen far behind schedule thanks to a hyperextended tendon. Then there is Jean Artigue, an acoustician who's traveling all the way from Paris to sonically map Studio A as part of some academic research project. In the midst of it all the Swiss soprano Constance Pik is flying in to perform with the Chicago Symphony, which means a concert, a CSO fundraiser, and a drop-in at Counterpoint where she recorded a set of Mozart arias, just after 9/11, that won her a Grammy. All of it will steal time from Willa Blount's sonata.

But already Ben feels the music sinking its hooks into him. It's like no piece of period music he's ever heard. Others were experimenting with dissonance in 1917, it's true, but the sonata's dissonant passages have an animal power to them that Schoenberg's bloodless investigations certainly never did. And the jazz passages—they're just inexplicable. Half a century ahead of their time, as if the composer had beamed into Birdland circa 1960 and taken everything he heard right back to the piano. To Ben's knowledge, some of the harmonic concepts behind them didn't even exist in 1917. The sonata is full of such mysteries. He'd like nothing more than to clear his calendar for it, to dig in and get to the bottom of things, but at the moment he doesn't have the luxury.

He gazes at the old cylinders standing before him on the dining room table. They gaze back, inscrutable and austere. One is turned so that the cameo of Edison is visible: the sly old inventor stares back from across the years, cagey and confident and by then unimaginably rich, Ben imagines. Even through the faded paper the ego sings out. Gathering the cylinders up gently, he crosses into the living room and arranges them on the music stand of the piano, where it seems to him they belong.

In the foyer the doorbell rings. He slips away to answer it, leaving the Edisons to confer in the gloaming.

Oliver Farahani stands on the stoop—taller than Ben at only fourteen, dark eyes flicking shyly downward, a platter of kebabs and rice in his hands. It's enough to feed a family of four.

"From us," the boy says and smiles nervously, slipping off into the murky heat before Ben can send back his thanks.

III.

ANA CLARA AT PLAY

IN THE MORNING Ana Clara Matta arrives late, as usual, for her Debussy session.

"Sorry, people," she says as she strides past the reception desk. "The bloody rain."

With an unapologetic smile she slips into the anteroom outside Studio A and stands her purple umbrella against the wall to dry. It's not the weather that's made her late; it's her tendency to operate on Brazilian time. Despite a childhood spent in London as the daughter of Brazilian diplomats, she's never lost her casual attitude toward clocks and calendars. It doesn't matter to her that the billing clock starts running from the scheduled session time rather than the time of her arrival; it's her record company's money, and once she sits down to play she rarely needs more than a single take to nail a recording. What Ana Clara Matta lacks in punctuality she makes up for in efficiency. She's famously well-rehearsed.

It's been raining since sometime in the night, the storm settling in for a methodical siege. Scattered all through the Counterpoint loft are drenched backpacks, rain-slicked ponchos, soaked tennis shoes propped against vents to dry. Half the staff are barefoot. Even for a Friday the mood is casual. As the artist gets herself organized, slipping off jacket and boots and shaking out her damp black curls, a roll of thunder overwhelms the traffic noise down on Clybourn.

The maestra sends Ben a sharp look—is the storm going to be a problem?

Though the recording suites are heavily soundproofed, thunder does occasionally bleed through, ruining a take. Ben isn't particularly concerned, having just seen to the installation of massive new bass traps behind the redwood walls.

"We're fine," he assures his artist. "How's the arm?"

"The tendon's shite. It's the damp." She holds out the slender forearm with its delicate gold bracelet and powerful hand, sliding up the sleeve and making a fist. "You see?"

He sees nothing amiss; only russet skin and a fine weave of muscles beneath it.

They sit down at the console to review her pieces. On the other side of the glass, Ben's assistant, Eliza James, bends over the Steinway in headphones, rechecking her mike positions. Though they've used the same setup countless times, each player's touch and body position are unique; the way a player hunkers down or rears back or sways with passion can subtly alter the recorded sound. It's Eliza's mastery of the nuances that makes her priceless.

Studio A is renowned for its flawless acoustics. The high, lovely redwood ceiling touches each note for a fleeting instant and sends it back sweetly, the 1.15-second reverberation time giving recordings just the spaciousness players crave. The thick Persian rug under the piano absorbs just enough of the ceiling's reflections to tighten the signal. Complex baffles on the walls, custom-designed by one of the best acoustic engineers on the planet, keep the midrange orderly and clean. The result is a recorded sound that might as well have been captured inside the player's own head. All this Eliza understands intimately. Meticulous and levelheaded, she's been at Counterpoint for nearly fifteen years. With her in the suite Ben can devote full attention to his artists.

Just now he's pretending to study the score for the *Canope* as Ana Clara walks him through it, cross-legged in black tights on the other chair, rimless bifocals perched on her small, beaked nose. She sings her way through certain phrases in double time, all business. At forty-six she's considered one of the world's foremost interpreters of French piano music; the Debussy CD will be her eleventh Counterpoint recording. Though her label has sprawling studios of its own in Los Angeles, she insists on recording here, with Ben Weil on the board. He's the only producer she'll work with.

Today's préludes are brief and impressionistic, and Ben has no real engineering concerns. What catches his attention, spurred somehow by the jasmine scent of his artist's damp curls, is Debussy's dynamic note at the top of the score: *Très calme et doucement triste.*

Very calm and gently sad . . . how well the phrase might have described the man Ben was in those first untethered days after uncovering Robin's affair, before the anger roared in. Debussy knew.

AT THE PIANO, Ana Clara pulls on her famous Punjabi slippers with their goat-leather soles and ornate beadwork. There can be no performance without them. She once delayed a recital in Berlin for forty minutes while a panicked minder dashed from the Konzerthaus to the Ritz-Carlton to retrieve the forgotten footwear, an incident that did not amuse the Germans. Now she stretches her body systematically, curling left and right, twisting gently on the bench, working her fingers one by one. The troubled forearm receives a brisk, expert massage. She goes through her paces like a runner preparing for a championship sprint, her concentration supreme, her thin lips drawn to a frown.

"Go," she says finally, nodding toward the control booth, and with a click of the mouse Ben starts recording. Debussy's music begins to flow from the Steinway's hammers, pulsing across gold-spattered microphone diaphragms through cables and into the mixing console where it sets a bank of meters in motion. On the wide computer monitor a green waveform begins to scroll by, tracking the heartbeat of the *Canope*.

Ana Clara Matta's artistry floods through the low-lit studio like sunlight through rain, the Steinway crystal-clear, the music ineffable. Ben is so easily seduced by such moments. They still move him as nothing else can. He lets out a long sigh, unaware that his breathing is falling into step with the left-hand part of the Debussy, shadowing Ana Clara's every move.

Without thinking he nudges a fader up, watching his meters. On the technical level all is well. The sound is sweet and true. It's the player's emotion that captivates him—and, hovering just over his shoulder, the composer's. He does feel Debussy, or his idea of him, in the booth: a smoker's voice, a staccato laugh, a scent of hair oil. A way of walking into a room. Fingers nearly as slender as Matta's, nails trimmed like a surgeon's. The music makes it all perfectly clear.

BEN STUDIES HIS ARTIST through the soundproof window. The sleekly tapered back, arched slightly above the piano bench. The nest of dark curls, tied back with a cream scarf to accommodate the headphones that she, unusually among players at her level, prefers to wear. The Punjabi slippers, sure and sensitive on the pedals. As she comes to a minor phrase she closes her eyes and turns her narrow face toward the ceiling, leaning into it, only to bring her head back down in a long arc as she resolves to major. The hint of a smile crosses her face. She has so much to say to the composer. As Ben listens, it's as if he's eavesdropping, so intimately does she converse with Debussy's ghost, all her sensitivity and intelligence devoted to its handiwork.

There's a toughness to Ana Clara Matta that's always appealed to him. He knows little of her private life, really, apart from what the music press prints and her fellow musicians hint at. Like any flamboyant player she's the subject of endless gossip. She's loved and she's hated. None of which seems to touch her: she glides through the clouds of envy and adulation unperturbed, at most faintly amused. When loose comments about her are made in Ben's presence he holds his tongue like a discreet maître d', it being part of his code not to take sides.

Only since Robin's departure has he allowed himself to wonder about Ana Clara's life outside the studio. He knows she divides her time between Chicago, London, and Paris when not on tour. She despises her native Brazil for its corruption, though she did give one triumphal concert in São Paulo some years back. She's fluent in several languages, which flit through her conversation freely, favoring the native tongue of whatever composer she's currently playing.

When it comes to her romantic life, it's common knowledge that she's capable of real cruelty. Most notoriously, there was the incendiary breakup with Horst Lörber, an Austrian cellist Robin knew, who fainted dead away and nearly tumbled into the orchestra pit when she accused him before a sellout audience in Munich of sleeping with a male student. There was the magazine interview in which she dismissed the huge, abstract paintings of another ex by remarking drily that what she found so tiresome about him was the way he was constantly trying to enlarge himself. And these were only the men. There are still the banal rumors of bisexuality—of an affair with an Italian writer spotted leaving Ana Clara's Florence hotel room at dawn, another with a beautiful nineteen-year-old pianist whose talent was suspiciously out of proportion to Maestra Matta's gushing praise.

There's little doubt that a good bit of the gossip is seeded by her manager, Sir Anthony Wooten, a British oddity as famous for his own sexual antics as for his alligator boots, rose cravat, and Anthony Eden homburg. It's Ant Wooten's job to keep the mantra *Ana Clara Matta* on everyone's lips, and he excels at it. He's almost certainly responsible for his client's latest moniker: The Animal. She's said to be quite proud of it.

BUT WHAT INTERESTS BEN is who she is when she's alone. He wants to know the mundane things. What books are on the nightstand in her Lincoln Park brownstone? What art on her walls? What food in her refrigerator? Does she use a pillow at night? Sleep on her back or her side? Talk in her sleep? (In which of her many languages?) What did she dream of last night as the storm rumbled in, knowing she'd be off to Counterpoint in the morning? Did Ben Weil flit through her unconscious, if only for an instant?

As she plays her way toward the final measures of the prélude, he tries to imagine her bedtime rituals. He watches her shake her curls out and slip her wiry body into a nightgown, brush her teeth with meticulous care while inspecting her sharp features in the mirror. Don the bifocals to delve into a book whose cover he can't quite bring into focus. In his fantasy she's exquisitely alone, her world solitary, under her perfect control. It's not occurred to him until this moment that the notorious Matta might sleep alone— but now his intuition tells him she does, even when there's a lover in her life. She'd protect the night's vulnerable, unguarded space for herself. She awoke alone today. He's almost sure of it.

"*Et voilà,*" she declares, the take finished. "What do you think?"

"Elegant," Ben says without thinking. The truth is, he stopped listening to the music halfway through. "Happy with it?"

"Not sure about the pedal on this bit." She plays a phrase adroitly. "Could be I lingered."

"I'll play it back."

"Let's hear it on the monitors." She sets her headphones on the bench and slips into the control room with him.

Together they listen, her fists balled on the chair arms, one slipper dropped carelessly to the floor. She's holding her breath with a sort of tantric concentration. When the passage in question arrives she leans toward the speakers and closes her eyes, lips moving silently, her whole body listening. Afterward she lets go of a long sigh that grazes his arm.

"*Ça marche*," she decides. "It works. Let's knock off the *Feux*."

But she stays where she is, eyeing him. "I think you don't like Debussy, do you? You might even be a Debussy hater, for all I know. Are you a Debussy hater, Ben?"

He nudges a fader up and down absently. Finds he can't look at her. There's some truth in what she says: Debussy's impressionism often feels shapeless to him. It's the same reason he dreads the obligatory pilgrimages, with out-of-town guests, to the Art Institute's Monets. He prefers cleaner lines in his art. But there's no need for Ana Clara Matta to know this. The truth is, Debussy's music moves him only when she plays it.

"I like him fine," he says.

"Liar."

The harsh word leaves him speechless. If there's one thing he's not, it's a liar. This has never been one of his failings. But when he steals a glance at her she's laughing.

"So serious," she says, and plays a feather-light arpeggio on his bare forearm. "Like some kind of *astronaut*." And with this she's gone, her jasmine scent lingering in the booth as she sits back down at the Steinway, his artist safely under glass once more.

IV.

DEEPER

WITH THE MATTA SESSION BEHIND HIM, Ben can't wait to get back to the Garnier recording. All through the humid afternoon it's played in the back of his mind, the music imperfectly remembered and all the more intriguing for it. In less than a day the French sonata has become part of his inner soundscape, a contour of his imagination.

At four-thirty he tells the temp to hold his calls and retreats back into Studio A, killing the lights in the suite. In the close, soundproof room the tinnitus in his left ear hisses like a gas leak. Ben's long since cataloged its variations: the ten-kilohertz scream, the midrange whine, the softer pink noise he's hearing now. He knows his companion's moods all too well. At the moment he's grateful for the milder weather inside his skull.

Ben takes his seat and cues up the sonata on a ten-second delay, tilting back and closing his eyes. Tonight it's the musician in him who wants to listen, undistracted by jumping meters and the busy scrawling on the computer screen. Tonight he'll let the music embrace him. It's not so unlike love, after all: he's a man entranced by a lover whose secrets have only been teased at. It's time to go deeper.

Before leaving last night he'd made a working copy of Willa Blount's original file and split off the noisy lead-in, pruning away the opening crackle so the music would begin immediately. And now it's here: Garnier's opening arpeggio comes swooping in through the monitors and hangs weightlessly in the close air, the notes ringing out from a past Ben's barely begun to imagine.

It's the fourth time he's heard it, more or less, yet the innocence of the opening phrase still deceives him. Even knowing what's to come, he lets himself be lofted up like a leaf on a rustle of wind, charmed by the simplicity of the four quiet notes. But it's only a feint. After the arpeggio comes the awkward rest, the music going oddly silent as if gathering strength, charging itself. Ben waits it out, the musical idea behind the long pause still obscure to him.

In the back of his mind he's counting. Five . . . six . . . seven beats of silence, then the first notes of real melody, the piece starting up in earnest. Despite the long delay there's an abruptness to the opening figure, a sense that the player's jumped the gun, launched into the first theme a beat too soon. Something in the meter is subtly off.

Finally Ben hears it: the seven beats of silence want to be eight.

It feels like an amateur's mistake, just bad counting. But given the rest of the sonata, the utterly masterful playing, Ben can only assume it's intentional. The weird rest is but the first of many a riddle to come.

THE MUSIC OPENS ITS HEART to him. Notes tumble through space, alighting gently in a quiet chord he finds inexplicable. A minor eleventh, he thinks, the sort of chord you'd hear Herbie Hancock play, not Debussy or Ravel or anyone else of Garnier's era. He has the urge to stop and analyze it but resists the temptation. If he halts the playback every time something intrigues him he'll never get through the track.

The pianist breaks left and walks the black keys down into darkness. For several measures the sonata lingers in melancholy. Ben slumps in his chair and knits his arms across his chest, brought low by the shift in mood. After a gradual descent the pianist lingers on two grave, methodical pulses toward the very bottom of the instrument's range, a low A if he had to guess. The music slows almost to a stop. He could be listening to the leisurely heartbeat of a whale hovering a hundred fathoms down. The final note drains into a hiss, leaving no hint that it was ever there.

Ben counts two silent beats; three. Then, without wind-up or warning, the sonata bursts into flat-out allegro. A long, virtuoso run drives the melody back above the water line, the whale breaching, the playing audacious. Ben feels his pulse rising. Galvanized, he rocks forward and clutches the arms of his chair. The pianist's technique is explosive, daredevil. For twelve or more measures the piece reaches into Liszt territory, fiendishly complex. In the faceless player, the composer has met his match. The notes explode in a fusillade of sparks, setting everything they touch on fire.

No amount of practice could have transformed Ben Weil into such a virtuoso, no matter how long he'd kept grinding it out in music school. This is no parlor amateur. These are gifted hands. Once again he sits awestruck in the deserted studio, nailed to his chair. The long-dead pianist might as well be tearing up the Steinway on the other side of the window, right here, right now. The playing doesn't seem humanly possible. The passage is halfway done by the time Ben remembers to breathe.

EVENTUALLY THE MUSIC RELAXES and a new theme appears. Flitting like a starling through clouds of suspended chords comes a simple folk song that takes the piece in a new direction entirely. If there was a whiff of the avant-garde in the first movement, then sheer flamboyant firepower in the second, now the sonata really begins to sing. The turn is full of grace. Ben listens with admiration as the pianist glides effortlessly from bravura into sweet lyricism, clearing the air, fingers weightless as starlight. . . .

Then trouble. There is a loud pop, then a painful scrawling pierced by a single piano note, a cry for mercy. The music is crushed. On the screen the problem reads like a wildly dangerous EEG. It's a shattering turn for the worse. But he knows from last night's session that there is music on the far side of the disaster zone. The pianist will return after several excruciating seconds, surprised in the midst of a complex phrase only slightly related to what came before. The sonata will move on but with something vital severed, the connective tissue ripped away.

Ben opens his eyes and pauses the playback, the engineer in him unable to resist getting down to work. Quickly he sizes up the situation. The damage to the wax has completely destroyed six seconds of the recording. Scrubbing through the waveform by milliseconds, he can find no musical signal at all after the last forlorn piano note. Garnier has been obliterated.

There is no software that can interpolate the missing audio, no magic that can divine the composer's intentions. Perhaps if it were a traditional piece, a bit of baroque clockwork, a musicologist could reconstruct the missing section, but for an experimental work like this it would be a fool's errand. The piece is just too strange for it. Ben clicks the mouse to move ahead, filing the issue away for later consideration.

The final passages of the French sonata hold more surprises. By now the composer seems capable of anything. As the pianist moves through another passage marked by airy chords and surprising silences, it's hard for the listener to guess where the piece will end up. Ben can only laugh in amazement, yet again, when the piano begins climbing through a series of rootless jazz chords—chords that remind him of mid-sixties Bill Evans more than anything—toward a grand flourish that can only be called a fanfare. Trumpets would not be amiss: it's as if a monarch has arrived in glorious, golden refulgence. No one would have predicted such a finale. It's bizarre but somehow it works perfectly. The pianist delivers a final, crisp triplet and the French sonata fades away, slipping back under its blanket of noise. It's over.

Or almost over.

Somewhere in the spew of static Ben detects a human voice whose words he can't make out. The speaker sounds like a woman although it would be hard to say for sure. Another voice answers, this one clearly male. The words themselves are buried—the muffled cries of coal miners on the wrong side of a cave-in.

It's no mean feat to extract intelligible speech from audio this corrupt. The piano speaks a simpler language. An E-flat is an E-flat. A bit of tossed-off speech, on the other hand, can pose profound challenges. All the nuances that make the human voice a wondrous thing make it the audio conservator's worst nightmare.

It's probably not worth the effort it would take to recover it. After hours of spadework it could turn out that the speaker is just telling the unseen recordist to stop the recording, or offering some bland compliment to the performer. With a mouse click Ben splits the file where the music ends and saves the spoken snippet to a file of its own. He'll get to it when he can.

The music is what matters most, as always. If there is a constant in Ben Weil's life—an unwavering faith—it's this. Never once has the music betrayed him.

V.

IN MY END IS MY BEGINNING

WITH GARNIER'S PIANO STILL RINGING IN HIS HEAD, Ben steps
into his compact little home and just stands for a moment, enjoying
the coolness, the soft flutter from the floor vent. As a fifty-fourth
birthday gift to himself he's had central air put in; little enough
in the way of self-indulgence, but something he and Robin never
managed to do. In a matter of hours, for the price of a vintage microphone, years of pointless suffering were reversed, summer after
summer of wrangling with the Chicago heat for no good reason.
It's a minor miracle that still catches him off guard. He settles his
bag under the etching of La Scala and closes his eyes, the better to
appreciate the soft touch on his skin, the tender welcome.

After the divorce, his life at a low ebb, Ben gradually convinced himself that such modest pleasures were his due. He had
the money, even after buying out Robin's share of the house; they'd
made enough over the years that the settlement left them both well
outside the danger zone. Counterpoint had brought in a sizable
income for two decades, while Robin, for her part, commanded
serious fees on the international circuit, her services as guest cellist
in high demand. Consumed by their careers and frugal at heart,
childless by undramatic mutual agreement, they'd never spent half
of what they earned. Over time the swelling of their assets came
to embarrass them. When they'd finally sat down with a financial
planner, goaded into it by Robin's brother, they were almost too shy
to look at the numbers.

"I see a lot of beautiful green here," the woman at the bank said
approvingly, thumbing through their documents. "There's certainly
no shame in that."

But for them there was a sense of shame, as if someone had told
them they were descended from robber barons, their lucre squeezed
from the souls of the poor. "It's not like it's anything to be proud of,

right?" Robin said afterward as they sat over noodles in a dimly lit Thai place. The good news had left her thoroughly dejected. "Think of all the people who have nowhere to sleep tonight—millions and millions, Ben." She eyed her plate with suspicion. "Think of the people with nothing to eat. Think of Sudan. Syria. The fact that we're clueless about finances doesn't mean the money should just rot in the bank. We need to give more of it away. Maybe a lot more." Ben didn't disagree. After paying the bill they'd hurried home to the computer and made hefty donations to Doctors Without Borders and CARE and the Red Cross, sticking with names they knew, ashamed they hadn't done it sooner. Ben closed the laptop, thinking they were done.

"But what about the refugees?" Robin said in dismay. She was still in her winter jacket, the color high in her pale cheeks, coppery hair tucked up under the Peruvian hat he'd given her the Christmas before. "And the homeless right here! I mean, those guys sleeping on steam grates on Lower Wacker are basically *internal* refugees, right? If we're going to help the Syrians, we've got to help the Chicagoans." Commandeering the computer, on a tear now, she clicked her way through websites like a Black Friday shopper. Ben gave up trying to track how much they'd spent. After an hour of ferocious giving, Robin slumped back in her chair, exhausted.

"You know what else?" she said later, changing into the thread-bare green pajamas she'd worn since college days. "I didn't like that bank lady one bit. All her *success plan* bullshit . . . it's not who we are, Ben. We're already successful, in the ways that matter to us. We don't need people like her. Right?"

And so, despite their considerable means, they'd continued to live like grad students, lugging out window air conditioners on the first hot nights of summer and blowing fuses—fuses—whenever the electrical service hit a glitch. In winter they ran a tippy space heater in the bedroom to banish the frigid drafts. The backyard was littered with broken cement slabs from a patio demolished by the previous owner; there was no garage for the Subaru, whose odometer had long since clicked past two hundred thousand miles. The kitchen floor was a patchwork of jaundiced linoleum that no amount of scrubbing could whiten, the cellar a forbidding catacomb.

Only the stately 1936 Bösendorfer parlor grand that dominated the living room hinted at their true means—though even that had been tax-deductible.

IT WASN'T AS IF THEY HADN'T EARNED a modest upgrade or two. Ben had built an international reputation and a thriving business doing what he loved most, his client list a who's who of the classical music world. Robin performed in concert halls around the globe, traveling business class with her precious Lorenzini cello riding next to her in seats paid for by her sponsors. Her recent South African tour had been a triumph. Only a few weeks before the truth about her affair came smashing down on him, the two of them had been featured in a *Chicago Magazine* cover story under the headline "A Classic(al) Love Story"—Robin resplendent in her green velvet concert gown and Cleopatra necklace, straddling the Lorenzini on the barren stage of Orchestra Hall, Ben hunkered hollow-eyed over the Studio A mixing board looking like he hadn't slept in days. Which he hadn't, as it happened, because by then he'd begun to suspect the truth about her and Alan Hurwitz.

In recent months they'd had almost no time together. Between touring and teaching she was rarely home, as likely to be in Vienna or Paris as Chicago—much later he'd wonder when she'd found time to sleep with Hurwitz, but by then it was academic. In the closing season of their marriage she'd played a nineteen-day stint in France and the UK, then headed straight off to Stockholm and Copenhagen, having spent her three-day turnaround in Chicago sleeping off a cold. Night after night Ben went to bed alone while she crisscrossed the Continent, their schedules too skewed for a goodnight call.

As fall trudged into winter, the skies overcast for weeks at a time, the dreary house oppressed him more and more. The ragtag furnishings and bad lighting were a burden he could no longer bear. After long days at Counterpoint he'd come home to his gloomy warren and change straight into pajamas and bathrobe, cold drafts coming off every window, the kitchen floor gritty under his slippers, and switch on a jazz station while he microwaved leftovers or poked at a bowl of cereal, unable to muster the energy to cook a proper meal. He'd be in bed by nine, only to lie awake to the sound of furtive rustlings in the kitchen—waiting miserably for a fatal snap—or the toilet gargling ceaselessly down the hallway. Meanwhile he imagined Robin in soft hotel beds and pin-clean bathtubs, room service croissants awaiting her, white Christmas lights wrapped around the manicured trees of whatever European town she was in—a precious respite from the rigors of her Chicago life, a parallel universe into which she escaped at every opportunity.

But no matter how often she went abroad, the pleasures of civilization never seemed to follow her home. The moment she stepped off the plane the familiar Chicago habits kicked in, the comforts of Edinburgh or Paris or Berlin left behind. Without missing a beat she'd switch on the space heaters and bundle up and get down to business. In the dungeon of a cellar she sorted laundry from the trip and coaxed the geriatric washer into action. With a run to the store she restocked the refrigerator and got the cooking back in gear. In the morning she ground coffee and scraped ice off the inside of the kitchen window, peering out into the broken backyard as if to reassure herself that nothing had been improved in her absence.

Anyone looking in on their daily life would have assumed they were barely hanging on, a missed paycheck away from calamity. They'd lived this way for years; it was all they knew. But as the marriage began to drift and take on water—Alan Hurwitz lurking beneath the waves, as yet faceless to Ben, present more as a sense of foreboding than anything—the bungalow's bleakness took on a more dangerous edge. Swaddled in an afghan one night, a glass of whiskey at hand for simple warmth, Robin somewhere in Scandinavia, Ben saw the truth: they were failing it, this union they'd built over more than two decades. They were starving it to death. The cheerless house had been screaming the truth at them for years now, if only they'd known to listen.

AFTER ROBIN LEFT HER SCARRED HOUSE KEY on the kitchen table and shut the door behind her for the last time, Ben came to see that he could make choices kinder to himself. Not that it would happen overnight; first there was anger to be burned through, grief over what he'd lost. And sheer disbelief: the sudden implosion of his life still made no sense to him. In the dismal, late-winter months after his wife moved in with her improbable lover and filed for divorce, the gloom of the bungalow for once suited his mood perfectly. Only with the arrival of spring—May stuttering forward in typical Chicago fashion, the daffodils thumped by smutty snow only hours after they emerged—did Ben look around his home and feel a tug toward action. Something had to be done if he was to move forward with his life. Even he could see it.

"Benjamin," his cousin Nikki told him one night over takeout, "you know I love you like a sister, right? The sister you never had? So I'm just going to say this. Don't hate me. No halfway sensible woman would see all this"—she swept her arm around the scruffy kitchen in a blanket indictment—"and not have serious alarm bells go off. Imagine! She goes on a couple dates with this cool guy, this *Chicago Magazine* cover story guy, and when she finally goes home with him he's living like a fucking mental patient."

It stung, but he took her point. When he surveyed the place through her eyes he saw nothing but despair. And so, with Nikki's help, he embarked on bringing the place up to par, upgrading the kitchen with cherry cabinets and granite countertops and stainless steel appliances, the price of the mammoth refrigerator so dizzying he had to sit down. But the kitchen was only the beginning. Nikki had grander plans.

"Look," she coached him when he quailed at the price of a bedroom set, "just do this. You can afford it." Then: "You won't always be sleeping alone, you know. I won't allow it."

The floors were refinished in a titanic four-day assault, the Sturm und Drang forcing him to relocate to her place for the duration. Afterward a tight-lipped old Pole, Mazur, labored for weeks to restore the Art Deco trim work and the painted-over transom window with its stained-glass lilies, humming snatches of Chopin as he worked. It seemed the parade of contractors would never end. But there was proper lighting in the house now, and a second bathroom, and a landscaped backyard with a rose garden Ben had no idea how to tend. A brand-new hybrid, nothing pretentious, sat in the brand-new garage.

And the air conditioning, of course: most of all, on brutal eve-nings like this one, the air conditioning, his first and best gift to himself at the dawn of his new life.

AFTER DISPATCHING A PLATE of Behrouz Farahani's kebabs left over from last night, Ben falls asleep early, the heavy meal pulling him down, his copy of the *Grove Dictionary of Music and Musicians* splayed open on the bed beside him. He's not been able to resist launching into some research. He's started with the performer on Willa Blount's recording, for whom he at least has a partial name. There are references to a number of Garniers in the *Grove*—a Belgian who barely survived the plague of 1480, an oboist from the Paris Opera who may have played at the coronation of Napoleon Bonaparte—but none with first initial J., and none alive in 1917. Whoever the stellar pianist was, he wasn't known to the editors of the *Grove*.

Just as Ben's drifting off he thinks he hears the sonata playing somewhere in the house, wafting through the ducts like a breath of cool air. Not the crackling, corrupted version on the audio re-cording but the pure and essential thing itself, as its composer must have heard it, as Garnier must have played it. The soul of the music unchained, roaming a modern world it must find outlandish. The playing seems to be coming from the living room where the old cylinders sit atop the piano like tiny Torah scrolls, the music trans-mitted directly from wax to ivory as the ghost of the dead pianist awakens—the whole riotous century dissolved at a stroke, banished by the lost sonata's first quiet notes.

BOSTON AND AIGREMONT

AUGUST 1915

VI.

A WOMAN OF HER WORD

ELISABETH GARNER SNAPS OPEN HER DAMP PARASOL, the sound crisp as a wingbeat, and stands it beside the cloakroom door. The cheerless corridor is dank with the smells of wet wool and oilcloth, some of the assemblers having arrived before the storm eased, caught in it as they hustled through the downpour. As for her, she's lucky to have run a bit late this morning: by the time she walked out, parasol at the ready, the deluge had sifted down to a fine mist. Shafts of sunlight were already breaking through, dashing the oil stains along Humboldt Avenue into kaleidoscopic colors, there and then gone.

As the streetcar swayed past the old burying ground she wondered whether the skies would clear in time for the Sanborn party. A part of her hoped the storm would swing back and sweep the Sanborn place right down off its hill. But after the miserable night she'd had, debating with herself endlessly in her stifling bedroom as the clock clacked away like some tropical insect, she was more confused than ever. Exhausted, too; so very tired. As she climbed the Bell factory steps she didn't know how she'd soldier through the day. What she wanted to do was go home and lower the flounced shades in her bedroom, then unlace her boots and unbutton her starched collar, unpin her hair and lie down with a cool cloth on her forehead . . . but none of this could be done. At the heavy door she lifted her chin and put the thought out of her mind. She wouldn't give in.

THOUGH THE RAIN'S BLOWN OUT OVER THE ATLANTIC, you wouldn't know it from the damp on the air. Elisabeth wishes they'd open the grimy casement windows, but Cyril Jones, the foreman, claims that the sea air is bad for the equipment—by which he means the polished metal components of three dozen half-assembled

Graphophones, neatly arranged atop high workbenches like a silver service laid for a princely feast. Eight Irishmen, two Scots, two Italians, a German, and a pale Polish girl in a hairnet hover over the parts under buzzing Edison lights, intent as surgeons, well aware that the famous founder of the Bell Company is due to pay a visit in just a few hours.

Elisabeth will miss him. Mr. Bell and his wife will surely have gone by the time she trundles back from calling on the Sanborns. A shame, as she's heard the great inventor is endlessly charming—a bearish, no-nonsense Scot who wears his genius lightly, far more likeable than Edison. She's studied the framed photo of him on the manager's wall. The genuine smile nestled in a Père Nöel beard; the eyes that strike her as playful but a little sad, too. There's a weight of age on Mr. Bell. Though she's never seen him in the flesh, her heart goes out to him the way it went out to her ailing grandfather when they bid him farewell, surely for the last time, at Le Havre.

On his last visit, famously, Bell smoked with the workmen on the back stairs, regaling them with stories of his work up in Nova Scotia on flying machines and scientifically bred sheep. These are stories Elisabeth would adore hearing. But today it's not to be. Instead she'll be suffering through the prattle of the idle rich—not a genius among them, if she's right.

CYRIL JONES MAY BE RIGHT about the salt air. When the breeze doubles back on the town there is a considerably nautical odor from the wharves. On humid days the fishy stench crawls right up Bantry Way, rubbing its squalid hindquarters against everything it passes. And so the windows stay shut, the airless third-floor rooms laden with a pungent brew of sweat, breakfast onions, tobacco smoke, and all manner of gossip—always gossip, some of it in accents Elisabeth thinks she'll never understand, no matter how long she lives in America.

This morning, after her sleepless night and the heartbreaking breakfast with her father, she has no patience for any of it. The unaccustomed morning coffee's made her jittery; there's a high-pitched whine in her ear. Something chutters like a locomotive in the back of her head. But she'll carry on for her papa's sake, if only to keep his mind off the war in France and all they've lost. She's made this promise to herself and she's a woman of her word.

"SHAME YOU'LL MISS THE GREAT MAN," says Tom Shea in his slippery brogue. "Rich as Pharaoh, he is."

He and Elisabeth are in the shipping room, occupied with preparations for the excursion out to Winchester. Shea's been loading crates with two Imperial Graphophones while she packs up three dozen wax cylinders, half of them blanks for home recording, half with music from the Edison catalog. There's a small problem with the blanks: some of the boxes contain the new blue cylinders rather than the standard blacks. Not the first mishap from the Edison factory, which seems to be overwhelmed of late. There's nothing to be done; they'll work fine on an Imperial. The customer surely won't know the difference.

It's the Edison catalog cylinders that really concern her. Just now she's fretting over whether to include #205, "Coon Songs from Ole Virginie"—a curiosity that will either amuse the Sanborns or offend them, if Tom's right about the meaning of the title. How's she to know? The Sanborns' set is as mysterious to her as a band of Fijian cannibals.

From time to time, as a girl in Paris, she met genuine aristocrats who glided through her father's music circles—she'll forever recall the kindness of the elderly, stale-smelling Comtesse de Plessis, who'd sit and interview her attentively whenever their paths crossed, shunning the other adults—but American aristocrats are another matter. It could be that "After the Roses Have Faded Away" (#2575) would be a safer choice than the coon song cylinder. She weighs them against each other anxiously, like cabbages sold by the pound.

On days like this, the idea of representing the Bell Company in the mansions of Boston fills her with a baneful panic. She worries that her French accent and fine features have fooled them all into thinking she comes from money—which is exactly the point, she knows, even if nothing could be further from the truth. "A classy looker's what they want," Tom told her bluntly when she took the position. "That's you, doll."

She's surprised he's found a situation at Bell, as ill-kempt as he is—the copper-wire hair perpetually out of sorts, the misbuttoned plaid vest with its tobacco stains, the crooked brown teeth packed with food. The coffee on his breath, which isn't whiskey, at least. When he asks about her Saturday plans she can almost hear the scheming in his mind. But Tom's had his trials, as he reminds her nearly every day. He's an Irishman, isn't he? Trials aplenty.

But he's not done with Mr. Bell. "Cursed with a wife like that . . . ye got to feel sorry for the old beaver, don't you?"

"What is it you find so lacking in Mrs. Bell?"

Tom brushes a bit of packing straw to the floor and regards her with mock surprise.

"Why, nothing at all. It's grand to be deaf as a stone." Her frown does nothing to derail him. "C'mon, girl. Don't be coy. Suppose you're the old man. You invent the telephone. The Graphophone. Brilliant. But at the end of the day, for all your trouble, what do you come home to? A woman with no use for any of it. Can't hear a word on the telephone, can't hear a lick of music. All your glory wasted."

"I'm sure Mrs. Bell doesn't need a telephone to communicate with her husband."

Shea leans in close. "Dead to rights, Liz. She'll read your lips like the Sunday papers."

Elisabeth is about to scold him when the bell from St. Brigid's tolls.

"Half ten! Christ," Tom says. In her exhaustion she's entirely forgotten the time. "We've a train to catch, girl."

VII.

IN DEEPER CHANNELS

ALL THROUGH THE SHORT RIDE out to Winchester Elisabeth thinks about the choker: her late mother's, with a cameo locket that once held a photo of her father and now holds a photo of Sylvie Garner taken before she fell ill. It's a fine Murat piece from Toulon, a family treasure from her grandmother's day. She possesses nothing finer. She's chosen it for the Sanborn visit for its elegance, but also because she wants her mother along to calm her nerves.

As the driver glides from the Winchester train station out to the estate in Oren Sanborn's maroon Silver Ghost, steady as an ocean liner—Tom Shea and the Sanborn gardener following behind in a Tin Lizzie loaded with the crates—Elisabeth perches on the back seat, rubbing the locket gently between thumb and forefinger, and asks her mother to help her find the right words this afternoon. Somehow she'll have to keep a cool head amidst the tycoons and society ladies, and with only a few hours of sleep behind her. At the moment she can barely keep her eyes open, the morning's dose of Chase and Sanborn faded now.

Elisabeth has another, humbler request. As the car passes one stately home after another, broad oaks dappling the hood with shadow, she asks her mother to please, please keep her from perspiring. *Mère . . . ne laissez pas la sueur trahir ma tenue!* It's far too hot to be wearing a button-up collar, bodice and corset, lace-ups and a hat, for goodness sake—she might as well be wrapped in a bearskin. But it wouldn't do for the Sanborns to notice her body's rebellions. Powder can only carry a girl so far.

ELISABETH KNOWS SHE TURNS HEADS when she walks into a room, but it's for all the wrong reasons. She'd like to be known as a woman of substance, not just a fresh young face—hasn't she earned it?

43

She's at home in the English language now, having embarked upon her twelfth year as an American, though the accents of her coworkers can still flummox her. What's more, she has a bachelor's degree from the Boston School of Social Workers and a fine letter of reference from the famous Dr. Brackett. Her father carries it with his sheet music in his oxblood portfolio. Only for safekeeping, he says, though she's caught him studying it with a smile, endlessly proud of her achievements.

Nor does her education stop there. Her knowledge of life runs in deeper channels. She's certainly seen more of the world than most American girls have. She's wandered the dreary Louvre and climbed the Acropolis; thundered through Atlantic gales and watched dolphins shoot like hooked carpet needles through the cold waters off Newfoundland. She's seen a man die, an elderly bicyclist dragged under the wheels of a Paris carriage for two horrifying blocks. And she knows serious music: thanks to her father she's heard the music of Debussy, Fauré, and Ravel played by the composers themselves—in Monsieur Debussy's case, on the family piano where she played her very first notes.

Everything she knows of music begins with her papa. As a girl of nine she'd sat next to him on the hard piano bench in the Saint-Cloud flat, hour after hour through a Christmas holiday blanketed in snow, while he played his way through a hand-copied score of Debussy's *Suite bergamasque*, stopping to explain its nuances as he went. It was genius, he thought, though Debussy the man still owed him two hundred francs from their student days at the Conservatoire. Elisabeth will never forget how the third movement, the Clair de lune, captured her heart. The unhurried opening, like something from a child's music box, chiming with the laughter from the kitchen where her mother sat chatting with her friend Agnès. The heady scent of the Christmas roast filling the flat. Snow mounting higher and higher atop the stone wall across the street, layered up delectably like icing on a cake. Seeing how the melody pleased her, her father asked if she'd like to learn to play it. And so she did, with his infinitely patient help—the right-hand part, anyway, while he took the left. Day after day, all through that Christmas week, they worked their way through it, Elisabeth learning by ear, the music growing inside her, expanding in her heart until she knew it from start to finish.

There is no piece of music she loves more. The floating melody comes back to her when she least expects it, a sweet signal from the past. To this day she has the notes firmly under her fingers. Not just the right-hand notes, now, but all of them. It's what she plays whenever a piano presents itself to her.

IN ALL THESE WAYS Elisabeth Garner is a laudable young woman. But in America she's never mingled with the well-to-do, and it's barely two months since she entered the vexing world of sales—a temporary expedient to help with the light bill until a position opens up in Mrs. Taylor's settlement house, where she can do the work she's trained for. Nothing in her life has prepared her for a day like today.

Apparently her predecessor was a dismal failure. Ty Perkins couldn't have sold farls to a starved man, Tom Shea says, his words nonsensical to her but his meaning plain enough. In hiring Elisabeth the Company's taken a different tack, using the fairer sex to gain entry into the best homes where a good word passed from one club man to another is worth its weight in gold. While Bell's army of pavement-pounders is out peddling the basic Graphophones at twenty-four dollars apiece, Elisabeth's sole charge is to sell the Imperial line with its De Beers diamond stylus, gold appointments, Honduran mahogany case, japanned black chassis, and mono-grammed nameplate. And, of course, the Company's personalized service, in the graceful person of herself.

At times the responsibility terrifies her. Do they realize she's only twenty-three years old? The Oren Sanborns would see through her like glass. Which was all the more frightening because the Sanborn patriarch, Oren's late father, had been a friend of Mr. Bell's when they were young men struggling to launch their businesses. A failure today would reverberate. Elisabeth lay awake for hours debating whether to resign her position, and resolved just before dawn that she would. She'd give her notice and find a position better suited to her education, if not at Mrs. Taylor's settlement house then at another. Today would be the day she set a new life in motion.

She told herself that it wasn't so much a matter of failure as of falling into a line of work for which she was ill-suited in every way. She'd get up and dust herself off and move on as people of character do, knowing that better work awaited her elsewhere. The Bell Company and the Sanborns, with all their coffee money, would do perfectly well without her. Of this she had no doubt.

None of which meant that she could just sleep in. Her father needed his breakfast before heading off to teach. This hadn't changed overnight, even if everything else had.

It was only five-thirty, but there was no point in tossing and turning on sweaty sheets for another miserable hour. Elisabeth washed and dragged herself to the cuisinette, only to discover, to her bafflement, that her father was already working away to put breakfast on the table. Her place was neatly set with an egg cup and toast rack and her mother's beloved china blue coffee cup and saucer—this last a peculiar choice, since she'd never developed a taste for the stuff and nor had he. Sylvie Garner had been the coffee drinker in the family. Everything about the scene was peculiar. What in the world was her papa doing?

He hadn't noticed she was there. She watched as he rummaged behind the washstand curtains in suspenders and undershirt, humming Strauss stealthily, in an excellent mood.

"Papa?" she said. "*Tout va bien?*"

He startled at the sound of her voice, knocking his head on the underside of the washstand. Poor, clumsy Papa—so brilliant at the keyboard, so awkward in ordinary life. With a palm to his forehead he turned to face her, the coffeepot in his hands and a smile spreading under his moustache.

"*Mon ange!* You're up early. Excited?"

"Papa, what are you doing?"

"Making your breakfast. As you see."

"But why?"

With a spry step he came and clasped her elbows through the sleeves of her dressing gown, eyes shining. "Because it's a very big day for you, *chérie*. Do you know how proud you've made your old papa?"

She hardly knew what to say. How could she tell him she'd be quitting Bell in a few hours? She smiled halfheartedly, looking away.

"Mademoiselle," he said, pulling her chair back like a *maître d'*.

She sat bewildered as he bustled about the kitchen, boiling eggs, slicing bread, putting the kettle on. She'd never seen such domestic industry in him. A moment came when he turned with a paper sack in his hands. She saw the smile in his eyes, the whimsy on his flushed face with its aquiline nose. He could barely contain himself.

"*Et voilà, ma fille*. For you." He presented the sack as if it held the jewels of Versailles.

"Papa. . . ."

"Open it."

She reached in tentatively, but something had already told her what she'd find. She was right: in her hands sat a red tin of Chase and Sanborn coffee.

"Oh, Papa."

Though her heart was heavy she found herself smiling at him. Amid the daily blood tide of terrible news from the front, his heart broken by the German invasion only months after Bright's disease took his cherished Sylvie, her papa's happiness was irresistible. Now he was in motion again, first at the icebox, then at the stove, then back at her side, this time to pour coffee and scalded milk into her mother's cup.

"Today is your day, Elisabeth," he said, stepping back like a discreet waiter.

She disliked the flavor of coffee, but she drank it to the last as he watched with satisfaction. Now there could be no question of quitting the Company; not today. She might as well slap her dear father in the face. And so she ate her egg and toast and went in to dress, her clothes laid out the night before, finally fitting the choker around her powdered neck and praying for the strength to get through the day.

VIII.

AIGREMONT

THE ART OF CALLING ON THE WELL-HEELED, according to Tom Shea, is to convince them that you're *almost* as high-class as they are—not quite in their set, but only one rung down. You want to seem vaguely familiar, like a second cousin they met as a child but can't quite place. Or, in the case of a lovely young woman with a French accent and European manners, the sort of cousin you wish you had. You're the plucky Gibson Girl who's always up on the latest fashions and eager to share her modern discoveries, be they teabags, zippers, dirigible rides, radium beauty creams or Imperial Graphophones. You're not there to sell them anything, heaven forbid; you've brought along a few curiosities only to spare your hosts the tedium of rummaging in shops. It's Tom you need to talk to if you want an Imperial for yourself.

Elisabeth rehearses the spiel in her mind during the ride through Winchester, whose grand houses size her up coolly from behind their vast lawns. Eventually the Silver Ghost turns into High Street and there it is, abruptly: the Sanborn place spread across a gentle hill, opening its blond stucco arms to receive her. As the driver glides up to the imposing entrance, a gardener touching his hat as they pass, Elisabeth nervously takes in the arched windows, the Greek columns, the snug-fitting gardens and sun-washed portico, wishing her corset would allow her to take a deeper breath. When they pull to a stop she touches her mother's locket for good luck.

The driver hands her down off the running board and escorts her up the wide steps, then rings the bell on her behalf, crows squabbling in the roomy sycamores down the hill. Before the door there's a pool of welcome shade. Elisabeth dwells in it for a bless-ed moment while waiting for the bell to be answered. It's cooler in Winchester than in Boston; this, too, must be something the

48

wealthy are able to arrange. By the time the door swings open to reveal a maid in a pleated cap her heart's finding a quieter tempo.

"Miss Garner?" the girl says with a genuine smile, friendlier than any French maid would dare be. "Welcome."

The door opens wider. From the corner of her eye Elisabeth notices Tom Shea being directed to the service entrance, lugging the crates with difficulty, sweat rings under his arms. In winter he moonlights as an ice cutter on the Charles, hewing and hauling blocks far heavier than the crates, but in high summer it's a trial. Lifting the hem of her skirt from her boot Elisabeth hands her parasol to the maid and steps into Aigremont, the Sanborns' world opening before her.

THE FOYER IS GRAND, though somewhat less grand than she expected. The maid excuses herself to announce her arrival, leaving Elisabeth to take in the house.

To the left is a curving staircase, its pediment trimmed with dark parquet. The floors are polished to a high shine, the walls papered with golden fleurs-de-lis. Beneath her feet lies a Persian rug as thick as any rug she's ever stood upon. She looks up: adorning the underside of the staircase is an ornate floral design in raised plaster. Above the landing, blooming with scarlet and green in the sun, is a stained-glass window with a garden scene. In her grandparents' day it would all have been quite chic, she's sure.

Through the double doors to her right Elisabeth hears the commotion of servants readying the house for the afternoon's festivities. But where are the Sanborns? As the wait drags on, she wonders whether Rena Sanborn will make a grand entrance down the staircase. Maybe Oren will come bursting through the parlor doors, peeling off his driving gloves. . . .

No, she tells herself, *not for me*. She's only a saleswoman—they'll know it, even if their guests do not. Though the friendship between the elder Sanborn and Bell should count for something, Elisabeth doubts it will spare her from making a fool of herself.

She prepares herself as her mother would have done. Adjusts her hat; checks her posture; smooths her blouse. She'd like to powder her neck, but there's nowhere to do it. She tries to make her peace with the uncertainty of the moment, readying herself for whatever manner of greeting the Sanborns might offer.

Something tells her she'll be better served if she's deeper into the house when they arrive. To wait just inside the door is to say she doesn't belong in such a fine home. With a few steps she positions herself over the ornate central figure of the Persian rug and clasps her hands high at her waist, as if tucking them into an invisible muffler, the wait dragging on and on. The longer they keep her waiting, the less convincing the masquerade will be. No young woman of means would be treated in such a manner. But she's entirely at their mercy now.

"Miss Garner?"

A woman's confident voice, finally, from close behind her.

"Has my mother kept you stranded here like a refugee? Gosh, I certainly hope not."

Elisabeth feels a touch on her arm and turns to find herself face to face with a woman no older than herself. Younger, in fact, twenty at most. This can only be the Sanborns' daughter, Helen.

It's impossible not to be struck by the girl's broad patrician face, something at once feminine and mannish about it, and by her wide, confident smile. Her orderly white teeth are a wonder to behold, her throat substantial and lovely. It's a moment before Elisabeth realizes the girl's in riding clothes, tan britches and boots and a green velvet jacket.

"You *are* Miss Garner, aren't you?" Helen says, thumb hooked in her waistband.

Elisabeth never imagined she'd be met by the daughter. At this moment it's a blessing. When Helen holds out her hand she nods and takes it gladly, surprised by the firm handshake that follows. The girl is so at ease in her world.

"I'm grateful for the invitation, Miss Sanborn."

The girl tilts her head inquisitively. A chestnut curl escapes her hairband.

"Is that a French accent I hear, Miss Garner?"

"You've a good ear."

"So, it would be Gar-*nay*, then?"

Elisabeth smiles. "It was actually Garnier, back home. My parents got tired of being called *Garneer*, so they changed it to Garner."

Something catches the girl's eye over Elisabeth's shoulder. She winks at someone and turns back to her guest with a flicker of amusement in her eyes. "But what should *I* call you, Miss Garnier-Garner-Garneer?"

"How about Elisabeth?"

Helen takes her hands eagerly. "That's my middle name! What a grand coincidence."

"*Mais oui*," Elisabeth says, feigning astonishment. It's only this and nothing more—a coincidence. But if Miss Sanborn finds it grand, so be it. Perhaps it will sell a Graphophone or two.

THERE'S SOMETHING DISARMING about the Sanborn girl's friendliness. In all her grim imaginings of the day, Elisabeth never guessed she'd be received with such warmth. Helen's set her back on her feet.

"Come on!" the girl says, squeezing her hand. "I'll show you around. Then I'd better get out of these clothes, hadn't I . . . though dressing doesn't take me a tenth the time it does Mama." Turning toward the parlor doors, the girl sends an appraising glance over her shoulder. "You're so elegant, Elisabeth. Look at that precious locket! French? I'd ask you whose face is inside, but it's none of my beeswax. Is it a beau?" With a frown she adds, "I'll never match your style. Never in a million years."

Elisabeth hesitates, the girl tugging at her hand. Should she let herself be waylaid by the daughter when her hosts haven't yet appeared? But Helen's friendliness leaves her no choice.

"Alright!" Elisabeth says, and lets herself be pulled along into the house.

IX.

WHERE THE MAGIC HAPPENS

THERE ARE SERVANTS EVERYWHERE, and freshly forced lilies, and enormous silver bowls of fruit, and purple bunting hung against the dark wood in graceful sashes. Everywhere Elisabeth looks, the house is exquisite. But in the parlor they come upon an old woman in a severe black dress.

"*Now*, Mr. Hiscox!" the woman snaps at a boyish server. "Step to it."

"Mrs. Dooley," Helen says under her breath, squeezing Elisabeth's hand. "Don't cross her. You've been dooley warned."

The tour is undertaken at lightning speed. The cozy parlor with its marble fireplace, which gives up a faint scent of woodsmoke. The double doors fitted with cinched curtains, which Helen throws open with a stagey flourish. The paneled study with its huge explorer's globe and rolltop desk and ugly electric chandelier, a man's retreat if ever there was one. On the sideboard Elisabeth notes a collection of crystal decanters, an enameled cigar box, a telephone. Nearby sits a Bell Dictaphone into which Oren Sanborn is said to be recording his memoirs. On the wall hangs a buck's head with shellacked antlers, glassy stare fixed on a pair of stuffed trout screwed to the opposite wall.

Elisabeth and Helen are alone in the room. With a mischievous smile the girl rolls back the lid of the desk to expose a jumble of papers, dozens of slips and scraps and crumpled bills, a stunning pocket of disarray in the midst of such immaculate housekeeping.

"Father," she says with a roll of her hazel eyes, and closes it again, tugging Elisabeth toward the next room.

"And now for the best part," she says, stepping back to sweep her arms toward the gold-coffered ceiling of a music room. "The place where the magic happens."

It's a lovely room. Three French doors overlook a garden of cream roses, each door crowned with a crescent window through which sunlight is streaming. The parquet floor sparkles like a mountain brook. Along the walls stand high-backed chairs, painted white and meticulously filigreed. But it's another furnishing that stops Elisabeth in her tracks: in the corner sits a snowy-white grand piano. Helen lays a hand along its flank as if calming a stallion.

"Mama's true beloved. A Mason and Hamlin—Papa bought it at Drury's as an anniversary gift, back when they still did things like that. Do you play?"

"A few little things. But my father . . . he'd fall in love with this in a heartbeat. He'd give anything to play a grand piano again."

"He plays quite seriously, then?" With an impish look the girl thunks a low ivory, the note bouncing against the walls.

"He studied at the Paris Conservatoire, under Fauré. He was going to be a concert pianist."

"And? What happened?"

"It's quite a long story."

"I'd like to hear it."

"Maybe I'll tell you sometime."

Elisabeth studies the piano to avoid the girl's keen gaze. She can so easily picture her father bent over the keyboard with eyes closed, Debussy or Chopin pulsing through him.

"I'm going to hold you to it. Your father's got to be more interesting than mine."

"Helen!" says a stern woman from the doorway. "You're not dressed?"

Elisabeth assumes it's strict Mrs. Dooley, but it proves to be a tall, imposing woman in a fine lavender dress. Across the matronly chest lies a string of the largest pearls Elisabeth has ever seen.

"Mrs. Sanborn!" Elisabeth says with a quaver, taking a clumsy step forward.

Rena Sanborn looks past her, glaring at her daughter.

"Hop to it, young lady. We'll have guests at the door any minute. I want no excuses."

With a curt nod toward Elisabeth, the lady of the house turns on her heel, off to deal with another last-minute emergency.

"It's only 'cause there's a party," Helen sighs. "Nothing to do with you." She leads the way through the French doors and deposits her guest at the outdoor portico, where Tom Shea is setting up the Graphophones beside a rostrum decked with white roses and bunting.

White everywhere, Elisabeth reflects. *The color of summer money in America.*

THERE'S WORK TO BE DONE. With Helen gone, the Company's business surges back, a seriousness coming over Elisabeth as she reminds herself why she's here.

From the portico she discreetly surveys the grounds. A phalanx of folding chairs has been deployed across the close-cut lawn, shielded from the sun by awnings supported on poles festooned with white gladioli. At a bar set up near the French doors, girls in wispy frocks take instruction from a dour steward with an Italian-looking moustache. Helen's friends, perhaps, conscripted to squire drinks around; perhaps, too, to attract the attention of eligible suitors. With war in the offing Elisabeth wonders whether the tempo of the hunt is quickening or slowing.

All looks to be in readiness. All, that is, but the Company's wares: Tom is struggling mightily with the telescoping horn of one of the Graphophones, a new design that allows the cone to be collapsed into a foot-long package. It appears that one of the segments is stuck. Some choice Irish language is spilling from her colleague. When she sidles up and asks if it's going to be alright, he snaps: "The feckin' thing's banjaxed!" Elisabeth moves on, afraid his distress will infect her when her nerves are already on edge. He's best left to do his job, and she hers.

She decides to stroll the grounds, taking a meandering flag-stone path alongside the windows. Rosebushes soften the stucco walls with a froth of loveliness. An orderly hedge of *buis* bakes in the sun, throwing off a pleasant liquor, though at the moment she can't recall the English name for it. The staff meanwhile bustle to and fro with platters of strawberries and petit fours, silver pitchers sweating with ice water, the last vases of flowers.

Through the dining room windows she spots two of Helen's brothers. It must be them: young men in short pants and monogrammed jackets, handsome but not too handsome, laughing as the servants steer around them. The older one draws a slim silver case from his jacket and takes out a cigarette, which he proceeds to tap smartly on the back of his hand and slip between his lips. At first he doesn't light it; he's too busy expostulating on something to his brother. The cigarette wags from his lips, a lighter flicking in his hand. His brother listens admiringly, hands jammed in his pockets, a cowlick out of sorts on the back of his oiled head. When the cigarette is lit at last, the older boy disappears behind a cloud of smoke, gone like a genie.

James, she reminds herself, *named for the old man. Probably they call him Jim.* She's researched the Sanborns as best she can. The smaller boy seems quite sweet, too young to have adopted any of his brother's modish airs. *Caleb. Or is this little Jack?* Elisabeth ducks from the window hastily, worried the smoker will spot her when he emerges from his cloudbank.

It occurs to her that her leisurely ramble through the grounds might be considered presumptuous. Does she really think she's a *guest* of the Sanborns', at liberty to wander about? It's not as if she's invisible. Slipping past the Sanborn boys, Elisabeth makes her way back to the portico, only to see that the first guests are arriving.

A YELLOW ROADSTER stops in the driveway, discharging a slim young woman dressed in a lilac gown that's pleated up to her scant bosom like a nightgown. A yard-long string of black pearls swings against her narrow hips as she's helped from the car. This is not a fashion known to Elisabeth. The woman's curls are held in place by a sash of lilac voile, through which lily-of-the-valley has been carefully woven. The footman races around to open the door for her companion, a tall stylish man with slick blond hair and white plus-fours who looks as if he's just stepped off the golf course. The couple make their way up the front steps like royals on holiday, profoundly satisfied with themselves.

Elisabeth's heart begins to throb in her chest. She can't imagine approaching people like this, making small talk, inching her way toward the topic of Graphophones. . . . *C'est absolument fou!* What has she been thinking? But she'll find a way to do it: she decides so on the spot. She'll meet the moment. She'll seek the couple out as soon as possible.

"May I see you in?" a reedy voice says to her right. "That sun really packs a wallop."

There's a man standing close beside her—how has she not noticed? He touches her elbow and she pulls away on reflex, realizing instantly that it's a mistake.

"Well!" the man exclaims. "I guess chicks pretty as you need to mind the roosters."

Annoyed, Elisabeth turns to find herself next to a weak-chinned man of fifty or so, his stringy hair combed haphazardly over a peeling scalp. There's a tumbler of whiskey in his hand but it's easy enough to spot the drink in his eyes. With a wavering gaze he surveys her, lingering on her neck and wandering down over her breasts, thinking the thoughts men think. He seems far too shabby to be a friend of the Sanborns. She'd like to be rid of him immediately—but now he's extended his hand.

"Oren Sanborn. You're one of Helen's girlfriends? You girls get foxier by the day."

Taken aback, Elisabeth lets him take her hand, seeing no alternative.

"Elisabeth Garner, Mr. Sanborn. What a pleasure."

Sanborn leans in close. "How about a bourbon, Liz? An Old Fashioned? No need for Mother and Dad to know. Or Helen, for that matter—the Hellion, I call her." He gives a little bark of a laugh and takes a gulp of whiskey.

Something in the man's easy corruption gives Elisabeth a lift of self-confidence. "I don't think whiskey's for me, thank you." Her host sniffs this away. "And I've only just met your daughter, who's lovely. I'm actually here on behalf of Mr. Alexander Graham Bell's company. I believe your father and he were friends."

It takes Sanborn some moments to organize his thoughts. His liquid gaze stays on her but she can't see much behind it. "Bell. . . . " he says, as if barely recognizing the name the whole world knows.

"My father knew him back in the day. A wonder he's still alive and kicking."

"He's at the Company this afternoon. Alive as you please."

"Saved by the bell, I guess. Ha!" The whiskey glass is drained. "Good for him. But let's find you a drink. Don't tell me you're not parched." With this Sanborn grasps her elbow and steers her toward the house, the party underway.

X.

ANOTHER HELEN

WHAT ELISABETH WILL REMEMBER MOST from the afternoon is this: Helen Sanborn transfigured from girl to woman before her eyes. The transformation begins at the moment when Rena Sanborn mounts the portico steps, welcomes her guests briskly, and with no further ado introduces her daughter, whose privilege it will be to introduce the day's speaker.

When Helen makes her entrance, Elisabeth is standing near the folding chairs, having held her tongue for twenty long minutes. To her regret she's attached herself to the tall blond man and the woman with black pearls who arrived in the yellow roadster. The man, who's introduced himself only as Helmut, says he's a banker from Berlin. His lady friend's from Providence, a well-heeled society girl by all appearances. Elisabeth's forced herself to stay close to the German, chained to him like a convict to a guard, waiting for some opening to introduce the topic of Imperial Graphophones.

In the back of her mind she's kept rehearsing her lines. *Elegant as a fine violin, you know. The stylus is a diamond! I'm certain you have one—everyone does.* Since detecting Elisabeth's French accent, however, the German hasn't let up about the war, pretending to take the French side but in the next breath bragging about how his father goes shooting with the Kaiser—she knows who the Kaiser is, doesn't she? A good man who can't be blamed for Hindenburg's blunders. Does she realize he's the grandson of the Queen of England? The best sort of Prussian, even if he's stuck on the wrong side of this damned war. . . .

It's astonishing to Elisabeth, this kind of loose talk, what with all the panic over German spies and submarines, with the sinking of the *Lusitania* and the horrifying German gas unleashed at Ypres only a few months ago. But the man is drunk. With each glass of champagne his ugly accent has worsened. Perhaps he assumes he's among friends who'd never doubt his loyalties. And would they? Elisabeth has no idea. She knows how her neighbors in Roxbury would handle him: the Italians and Swedes would show the man what a working man's fists can do. Already they've burned a Bavarian brewery to the ground.

She's glad her father doesn't have to listen to the German's rubbish. When the news about Ypres came, he sobbed at the kitchen table all evening and into the night, inconsolable, the thought of all those gas-blinded French boys too much to bear. She'd not seen him so bereft since the miserable months after her mother's death. For several frightening days she felt him wrestling with an urge to go home, to join the fight despite his age, though he spoke not a word of it to her.

And now to think that his own daughter, champagne glass in hand, is making conversation with a German whose father hunts with the Kaiser! She'd be ashamed to tell him. She won't tell him.

IS THERE ANY REASON to believe the German isn't a spy? And the American girl, this silly Betsy or Franny—how can she stand him? He's handsome, of course, in a way American girls swoon over. He smokes in a curious way, the gold-banded cigarette dandled just below the buffed nails, the smoke drilling precisely from his narrow nose. She wishes she'd never given the man her calling card.

By the time Rena Sanborn takes the stage, Elisabeth's on the brink of speaking her mind. *And what do you think of how you Germans gassed our French boys at Ypres?* As Rena waves gracefully to get her guests' attention Elisabeth continues to play it out, imagining how the smug look would abruptly fade, how the athletic shoulders would stoop, if only for a moment. . . . He'd take another sip of champagne to buy time, avoiding her eyes, caught out with no good answer to her direct question. She'd wait it out coolly, secure in knowing that only hours ago she was ready to quit her job for good. But Elisabeth forgets all this when Helen Sanborn appears.

The girl seems to have melted clear through her mother's earlier sternness. With a proud smile, Rena ushers her daughter to the rostrum and retreats into the shadows at the edge of the portico.

There's a charming modesty in the way Rena so tactfully gives way to Helen. With a few small steps backward she reveals another side of herself entirely.

And Helen! Elisabeth can barely believe what she sees. The playful girl in her riding britches, the rambunctious little sister who tugged her by the hand through the mansion, has been startlingly transformed into a sober young woman in an elegant white frock and white shoes trimmed with tiny pearls. Under the dome of the portico she takes the stage confidently, the guests going quiet as if Bernhardt herself has stepped from the wings. The silence is broken only by a flutter of birdsong in the hedge.

"Boxwood!" Elisabeth whispers, the English name for *buis* finally coming back to her.

Her unpleasant companion says something in German, drawing a sharp look from a matron seated nearby. The woman mouths something at him: *Hun!* is what Elisabeth reads on her lips. Again the man says something, this time with a sneer. "Speak English!" the woman huffs, and turns away to whisper to her husband, who cranes around her wide hat to size the foreigner up for himself.

"Filthy Heinie," he says. "Some nerve, to come here."

Elisabeth can feel the chill around her. A patriotic cloud has passed over the sun. But Helen is too far away to detect any of it. Birds chitter; the young heiress grips the lectern, head tilted back like a head on a Roman coin. Elisabeth notices the two brothers leaning in the doorway—a smirk on the older one's face as he watches his sister pose for the crowd, the younger boy trying to catch a moth in his hand.

"Let me echo my mother's gratitude," Helen says, her voice a bit too loud. "Thank you all for coming out to support a cause that's very dear to us, and I'm sure to you."

Elisabeth hears a mild snort behind her. Apparently the gathering is to be more than just a garden party. There's to be a speech; something political. In the bushes below the portico Tom Shea crouches between his two Graphophones, ready, at last, to record the speaker.

As Helen waits for a smattering of half-hearted applause to subside, Elisabeth notices a dark presence next to Rena Sanborn, a compact young woman in a drab, prison-matron skirt and starched white blouse. Her black eyes make her quite beautiful. Just now they're surveying the assembled party, unimpressed. She can only be the guest of honor.

"It's my privilege to introduce a true visionary," Helen says, "a woman who believes with every fiber of her being that suffrage for women will make America the envy of the world." She stops for dramatic effect and scans the faces before her. "Surely no nation can be called a democracy when forty million of its citizens are denied a place in the public square."

Helen stops for applause but this time there's precious little of it. A few of the younger women clap discreetly, along with an imposing trio of elderly women who applaud with startling vigor. Elisabeth herself has the urge to clap but she's not quite so reckless as that. Helen waits with a fixed smile, clearly enjoying the little shock wave she's sent out.

"Overplayed her hand, I'd say," a voice mumbles in Elisabeth's ear, steadfastly drunk. She can smell the whiskey. "Not the best time to sound unpatriotic, with all this fucking trouble in Europe. But the girl says whatever she thinks. Takes after her mother."

Sanborn hovers beside her, a whiskey in one hand and a cigarette smoldering in the other.

"There's a match out there for her, God willing," he allows. He sweeps his cigarette across the seated guests. "Not that she's improving her chances any at the moment."

Helen waves her guest forward.

"Please extend a Winchester welcome to Miss Alice Paul, PhD, lately back from England where she had the honor of being jailed with Mrs. Pankhurst herself." Amid uncertain applause the black-eyed woman strides over, head bowed in titanic concentration like a Puritan preacher. She's a dynamo, obviously—even the way she walks says so.

But Elisabeth is still pinned between two aggravating men. Sanborn slouches to her left; the German soars to her right. What's more, the day has grown steadily hotter. Under her hat she feels beads of sweat sprouting at her hairline. It won't do.

"Will you excuse me?" she says to no one in particular, and slips past Sanborn toward the house.

In the ornate washroom she reapplies her powder, then makes her way into the dining room, lingering at some remove from the open French doors. The speaker's strident voice must be carrying all the way into town. Elisabeth happens to find it invigorating. The sheer force of Miss Paul's presence compels. Helen too stands transfixed, unable to take her eyes from the woman with the flashing gaze and brandished finger.

Elisabeth feels a jealousy flare in her chest, certain that Alice Paul's oratory will erase all thoughts of Elisabeth Garner from Helen Sanborn's mind. In these brief hours at Aigremont, Helen has been the only ray of light to fall. Now, in the presence of true greatness, a mere saleswoman surely counts for nothing. What ever made her think that a Sanborn would remember her?

From her discreet post she watches the guests fidget in their chairs. Alice Paul's lost them decisively. A few of the women nod as she makes her case, but the rest sit fanning themselves with glacial smiles. The men confabulate openly, chuckling over club gossip or motorcars or the war, as if they've crossed paths at Parker's raw bar. Someone near the back is quite audibly snoring.

Meanwhile, squatting at the very edge of the portico, poor Tom Shea struggles to keep the Graphophone's cone in front of the mercurial Miss Paul, who tosses her head and leans over the rostrum and won't stand still for any of it. As another cylinder runs to its limit, Tom scrambles to swing the second Graphophone's cone into place, something at once clownish and acrobatic in his performance. It's a high-wire act, a vain attempt to catch a lightning bolt. What's actually being captured on the spinning wax is anyone's guess.

It occurs to Elisabeth that Tom's heroic exertions have enthralled the crowd far more than Alice Paul has. Watching Tom, you'd think only an equilibrist could manage a Graphophone. In the next instant she realizes that the whole excursion is hurtling toward failure. Soon she and her colleague will be on their way, the Sanborns left with their monogrammed Graphophones but Tom's order pad untouched. The awkward afternoon will fade into memory as Elisabeth rides the train back and catches the trolley for Roxbury, a quiet evening with her father ahead, a life cut to her own measure.

She sees it clearly now, standing in the Sanborns' dining room surrounded by cream roses and petit fours and frocks worth more than her father's made all year from his piano teaching: she won't sell a single Graphophone today. What a relief it is to know it.

Second Movement
Allegro

Chicago

September 2018

XI.

A ROBIN'S FLIGHT

SATURDAY MORNING brings a blessed break from the heat. Ben's up early, buoyed by a softer sun, feeling better than he has in weeks. But it's not just the change in the weather that's brought him back to life. Two long evenings immersed in the Garnier recording have renewed him. Standing in the shower, toweling off, bending to pull on shorts, he finds that his balance is almost perfect; the ringing in his ear is as quiet as it ever gets. The day is bright and blue. Feeling bold, he decides that a jog along the lakeshore is in order. Then it will be back for a shower and off to lunch with his cousin.

He's steaming milk for a cappuccino when the phone trills.

"Me," Nikki says, in the telegraphic way he loves.

"Hey, you."

"Shitty weather."

"Never worse." Ben switches to speakerphone and takes his cappuccino to the kitchen table, sitting down in a wash of sunlight. "We still on for lunch?"

"Alas, no—Robin just called me in a panic. She *has to see me*. Sounds like an emergency." He imagines her gray eyes narrowing skeptically. "Boy trouble." After a moment she says: "I mean, not to minimize what she's going through. For her it's real as fuck."

Nikki and Robin have been friends since long before Robin came into Ben's life, having met at a summer orchestra camp as teenagers and later roomed together at Juilliard. It was the summer after that first Juilliard year when Nikki introduced Robin to her cousin Ben. Already a standout player, Robin had just transferred into the Northwestern program to follow a beloved cello mentor there; come fall, she and Ben would be classmates. Of course they should meet. But the introduction felt forced, Nikki's hand too heavy in bringing them together, and neither made any effort to cement the connection. Their mutual shyness blocked the way. It would be winter term before they even met for coffee, and this only because of a chance encounter in the checkout line at the student union.

By spring Nikki would abandon her violin studies, having concluded with her usual frank lucidity that her future as a musician would be limited to playing in small-town orchestras and giving lessons to beleaguered children and hopeless late bloomers. After two years at Juilliard she knew just where she stood. She'd stared down the reality of it without flinching. On the very day Robin was invited to join a master class with Yo-Yo Ma in Vienna, Nikki withdrew from Juilliard and bought a ticket to Costa Rica, her violin abandoned like a jilted lover. It would stay in its case for nearly a year.

She returned from her travels fresh and fit and centered, ready to re-engage. In Costa Rica there had been yoga in a cloud forest, in Belize a marathon stretch of scuba diving. Neither Ben nor Robin—in the first flush, finally, of love—could detect a trace of regret over her decision to abandon a music career. Things had played out as they were meant to. Besides, another vocation was calling: that fall Nikki began work toward a master's in clinical psychology at Loyola. In this she could excel, and did.

For some years now she's run a therapy practice focused exclusively on teenage girls. Cutters, depressives, failed suicides, gender shifters, sufferers of every sort of adolescent torment—tough work, draining work, but she's suited to it. She listens acutely, her memory for detail prodigious, then speaks with tonic directness. Ben knows this not because he's watched her work, but because this is her way with everyone. He has no doubt she's very good at what she does.

Since the divorce Nikki's walked a tightrope between her cousin Ben and her best friend Robin, managing it as well as anyone could. Having thrown herself into helping him get back on his feet after the divorce, she's lately pivoted to give Robin her due.

"Shit, I'm sorry about this," she says on the phone. "This is like, what, the third reschedule of this lunch? And tomorrow I'm off to Belize. I'm not even packed. Can't find my fucking regulator." Ben hears her walk across the kitchen, flipflops slapping. "Look, let's have dinner as soon as I get back. I'm dying to try that place in Ukie Village with the kickass gnocchi. I'm buying. No arguments."

"You'll hear none from me."

He expects her to sign off but she lingers on the line.

"Hey, listen. There's something you should know. You shouldn't hear it through the grapevine."

Ben's first, bracing instinct is that she's sick, that she's been handed some terrible diagnosis that will steal her away from him. His stomach tightens.

"Tell me."

"She's moving to Boston, Ben. With the boyfriend. The day I get back, actually. Which is why I need to see her today."

Ben circles the rim of the cappuccino cup with his fingertip, relieved the news isn't about Nikki. Since the deaths of their fathers—twin brothers felled by matching strokes only months apart—they've been closer than ever. No one was kinder to him in the aftermath of the breakup. He does think of her as a sister.

As she waits for him to absorb the news, he senses something shifting in his heart—a quiet rearrangement of his feelings toward his ex-wife. It isn't anger or envy or anything of the sort. No: what he feels for Robin is simple concern.

"You think that's a good idea? I mean, her moving across the country with this guy, after everything she's built here?"

"Career-wise she'll be fine. She's nailed a teaching gig at Brandeis, and she's got her eye on a cello chair at the BSO. Someone's dying, though not as quickly as some might like, apparently. There must be a million players sharpening their knives for it, but you know how well she auditions. Professionally it'll be good."

"And? Personally?"

"Who the hell knows. Alan's moving out there to build his empire. I think it's crazy, between you and me. Can you imagine the competition, with all the universities? There's a café on every corner. But he's sold her on the plan. She's a true believer. Until I hear otherwise, anyway." She says something under her breath, perhaps to her Weimaraner. "She's being really hard-headed about this, Ben. Defensive. Not like herself at all."

"Which can't bode well."

"Thing is, Alan's young. Overconfident. I don't think she sees it, weirdly. If you're asking my opinion, which you're not, my guess is he'll leech off her for a year and come running back with his tail between his legs, with a lot to answer for. His investors won't take kindly to a flameout. These are hardball players. First-class alphas. So I really don't see a future there, no." Nikki takes a breath. "I'm not betraying any confidences in saying this, by the way. These are my opinions, not hers."

"You've said all this to her, I'm sure."

"Delicately. But she just shuts me down. Fucking ghosts me, her oldest friend! It's a huge move—she's nervous about it. She should be." The dog gives a sharp bark; she shushes it in Yiddish. "But after this call I just got, I'm wondering if I finally got through to her. She's not always as strong as she seems, you know. But of course you know."

Again Ben feels a softening toward Robin, her wellbeing somehow still his concern. Despite betrayal and divorce he knows her better than anyone in the world. After so many years together, a true release will take time.

"So," Nikki says, "now I've told you. I thought you should know."

After hanging up he stands and stretches, watching absently through the kitchen window as Eva Farahani tends her basil pots next door. Nikki's given him much to think about. With Robin's abrupt decision he wonders whether he actually might be in a better place than she is—that blowing up her marriage to run off with Alan Hurwitz might have left her in a sort of freefall. Yet nothing about it feels like a victory. In the end, despite everything she's put him through, Ben wants her to be well.

XII.

COFFEE BARON

THOUGH HE'D NEVER ADMIT IT to anyone, it irks Ben that his usurper is just a glorified barista. Hurwitz's smug little café lies between the Jackson El stop and Robin's rehearsal studio, a block from Orchestra Hall. By Ben's tally she must have passed by it a hundred times or more since leasing the space two autumns ago, the location opportune in ways he never suspected.

Since the breakup he's imagined their first encounters in extravagant detail. Robin gusting in for her daily macchiato on a brisk October day, cheeks flushed from the climb down the station steps and the brisk walk along State Street. The tall, shaven-headed proprietor in his black tee shirt coming on to her casually as he pulls her coffee, quickly learning her order by heart, Robin blushing at this small attention to her desires. Bossa nova on the air, probably; a clatter of stools scraping across the varnished floor. The *whoosh* of a steam nozzle plunged into cream. Robin fumbling for her wallet, the exquisitely trained fingers charmingly clumsy. The momentary panic of a spilled coffee somewhere behind her, a bracing curse in a nasal Chicago accent, the marble tabletop hastily swabbed. Robin noticing none of it as she drops a crumpled dollar in the tip jar, being sure to wait until she has her barista's undivided attention. Hurwitz nodding, not so much for the tip as to convey a small intimacy, something already kindling between the two of them—a nod toward a future in which the café will not be the only place they meet. Soon, perhaps, Hurwitz will nod like this when she unbuckles his belt, kneeling before him, a mischievous smile in her eyes.

Really? Ben thinks, unable to shake the images from his mind, even after all this time.

Beyond the plain sexual jealousy, he feels something deeply out of balance in the affair. Robin is an internationally renowned musician, at the top of the second tier of cellists and bidding to enter the first. What's Alan Hurwitz, besides a decade younger and a head taller than her husband? Surely it can't be just the barbed-wire tattoo across the bulky bicep as he pulls her espresso? The flat stomach and the skin-tight black tee shirt that calls it out? It isn't that Robin is blind to such enticements. It's that she's always dismissed them, reaching for character. For substance. How many times has she scoffed at a perfect body, male or female, dismissing anyone who'd invest such time in sculpting their appearance to the neglect of more serious pursuits?

Now Ben wonders if this was ever the whole story. There must be more to the man than a pumped-up body; he respects Robin too much to doubt it. It's simple hurt, he suspects, that's made him so scathing, so dismissive. Then again, it may be that her attraction to Hurwitz is a mystery he doesn't care to solve.

Robin has shed no light on it, of course. She'd certainly never have shared her fantasies of other men while they were together. She'd have spared him such small cruelties only to hit him later, ironically, with the enormous cruelty of walking out on him after twenty years together. She'd have done this not out of some vindictive urge but out of kindness. And so Hurwitz had snaked down onto Ben like a missile out of a clear blue sky as he went about his life, oblivious to the annihilation to come.

THE WORST MOMENTS usually arrive late at night, though they've also come while he's sitting in the sun amid his bedraggled roses, or jogging past the Goethe statue at the end of Diversey, or trawling Twitter while finishing off a solitary biryani up on Devon. He'll be going about his life as if Robin Weil never existed, only to be hauled back into the past and deposited into Hurwitz's accursed café once more, condemned to watch their flirtation on an endless loop.

She and Hurwitz are always there waiting for him, performing under a spotlight of morning sun, her unfussy beauty a thing to behold. It's always October, though in fact he has no idea when they first met. Ben feels the charge between them as if he'd been there to witness it first hand, standing behind Robin in line, maybe, or camped out at a table with a cappuccino in front of him and Bill

Evans in his headphones. He can't help but detect the germ of intimacy in them, the tidal pull toward betrayal. At best he's a prisoner of memory. At worst a ghost, eternally condemned to return to the place of his undoing.

Robin would have stood out from the crowd, surely. Through her late forties his wife's beauty had been gradually distilled down to its essentials, refined by time into something subtler, more magnetic. The red hair muted to bronze, the pale, freckled skin slightly transparent. The narrow, lovely hands more sculptural, their fine bones and veins more defined. But the transformation wasn't only external. As time went on, certain youthful scores had been settled in her heart. Robin began to radiate a mature self-confidence, a luster of experience. Her command of the repertoire was broad and thoughtful, her professional standing secure. By the time she met Alan Hurwitz her résumé was studded with competition wins and guest turns with prestigious orchestras all over the world. Every year there were performances in storied concert halls: the Vienna Musikverein, the Concertgebouw in Amsterdam, Teatro Colón in Buenos Aires. Carnegie Hall was familiar ground. Her students had gone on to win first-chair seats in solid regional orchestras, and in one case a very fine German one.

She wore her victories lightly, without the faintest whiff of arrogance or false modesty. There was a grace about Robin that wasn't feigned. The shy young woman who'd close her eyes nervously while speaking to a stranger, unable to hold a direct gaze, had given way to a woman in full control of her self-esteem. In his solitude Ben's come to see that all this would have been immensely attractive to other men. Her poise and quiet elegance must have caught Hurwitz's eye immediately. Her loneliness too, no doubt, her need to be someone's lover again. It must have been written on her face, even if her own husband had somehow failed to notice it.

HURWITZ HAS HIS OWN ACCOMPLISHMENTS, to be sure. In a few short years he's parlayed the original Café Métro into three more stores, putting down stakes in Streeterville, Roscoe Village and Hyde Park. Something art deco–themed is being rolled out in Evanston; Ben's driven past it. His obnoxiously expensive, private-labeled coffees are popping up in groceries all over the city. Hurwitz is on the upswing.

All this Ben has known, vaguely, for some time—he himself was a fan of Métro's Gold Coast Roast, in fact, until his wife's betrayal turned it to poison. He'd once slogged through a long *Reader* article about Hurwitz's entrepreneurial saga while waiting to collect Robin after a colonoscopy, only because he'd read absolutely everything else in the issue. Dull as it was, the article did contain one detail that caught his eye: apparently the sharp young businessman held a PhD in astrophysics, from MIT no less, and had co-authored an important paper on gravitational waves in dark matter. A little buried surprise that would have pleased Robin, no doubt, even given her some comfort as she fell into his bed. She would have admired Hurwitz for it, would have asked him question after question about his work, educating herself, when they weren't occupying themselves in other ways. It would have delighted her to discover that there was a respectable intellect behind the self-satisfied gaze. It would surely have been a relief.

None of which changed the fundamental fact that Hurwitz had dropped out of academia to squander his gifts on building an empire of cafés. Galactic dark matter had given way to the kind of dark matter that issued from the nozzle of an espresso machine. Perhaps this wasn't the only transformation, either. Had Hurwitz the cosmologist actually walked the MIT campus with such ripped abs? Had his studies left him time to spend hours at the gym every day? Hard to imagine, though you never knew.

Ben had mostly forgotten the *Reader* article, though it was true that the bit about Hurwitz's alter ego as a cosmologist had crossed his mind once or twice while waiting in line for his Gold Coast Roast. Until the breakup he neither knew nor cared, particularly, about the man's personal life. Matters came into stark relief only when Robin confessed that she'd been sleeping with her barista for the better part of a year. It was only weeks after their *Chicago Magazine* cover story ran. She'd long since met Hurwitz's two young children, even his ex-wife. Apparently the affair was old news to everyone but Ben. Confessing it to her husband was almost an afterthought.

Ben did the math. Though his sexual life with Robin had flagged over the years, derailed by her constant touring and the pressures of his work, she must have traded off lovemaking between him and Hurwitz for months. Perhaps she'd slept with both of them on the same day—who knew? Hurwitz in the afternoon, then her unsuspecting fool of a husband on the drowsy slide into sleep. The thought made him physically ill.

How on earth had he missed the warning signs? Robin herself couldn't believe he had. After delivering the news she'd shaken her head in amazement. "You mean you didn't *know*? Jesus, Ben." As if she'd left a note about the affair taped to the refrigerator door: *Ben - Sleeping w/ Alan Hurwitz. Won't be home for dinner tonight. Maybe not ever. Love, R.* As if she'd casually introduced Hurwitz to him as her lover one day, two fingers tucked fondly into the man's razor-strop of a belt. *You know my boyfriend Alan, don't you, Ben?* Mooning up at her barista who'd be grinning proudly down on her, snaking a meaty hand through her fine red hair. It should have been obvious, no? *Jesus, Ben.*

"Fuck no!" Ben had said through his tears on that first horrible night, chastened and embarrassed, as if he'd been the one caught cheating. "I *didn't* know. I trusted you, Robin."

Only in hindsight would he see the countless clues. The faded Café Métro tee shirt she refused to share with him as they routinely shared others. The private-batch blends she'd bring home in canning jars rather than Métro's gold-foil bags. The ever-lengthening hours at the rehearsal studio even as she let go of students, no longer needing the money. (Did she and Hurwitz make love there, knocking over music stands to fuck on the threadbare kilim she and Ben had bought together when fifty dollars was a fortune?) The evidence had been mounting—the deadly gravitational waves surging through the dark matter of their life together—yet somehow Ben was blind to it all. How naïve he'd been. But he could never have imagined the painful details. Only the vacancies of bachelorhood gave him time to do that.

AND NOW THIS RISKY MOVE WITH HURWITZ, this evacuation to Boston and a new life. He can almost hear the debate that must have played out in Robin's head as she inched toward the decision. Even now, if Nikki's right, the matter may not be as settled as she'd thought.

Ben can imagine her high anxiety, her heart at war with a sensible, last-minute trepidation. The professional opportunities in Boston will be pulling at her powerfully, but the idea of abandoning Chicago for a lover—a much younger man whose world is not her world—must be giving her pause. How will it feel to call home from Stuttgart or Santiago, bursting with excitement over the chance to play with some personal hero of hers, only to have her lover respond vaguely, the name meaningless to him? Ben knows the players, the repertoire, the concert halls; Hurwitz would only be guessing. Furtively Googling, faking it. Is this the sort of partner she wants? The Robin Ben knew would've moved heaven and earth to talk a friend out of taking such a leap.

She must be packing up her apartment at this very moment. Coming across a hundred mementos from their decades together, deciding whether to ship them halfway across the country, to inject them into her new life. With her final days in Chicago upon her she must be wrestling with some complicated feelings.

Or perhaps Ben's giving himself more credit than he deserves. Perhaps she's relieved to be done with Chicago. With Ben Weil; with all of it. Happy to be gone.

XIII.

A QUESTION OF BALANCE

WITH LUNCH POSTPONED, the afternoon opens wide. After a careful but steady jog along the lakeshore, the elms and oaks still heavy with the previous day's rain, Ben takes the short way home and heats up Thai leftovers, eating at the kitchen counter in his running clothes. He doesn't bother to shower before sitting down. When he was still a married man, it was the sort of thing he'd do only when Robin was on the road—a rebellious descent into male barbarity as his famous wife soaked in hotel bathtubs in Vienna or Paris. Now he does as he pleases.

As he eats he begins to feel lightheaded again. The heat, he tells himself. Simple dehydration. But as he walks to the sink to refill his water bottle he has to admit it's more than that. He feels himself veering to the right, his center of gravity oddly shifted. At the same time the ringing in his left ear returns, the high-pitched whine he judges to lie somewhere in the ten kilohertz range. With a conscious effort he corrects course, takes two more steps, and turns to walk back across the gleaming floor. The disorientation and ringing fade as abruptly as they came. Ben stops and stands in a square of sunlight; nothing amiss now. The moment's passed.

He wishes he knew how concerned to be about these episodes. Their fickleness is confounding. Sometimes he'll go for a week or more before trouble strikes, only to be caught off guard by a sudden bout. Often it's in the midst of a deadline project that has him pounding out long hours at the studio, which makes some sense, at least. But then an episode will come over him when the workload's been light, when he's been sleeping well, and his blithe hypothesis is shattered at a stroke. None of it adds up to a pattern he can make sense of, but clearly something isn't right.

The ringing in his ear worries him as much as the dizziness, because his carefully attuned hearing is his livelihood. It's what he's esteemed for. If the tinnitus worsens, he won't be able to work. It's as simple as that. And without the work, who would Ben Weil be? He can't begin to imagine.

He tosses away his carryout boxes and tells himself not to over-react. In the next breath he comes up with what seems a reasonable plan, a compromise of sorts. If he's still having the episodes of dizziness when he meets Nikki for dinner after Belize, he'll tell her what's been going on. If she urges him to see a doctor, he will. In the meantime he'll refuse to panic. The day is lovely, his meandering rooms dappled with sun, the Farahani kids playing in the sprinkler and squealing with delight. All will be well for this day, at least.

AFTER LUNCH HE GOES TO THE BÖSENDORFER, the sharp-eyed Edisons poised on the music stand where he stood them the other night. There's a whiff of arrogance about them, a pride in their own relentless genius. There will never be another Edison, they proclaim. Before playing a note Ben turns the cameo portraits to face the stand like scolded schoolboys. "Better," he says to no one in particular, and settles himself on the bench.

The sonata was playing in the back of his mind while he ran along the lakeshore this morning, but what his hands find on the keyboard now is "Round Midnight," the old Thelonious Monk tune. Sometime in his late thirties, perhaps as a statement of some kind to Robin, he'd largely given up the classical repertoire in favor of jazz standards. Like many classically trained players he found it a struggle to get the rhythms under his fingers. Time and again he'd catch himself playing to a metronome in his head, flattening everything into straight time. He assigned himself homework: Coltrane's melancholy ballad, "Naima," to help him stretch out his legato; a handful of Monk tunes for broken syncopation. Blues to loosen his wrists up. He'd never be a natural jazz player, but in time he became a better one.

Jazz became his music of reflection and solace. He played nothing but ballads in the weeks after Robin left, the music helping him think through his next moves. It was "Giant Steps" that convinced him to undertake the kitchen remodel, "Autumn Leaves" that gradually neutralized his corrosive fury over Hurwitz. Now, as he plays through Monk's brooding changes, he feels a certain tranquility settle over his heart.

For some minutes he improvises, letting instinct guide him. The more he's played jazz, the clearer it's become that this sort of free play is what feels most natural to him musically, most heartfelt. By the time he works his way back to the Monk tune, he's touched something inside himself that years of classical training never uncovered. He could stay at the piano all afternoon, sitting in his running shorts with stocking feet working the pedals, the music flowing through him effortlessly, the day gently passing.

In time his quiet mood leads him to the French sonata's opening notes. Quite unexpectedly the familiar arpeggio chimes in his living room. He stops and sits back on the bench. Somehow the thought of actually playing the piece has not occurred to him, yet here it is under his fingers, beckoning quietly. The music seems to have a plan for him.

Ben lowers the lid over the keyboard and takes a long shower, then scrounges up some blank music paper and sits back down at the piano with his laptop open on a chair beside him, Garnier's recording cued up and at the ready. After hesitating a moment he plays the opening arpeggio again, then scribes the notes on the page, taking dictation from the past, his blood quickening in the Saturday sun—the lost sonata emerging in black and white before his eyes.

By SUNDAY EVENING he's managed to transcribe the first two minutes. After listening many times now to the full recording, he's still unclear on how to divide it into movements. The tempo and thematic changes are slippery. Apart from the allegro passage it's not clear where the boundaries should be drawn. None of which matters, for now. At the moment he has his work cut out for him just getting the notes down on paper.

As the hours clock by he works tediously from the recording, playing back a few seconds on the laptop and then working the music out on the Bösendorfer note by note, bar by bar. It's exhausting. He's never been any good at scoring, and he's woefully out of practice.

The shifting time signature gives him particular trouble. It takes him twenty frustrating minutes to decide that the opening passage, with its weirdly staggered pacing and seven-beat rest, is in 5/4 time. Sometimes the corruption of the recording makes individual notes impossible to discern. But as the composer's style soaks deeper into him he begins to find the notes more quickly, the piece unfolding phrase by phrase until he's filled six pages with a working score. Riddled with errors, no doubt, but a solid start.

Which brings him to the cusp of the allegro section. After a journey through the deep bass register, Garnier bursts into a breathtaking series of runs, a blizzard of thirty-second notes flying by at breakneck speed. In the face of this explosion Ben is stopped cold. He can't possibly play it, much less transcribe it. He plays the recording back at half speed but even then it's overwhelming. He's swamped. Garnier's command of his instrument is on par with any of the greats. Ben might as well be chasing a racecar on a bicycle.

Nevertheless he takes out a fresh sheet of manuscript paper, titles it SECOND MOVEMENT: ALLEGRO, and sets to work. He can at least make a start.

For an excruciating hour he labors over the first ten seconds, replaying the music at half speed again and again, trying to capture the opening sequence. There are two ill-placed crackles in the midst of the first soaring run, each obliterating a daisy chain of notes; only by skipping forward to the next run can he infer the missing music. In several places he writes in and then scratches out accidentals, not understanding the chromatics at first, the composer's harmonic concept still opaque to him. No doubt he's making serious mistakes.

By eleven o'clock he's ready to give up. There are just too many notes. The ten-second opening sequence is only that: an opening sequence. Beyond it lies a jungle crawling with danger. It's been tedious enough to get down the introductory themes with their sparse melodies and unhurried pace. The allegro passage could cost him weeks of thankless labor, with no guarantee that he'd get it halfway right. Ben jots the heading THIRD MOVEMENT on a fresh sheet and shuts the laptop down. He'll come back to the vexing allegro later, with a clearer head—it will be waiting.

Eyes bleary, Ben eases into "Naima" at a relaxed tempo, turning back to the comforts of jazz after the long hours of wrestling with Garnier. His fingers find the wistful melody effortlessly and then wander into a low-key improvisation. The music comes easily, exhaustion opening him to new possibilities. The night's tedious work lets him go.

For a good fifteen minutes he strolls through Coltrane's lush garden, circling back to the melody when the mood strikes, varying, modulating, spinning out his own ideas until the chorus gradually twines together with another piece of music close to his heart. He doesn't see it coming until he's well into a segue, but eventually Coltrane follows his muse into the final passage of the Garnier sonata, Ben's left hand leading the way into the sequence of big modal chords with a dark, exploratory E-flat.

When he realizes what's happening he laughs in delight. Why *not* riff on the sonata? From the beginning, after all, he's felt a rare sense of freedom in the piece, an openness to the radically new, the evanescent idea—the spirit of jazz, in a word, though jazz of Coltrane's sort was still half a century in the future when Garnier sat down at the piano. It's one of the most baffling things about the piece. Ben doesn't know the final run of chords well enough to play them through, so he just keeps improvising, quoting Garnier only in loose translation. To his ear it all works beautifully. It's not the sonata he's playing but his emotional impression of it, the ideas flowing smoothly from his hands until he finds himself riffing on the final chords of the recording, a circle of fifths that puts him in mind of "Autumn Leaves." Even the Bösendorfer seems to appreciate his spontaneous cadenza, holding Garnier's last airy, unexpected notes for ages.

XIV.

LILI'S DESCENT

THE NEXT DAYS pass in distraction. He's only going through the motions at Counterpoint, running out the clock until he can go home and forge ahead with the real work. The sonata tugs at him like a needy child. Garnier's faceless ghost hovers in the conference room while he meets with the accountant, then leans over his shoulder, humming the folk melody from the third movement as he swaps out a shorting fader on the Studio B console. On Tuesday afternoon Ben sits impatiently through a presentation on the new profit-sharing plan, playing arpeggios on the tabletop as the sonata cycles in his head. At the earliest decent time he packs his things and steps outside into the volcanic heat. He couldn't care less what his employees think. His fingers are itching to get back to the Bösendorfer's keys.

He begins to listen more carefully, filling a notebook with ideas.

MOVEMENT I

Stillness. Delay 5+ sec — seven beats. In 5/4! Weird. Aggressive use of silence.

Satie Gymnopédie 1. Ravel? Resolve minor to sus2 =imperfect?

Leaves the door TOTALLY open.

~~Modal?~~

Underlying pulse in measures 6-9 — Fauré Nocturne 1, but unsyncopated; performer decision? How to score? Griffes?

Probably NOT Debussy — not really impressionism as I understand it.

This isn't visual language. (Is this right?)

After listening to nearly all the early twentieth-century piano music in his ample collection, Ben is no closer to guessing the identity of the composer. He's no musicologist, but he does know enough to make certain informed judgments. The opening movement, for example, sounds very much like the Satie of the *Gymnopédies*, but the Allegro section all but rules him out. Satie never would have written it. Debussy? Too prone to odd silences. Ravel, Fauré, Rachmaninoff . . . issues with each of them. The music doesn't line up with any of the major composers of the time. Unless, of course, the sonata was someone's early or late work, radically different from the canonical pieces—which would make it a discovery of great interest indeed. Ben continues to listen, filling the house with piano music, his frustration rising as the unknown composer finds ever new ways to elude him.

IT'S NOT THAT THERE AREN'T MOMENTS OF INSPIRATION. Close encounters, near misses. And then, at last, a solid clue.

Late Wednesday evening, as Ben lies on the couch listening to Emile Naoumoff's recording of the little-known Lili Boulanger's *Trois morceaux*, his mind wandering, the city filtering into the room through an open window, something makes him sit up abruptly. He's certain he's heard a passage he recognizes from the Garnier sonata. It comes at the end of the first *morceau*—a thoughtful, dark, stepwise descent into the deep bass register of the piano that ends in two low pulses, exquisitely pianissimo. He dons headphones and plays it back. The intervals, the passing dissonances, the pedal work with its lush sostenutos and bold stops—it's not quite identical, but it's very close to the sonata's descent at the end of the first movement.

This much he's already transcribed. He goes straight to the Bösendorfer and finds the manuscript page, playing it through slowly, the Boulanger sounding in the back of his mind. It is indeed quite close, right down to the two final pulses, doubled As.

Wide awake now, Ben finds the sheet music online and prints it out, then lines it up on the kitchen counter beside his handwritten manuscript of the sonata. Under the bright lights he sight-reads the Boulanger, tracing it with his fingertip and humming the melody line until he locates the descending passage. The composer has marked it *grave et doux*—serious and sweet. Exactly right.

The two pieces step down hand in hand along the black keys, slowing from eighth notes to quarters as the mood darkens, a sparse right-hand melody line urging them on. They track closely across eight full measures, the sonata's harmonies a bit more dissonant, Boulanger's tempo more halting in Naoumoff's reading, but all in all as kindred spirits.

"Yes!" Ben shouts when it's done, and brings the flat of his hand down on the countertop. He's ecstatic. It's not clear what it all means, but it feels hugely significant. In the next instant he looks down the hallway, about to call out to Robin, to share the breakthrough. Hearing the thrill in his voice, she'd drop whatever she was doing and come running, her eyes reading his face, studying him eagerly as he tried to explain the discovery. *"What?"* she'd laugh, "Spit it out, mister! You're killing me!"

But Robin is gone. Gone from his house, gone from his life. It's only him, the smug Edisons, and the ghost of J. Garnier—and now, perhaps, the ghost of Lili Boulanger, too. A garden of the dead.

AT LAST he feels he might be on to something. Going back to the computer, he reads up quickly on Lili Boulanger and discovers that the *Trois morceaux* were composed in 1914, shortly before Garnier made his recording at the Sanborn mansion. The sickly Lili died just four years later, at the age of twenty-four, as the Great War entered its most brutal turn, leaving her sister Nadia to become the Boulanger everyone would remember. Perhaps Lili's somber *morceau* was an early warning of her final illness, or a response to the outbreak of war. A profound darkness runs through it, and through the unknown sonata, too.

Later, as Ben lies in bed trying to sleep, he struggles to make sense of what he's discovered. Only one passage ties the two pieces together, and not quite note for note. He doesn't know much about

Lili's work, but he'd be surprised to learn that the other movements of the Garnier recording were hers too, particularly the jazz passages. A radically different sort of imagination is at work in the other movements—a more brilliant one, perhaps.

The good news is that Lili's oeuvre can be quickly surveyed. She died so young. In the morning he'll get his hands on everything and begin listening. Perhaps there's something else lurking in another of her pieces, another reflection of the sonata waiting to be found. Or perhaps the fleeting passage is just a coincidence, a parallel invention. Or simple plagiarism, for that matter, though in which direction he can't guess. Or then again—most charitably—an *hommage*, one composer quoting the other admiringly.

Anything is possible at this stage. All he knows is that the two pieces seem to share a slim strand of musical DNA. He's in the hunt at last.

On Sunday the rain returns, puttering along as he listens his way through the Lili Boulanger catalog searching for clues. There are only twenty-one published works, nearly all of them brief and many of them choral. The entire span of her piano repertoire can be covered in a few hours of listening. Though he's set aside the day to acquaint himself with the work, he's finished by early afternoon.

In listening to everything once and then a second time, Ben hears no echo of the Garnier recording apart from the eight measures in the first *morceau*. Deflated, the whining in his ear worsening by the hour, he decides that he needs to get out of the house and clear his head. It's time to mull over the evidence he's assembled.

After a quick lunch he takes up his umbrella and spends the rest of the afternoon walking in the rain, ducking into used bookstores, sniffing cheeses at the local deli, stopping for baklava at a Greek bakery packed with sullen backgammon players. Wanting a coffee, he steps into a café but leaves when he sees the placard displayed next to the espresso machine: Café Métro Blends Proudly Served Here. Instead he stands before a kiosk just outside, inspecting a year's worth of concert posters peeling away in the damp, a soggy palimpsest of the city's life. The rain shows no sign of letting up. Through it all he turns the Lili Boulanger question over in his mind.

The likeliest explanation, it seems to him, is that the mirrored passage is a case of parallel invention. There are meaningful differences between the Garnier recording and Lili's piece; who's to say either composer was aware of the other's work? The evidence is just too thin to support it. The two pieces have nothing in common beyond the eight brief measures that first caught his ear.

But there is the matter of their nearness in time. Lili's *Trois morceaux* were published only three years before Garnier sat down at a piano in the Sanborn mansion and recorded the *Fr. sonata, American debut*. Perhaps the composer of the lost sonata had heard Lili's piece and unconsciously borrowed from it, the resulting work somehow making its way across the Atlantic to a Boston drawing room? Such things happened, sometimes with brilliant results. One hears it all through the Baroque repertoire. It's not a matter of thievery so much as a subtle call and response. But how, in the case of a nameless composition engraved into five bruised wax cylinders, could one possibly know the artist's mind?

As Ben wends his way home through the rain the whole venture begins to feel pointless. He lets himself into the house and changes into dry clothes, then brews the cup of coffee he's been craving all afternoon, watching the drizzle spatter against the kitchen window while he considers his next steps.

Boston and Aigremont

August 1915

XV.

WELL IN

IT'S CYRIL JONES who gives Elisabeth the news, not that he really intends to. It's the Monday after the Sanborn garden party and she's arrived at the Bantry Street offices in a nervous state, certain she's to be let go—Jack Rimes, the general manager of the Boston operation, having summoned her to his office for a chat. She hasn't sold a single Imperial. How can they keep her on?

Perhaps it's for the best. The real question is what to tell her father: it's not a matter of losing her meager contribution to the grocery budget, but of his proud hopes for her. The news from France has been so abysmal, so frightening, so very sad; her position with the Company has given him something to grasp onto, the sense of a future. He has a few talented piano students who lift his spirits, but it's nothing like seeing his daughter flourish. To watch her leave in the morning dressed like a proper young lady, to kiss her powdered cheek as she goes off to the streetcar—this is what he needs.

She's been glad to help him in this way, just as she's glad to rub his shoulders while he sits slumped over the newspapers in despair, reading every snaking line of bad news about the war, the personal letters reprinted for the news they carry, the grim dispatches from London and Petrograd and Gallipoli. "Jousselin's been killed!" he cries, gripping the table like a passenger on a wildly rolling ship. "The British have deported the Kaiser's *pianist*." "Elisabeth—starving Hungarians are eating soap to survive!" Each day brings more outrageous developments. She worries that her papa is drowning in all the misery, but doesn't feel right standing in his way. France is his mother, and she's dying before his eyes. How is it her place to keep him from his grief?

And so she's been happy to let him relish her advancement in the world. What would become of him if even this consolation were taken away? When the Company lets her go, she thinks, she'll continue to dress in the morning and leave at her usual hour, pretending she's off to work . . . she'll stroll the park until he's safely at school, then double back and hole up in the hot apartment, or take the streetcar into town and window-shop the fall styles, all the fine frocks she'll never be able to afford. She'll do whatever it takes to keep her father whole. Tomorrow the masquerade will begin.

But as she walks through the assembly room Cyril Jones waves her over, a rumpled order form in his hand.

"This ain't right, is it? Cody's cutting the plate and he don't want to spell it wrong."

Jones points to the line on the form where customers write in what they'd like engraved on the nameplate of their new Graphophones. There, in a precise hand, Elisabeth reads something that makes no sense to her: *To Anna, mein Schatz — from Helmut.* Beside the name *Helmut* someone's printed in blunt pencil: H-E-L-M-I-T. Cyril's dirty fingernail points to the editorial correction. "Helluva name but it sure ain't spelled like that. Should be H-E-L-M-I-T, like a doughboy's. Right?"

It dawns on Elisabeth what she's looking at: her first sale.

How could it be? She wracks her brain, trying to understand—then remembers giving the German her card at the Sanborns' party. The card says nothing about the Company, by design, but it does list the Bantry Street address and the telephone number, LEXington 4826.

"How did this order come in?" she asks Cyril.

"Fella stopped in yesterday after you left, asked for you. High-hat sort. Surprised by the operation." Lowering his voice, he adds: "A *Hun.* The boys wanted to deck him. But Rimes was out of his office fast as you can say Jack Robinson. Saw the cut of the man. Poured him a whiskey and had a check in hand in twenty minutes flat." Cyril rummages on his workbench, finds an oversized calling card with a grubby thumbprint on it. "Left this for you."

In Jack Rimes' office Elisabeth is handed an envelope with twelve dollars, her first commission. Far from letting her go, Jack is full of praise. In two days' time she and Tom will call on the Cabots, then on Saturday will ride out to a polo party at the Robert Gould Shaws, in Wellesley—it's already been arranged. "The Sanborns were just the warmup pitch," Jack says. "Now I want you to knock it out of the park."

As Elisabeth walks home from the streetcar, the envelope with its prize clutched in her hand, she wishes her mother were home to hear her news. "*Ça ne m'étonne guère!*" she'd say proudly, untying her apron to embrace her daughter. "You shine like a star, *ma fille.*" But Sylvie Garnier is gone. This Sunday, as every Sunday, her daughter and husband will leave flowers at her grave, the stately elms and manicured lawns unable to soften the memory of her final days, the jaundice and the painful mercury treatments, the opium funk and delirium, the sweaty hair and last convulsive breaths. There is a familiar hollow in Elisabeth's chest at the thought of her mother, an ache that sometimes sharpens to something far more dangerous. One day her heart will break wide open at the thought of her. Her father's must break every time he awakes to find her side of the bed empty.

As Elisabeth nears home she feels for the German's calling card, stashed in the pocket of her skirt. Cyril Jones's oily fingers have left their mark. With a deft motion Elisabeth tears it to pieces, scattering the scraps in the alley among the stinking trash bins. Today, of all days, she knows her heart, and there is room in it for only one man. He'll be waiting for her upstairs, collar unbuttoned and a warm lemonade in hand, never suspecting what good tidings she carries.

WHEN A TELEGRAM COMES from Helen Sanborn, Elisabeth's not entirely surprised. For a week now, since selling her first Graphophone, she's felt movement under her feet, the world opening to receive her. A change is in the air. When Jack Rimes strides from his office with a telegram in hand there's an admiration in his eyes that was never there before. "For you," he says, handing it to her with a hint of formality. "The Sanborns."

DARLING ELISABETH –(STOP)-
YOUR PRESENCE REQUESTED AS MY GUEST AT
CALUMET CLUB SATURDAY
1 PM LADIES LUNCH –(STOP)-

RSVP TO PROVIDENCE 3267 –(STOP)-
AFFECTIONATELY HELEN SANBORN –(STOP)-

Elisabeth reads it again, then looks at Jack, who begins to laugh. "You look like you've seen a ghost, Liz," he says, and squeezes her arm. "You're well in now. Good work."

When Elisabeth slips the telegram in her pocket it radiates a sort of heat. It's as heady as an order commanding an army to march, though its real meaning will be revealed only gradually, as summer fades into autumn and one year passes into the next. When she shows it to her father over dinner he'll study it like a score, then gaze across the table and reach for her hand—her dear, emotional father, so French, so quick to tears.

"Don't forget me, *ma fille*," he'll say with a tight-lipped smile, and take up a napkin to dry his eyes.

XVI.

VERY MUCH A GENTLEMAN

IN THE WEEKS THAT FOLLOW, Elisabeth will feel time quicken. At night she'll lie awake while the events of the day scroll past her inner eye, too swift to make sense of. Half a dozen society girls, friends of Helen Sanborn, sitting around a flower-bedecked table at the Calumet Club that first Saturday, testing their boarding school French on her and frothing over with invitations to polo matches, motorcar outings on the Cape, charity auctions. The clink of crystal glasses; Delmonico steaks and halibut brought in on monogrammed plates, materializing from beneath silver domes. Long Sunday treks out to Aigremont to go riding with Helen or gossip over iced Coca-Cola in her girlish bedroom, meanwhile fending off the attentions of the rowdy Sanborn boys when Rena isn't around to ride herd on them. A terrifying sail up to Nahant in Oren's sailboat, the seas rough and Oren three sheets to the wind, the boom swinging back and forth like a wrecking ball as he tacks wildly and tilts the boat so far over that Elisabeth can skim the water with her toes.

"Between us, Elisabeth," Rena Sanborn will tell her one afternoon as the two of them stroll the garden cutting roses for the table, "I'm delighted that Helen's found a friend in you. A girl who's not afraid to earn her keep . . . it's a rare thing around here. I like the ideas you're putting in her head. It's a fine example you set."

This will surprise Elisabeth—her work with the Company is something she never speaks of at Aigremont—until she recalls Jack Rimes saying that Rena may have first entered the Sanborn household as a domestic, a cook or housekeeper. She too is a woman who would have known how to earn her keep. The more time they spend together, the more Elisabeth admires her, as much for what she doesn't say as for what she does.

In spite of what Rena thinks, though, Elisabeth can't see that her own style of life is making much of an impression on young Helen. On the last day of August, Helen takes her hands in hers and confesses that she's been called upon several times by H. E. Rollins, a gentleman from a family of judges and political men down in Savannah, Georgia. Apparently he's come up for a special course at Harvard Law, though Helen's vague on the details.

"Hugh's his real name, but he goes by H. E. down south," she says with a knowing look. "He wouldn't tell me what the E. was until I said I'd dine with him at his club."

"You're sure that's all it took?"

Helen lets go of Elisabeth's hands to swat them. "Shame on you! How much do you think a silly middle initial is worth, anyway? A half-burnt chop in a roomful of Harvard men was sacrifice enough, believe me. Not that he didn't apologize for the food—he was mortified. But next to those boys Hugh came off like royalty. Perfect manners and a John Barrymore profile. Not a hair out of place. And that accent! Soft as *buttah*. I could listen to it for hours. We strolled all through the quads afterward and he was a perfect gentleman every step of the way."

"Did you find out what the *E* stood for?"

Helen scowls teasingly. "Ready, Liz?"

"Ready."

"It's for *Evelyn*." Helen bursts into laughter. "Priceless, isn't it?"

"But that's a woman's name. In France it is. We say *Aveline*."

Helen nods through her laughter. "He was so embarrassed to admit it—it was sweet. He's forbidden me to speak it aloud. But in England it's quite a distinguished name for men. There're dukes and viscounts. Very highbrow. Since Hugh's from an old Southern family, I guess I'm not surprised." Taking Elisabeth's hands again she says, "In some ways they're a hundred years behind us down there, barely modern at all, but if that means chivalry isn't dead I'm all for it."

"When do you see Mr. Rollins next?"

"He'd like to know that, I expect."

"So you're keeping him guessing. You must be really serious."

Helen's eyes go vague.

"Yes," she says, almost to herself, "I think I am. Deadly serious, possibly."

LATER, UPSTAIRS IN HER BEDROOM, Helen shows her the letters Rollins has written her, a fat bundle of ornately addressed, squarish ivory envelopes bound with pink silk ribbon. She's hidden them, along with a diary and certain other precious possessions, in a cubby she accesses through a loose strip of baseboard behind the nightstand. When she takes up a letter-opener and gently pries the baseboard loose, revealing a two-foot-wide void behind the wall, Elisabeth looks away, embarrassed by the brazenness of her young friend's faith in her. Though she'd certainly never betray Helen's cache to others, she'd feel better if Helen made her swear not to. It's too intimate a revelation to let pass in silence. But all Helen cares about is her paramour's letters. From the cubby she retrieves a briefcase made of some lacquered, diamond-patterned hide.

"This?" she says, seeing Elisabeth's surprise. "A hand-me-down from my aunt, who brought it back from a coffee-buying trip in Costa Rica. It's iguana." From deep inside the cubby she retrieves a key and unlocks the case, drawing out the thick bundle of letters. "Just look at these!" she says, handing them to Elisabeth. "H. E. writes me *twice a day*. He sent me six letters before I'd even agreed to see him."

Elisabeth weighs the bundle on her palm, cologne wafting from it. "This man knows just what he's doing," she says with a grave look.

"Don't I know it."

"He has a battle plan, Helen. You're under siege, actually. Be careful, won't you?"

"I am careful," Helen says with a defiant little frown.

"I'm sure you are. It's just that a man like this . . . he's obviously experienced."

Helen snatches back the letters, returning them to the briefcase and sliding it into the nook. Deftly she snaps the baseboard back into place and shifts the nightstand in front of it. It's quite a good hiding place, Elisabeth thinks. *Brava*, she tells Helen silently.

As they say their goodbyes it occurs to Elisabeth that she herself has never had such a hiding place. Not in Honfleur, not in Saint-Cloud, certainly not in the Roxbury flat. She's never needed one. As a girl she had no prying brothers or sisters to worry about, and what few secrets she did have dwelt only in her thoughts. She felt she could talk to her mother and father about almost anything; they'd given her this gift at an early age. Only since her mother's passing has she begun to worry that it's made her a bit of a naïf, defenseless in a world unworthy of such trust, a world that doesn't always have her best interests in mind. As the train carries her back to the city, Elisabeth considers her open heart and wonders if a day will come when someone breaks it without a second thought.

HER SOCIAL ENGAGEMENTS begin to spread her thin. Unlike her various hosts, she works for a living and sometimes has to drag herself out to Friday evening dinners that don't begin till nine, or Saturday garden parties that are a trolley and two long train rides from Roxbury. And there is her papa to consider. As she sits in fine parlors, playing dull hands of whist while listening to well-heeled girls gab about sailing down to Bermuda or gambling in Havana, she thinks of him alone in the apartment, scouring the papers obsessively or wading through Shakespeare in the original, a challenge he's set himself as other men resolve to climb the Matterhorn. She's learning to say no to invitations, on his account: to plead competing engagements, when really all she wants is to cook her father a pot of *moules* and talk away the evening with him, as they've always done.

As the hot summer flows into a crisp fall and the social season swings into high gear there are ever more invitations to cope with, not just from the Sanborns and their friends but from other clients, too—even the Cabots, once, who invite her to steam to Ireland with them on a shooting holiday in Galway. The pace of her new life is exhausting and exhilarating all at once. Sometimes it seems she's away more often than she's home.

HOW, THEN, CAN SHE NOT WORRY when she arrives late in the evening to find the apartment empty? Sometimes her father will have left a note saying he's dining at the home of one of his students, or attending a symphony concert with his violinist friend Martin, but more often there is no note at all. The apartment is small; from her room she'll hear him turn the key after midnight, quiet as a cat burglar, and go straight to bed. In the morning he'll ask about her evening in a stream of questions that leaves her no opening to ask about his. It's clear that he'd rather keep his movements to himself.

She wonders whether there is a woman. It's the simplest explanation for the long evenings, the stealth, the evasiveness. He'd be too proper to share such a development with his daughter; he'd never volunteer such information. But if it's a woman, why hasn't his mood improved? If anything, there's a darker cast to his eyes, a deeper preoccupation with thoughts he won't share. And he's been losing weight: his drawn face and loose-fitting trousers worry her as much as his downcast eyes do.

Elisabeth senses they're both changing, but his change seems to be for the worse. She can't get him out of her mind, whether brushing off Tom Shea's banter at work or making small talk with some Cabot or Sanborn. Her father is always with her. All she wants is for him to find some happiness, or failing that some peace, but she barely knows how to help him search for it.

An afternoon comes when she confesses her worries to Helen. They're sitting together in a loveseat under the garden pergola, grapes and purple clematis twined above, a pitcher of punch before them despite the touch of fall in the air. It's October, with a scent of burning leaves about. Along High Street, and all down the narrow lanes that meander to the Mystic Lakes, the maples are losing more of their scarlet with every wisp of breeze. Mrs. Dooley has brought them cashmere wraps, just right for a day that can't decide between summer warmth and autumn cool.

"Your father must think of home constantly," Helen says. "I certainly would."

"It's all he thinks about. He can't understand why Wilson is keeping out of the war. Coddling the Germans, waiting for them to explain the Lusitania, as if it were any mystery what they're up to. It disgusts him."

99

"All my brothers want to ship out, though of course James is the only one old enough. I think it's all to impress the girls. Hardly your father's motivation." Helen laughs suddenly, too brightly. "Can you imagine my big brother in the trenches, with no one to feed him? He wouldn't last a week."

With her father's dark mood weighing upon her Elisabeth finds it difficult to share in her friend's amusement. "I think my papa wants to go over there too. He's almost fifty years old! And can you imagine a pianist with a rifle in his hands?"

Helen senses her guest's annoyance, or perhaps hears her own glib words echo embarrassingly in her mind. In a softer tone she says, "He seems such a refined man, from all you've said. A gentleman in the best sense."

Elisabeth has been around enough society people now to hear the question hidden inside her friend's remark: Is your father a noble? A gentleman in *that* sense? The unspoken question comes as no surprise. The Boston arrivistes are fascinated by the moldy old hierarchies of Europe. For them it's as if the Revolution never happened.

Elisabeth's said little to the Sanborns about her own family—the Garniers being hard-working, educated, no-nonsense bourgeois from a small Norman town, nothing more, nothing less. Just now it seems to her that to hide her origins is to insult her father.

"He's very much a gentleman," she replies, "educated, well spoken, kind. But the Garniers are ordinary folk, you know, just good working people. It's my father who went off to Paris and distinguished himself."

Helen nods thoughtfully. "As a musician?"

"He was a classmate of Debussy's at the Conservatoire. He gave recitals in the Faubourg Saint-Germain—I think he was a bit of a ladies' man, very handsome, very talented. At some point he was invited to play for the Duchesse d'Uzès, which is how he came to meet Maestro Warren, a friend of hers."

"Warren? That's not French."

"He was American—Professor Severn Warren, the music chair at Harvard until he crashed his roadster into the Charles. A brilliant pianist. He died only two weeks after we arrived here. He'd met my father at the Duchesse's château down in the Vaucluse, while on tour in Europe."

Helen lights up. "Wait, Warren . . . he played in our old Sheffield Road house! I'm sure of it. Years ago, at one of my mother's candlelight teas. There's a photo. A thin sort with a cigar and bushy eyebrows. Snow on the ground. I could show it to you."

"Unfortunately he didn't live long enough to defend my father's appointment."

"How do you mean?"

"We came over because Maestro Warren promised him a teaching post at Harvard, a place with a chamber group he'd founded, guest appearances with the Boston Symphony . . . all for good money, and with opportunities to go back to Europe regularly on tour. It was exciting for a young musician. Flattering."

"But he was doing so well in Paris."

"Yes, but he wasn't actually making much money, and he disliked the nastiness. There were some ugly people in that world. Geniuses, too, of course—Debussy, Fauré, Ravel . . . he knew them all. It wasn't easy to stand out in that kind of company. In America he'd be in the limelight from the moment he arrived. So he convinced Mama they should take the offer. We came over on the *Bretagne* when I was twelve."

"Only to have Warren drown himself in the Charles. It all fell to pieces."

"It turned out that the Harvard post hadn't actually been approved by the faculty, who apparently hated Warren to a man. Withdrawing my father's offer was their first order of business."

"Vile! Was there no chance of appeal?"

"For an immigrant who didn't know a soul here? Who was brought over by a man they despised? There was no appeal. And as soon as Harvard fell away, all the other promises fell away too. The Symphony, the chamber group, all of it gone, just like that."

"What on earth did he do?"

"What he still does. He taught piano at Boston Latin. Took private students, too."

Helen lays a hand on hers. "Oh Elisabeth, I didn't realize."

"It's not that he dislikes the work. Until recently, I think, it gave him satisfaction. Of course, it's not Paris . . . of course there is disappointment. He could have taught there, if nothing else, and who knows where that might have led."

"Why didn't he go back?"

"He'd cut all his ties to that world. He'd made such a point of walking away. He'd burned his bridges behind him. And he had a wife and daughter to support. So when he was offered the Latin post he took it without a second thought, just to have a steady income. My parents had nothing else. Eventually, I suppose, they decided to raise their daughter as an American."

"My good fortune!"

"But now with the war, with Mama gone. . . ."

"Now you wonder whether he'll stay or go."

"I do."

Elisabeth feels tears coming on. Until now she's not confessed her fears to anyone.

Helen slips an arm around her shoulders and pulls her close. When a shiver runs through Elisabeth's body, a little chill of sorrow, Helen lifts her cashmere wrap and gathers her friend to her bosom, rocking her slowly, shushing her, the scent of her lavender bath water and the swell of her breast a comfort. For a time Elisabeth floats in the warm pool of her friend's affection, a lily serenely tethered. Helen strokes her hair; traces a tiny vein across her temple, her fingertip feather light. If time is passing, Elisabeth isn't aware of it.

Eventually Helen whispers, "I have an idea."

Elisabeth tilts her head to see her friend's broad face hovering above her, a light flickering in her eyes. Again a scent of burning leaves comes, of the season passing.

"Tell me."

"We'll invite your father to play here. You said he'd love to try out the grand piano. . . . Let's give him that opportunity. Just a relaxed affair. Maybe we can lift his spirits, take his mind off the war for a little while. Give him a chance to do what he loves most. And how wonderful it would be for the rest of us!"

"Oh—" Elisabeth sits up, feeling a collision in her chest. Her two worlds have never touched in this way. At the same time she knows how it would thrill him. He's not touched a grand piano in years, much less given a recital. She tries to picture him in the Sanborn music room in his modest teacher's suit, with his unruly hair, Oren and the boys fidgeting as he plays, Helen and Rena looking on with satisfaction, the music room reverberating with his artistry. Helen's right: to play again would bring him tremendous pleasure.

Helen warms quickly to her idea. "Liz, we could record him on the Graphophone. What would you say to that?"

It's terrible, but in the clarity of the moment Elisabeth sees it this way: Jacques Garnier's passion should be preserved—yes!—because the time will come when he can no longer play. On some bleak day she'll lose him forever. . . . This is the hard truth of the matter. With a recording, at least, she'll always have his music, even if she can't have him.

"It's a splendid idea, a wonderful idea," she tells Helen, and does her very best to smile.

Chicago

October 2018

XVII.

ALLEGRO FOR FOUR HANDS

It's well past time to report in to Willa Blount. Ben's put it off for as long as he decently can. With a coffee close at hand he picks up the phone and dials the number for the Wooden Arabian.

He halfway expects the shop to be closed, as it's after six in Maine. But the phone is picked up immediately by someone who sounds like a chirpy teenage girl. Ben asks for Ms. Blount and after some moments an older voice comes on the line, contralto and confident.

"Mr. Weil," Willa says before he's identified himself. "I'd thought you might come up for air just about now. And so you have. I've got you in my phone as a VIP, you know."

He can't help but laugh. "This thing must be pretty important to you."

"More than you know. What news do you have for me?"

Willa Blount speaks with a brisk New England accent, businesslike even when dispensing pleasantries. He pictures her sitting on a high stool behind an antique brass cash register, a honeyed early-evening light seeping through the window, postcard-perfect lobster boats bobbing in the harbor across the street. Evening settling in; tourists strolling. Sturdy brick warehouses opposite the wharf; an ancient general store with warped floors. As for the Wooden Arabian, Ben can see it as clearly as if he passed through its jangling door only yesterday.

He knows what Willa Blount looks like, too. After receiving her first letter he'd hunted down several photos of her on the internet. His correspondent was wiry and compact, in her hale early eighties, he judged, with the good posture and surefooted grace of an aging athlete. Through the photos he peered into her world. Willa manning a table at some town festival, her gray hair clipped short and an Ask Me About the Good Old Days button pinned to her cream jacket. Willa rising in a town council meeting to make a point, legal pad in hand. Willa posing in Victorian costume, powdered and bewigged, the hint of a smile saying that she's perfectly aware of how ridiculous she looks. Ben noticed early on that her eyes somehow formed the precise focal point of every photo: there was something uncompromising in Willa Blount's gaze, a quickness to be reckoned with.

And now she's waiting for his report. He thinks it best to lower expectations.

"It's slow going, but I'm getting there. Proceeding step by step. It's how I work."

"I'm sure a methodical approach is best. How far have you gotten?"

"The recording's in much better shape. Listenable musically now, with some issues."

"That alone is an accomplishment, I suppose." A phone trills in the background; Willa's young assistant picks it up. "Mr. Weil, I know it's early days, but do you feel the recording might be of historical interest? I'm perfectly prepared to hear that it's not."

"Really too soon to say." He could tell her he's been transcribing the sonata, picking it out on the piano in every spare moment, but he holds back. "It's a strange piece. Not Impressionism in Debussy's sense, though there are whiffs of that. I thought about Satie, but the Allegro wouldn't be like him." He has no idea how much Willa Blount knows about music. Perhaps the names mean nothing to her. "What's amazing is how all those elements are blended in such a modern way—you just wouldn't expect that in 1917. There's actually jazz in it, and I don't mean Jelly Roll Morton, either. Something much more experimental. Mid-century. I don't know what to make of it, in all honesty."

"I do appreciate honesty. Any luck tracking the elusive Garnier down?"

"I haven't put much time into that aspect, honestly."

"You're very intent on honesty, Mr. Weil, I have to say."

Embarrassed, Ben smiles nervously into the phone, as if Willa Blount could see him.

She says, "A question for you. Does it make sense to play the improved recording for some of the musicians you know? Take a sounding, if that's not too bad a pun?"

"I'll do that soon," he replies, though he wonders whether he actually will. For some reason he's hesitated to reveal the sonata to others, even others who surely know the period better than he does—Ana Clara Matta, above all. "I want to take the audio restoration as far as I can before I ask people to invest time in it. Their time is so valuable."

This is met with a silence long enough to become awkward. "I know you'll use your best efforts," Willa says at last. "Please do keep me updated on your research." He hears the shimmy of a door chime in the background. "And now I've got someone here to pick up a bedstead. I appreciate the call, Mr. Weil." After a beat she adds: "Honestly."

"My pleasure. And please call me Ben, if—" But the line's gone dead.

AFTER THE TALK WITH WILLA he's drawn back to the question of Garnier's identity. As little as he's been able to discern about the sonata's origins, he's got even less to report about its stunning interpreter. Apart from a drowsy evening spent thumbing through the *Grove* he's done little to hunt down the virtuoso behind the recording. Obviously there are better ways. Sitting down at the computer he types *J Garnier* into a search box and begins to scan the results that come flying back, hoping to stumble over something that will part the veil.

There is precious little to be found. After an hour of trolling through websites he's learned about various Garniers, but none of them a turn-of-the-century pianist. Ben makes the acquaintance of Jean Garnier, a minor sculptor of romantic bronzes who died in 1910, then wastes far too much time browsing through auction photos of Pierrots and ruffians with violins and ewers engraved with flying pixies, none of which suggest that the sculptor had a sideline as a virtuoso pianist. Then there is Charles Garnier, architect of the Paris Opéra, *aka* the Palais Garnier: this might have been the distant bell that rang when he first saw the name. He and

Robin saw *Rigoletto* there on their honeymoon. But the Garnier of Palais fame is no more the one Ben's looking for than is the etcher of flying pixies.

Disheartened, he leaves the mystery for later. For once the internet has nothing to offer. But in the end it's the music that matters most. His priorities couldn't be clearer.

DEEP IN THE NIGHT a dream awakens him sweetly. He's sitting at the Bösendorfer where he's spent so many hours since Willa Blount entered his life, the sonata score spread flat across the piano top. The entire piece has been neatly transcribed, even the Allegro section his waking self has abandoned for later. It's this section the dreamer is playing, hands flying over the keyboard in a blur of inspiration too fast for the eye to track, the music exploding from the piano . . . his playing volatile, dangerous, infinitely far beyond anything Ben would be capable of in waking life. In the dream he leans forward, putting his back into it, and the music comes faster and faster, unstoppable in its ecstatic complexity, until the Allegro gives way to the third movement's folk song. The pianist shifts mood effortlessly, softening his attack with perfect grace and control.

As the sleeping Ben plays on, he becomes aware of two hands coming to rest lightly upon his, the way a piano teacher might guide a child. A trace of warm breath touches his neck; there's jasmine on the air. A woman's slender fingers steer his left hand as it plays the simple bass figure, finger pressing on finger as if playing a human keyboard, a fine gold bracelet laid against the narrow wrist. The folk melody begins unfolding into its variations, the invisible accompanist leading the way, until the music stops cold at the precipice of the six-second gap. The tawny hands clutch his as if to keep them from touching the keys, to prevent a stray note from shattering the silence.

Ben awakes to find the dream still in his body, the thrill of the Allegro thrumming in his veins. The music is inside him as never before. He can still feel, too, the woman's hands guiding his, the nearness of her, her tactful patience with him. In the semi-darkness of his bedroom he forgets for a moment where he is, like a traveler startled awake in a foreign port, the world beyond the window alien and hyperreal. Only the hands feel familiar.

XVIII.

NIGHT MUSIC

IN THE MORNING he awakes with a raw throat, feeling as if he hasn't slept at all.

Exhausted, he lies watching the locust tree through the bedroom window as it shivers its mane of gold. Fall has come to Chicago almost overnight. All along the lakeshore the parks are aglow with autumn hues, the air brisk as ice water once the sun goes down. It's Ben's favorite time in the city. If he felt better he'd take a quick turn around the neighborhood before leaving for work, but instead he lies still and takes stock of his condition.

He's not well. He can't pretend he is. Something's invaded his body overnight, really dug in. His sinuses are filling up, which seems to be worsening the tinnitus, the tiny engine charging along louder than ever. When he finally swings out of bed his joints complain like an old man's.

"Who kicked the shit out of you?" he asks the hangdog reflection in the mirror, alarmed. He dreads being sick—always has—but more than this he dreads being sick alone. There will be no Robin to shoo him back to bed, to bring him lemon-ginger tea, to call during rehearsal breaks just to make sure he's alright. Even Nikki's gone off to Belize. He could die in his bed and not be discovered for days.

In the shower he loses his balance for several seconds, his head spinning when he closes his eyes. It's so severe that he has to brace himself against the tile wall to keep from falling, then squat like an umpire until it finally passes. Afterward he dresses haphazardly, unable to make simple decisions, and finally pulls on yesterday's rumpled Counterpoint tee shirt. It will do.

Against his better judgment he drags himself to work. There is the monthly all-hands meeting at nine, then a meeting with the acoustician, Jean Artigue, who's come all the way from Paris to study Studio A. Artigue's gear has been shipped ahead in locked cases and awaits him in the storeroom. It would be poor form to stand the man up after he's traveled thousands of miles to meet the renowned Benjamin Weil. And there is Ana Clara Matta, who plans to drop in at some point and collect a disc with premasters of the Debussy préludes she's recorded so far. Ben wants to hand the CD off in person; he's made gain adjustments to the *Ondine* that are worth discussing before she auditions the recordings. But more than this he simply wants to be in her presence. There is no doubt in his mind as to who last night's gentle piano teacher was.

His laptop is still sitting on a chair next to the piano where he's been using it to play back the sonata as he transcribes. As he zips it into his messenger bag his eyes stray to the manuscript pages. On impulse he tucks them in with the computer, another spell of vertigo coming over him just as he turns to leave the room. His head is pounding with a sinus headache, his left ear roaring, his stomach queasy.

"Jesus! Enough," he says in exasperation, but as he walks to the front door the balance problem dogs him with every step. He tacks to the right without intending to, then falters when he corrects for it. The trouble is out in full force. What's usually a passing sensation has dragged on for an hour now.

He thinks the head cold must be putting pressure on his inner ear. He tells himself there's no cause for alarm. But something is changing; with each passing day it's becoming harder to dismiss it. He isn't at all pleased with the fractious new music in his head. Robin surely would have forbidden him to go in to work—would have made a doctor's appointment for him and driven him there and sat holding his hand in the exam room, insisting they get to the bottom of it. But Robin's made other choices for her life.

Out on Lincoln, Ben hails a cab rather than walk the half hour to the studio, although the return of the sun gives him a momentary lift, the atmosphere scrubbed clean by yesterday's rains. The thought of navigating the commotion of the streets is exhausting. The day has just begun and already his energy is nearly spent. As the blocks lurch past he toys with telling the driver to turn around and deposit him back on his doorstep, but the day's business pulls at him, uninterested in his complaints. Better to power through till quitting time and turn in early. Better to stay on a proper cycle.

After paying the driver he walks quickly through Counterpoint's common area and shuts himself in his office. In the enveloping quiet he closes his eyes and lets the sun sing through his body, his head spinning down. Gradually the howling in his ear fades. He'll take it slowly today, see how he feels by lunchtime. Getting this far already feels like an accomplishment.

Jean Artigue arrives toward the end of the staff meeting. Ben shows him straight into Studio A and asks the intern to wheel his gear in from the storeroom. Though he's just flown in from Paris, the wiry man in the wrinkled shirt is alert and engaging. He's been working toward this moment for the better part of a year now.

Artigue's angular face is lined and tired under its thatch of gray, but his hazel eyes are on the qui vive. Carefully they survey the control room, the layout of the recording suite, everything that might play a role in the famous Studio A sound. At first Ben finds his energy tiring, but the man's enthusiasm is irresistible and soon he feels buoyed by it, happy to be carried along. Though his plan was to get his guest situated and leave him be, Ben decides on the spur of the moment to stay with him and learn what he can. The research is intriguing, actually, as it will compare Studio A's acoustics with those of other top-tier studios around the world. Solid empirical work, not just subjective impressions. Artigue has promised to share results as soon as he has them. While he sets up his custom-built gear Ben asks him a string of questions, putting the fatigue out of his mind. He's pleased to hear that Counterpoint first came to his guest's attention through Ana Clara's Ravel CD; Artigue's wife, a musicologist at the Sorbonne, couldn't stop listening to it. Jean himself, while not a musician, seems to have an impressive knowledge of French modernism. For some minutes he enthuses over Messiaen's ear for birdsong. By the time the temp appears in the doorway to take their lunch orders, it seems impossible that two hours have come and gone.

At four-thirty, with the work completed and Artigue's gear packed away, Ben collapses onto the leather sofa in the reception area. The Frenchman is saying polite goodbyes to the staff, making his way methodically through the suite like a bridegroom thanking guests. Ben likes him; in the course of the afternoon he's observed a deep vein of perfectionism in the man that mirrors his own. They're both connoisseurs of sound at its most refined. He's learned things from Artigue as well, crouching by his side as the equipment probed every inch of the performance space in search of tiny variations in resonance that might contribute to the Counterpoint sound. Now and then his guest would exclaim under his breath in French, struck by some nuance that had caught his attention, then stop and patiently explain the discovery in his near-perfect English. The two of them climbed ladders to inspect the intricate ceiling baffles, because these too had to be mapped in fine detail. Throughout the process Artigue took photos on an expensive-looking Nikon, at one point asking Ben to pose by the Steinway. The whole afternoon was an education, a pleasure.

As his guest makes the rounds Ben toys with asking him to dinner. Though he's dog-tired and the cold has moved into his chest, it would be the proper thing to do, and the seeds of a genuine friendship might be sown. He ought to just go home and go to bed, hoping to kick whatever's ailing him, but the moment should be seized. Artigue will be off to New York in the morning to analyze a studio in Soho, then back to France Wednesday night.

His visitor settles the matter for him. "My friend," he says, sitting down on the couch and laying a hand on Ben's shoulder. "I am so grateful for today. Thank you." The smile is sincere. Sincerely exhausted, too. "I was going to treat you to dinner—I have reservations for us at Spiaggia. But I'm afraid I'm not such good company tonight. I think I have just the energy to find my hotel and put myself to bed. Can we find another time? Perhaps in Paris? You'll be my guest, of course. Say you'll come."

BEN SHOULD GO HOME but something is drawing him back to Studio A. Perhaps it's that Artigue's uncovered a bit of its magic, like a gifted teacher uncovering the hidden brilliance of a shy child. The day has been one of quiet discoveries. Though he's spent thousands of hours behind the console recording others, Ben has rarely made time to listen to the room from the musician's seat. That is Eliza's inviolable domain. They work on opposite sides of the glass, masters of their own realms. But tonight Ben wants the whole of the place to himself.

He sits down at the Steinway and cranks the bench a notch higher, settling in. For a long moment he sits listening to the room itself, the ringing in his ear mercifully quiet, the redwood walls ranged around him like watchful desert cliffs.

Every room has its ambient tonality. There is a baseline soundscape even in the most well-treated spaces. In Studio A he hears something like the faint rush of a far-off river, or perhaps of blood through a heart valve, nearly imperceptible, a certain richness on the air. In his exhaustion his perceptions are keen and undistracted. All is laid bare. He lets the room speak to him, lets time pass frictionlessly, and finally lays his fingers on the keys of the Steinway to play the lost sonata.

HE PLAYS WHAT HE CAN from memory, the music more lucid than ever in his mind, then pauses to retrieve the score from his bag. With care he spreads it across the stand. He might be feverish but it doesn't matter. Did illness stop Lili Boulanger from playing the music in her head? Everything says she was only pushed to new heights by it.

Ben scans the first page of the score and begins again at the beginning, taking his time, gliding his way through the opening's suspended chords. He barely glances at the score. Without realizing it, he's learned much of the piece by heart. As the opening theme flows into the first variation he closes his eyes, trusting his memory, the Steinway full-throated in one moment, silken in the next, responsive to his touch in a way the Bösendorfer simply isn't. His parlor grand is a fine instrument but it can't stand up to a Steinway concert grand in an acoustically perfect room.

As he plays, he begins to have a different sort of conversation with the sonata, the soft hammers speaking for him, the room speaking back. It's been a long time since his musical heart has felt so open while playing a classical piece. Even in the thick of his piano studies at Northwestern, thirty years ago, he rarely let the music carry him away like this.

In those days his playing was plagued by a tightness he couldn't overcome. In the scrum of outsized egos he'd assumed it was just nerves, but it wasn't only that. There was something fundamental to his nature that stood in his way, something he understood only when Robin Masters slipped into his life. What was really blocking him was his stubborn modesty. His inner life had never been open for public inspection—not out of any sense of privacy, but because he doubted anyone would be interested. The idea of laying his heart bare at the keyboard was nothing short of terrifying, though he knew perfectly well that it was the gateway to true artistry.

Robin suffered no such inhibitions. To watch his lover play Bach, whether she was perched on the sofa in one of his rumpled tee shirts, her red hair awry after a night in his bed, or straddling her cello on a spotlit stage, was to be profoundly and identically aroused. There was no daylight between the passionate Robin of the bedroom and the passionate Robin of the concert hall. It had quickly made her the darling of the faculty and the envy of her fellow students. It had made Ben Weil fall in love with her.

But sometime during their first December together, with scant warning, the music went cold in him. He felt it like the death of a close relation. Robin couldn't be blamed, of course; she was only being who she was, doing what she did so very well. By the time the campus oaks leafed out Ben had admitted the truth to himself: he'd never be able to expose his heart the way a true artist must. The fearless immodesty of it was beyond him. Six months to the day after first kissing Robin Masters he withdrew from the program, the start of a painful reckoning that led haphazardly to Counterpoint and all that was to follow. His real talent, it turned out, lay on the other side of the glass.

Tonight it's a different story. Tonight he's playing as soulfully as anyone can, the big Steinway his subtle and responsive lover, the sonata a love song. It may be that he's never played with such emotional honesty. The signal is pure and strong. Perhaps it's the flu that's left him so utterly undefended, but it doesn't matter. It's not a moment for speculation. His body's doing all the thinking tonight, channeling the music like a silver wire in a lightning storm.

He's reached the descending passage where the sonata intertwines with Lili's *morceau*. Ben turns the page of the score and takes a shallow breath, prepares himself. Begins. With deliberate care he steps down through the chromatics, playing more slowly than Garnier did a century ago, feeling his way into the uncertain darkness. After three brief waystations of dissonance he reaches the single major E chord, bright and strong—and banishes it, stepping down, down into darkness, the going treacherous, slow. His fingers creep from one black key to the next as his right hand throws out little warnings and flourishes, the spare countermelody that flits above the bass line. . . .

Then the false floor: a solid A, persisting as if the descent has finally reached terra firma, only to be answered by a tatter of sixteenth notes in the upper register and then a long rest. All that remains now are the final two pulses. Ben lets them ring until they fade away, the Steinway pouring its heart into the melancholy of their passing. The studio reverberates around him. By the time the music folds into silence Ben's forehead is resting against the piano top, the dying vibration transmitted straight into his skull—the unknown composer's genius richly and fully his own, if only for a few moments.

"Brilliant. Absolutely brilliant."

A woman's voice startles him from his reverie. His hands are still on the keys; by clumsy reflex they stumble into a sour discord. Ben turns on the bench to find Ana Clara Matta standing close behind him, arms loosely crossed. There is a look of bafflement on her face, a faint smile on her lips.

"What *was* that, Ben? What did I just hear?" She cocks her head. "I'm sure I've never heard this music before."

"It's nothing much," Ben replies, but so quietly she doesn't hear him.

"Move over," she says, and sits down beside him, the two of them squeezed together on the bench, her thigh against his. "May I?"

Sight-reading effortlessly, she plays the descending passage again, exclaiming quietly as she goes. Certain notes seem to move her especially. "*Oui!*" she whispers when she comes to the hopeful major chord hidden inside the minor progression. Ben listens with one hand clutching the edge of the piano bench, overcome by the sensitivity of her playing. As her feet work the pedals he feels a ripple of movement where their thighs touch. He should shift on the bench and give her more room but something roots him where he is. He's surprised she's kept on with it, this physical connection, but he's glad for it.

In all the time they've worked together they've never sat down at the piano like this, as fellow musicians. She knows that he plays, but he's certainly never dared to play for her. To be surprised at the keyboard, ambushed like this . . . it's the only way it could have happened. On any other evening it would have humiliated him, even angered him, but tonight he's played far beyond his abilities, inspired by the Steinway, the resonant room, most of all the sonata. If she were ever to hear him play the piano, he's glad she's heard him play tonight.

She's reached the end of the descending passage. With an efficient snap she turns to the next page of the score, only to discover a barren span of nearly empty staves. SECOND MOVEMENT, the handwritten title reads, ALLEGRO. Below lie the first daunting measures, all he was able to transcribe before abandoning the work in despair. In a tiny hand he's written out the opening blizzard of thirty-second notes with a gaping crescendo sign below them, then the bold, fortissimo discord that puts an end to the run. In several places he's written in accidentals then scratched them out, the Garnier recording marred by crackles that leave the underlying notes unclear. The manuscript is a mess.

Ana Clara regards the page with bafflement, then turns past it to the next, which begins the third movement with its relaxed folk song. Without much thought she plays the first measures, a simple figure in quarter and eighth notes, and stops. Unsatisfied, she turns back a page and leans in to read Ben's scrawl, playing the opening run at half time, then at its full blistering speed, until she reaches the dissonant chord at the end. Letting it ring, she leans back and shuts her eyes. She must be trying to hear the music that comes next. Surely there is more to the Allegro than these scant few measures.

When the chord dies out she pages back to the beginning of the score. Ben has given the piece no title other than French Sonata. Seeing this, Ana Clara makes a small sound and plays the opening arpeggio, so familiar to him now, then enters the long tunnel of silence that follows, the strange seven-beat rest that still confounds him. He feels her counting it out and wonders what she's thinking, how her musical mind, with its encyclopedic grasp of the twentieth-century piano repertoire, is analyzing it. But then she moves into the short minor phrase and lands on the first of the suspended chords, her articulation confident, her touch sublime. She plays out the movement with exquisite lyricism, grasping the music immediately. It shouldn't be surprising, as she's built a career on interpreting the period's masterworks, but Ben sits next to her enraptured, utterly transported by her artistry.

Near the bottom of the fourth page she stops in mid-phrase and swivels to look at him, her face closer than it's ever been despite all the time they've spent together huddled over scores. There are flecks of gold in her dark irises. The scents of her hair, her skin, her breath play over him. He sees her sharp mind working, her eyes searching his. With care she lowers the keyboard cover, never breaking his gaze, a hand planted on the bench behind him.

Ben holds his breath, not knowing what to expect. He can feel the Garnier recording slipping from his grasp, a secret no more. But then he sees a change come over Ana Clara Matta: a slight rise in the plucked brows, a softening around the compact mouth. A glistening in her brown eyes. A smile in which he sees only admiration.

"My God, Ben," she says in wonderment, "this is *yours*, isn't it? You *wrote* this."

Wrapped in the soothing embrace of Studio A, alone with a woman who's lately crossed into his dreams, Ben says not a word.

"It's got to be heard," she says. "By everyone! I can make that happen. You know I can."

Still he's mute, something collapsing inside him.

She covers his hand with hers on the bench. "Look, I know it's not done yet. You have to finish the Allegro, which is brilliant so far. But when it's done, when you're ready, we're going to take this out into the world. I'm going to make sure it gets heard. And I'm going to make sure you get the recognition you deserve."

He shakes his head helplessly.

"Ben! Don't you dare say no. Be proud. This is inspired work. Really. I don't have to tell you that. Or maybe I do—maybe you need to hear it from someone who knows. So, now I'm telling you: this is going to floor people. There's real genius here." She lays a hand on his hot cheek. In a quieter voice she says: "The world needs to know about Ben Weil and his *French Sonata*. It's time for him to come out of hiding, don't you think?"

Later he'll invent a dozen reasons for his silence in that moment, but none of them will excuse it. Instead of simply telling Ana Clara about the Garnier recording, instead of enlisting her help in tracking down the real composer, Ben Weil lets her honest mistake harden into a lie of omission, staring dumbly into the searching eyes before him like the worst sort of fool.

Although he's been sitting perfectly still, he feels the dogged vertigo rush back in. Suddenly he's lightheaded enough to faint. The devil in his left ear lets loose a tiny scream. He's never been so tired, never in his life. But she's still waiting, her eyes on his, a smile playing at the sharp corners of her mouth. Her heart opens wide before him. She isn't going to let this go.

Ana Clara shakes her head slowly.

"I had no idea," she says under her breath, more to herself than to him. "*No* idea."

In his shame and confusion he can only close his eyes. If he feels a brush of soft lips on his in the darkness, it is only to seal his misery.

THIRD MOVEMENT
Adagio

AIGREMONT

SEPTEMBER 1918

XIX.

SERVICE

THE MUSIC ECHOES UP THE MARBLE STAIRCASE at odd hours. Mostly, though, it arrives after nine in the evening, when the night nurses are making the rounds to sponge down the feverish and the day crew have collapsed into their sagging cots. The servants' attic quarters are allocated to the nurses and cooks; the orderlies and mortuary men are squeezed into the music room like submariners, each with no more than a few feet of space for himself. Not that the tight quarters matter. They're asleep almost as soon as they lie down, the way shot soldiers are sometimes dead by the time they hit the ground.

The piano music makes its way up the hill from the carriage house along the meandering driveway until it reaches Aigremont's French windows, left open to dispel the reek and to bathe the stricken with autumnal coolness. Drifting over the cots in the ball-room and study, it enters the foyer where it regroups and climbs the wide staircase toward the family bedrooms, deserted now but for Mrs. Sanborn in the master bedroom and Elisabeth in little Caleb's room.

One never knows what sort of music will come. The whims of the unseen musician are changeable. Sometimes it's a casu-al arrangement of "After You've Gone" or "I'm Always Chasing Rainbows," sometimes a bit of jumpy ragtime, once even "Für Elise"—the unseen player's taste catholic, his touch fluid and easy, his skills rusty from the war but far from forgotten.

It really doesn't matter what he plays. The music lulls Elisabeth to sleep, calming her nerves when nothing else can. The sound of the grand piano itself, its stately and full-throated timbre, consoles her. It takes her home, if only in her heart. She can't get enough of it. If she can't have her father, at least she can have this.

She wouldn't be here, ministering to the ill and the dying, if she hadn't already lost nearly everything that mattered to her. Back in Roxbury, events had brought her so low as to consider what sort of death it might be to throw oneself under a streetcar, bracing herself one morning as it screeched toward her, even taking a step forward until someone pulled her back with a terrified "*Miss!*" She'd stood on the wharf near the Bell factory and gazed down into the sloshing bilge and sobbed like a child, the filthy waters calling to her. But though the hard times had ground away whatever slender faith in God her parents left her, she was too Catholic to take her own life. It was too deeply ingrained in her, this cruel conviction that she must bear her allotted burden as Christ bore his.

Here at Aigremont there is another possibility. If the influenza were to take her, it wouldn't be her own doing. She would not be culpable. She'd be forgiven, even blessed, if the Almighty should prove to exist after all. She's thought it through quite carefully. To earn such grace she must not invite death in, nor incline toward it; her intentions must remain pure. And so she wears the cloth mask, she washes her hands between patients, she takes the sensible precautions. All while hoping, in her darkest moments, that it will be for nought. There's an odd consolation in the idea.

On nights when she's fallen asleep to the sound of the distant playing, she awakes without fail the instant it stops—the abrupt silence another loss, another failure she can't abide.

SHE'D HAVE PREFERRED to bunk with the nurses but Rena Sanborn insists that she sleep on the second floor. She's all but family now, the mistress of Aigremont says—though Elisabeth suspects that with Oren banned from the house, the boys shipped off to Maine, and Helen marooned in New York, pregnant by a husband who's already left her, Rena Sanborn just wants someone down the hallway at night. Whatever the case, Elisabeth's come to love little Caleb's room, its cozy scale, its boyish charms. It's a perfect refuge from the frights of the first floor. Though Rena's gently prodded her to move into Helen's room—one more suited to a young woman's style of life—she won't hear of it. She's happier in Caleb's world.

The invisible pianist is one of the three doctors. He must be. They're the only ones allowed into the carriage house, where they sleep on rollaway beds and play cowboy pool on Oren's slate table while drinking his whiskey, or so the rumor goes. The quarters are unimaginably luxurious, no doubt, compared to the field hospital behind the Belleau Wood line where they worked side by side in the blood and muck until a German mortar sent them all home, shrapnel lodged in their hips and legs. Were it not for the influenza they'd be convalescing quietly in some Red Cross hospital in Ohio or South Carolina or Texas. Instead they've been shot from the heat of one battle into the slower burn of another.

All three have limps. Anyone can see they're in pain, but they don't let it slow them down. They work long days with irregular hours, crossing paths at the carriage house only when their shifts happen to line up. Mostly they sleep when they're together, despite what the rumors say. This Elisabeth will learn in time; for now their movements are a bit of a mystery, the little carriage house at the foot of the driveway off limits to everyone but the three men and the Italian housekeeper who's been Mrs. Sanborn's most trusted servant since the passing of the formidable Mrs. Dooley.

The youngest of the doctors, Lance Corporal LeBlanc, lost his left eye at Cantigny and isn't allowed to operate, his depth perception ruined. Stitch, they call him, his suturing as good as any Jewish tailor's, somehow, despite his disability. Stitch has a girl back in Baton Rouge who looks far too much like a sister, in the wry opinion of his colleagues—the same red hair as his, the same sharp cheekbones, the same pronounced canines. He hasn't brought himself to tell Doris about the eye as yet. She writes with the regularity of an ocean tide, a letter arriving every Monday, her handwriting ornate as a fleur-de-lis, something old and antebellum about it. It galls LeBlanc that she's only a train ride away now, both of them pinned down by an epidemic they can't control any more than they could control the war that once kept them an ocean apart.

Sergeant First Class Stan Lazar, a heavyset Brooklyn man with hollow eyes and shoulders slumped like flour sacks, is completely deaf in his right ear and hard of hearing in his left, but this doesn't stop him from thinking faster than any of them in an emergency.

He's saved more boys than anyone can count. They say the influenza is rapaciously fast and lethal, but for Lazar it's insufferably slow and dull. He resents the work because there's little he can do for his patients except watch them spiral down into pneumonia and die. If they'd have let him stay on in France after his own brief hospitalization at Reims he'd gladly have done so, trudging straight back to the front lines, plunging his hand back into the fire. It's Aigremont that's the hardship tour. The irony, he tells everyone, is that the name of the grand house sounds as if it could be the name of a French battlefield.

And then there is the third man. For some days now Elisabeth has been convinced that the nocturnal pianist must be Captain Charlie Westerlake, the only one of them who's a full medical doctor rather than just a medic, although he's not much older than she is. She can picture him perfectly tonight as she lies in Caleb Sanborn's narrow bed listening to the far-off music, the boy's little wooden oxen team and painted roosters and scale-model racing sloop arrayed on the dresser before her in the moonlight, her linen mask and nurse-assistant's cap folded neatly beside them. She keeps her hairpins and badge in the petite silver loving cup the boy seems to have won in an equestrian competition. Elisabeth watches the little urn catch the moonlight as the pianist plays on, her eyes half closed, the collar of her nightshirt undone. She's lying still enough to feel the pulse in her long neck, the soft and lyric beat of life.

Tonight's music is a lilting waltz she can't quite place. The melody is carried entirely by the right hand, a tune as simple as a children's song. She needs music like this desperately just now, its lightness: three of her patients, two farm brothers and a chestnut-haired girl from Stoneham, children all, died on her watch today. At dinner she couldn't eat a thing. By the time she went up to bed the dead children's cots were already occupied by new arrivals.

She closes her eyes and imagines Captain Westerlake at the keyboard of the grand piano. It's the white Mason and Hamlin that Mrs. Sanborn had moved from the music room to make way for the men's sleeping quarters, the piano on which Elisabeth's own father played his final recital a few weeks before sailing for France. Hard to see how the servants wedged it into the carriage

house with the billiard table and other furnishings, but somehow the feat was managed. Now, she imagines, Westerlake will
be sitting on the white bench with eyes closed, slipping grate-
fully into the unassuming little waltz like a bone-tired soldier
slipping into a hot bath he had no reason to expect. Perhaps his
colleagues are listening from their beds. More likely they're with
patients or in the town, the pianist alone for the time being.

Westerlake is a tall and quietly imposing man, stocky but not
overly so, a man who could wear full whiskers to handsome effect
but chooses to go clean-shaven. His wide-set gray eyes are almost
transparent in low light. When he visits one of the soldiers he drops
into a crouch beside the cot, coming right down to the man's level;
Elisabeth's observed it time and again. She's never known a doctor
to do this, much less with patients dying of contagion. Though he
wears the obligatory mask, he is unafraid, which gives her some
idea of just how bad things must have been in France.

She'd like to hear his war stories but can't picture such a conversation with Charlie Westerlake, who keeps to himself and doesn't
mingle. Nor is it a time for looking backward. Elisabeth herself
couldn't possibly take on more suffering, even someone else's recollection of suffering, while the influenza is still about its deadly
business. She knows herself well enough to understand that this
is another reason she's moved out to Aigremont, shuttering the
Roxbury apartment and taking leave from the Bell Company in
order to work with the sick and dying. The exhausting trials of the
infirmary leave her little energy to tally her losses.

In the three weeks she's been here, she's done her best to focus
on present matters. Some days she succeeds for hours at a time, until the press of work slows for a few minutes and something brings
back memories of simpler times, afternoons gossiping with Helen
about H. E. Rollins or eating chilled oysters with her new friends
at Helen's club—or, painfully but also sweetly, quiet evenings spent
reading and chatting with her father in the Roxbury flat, news of
the war closing in with its engulfing darkness. When such memories strike she immediately goes to the nearest nurse or doctor
and asks what she can do to help. There is always another task to

absorb her, to lift her back into the present. The need is infinite and unflagging.

She likes Charlie Westerlake's methodical way of speaking and moving, the care he takes with the physical world. There's a feline economy to the way he walks, even the way he smokes on the stoop outside. She's never known anyone to live in his body with the ease Westerlake does. Even with the limp from the mortar wound he makes his way with grace. It's these qualities that have convinced her that he's the nocturnal pianist, because they hint, obliquely, at an artistic sensibility. All the nurses are half in love with him.

Sleep is overtaking her now, the piano music and cool September air rallying to its cause. She's exhausted, as usual, and soon enough she's dreaming. Tonight finds her in a green-striped deck chair on the SS *La Bretagne*, crossing from Le Havre to Boston to begin her new life in America, the foredeck crowded, oddly, with strolling nurses in white smocks and surgical masks. Their aprons are wildly spattered with blood, which for some reason doesn't alarm Elisabeth in the least. In the distance a pod of dolphins leaps and frolics, gray as Norman doves. Though the seas are calm the huge ship has begun to rock gently, gradually carrying her off to a dream within a dream, a slumber within a slumber, a white piano playing faintly in the background.

When the music stops she surfaces into Caleb's room and in her foggy half-awareness realizes that the unseen pianist has segued into Beethoven. It's the "Moonlight Sonata" that ushered her into her dreams, she's sure of it. Beethoven's opening triplet, so sober and lovely, rings in her head until she slides back into sleep, dreaming of nothing this time, sleeping the spotless sleep of a child.

XX.

NEEDLE OF THEIR DESIRE

IN HER BETTER MOMENTS Elisabeth doesn't fault Helen Sanborn for staying well away from Aigremont. If she were in her friend's straits she'd do the same. Not that Rena Sanborn would allow her daughter to return home, it should be said: an expectant mother should hardly take up residence in an influenza ward. Perhaps Rena could pack Helen off to Maine, to join her brothers in isolation at Elmwood, the family horse farm . . . but this wouldn't make sense either. What woman of means would allow her daughter to give birth under the care of some country midwife or hayseed doctor? New York may be rife with immigrants but it's clearly the better option, as long as one is set up properly. Helen surely is; she wants for nothing. She has no reason whatsoever to venture into the thronged and dangerous streets. Influenza is the last thing she should worry about right now. She has troubles enough without it.

Rena has made her opinion on all this clear to Elisabeth half a dozen times. She won't let it rest. The decision must still be tearing at her despite her insistence that the matter is closed. Elisabeth feels for her: she can see that a tender heart, the heart of a worried mother, beats behind the sometimes stern exterior.

Rena raised the matter again just this morning, when they chanced to meet on the grand staircase en route to breakfast. It was seven-fifteen, near the end of the overnight shift. Just below them in the foyer, an exhausted orderly dozed in a wash of morning sun, sprawled across a chair embroidered with the Sanborn coat of arms. In normal times he'd have been given the bum's rush. Not today.

"She's better off riding this out at the Knickerbocker," Rena said, clutching the banister with a beringed hand. "She can go to ground there, be properly taken care of."

Elisabeth pictured her friend in a well-appointed suite with room service, ice buckets with bottles of champagne, sanitary linens, a Chinese laundryman at her beck and call—properly taken care of indeed.

"Not to mention that there's a house physician on duty round the clock. They've taken all possible precautions, obviously. Their reputation depends on it."

"I'm sure you're right," Elisabeth said, too tired to discuss it yet again. The stench of the ward crept upstairs as they chatted under the tall stained-glass window. In happier times Aigremont had smelled like a florist's, cut flowers everywhere one looked. Now it smelled like a butcher shop in a bad neighborhood.

Rena leaned in and lowered her voice. "Helen says the entire staff wear monogrammed satin masks, with the exception of the maître d' and the sommelier. One imagines the difficulty for a sommelier." She adjusted her large ruby ring, lining it up with the knuckle. "Someone's been thinking cleverly about how to make a clean breast of this, I can tell you. I can't imagine a safer place for Helen at this moment. Can you?"

Elisabeth had heard all this before, nearly word for word. But what no one would say aloud—not Rena, nor Elisabeth, nor even the doctors—was that nowhere was safe. Not the Astors' hotel, not sleepy Winchester, not even Maine. The flu was hunting down victims everywhere, rampant as a band of Bolsheviks. In tiny Winchester alone there were four hundred cases. They were burying local citizens late into the night just to keep up. Elisabeth knew this and so did Mrs. Sanborn, but neither spoke the words. Everyone, these days, kept their fears to themselves.

With a confidence she didn't feel, Elisabeth said: "Your daughter's just where she should be, Mrs. Sanborn. I'm certain of that. Really."

She touched the older woman's elbow to remind her that it was time to go downstairs. They descended side by side, Elisabeth in her nurse's apron, white cap pinned to her dark French braid. Mrs. Sanborn wore her usual iron-gray dress and gold brooch—her version of a uniform suitable to the occasion, the brooch declaring, like a badge, a certain authority over the proceedings. One expected no less from the lady of the house. Elisabeth found her choice of clothes inspired. Real thought had gone into it, she could see.

In the children's dining room, reserved now for the exclusive use of Elisabeth and Rena, an urn of Chase and Sanborn coffee would be waiting along with an elegant breakfast, which Elisabeth couldn't begin to take on board, the odors from the ward on the other side of the swinging door making the thought of food unpleasant in the extreme.

THE INFLUENZA IS PERVERSE. While it claims some within hours, others linger for days, many of these eventually able to walk back out into the world unassisted. After three weeks at Aigremont Elisabeth can predict the ultimate outcome nearly from the moment a patient arrives. At the triage desk the symptoms are noted down: fever, a scarlet throat, trouble breathing, a wet cough—and perhaps the dread brown blotches, whose presence can send the patient straight to the unfortunately named Grave Cases ward in the basement. It's a short walk down an ill-lit corridor from there to the holding morgue, cooled with blocks of ice brought in every few hours. Elisabeth's heard the orderlies describe the scene below but hasn't yet seen it for herself. Her duties lie upstairs, a small mercy for which she's grateful.

Apparently the traffic between the basement ward and the morgue is nearly constant. As places become available in the hospital mortuary, Aigremont victims are carried past the coal chute and up the back stairs into a waiting baker's cart, never more to be seen by the upstairs staff or other patients. She understands that it was Lance Corporal LeBlanc who devised the system during his first days at the house, an assembly line worthy of Ford, every detail thought through. Only once, while airing her lungs outside during a short break, has Elisabeth caught a glimpse of the proceedings: a litter carried by orderlies to the waiting cart, a body swaddled in a white sheet but for a dangling arm clad in striped pajamas, a blood-soaked towel tumbling to the flagstones. It was enough to convince her she didn't want any part of it. She didn't know how they bore it day after day, the orderlies and doctors and Red Cross nurses who worked in the bowels of the house among the swiftly dying.

This morning she's been assigned to the soldiers laid out in Oren Sanborn's study, boys brought in from Camp Devens. Some have been over to the war; others are recent inductees, callow New England boys stricken in the midst of boot camp. She's grown better at telling the difference between the two: it's the panic in the eyes of the trainees that gives them away. The men back from the front have seen far worse than the flu. Here, at least, there are no amputations, no bodies pulped by bombs, no gas snaking through fetid trenches. Despite the relentless fever, the suffocation, the blood pouring from throats and ears, the flu is a more merciful killer. Dismemberment by one's fellow man lies in a different circle of hell entirely.

Elisabeth's first patient of the day is a young Irish private named Mulroney, from County Cork by way of Medford. He can't be more than eighteen. The chart clipped to the cot says he's just back from the front—Flanders Fields—though her intuition has already told her as much. As with all new patients she's taken a moment to observe him before approaching, to judge his condition in advance. She's found that this little pause helps her present her best self to the patient. Her new charge's condition, she's determined, is just short of dire.

When she arrives at Private Mulroney's bedside, he's hacking bright blood onto the counterpane, his ration of two spit rags crumpled on the floor, saturated long ago. The boy's face is wrenched from the sheer physical effort of trying to catch a breath, but when the hacking subsides for a moment and he looks over to see the pretty nurse-assistant he manages a weak smile. His crooked teeth are edged with blood.

"Joseph, Mary and all the saints," he says in a half-whisper, throat raked raw. "And aren't you a sight to behold." His accent is like Tom Shea's but softer, perhaps from another part of Ireland. Or perhaps it's only been softened by exhaustion. For a fleeting moment Elisabeth thinks of Tom in his uniform on the day he shipped out, bright as a June morning, and wonders if he's still alive. The last letter she had was from Cantigny, a week after he arrived in France. Not a word since then.

Over the mask Elisabeth smiles with her eyes, scooping up the spent rags—blood on her hands with the very first patient of the day.

Mulroney pulls a face, still somehow capable of joking, and rasps out: "I ain't *died*, ain't I? Because there's a angel about, yeah?"

When she takes his wrist to get a pulse he somehow maneuvers her hand into his, which is clammy with fever. Just as dexterously she extricates herself and gets to work, drawing the Red Cross stopwatch from her apron pocket and counting out the sickly beats. She grants him a tiny smile but keeps her eyes on the watch, having been through this drill before. The boys are so starved for love, for simple kindness. She has to thread the needle of their desire carefully. She could never live with herself if she were to break a dying heart unknowingly. When she's gotten the pulse, she moves on to take Mulroney's temperature, his eyes on her constantly. He's carrying a fever of 103°, up two points from the 11:00 p.m. reading. Elisabeth wipes a bit of missed blood from her cuff and notes her findings in the chart while her patient plunges into another bout of wet coughing, gasping for air, drowning in his own fluids. Soon, she knows, he'll turn from red to blue, starved for oxygen. She's seen it countless times now. It can happen in a matter of minutes.

"Now, Mr. Mulroney," she says when the attack subsides, "I'm going to send an orderly round to change these sheets for you. How does a bit of ice sound?" She bends to blot his brow: she can give him this much.

"If *you* bring it, Miss," he says faintly, eyes bloodshot and hollow from the gargantuan struggle to breathe. There's a gurgle in his throat that doesn't belong there.

Elisabeth knows how this ends, unless the fever breaks. By noon he'll be moved downstairs to the Grave Cases ward, by suppertime to the morgue. There will be another young soldier here in the sagging cot, equally in need of her care. As she moves down the row to the next cot her heart is as heavy as a stone, and it's not even nine in the morning. Even the sight of Dr. Westerlake, bent over another of the soldiers with a stethoscope to the boy's chest, his eyes shut as if in prayer, barely moves her. The captain must suffer too, she thinks, must leave his shifts with the same heavy heart. But at least he has the piano. At least he can play.

THE STAFF SWAP RUMORS AND FOOLISH IDEAS like playing cards. Elisabeth can scarcely believe some of what she hears.

A pouch of camphor hung under the nose of a child is proof against the contagion.

The Bayer company, a German concern, has been lacing its aspirin with influenza.

Gargling salt water laced with cinnamon keeps the disease away.

A face mask soaked in urine will prevent the effusion of blood from the nose.

A pouch of mothballs, held against the heart, scares the flu away.

Woolen drawers break a fever.

Women with pronounced moles are immune.

Jews are immune.

Jews invented the influenza while masquerading as Christians in Spain.

The flu was sent by God to end the Great War.

If a clove of garlic inserted into a woman's pudenda dissolves, she cannot catch the flu.

The only time Elisabeth's seen Dr. Westerlake lose his temper was when one of the nurse-assistants asked, on behalf of a patient, whether there was any harm in keeping a camphor pouch around one's neck. The woman had caught the captain in the foyer, on his way back to the carriage house for the night. He was beyond exhausted; Elisabeth could see it plainly. His eyes were hollow like a starved man's, his face gray as cement and nearly as hard. For a long moment, he frowned as if considering the question seriously, his long fingers absently tracing the carved door molding. The meek nurse-assistant, who struck Elisabeth as a country girl only lately arrived in Boston, waited with a chart clutched to her breast like a battle shield.

When Westerlake finally spoke, it was for all to hear. In a furious voice he said, "Tell your patient it's horseshit. Camphor will displace his oxygen. If he doesn't like it he's free to go. We could use the bed." The captain reached for the doorknob, then turned on the nurse-assistant. "And you! Don't you know better than to waste my time with this kind of nonsense? Show some judgment."

The poor woman burst into tears. Westerlake left the house without seeming to notice. But in the morning Elisabeth saw him guide the woman gently through the library and out to the portico, speaking quietly to her all the while, humbly stooped so she could hear him. Later the woman told Elisabeth and the others that he'd apologized like a true gentleman, with real heart.

"It's the misery," she said. "It's got under his skin. How can you blame the man? I worry for him." Which were Elisabeth's feelings precisely. Forgiveness, in times like these, seemed a virtue above all others. Whatever toll the conditions were taking on everyone else, the burden seemed to fall heaviest on Drs. Westerlake, Lazar, and LeBlanc, who looked more shell-shocked every day but nonetheless carried on.

XXI.

NOBLESSE OBLIGE

So MUCH HAS CHANGED, and so quickly.

Elisabeth can't remember when time has moved at such a breakneck pace. Even Helen Sanborn's life seems to have gone off the rails, the headlong rush of her changing fortunes over-taking her. Hard to imagine that it's been barely a year since H. E. Rollins moved his fiancée to New York and wed her in the gilded ballroom of the Knickerbocker, somehow convincing Caruso, who lived on the fifth floor and met H. E. in the lobby bar daily for martinis, to sing at the reception. Hard to believe, too, that only four months have passed since Helen learned of her husband's brazen infidelity—word having come through the selfsame Caruso, who personally apologized to Helen for having introduced H. E. to the twenty-three-year-old soprano who'd been entertaining her husband for some weeks, apparently, in a Chelsea walkup. (Helen had taken a carriage out to surveil the unsightly brownstone, her fury concealed behind a borrowed widow's veil.) Worse yet, it seemed that everyone in their set had known of the affair for some time. Helen recognized the faint smirks on the society ladies' faces, the false sympathy of consoling hands on hers, the general mirth of them all. . . . No wonder she'd retreated to her room for days afterward. It was a humiliation the like of which she'd never experienced.

And now Helen was to bear the philanderer's child! Thanks to the influenza, she'd be forced to rely on an acquaintance of her mother's to usher her through her confinement—H. E. and his girl shacked up somewhere in Amagansett, sheltering from the epi-demic in a manner the expectant mother preferred not to contem-plate. Events have unfolded with breathtaking speed and fearsome gravity.

Lately Helen's direst fear is that she'll open the newspaper one morning, the silver breakfast tray balanced atop her growing belly, only to discover her name and Rollins' imprisoned together in a *Table Gossip* notice, her private tragedy emblazoned there for all to see.

All this Elisabeth has learned from the long, jumbled letters Helen writes her on gold-embossed Knickerbocker Hotel stationery. By her correspondent's own account, the act of writing helps her organize her thoughts, though the scattershot style of the latest communiqués casts this into some doubt.

Before moving to Aigremont Elisabeth would read the letters in her father's armchair, the Roxbury apartment cold and empty without him, the Edison bulb sputtering above. She was still working for the Company when Helen began writing, putting in relentless hours to keep her mind off things—her plan to take a position as a social worker at Mrs. Taylor's settlement house derailed by the urgency of earning a living wage in her father's absence. Mrs. Taylor could never match what she earned at Bell. Often as not Elisabeth had trouble keeping her eyes open past nine, the exhaustion of the long days fusing with her grief until she could barely find energy to undress. Nonetheless she did her best to keep up with the barrage of Helen's correspondence and once a week or so managed to send a short note of her own.

Helen's early letters read like dispatches from the society column, packed with bright talk of Caruso's wit and glittering evenings in Carrie Astor's box at the Metropolitan Opera, of fine wines and leisurely drives out to Long Island, of H. E.'s sweet, clandestine runs to Tiffany's on her behalf. In every dispatch, it seemed, there was a description of some stallion or filly Helen had fallen in love with while riding in the country, the horse talk at times so specialized as to be impenetrable. Elisabeth wrestled with every one of these blithe reports. In her grief she couldn't share her friend's excitement, but they did take her mind off her own situation for the few minutes it took to read them.

It wasn't that she resented the casual descriptions of her friend's high-toned acquaintances. Helen had always inhabited a world that would never be hers. It was the sheer happiness of the young bride that would bring her to tears, and the way her friend's questions about her own situation seemed to come as afterthoughts. Helen's life was an ocean liner steaming off toward the horizon, Elisabeth left standing in the embers of a fallen world.

As far as Elisabeth could see, the spring of 1918 was no time for happiness of any sort. France was on fire; the war was never-ending. And now she was truly alone in the world, her mother and now her dear father gone. She had barely a friend in the world outside the small circle of Helen's friends, whose invitations dwindled the moment Helen left for New York. Elisabeth had understood her mistake, finally: she'd relied far too much on her adoring mother and father, on their pride in her studies and her modest forays into the world, to give her life purpose. Now it had all been dashed away. She'd been left starkly exposed. There was nowhere left for her to stand.

The truth was, she'd never learned how to be alone. How naïve she'd been! What a perfect fool. Sometimes it took days for her to find the nerve to slit open Helen's latest cheerful missive and take on the next onslaught of good cheer.

But then the stream of happy news suddenly turned to a flood of fury over the perfidy of H. E. Rollins. Just below its angry surface Elisabeth could smell her friend's fear. With a single letter the lighthearted banter was banished forever.

Helen's outrage leapt from the page. *A SINGER!* she wrote, *A SHOW GIRL!!! They are all loose, as everyone knows.*

Never mind that only a few lines before this the girl in question had been an opera singer groomed by the greatest tenor of the day, the legendary Caruso. Now, abruptly, H. E.'s lover was nothing but a common hoofer. No matter; the writer was white-hot angry. She had a right to some exaggeration.

As Elisabeth raced through the letter she recoiled in disgust. Her heart broke for her friend. And to be left pregnant, on top of everything else . . . during an epidemic! *Ça, c'est le comble!* What a despicable man Rollins must be. She read the letter twice through just to be sure she had the basic facts right, so cruel and improbable did they seem. Elisabeth fetched paper and pen and sat down to write her friend a consoling letter. It took time to find the right tone. Though she was furious on Helen's behalf, to throw kerosene on the fire seemed unwise. What Helen Sanborn needed was a voice of reason. In the end Elisabeth had seven tight-knit pages. Though it was near midnight and her eyes were bleary she dressed and scrounged up a two-cent stamp and walked to the corner to post the letter, not wanting to delay its journey by even an hour.

How sweet of you, ma douce amie, Helen wrote back after some days. *Your passion astounds. Merci, merci, merci—tu as un coeur fidèle et constant.* Enclosed, to Elisabeth's horror, was a check for two hundred dollars. The memo on the check read: *Dedicated to a true friend.*

About the check, Helen's letter said not a word. When Elisabeth sat down to write back this time, she couldn't think how to begin.

HAD HELEN ABANDONED NEW YORK and returned to her childhood home, she'd barely have recognized it. Not since the height of the social season had there been such a crowd in the house. But unlike the usual guests in their elegant attire, these visitors were bedridden and feverish, flushed and sweating, the influenza's mahogany blotches marring face after face. With barely a second thought, Rena Sanborn had transformed her comfortable mansion into a plague ship. The speed and bravery of the decision still took Elisabeth's breath away. Say what you would about Rena, there was a fearlessness about her that one could only admire.

Within ten days of the influenza's first appearance in Winchester Rena had bundled Jack and Jimmy and Cabe off to the Sanborn thoroughbred farm in Maine, permitting only a cook, a maid, and a groom to stay on there. The boys had insisted on bringing along Sammy, the family Dalmatian. A few days later, after an emergency meeting of the Winchester Hospital board in which it was made clear that there weren't sufficient beds to receive the frightening surge of cases, Rena resolved to convert her home into a spillover infirmary. The large kitchen would produce not only food for the medical staff and patients but considerable quantities of beef broth, which she herself would assist in delivering, each noontime, to the hospital proper. Aigremont's ballroom, study, library, and game room would be converted into sick wards, the parlor into a triage station, the wine cellar into a morgue. The music room and third floor would be converted to sleeping quarters for incoming staff. With astonishing speed Aigremont was transformed into a kind of field hospital, the rows of cots filling quickly with every sort of patient, from farmers to homemakers to the local Presbyterian minister, Reverend Guthrie. The study was reserved for doughboys taken sick at nearby Camp Devens, whose own infirmary could no longer carry the load—already more than eight hundred cases, a number Rena found alarming in the extreme.

Through the good offices of the Boston Red Cross, a detachment of nurses took up residence in the house and the intake of patients began, the cots filled to capacity in a matter of days. What was lacking was a doctor to oversee things. With forty-two patients it had quickly become clear that daily rounds by the hospital doctors would not suffice. The death of Reverend Guthrie on the infirmary's second night in operation so shook Rena that she prevailed upon a doctor friend to telegraph the Mayo brothers in Minnesota, pleading with them to send someone from their new clinic—Rena would pay the first-class train fare and provide suitably private accommodations in her carriage house. None could be spared.

Only after a conversation with Major Mahogue, medical director of Camp Devens, did a solution present itself. Under Mahogue's care were two medics and a gifted doctor, recently shipped back with mortar wounds sustained at Belleau Wood, who might fill the need. Captain Charlie Westerlake was dispatched to tour Aigremont—firmly suggesting, as he limped impressively through the house, the separation of cases by severity and an ironclad policy regarding the use of surgical masks. Officer that he was, he took charge immediately. A few days later he returned with Lance Corporal LeBlanc and Sergeant First Class Lazar in tow, each man with an Army duffel slung over his shoulder.

Mrs. Sanborn had her doctors—or one doctor and two battle-tested medics, to be precise. She decreed to the staff that all three would be addressed as *Doctor* out of respect for their sacrifice in France. The next challenge was to find enough volunteer orderlies and nurse-assistants to support them. The small band of Red Cross nurses couldn't do it all. She applied herself to the task immediately, corralling Mrs. Berger, her fellow hospital board member and a judge's wife, into putting the word out by all channels.

When Elisabeth read Helen's account of this grand mobilization, as relayed to her by her mother, she knew what she had to do. With a telephone call to Mrs. Sanborn and a brief discussion with Jack Rimes, her manager at the Company, it was quickly settled. Jack was shipping out himself; he could hardly deny her patriotic request for leave. Mrs. Sanborn would cover all her expenses, including rent on the Roxbury apartment, to free her for volunteer work. The very next day Elisabeth made for Aigremont, her feet solid and sure on the ground for the first time in months.

XXII.

Le Clair de Lune

Elisabeth has fallen into the habit of strolling the neighborhood before going up to bed. After joining the others for supper in the kitchen at the end of her shift—Mrs. Sanborn, her faithful breakfast companion, preferring to dine in her suite upstairs—she changes into a looser blouse and skirt, unpins her hair, dons her woolen wrap and lets herself out through the grand front entrance. There's a little thrill in opening the heavy door, as if she can't quite believe she's free to come and go at will. Aigremont may be her home for the time being, but the young Bell Company saleswoman who stood nervously on these same steps three summers and a lifetime ago would have laughed at the notion. Yet here she is.

She may not enjoy the same status as the doctors, but as Helen Sanborn's good friend and Rena Sanborn's protégée, Elisabeth Garner inhabits her own place of privilege. She's never invited to go along on the other nurse-assistants' excursions into the town. It's just as well: by the end of a long shift saturated with suffering and death, she's far from good company. She can barely speak at all. She doesn't know how the others manage it. Some of the younger staff leave the ward japing and giggling like schoolgirls off on summer holiday, the misery of the patients put behind them without a thought. Elisabeth, on the other hand, leaves the ward barely breathing, as if her patients' struggle for air has seized hold of her too. In the evenings she needs silence and calm, not banter and gaiety.

Nor does she care to expose her thoughts to strangers. In particular she'd confess to no one the disturbances that have invaded her dreams for three nights running now, the snatches of distorted memory, the flashes of raw panic. Black-bordered telegrams bearing her father's misspelled name; her mother's sweaty forehead and jaundiced eyes. A German U-boat snaking under the keel of a steamer packet, silent as moonlight, at the very moment a passenger's white boater lofts on a breeze and settles onto a sea swell. A white piano with keys crooked and yellow as an old farmer's teeth. And the boys, of course, night after night the boys: blotched faces, sweat-soaked heads of hair thrashing on hard pillows, breath stale as rubber. The boys come into her dreams nearly every night now.

None of this can be put into words, exactly, not into French and certainly not into English. The language of Elisabeth's vexation is an alien tongue, untranslatable, harsh and esoteric, impenetrable even to her.

AND SO, AS USUAL, SHE STROLLS ALONE tonight, untethered. Cast adrift under a saffron-red harvest moon, the brisk fall air its own reward. As she descends the wide marble steps the sour odor of the wards falls away and a scent of damp leaves takes its place, even this little bit of nature a godsend.

Back at the house, she knows, a crisis is underway, and she's relieved to be walking away from it. As she passed by the library she saw both Lazar and LeBlanc laboring over a bespectacled old man whose temperature had been soaring all afternoon. The patient had been in delirium since two in the afternoon, raving and pleading until another patient finally shouted him down. This was bad enough, but complicating matters was the fact that the old man was beset by a foul-smelling diarrhea the like of which Elisabeth had never before encountered. Earlier in the day she and one of the orderlies had spent nearly an hour cleaning him up and improvising a diaper from tea towels, the work made infinitely filthier by the fact that the patient wouldn't stop thrashing about. Then, as they were fitting the diaper, they discovered that the man was also suffering from acute stomach pain: when Elisabeth happened to press on his lower abdomen he screamed wildly and swatted her hand from his belly, which they saw was covered with a virulent rash.

It was heartbreaking. The old man could have been anyone's grandfather. Yet despite his distressing symptoms he seemed to have no trouble getting air, unlike every other patient on the ward. If it was influenza, it was a strain they'd not seen before. She and the orderly summoned LeBlanc, reported their observations, and moved on to the final patient of their shift, relieved to hand the old man off to someone who could make better sense of things.

But that was nearly two hours ago. By now, surely, their patient had been moved downstairs to the Grave Cases ward or else given up the ghost. And so as she passed the library Elisabeth was surprised to see Lazar and LeBlanc at the old man's bedside. Two of the three Aigremont doctors on a single case—this she'd rarely seen. At that moment Lazar was palpating the patient's abdomen, the man screaming like a flayed martyr. LeBlanc had collapsed into a chair in exhaustion. She was glad to put the scene behind her and step into the quiet night.

There is woodsmoke on the air. She pauses at the top of the drive to choose a direction, the scent coaxing her toward the maze of lanes across High Street with their pretty houses that meander down toward the twin Mystic Lakes, only to lose their way in cul-de-sacs and dead ends as if not quite certain where the water lies. She's made the walk a dozen times, invisible in the darkness, the narrow lanes wooded and serene. She'd never walk alone in such an ill-lit place were it not for the influenza, which has made her a bit fearless. Although Winchester is hardly Roxbury; it's hard to imagine a Winchester man lurking in the shadows, watching her, waiting for his moment. The place is as safe as the Honfleur of her childhood ever was.

Elisabeth decides she'll take the long way to the Boat Club, the dense and secretive greenery of Myopia Road suiting her need for privacy on this difficult night. Even a few minutes standing by the shuttered boathouse and looking out over the flat water can settle her heart. But as she makes her way down the gravel drive, the lights of the house giving way to an amber moonlight, the piano in the carriage house begins to play.

The unseen pianist has started into a melody as sweetly imprinted upon Elisabeth's soul as the sound of her father's voice. From the open window she hears Westerlake—for it can only be he—pick out the weightless melody of the *Clair de lune*, Debussy's sweet, bemused music ringing out into the night. Elisabeth is stopped in her tracks, her heart fluttering from the first unmistakable notes.

Before she's quite realized it she's transported back to a Paris Christmas long ago, to the piano in the Saint-Cloud apartment where she sat next to her father as a girl of nine and learned to play this same melody. Her father took the left-hand part, she the right. The memory is precise in all its details. The December snow building tiny hills against the mullions of the second-floor windows. The narrow street impassable down below, the unusually frigid air and the snowstorm paralyzing the city. In living memory there has not been a December as Arctic as this one. But in the warmth of the apartment she nestles against her father on the piano bench, the sluggish siege outside somehow clarifying the music that's flowing from his hands. There is a scent of bay rum at his collar, a faint scent of breakfast on his breath as he counts out the meter for her edification.

The music itself is brand new, a half-secret known only to a few in her papa's circle of friends. On the music stand sits a handwritten copy of the score that Debussy himself has given her father to settle a debt; a few years later, during the hard early days in America, her father would sell it for grocery money at a pittance, Debussy by then a famous man. How careless the composer's manuscript is, unkempt as his wiry beard and rumpled suits—the stiff pages marred by ink blots and furiously crossed-out sections, the notes cluttered across the staves. But her father finds his way through it without any trouble, seeming to know exactly where the music is headed.

After only a few bars of Westerlake's playing Elisabeth finds herself in tears, as if her papa's ghost has suddenly appeared to take her in its arms. She picks her way carefully over the short grass, drawn ineluctably to the music. Half in a dream she pauses near the carriage house to listen, hidden in the shadow thrown by a sycamore tree. But just as she takes her place, the music stops. She can feel the notes in her hands, her fingers needing to play. Her thumb and ring finger find the opening F and A-flat. After a pause Westerlake begins again, getting a little further this time, his touch a bit heavy and uncertain. It occurs to her that he must be sight-reading from a score. Perhaps he's discovered the sheet music Rena and Helen keep under the hinged seat of the piano bench. Elisabeth listens as he moves into the first variation, slowing down, feeling his way. She barely realizes that she's begun to sing the notes aloud, as if to guide his fingers. This is how she learned the piece on that snowy Christmas long ago: singing nonce syllables as she slowly picked out the melody, her voice training her fingers until they had it by heart.

Westerlake advances with more confidence toward the first crescendo. Under the sycamore his unseen tutor sings along, her smooth voice rising to meet the swelling music, the beauty and familiarity of Debussy's composition easing out something that's been locked away inside her since she arrived at Aigremont. When the piano abruptly halts again she goes on singing for a measure or two, her voice suddenly naked in the shadows.

"*Que c'est beau*," a man's voice says in French. "*Tu chantes du cœur.*"

Startled, Elisabeth dries her eyes and looks up to see Charlie Westerlake perched on the windowsill, smiling down at her.

"Don't let me stop you, Miss Garner. Please."

She can't think what to say. The thought of what she's done mortifies her. She's amazed, too, that he knows her name. She takes a step backward into the sycamore's shade.

Westerlake laughs, indulges her nervousness.

"I didn't mean to scare you off, you know. Just the opposite, as a matter of fact."

"No," she says, but only to herself.

"Probably my bad French. Soldier's French, you know. The worst kind."

He shifts off the sill now and disappears from the window, only to reappear a moment later when the carriage house door creaks open. The tall captain fills the doorway. Elisabeth notices the white sleeves rolled up over his strong arms, the slight cant to his large head. Even when standing he favors the wounded hip. For a fleeting moment she wonders how much pain it gives him. Whether it keeps him awake at night, aching where the shrapnel dug in.

"Do you play? A well brought-up French girl—I'll just bet you do."

Tongue-tied, Elisabeth nods.

"I wonder," Charlie Westerlake says in a quieter voice, "if you'd be willing to show me the rest of that Debussy. It's so damned beautiful I can't seem to get it under my fingers. Whenever I try to focus on the notes, my mind just wanders off someplace else. Paris, maybe, or some little French village, before the war. Do you ever feel that way? If I miss France, you must miss it like hell."

Elisabeth says not a word.

"Come on now, Miss Garner," he continues with mock sternness, "no need to lurk in the shadows. Not when the *clair de lune* is so lovely. It's not so often you see moonlight this color." He glances up toward the orange harvest moon, a private smile on his lips, then looks past her toward the mansion. "If you're worried you'll be seen here, don't be. No one's watching. And it's only a piano lesson. I promise."

Allez, ma fille, says her papa's voice in the silence of her mind. *Go.*

"Miss Garner," says the doctor, his eyes holding hers, flicking away, returning. "It's hardly a time to refuse a weary soldier a bit of beauty. Wouldn't you agree?"

Allez, ma princesse. Va là-bas.

Elisabeth walks out of the shadows slowly, aware of the moonlight settling over her shoulders. Charlie Westerlake's eyes are on her as he steps aside to let her into the little house with the white piano her father once played.

"Good," Westerlake smiles, and closes the door behind her. "Good."

Chicago

November 2018

XXIII.

ENTIRELY BEYOND HIM

BY THE TIME BEN AWAKENS she's up and making breakfast, chef's knife clicking like a metronome in the kitchen. For a few minutes he lies as still and stealthy as a hunter in a blind. Sprawled across her bed, the scent of her rosemary lotion on the pillow, he takes his bearings, baffled by the abrupt turnabout in his life.

Through the sari-cloth curtains the winter light is sluggish and diffuse. All the sun, he knows, will be pooled in the east-facing living room with its African masks and bubbling aquarium and polished Steinway, its expensive views of park and lake. It's where the sunrise found him after their first night together—the lovers never having made it to the bed, a tribal rug and enveloping leather sofa world enough for them. On that morning, too, she was up well before he was. It was the scent of coffee that had roused him, the aroma from a French press pot on a hammered-brass tray balanced in the hands of a kneeling woman who proved, incredibly, to be Ana Clara Matta. It was incomprehensible that she was there—no, that *he* was there, brazenly naked on a sofa in her Lincoln Park brownstone, the furniture disarranged as if he'd somehow slept through a home invasion.

Perhaps she felt the improbability of it too. In her eyes was a slightly startled look that wasn't at all like her, as if he'd been the one to surprise her in her sleep and not the reverse. The dark curls spilling over the collar of her kimono were damp from a shower, haloed in sun. He realized that she wasn't wearing makeup, an intimacy somehow in keeping with what had happened the night before.

"How long have we known each other?" she asked in a musing tone.

Ben thought back to her first Counterpoint session, when she'd filled in for the ailing pianist of a chamber group. She was barely thirty, far from famous.

"Forever," he replied, drawing a fingertip experimentally along her bare leg to convince himself she was real. "Must be fifteen years now. Kenji Aoi's Brahms session."

She frowned darkly and set the tray on the coffee table. For a moment it seemed to him that something might be wrong. The frown spelled trouble. Perhaps she'd had second thoughts about sleeping with him—who could blame her? Once he'd finished his coffee she'd ask him to leave in terms that brooked no objection. It would end up as nothing more than a one-night stand, never to be discussed again.

In the silence that followed, Ben felt himself starting to let go of it, of the doomed thing between them. But then came an apologetic smile; then came a kiss. She cupped his unshaven face in her hands.

"After all this time," she said, "can you believe I don't know how you take your coffee?"

AT THE FOOT OF THE BED hangs a mirror where he likes to observe her while they're making love, the rise and fall of her shoulders and tapered back, her spine like braided ropework when she leans forward to kiss him, a little cry caught in her throat. Occasionally she'll shake out her curls like a mare shaking off rain, or catch them in a hand and hold them atop her head as if to cool her nape, her small breasts lifted by the gesture. Ben wonders what's possessed her to hang the mirror exactly at the level of the mattress. Clearly it's aimed at the bed—a player's-eye view of the field. But what about when she's alone? From where he lies he can see himself a little too well. A flicker of caution passes through him, a faint question about her that he cannot yet answer.

He's known her for years, it's true, but he's only just begun to discover her as a lover. Though the woman he now knows simply as Ana inhabits the same body as the Ana Clara Matta of his professional acquaintance, she inhabits it in entirely different ways. The voice, a little deep in the way of many Brazilian women, goes deeper at night, throttling down. A soft bite crosswise on the nape electrifies her. Her breasts, on the other hand, carry no charge at all. Before going to sleep she insists, without fail, on executing a fifteen-minute regimen of dental care involving a number of machines and colorful fluids, her domestic rituals non-negotiable even in the first heady days of a love affair. All this he's uncovered in the course of these three nights in her bed.

She materializes in the bathroom mirror as he's relieving himself, bleary from her top-drawer scotch and the short night of jagged sleep. The whine in his ear is back in force; a whip of vertigo cracks inside his skull when he leans over to flush the toilet. Tomorrow, finally, he's to learn whether anything can be done about his body's accelerating collapse. Despite all that's happened with Ana, he's not been able to drive the coming doctor's visit from his mind—not since the neurologist called to say his MRI results were abnormal, that it was time to see a neurosurgeon.

For almost a week now the alarming news has been ramping in him like a fever. He can feel it in his gut, his arms, his fingertips, his whole body inflamed by it. If he's plunged headlong into Ana's world in hope of distracting himself, forgetting it for a time, the strategy's failed miserably. Even in her bed he's felt the dark heat rising—especially in her bed. He wishes he could confide in her, but something tells him he shouldn't. She suspects nothing. He's concealed it well.

Just now she's leaning against the doorjamb in yoga tights and an artfully torn Pretenders tee shirt, cradling her elbows and studying his body appraisingly.

"You like to run, then?" she asks, as if continuing a conversation they haven't yet started. "I see a runner's body."

"It's the only exercise I can stand."

"So, when you get tired of me you can get away fast."

"And why would I do that?"

"Men run away from me all the time. Surely you've heard."

Ben's not ready for this conversation. "Is there coffee?"

"It's not good for you, coffee. And that's coming from a Brazilian. I'll make you an açai. You'll drink it and you'll like it."

"Is there coffee?"

In the mirror she flashes a smile that feels mirthless to him, then hands him a monogrammed towel off the rack. "When you're ready."

It's Sunday; he could stay for a lazy breakfast but feels the need to leave quickly. He's promised himself a day of solitude to prepare for the doctor's appointment tomorrow—for whatever news it brings—but it's not only this. Since his first night here he hasn't been able to shake the feeling that he doesn't belong in Ana Clara Matta's private world, that he's nothing but a trespasser. An imposter with no right to be where he is, no right whatsoever.

IN THE LUMINOUS EARLY DAYS WITH ROBIN they'd stay in bed until noon, lingering over bagels and pots of coffee and putting off for as long as possible the moment of parting. This is entirely different. On these first mornings at Ana's place he's felt an awkwardness, even a danger in the air. Things are simpler at night. Three fingers of Lagavulin, then hours of heroic bouting on bed and floor and countertop. A late-night bowl of cold sesame noodles in her gleaming kitchen. On Friday evening, a private recital just for him, the *Clair de lune* played with simplicity and grace, her communion with Debussy never finer. A lazy, post-coital hour spent laughing at late-night comedians on television, her stomach rumbling from something she'd eaten. Eventually a dead man's sleep overtaking him, the body reduced to its simplest needs.

But the sun brings troubles he can't ignore. All the night's passion goes bloodless. He feels off balance in body and soul, his footing unsteady as he rolls from her bed, his dizziness on a tear. And so he's made his excuses and taken his leave swiftly. Endured her look of disapproval, the whiff of disappointment in which he detects, he's sure of it, a barely managed loneliness. In the lobby he's ignored the doorman's catty smile, a wave of relief combing through his body the instant the lobby door slams shut. Obliged to head up to Counterpoint Friday and Saturday for long-scheduled sessions, he's hurried toward the corner to hail a cab, putting his complicated lover behind him as fast as his feet will carry him. It shouldn't be this way, but it is.

On this particular morning there's another reason to make a clean getaway. As he hangs his towel on the rod, Ben feels a twinge of panic he can't account for, at first, something jabbing through the background fever of his medical worries. Silently he looks for its source, rummaging about in the fog of his head, until he recalls last night's perilous talk—the only time they've discussed the French sonata since Ana first heard it in Studio A. It's a conversation he doesn't care to continue.

"You're going to stand me up for breakfast again," her reflection declares from the mirror, the British vowels tightened into something stern. "I've got Henry & Dalton pears in, you know, though God knows where they get them this time of year. A gift from some poor piano teacher in Iowa. Half her month's wages, one imagines." She purses her lips with distaste and adds: "I even bought you bagels—the first time a bagel has entered this house, you can be sure. You see how I'm willing to sacrifice for you."

He turns and lays a hand on her hip. She's faux-pouting, narrow features drawn to a point. When he leans in to kiss her she gives him her cheek.

Difficult, he thinks, though he knows he has an equal part in it. He's lied to her, after all.

"It has nothing to do with you," he says. "You shouldn't take it personally."

"How else should I take it? You get up and fly out the door like a bloody thief. No breakfast, no conversation, nothing. You don't let me take care of you. I want to *cook* for you, Ben. I don't cook for anyone. But you don't fancy me, apparently. Not in a domestic way."

"Not true."

"Then why?"

"Because . . . this is all so new for me. I never thought I—"

"You never thought what? That you'd wind up in the famous Matta's bed?" She sends him a brittle look. "You should have a higher opinion of yourself, *amor*. And a more realistic opinion of Ana Clara Matta."

"Ana—"

"You should be making love to me when you wake up, not bolting off."

She steps back and puts her hands on her hips. "You know what? I'm not just fucking around here, Ben. This is real. Or I thought it was." There are sudden tears in her eyes. Another alarm goes off inside him: he may not have room for this in his burdened heart. His head begins to spin again, although he's standing perfectly still. It's good there's no food in his stomach.

"I know it's real," he says, but they both hear his hesitation.

His words hang in the air. She palms her tears away deftly.

"*Ai! Que vergonha,*" she says to herself. "I'm a disgrace."

"I'm sorry, Ana. I'm just trying to figure all this out."

She slumps against the door frame with a defeated look. A bare foot tucks behind the other's heel. Silence rings between the hard tile walls, the tinnitus blaring in his ear.

For some moments Ana considers his words, eyes shut tight. He's reminded of the way she closes her eyes before launching into a performance, gathering her thoughts, concentrating her essence, preparing. He's always wondered what's going through her mind in those moments. He's wondering the same thing now.

Seeming to reach a decision, she opens her eyes and pushes away from the door frame and takes his hands, reeling him in. All her hardness drops away. There is a light about her now, a change in weather. These abrupt swings of hers confuse him every time.

"Ben," she says, "listen to me. Here's the heart of it. There was always an attraction there, whether you knew it or not. Quiet men get under my skin. Opposites, right? So let me ask you a question: Did you really think my working with you all these years was only about the music? Yes . . . but no. Not only." She pauses to let this sink in, smiling up at him. "But now . . . *now* . . . there's this brilliant thing in you, something I never guessed was there, though I respected you in so many other ways. Do you know how exciting it is for a woman to suddenly discover genius in a man she thought she knew so well? Don't you see how erotic it is?" She hesitates. "How bloody *romantic*?"

He feels a gorge rising in his throat. "You're giving me far too much credit."

"No! Exactly, precisely no. You have to believe in yourself as an artist. I can help with that, Ben. There are people who need to

hear this sonata of yours. I can make that happen. You know I can."
She eyes him askance. "Unless you just wanted to fuck Ana Clara
Matta, in which case there's the door."

He isn't ready for whatever is happening between them. Even
in the worst of times with Robin there was no room for this kind
of drama. These whipsaw swings between grievance and sweetness
are entirely beyond him, especially now. But worse than all this is
the matter of the sonata—the lie. He can't imagine what she'll do
when she discovers it's not his.

She stretches up to kiss his lips, tender now. Takes him in her
arms. She seems to have forgotten the anger of a few moments
before.

"You have to believe in this fantastic music that's in you, Ben. I
won't let you ignore it."

The ringing in his ear shifts to a higher pitch. The first spike of
a headache shoots through his spinning brain. Ben feels he might
be sick, here and now, in her presence.

He'll have to come clean, because he's not a liar. He will have
to tell her. Even lies of omission must be undone . . . all the more
so when they threaten to escape into the wider world, to set fire to
everything in their path. Somehow he must confess what he's done.
But at this moment, depleted and in pain, with a menacing MRI
gnawing at him and his body failing in real time, he'd only make a
mess of it. Now is not the moment for such a delicate conversation.
Besides, in just two days' time she leaves for a month in Europe—a
fall tour whose timing feels nothing less than merciful.

When the moment is right, when he feels more in control, he'll
tell her. He'll think it through with a level head and say what needs
to be said. He will apologize with clarity and sincerity and take the
consequences. But not now, on this cold November morning, with
his head spinning and his stomach in open revolt.

Instead, obeying some perverse impulse, he gives more oxygen
to the lie.

"Look," he tells the woman in his arms, "it's just that I need to
go and work. You can understand that, can't you?"

She searches his face, not hiding her disappointment. "Work is more important than me? When I'm about to leave town? It's Sunday, Ben. The bloody studio's closed."

"That's not what I meant. I mean my other work."

He sees the realization unfurl in her brown eyes, the delight. She smiles beautifully up at him. With delicate fingers she touches his lips as if the two of them are standing in complete darkness. Traces his mouth carefully. Rises up on her toes to kiss him.

"Then go, *amor!* Work on your Allegro. Give me something beautiful to play. Finish." She squeezes his hand. "I won't disturb you. Come to me when you're ready."

At the door he accepts a paper bag she's produced from the kitchen.

"Take these," she says. "Sesame and some other kind. I'll just toss them in the bin."

A moment later he's back on the street with his armful of bagels, the shadow of his deceit close on his heels. Lincoln Park West is nearly empty; the air's too brisk, the hour too early for casual walkers. At Fullerton he turns and walks over to the harbor, the wind against him, granular snow blowing in off the lake. The sheer physical effort of it, the contrarian route he's taken, calms the vertigo and begins to settle his stomach. The body rallies to the challenge. At the breakwater he heads north along the bike path, a slurry of half-frozen lake water sloshing against the concrete rip-rap. His cheeks are aching—his heart is aching—but this, he tells himself, is only what he deserves.

XXIV.

TABLE TALK

SHE'D TREATED HIM TO DINNER at Mon Ami Gabi on their first evening together, supposedly to celebrate the completion of her Debussy recordings but really to drink him into bed. It was the thinnest of pretexts, this idea of a celebratory dinner. Seven weeks had passed since the final session; the masters had long since been delivered to her record company. While it was true that she'd done a brief Canadian tour in the meantime, her schedule crowded and complex as the fall concert season picked up steam and the longer European tour loomed, they both knew what was afoot.

All through the final Debussy sessions they'd circled one another warily, her spontaneous kiss in Studio A exerting a slow centrifugal pull. As late summer slid into a chilly fall they worked together hour after hour in the very place where she'd eavesdropped on his playing, neither of them saying a word about that surprising evening. The sonata, like the kiss, hung in the air as an open question to be taken up later, when the press of work was done.

She was already late turning in her Debussy masters. They had to push ahead. And so they sat side by side at the mixing board, pilot and copilot, eyes shut to A/B takes or review passages that worried her, the Steinway's commanding voice filling the room to the brim. In her usual way she'd pronounce quickly upon her work, then spring up and go back to the piano for more—though now, on occasion, she'd sink back in her chair and ruminate aloud on some matter of interpretation, some question of dynamics or tempo or compositional intent, then turn to Ben and ask what he thought. This was a side of her he'd never been allowed to see. While he answered her questions—with scarcely concealed dismay, having been put on the spot by a true maestra—she'd study him intently, fingers interlaced, seeming to hang on his every word. But if he sensed a new deference in his artist, a willingness to involve him in her creative process, he made little of it. He could say whatever he liked; at the end of the day Ana Clara Matta didn't defer to anyone. She trusted her judgment supremely, and so did he.

By the third week of September the Debussy CD was a wrap. They parted amicably, with only the faintest hint of mischief when she lingeringly kissed his cheek goodbye. How could he have known that she'd been thinking about him constantly since that startling night in Studio A? The notion would never have crossed his mind. But it was true: from the moment she'd heard him play the sonata she'd seen him in an entirely different light. In a matter of minutes she'd found herself profoundly attracted to him. Fascinated, in fact, by this measured and polite man, nearly a decade her senior, who'd never been more than a colleague to her. She couldn't deny what she'd felt in that moment. The world had shifted. In her imagination there was no going back.

All this he'd learn later, lying on the floor of her living room with his new lover tucked into the crook of his arm, her tropical fish darting in their tiny, blazing world next to the bookcases. At the time he didn't suspect a bit of it. She, for her part, certainly wasn't telling.

ONCE THE DEBUSSY WAS DONE he'd heard nothing from her for weeks. He barely noticed; no sooner had he sent off her masters than he was plunged into a new round of deadline work for another client. By the time he'd roll into an Uber at ten or eleven at night, too beat to walk all the way back up to Ravenswood, he was asleep on his feet. There was no time to think about Ana Clara Matta, much less wonder whether she might be thinking about him.

He knew that she was as busy as he was. In listening to her run through her calendar aloud, frowning at her phone as they arranged session dates, he'd gleaned the outline of her fall schedule. By now she'd be in rehearsals for her Canadian tour. Then, after only a brief stop in Chicago, she'd leave for Europe, where she was to undertake a four-country tour as guest soloist with the Ensemble Morisot. In January, back in Chicago again, she was to début a commissioned concerto in what would surely be one of the marquee events of the season—though this particular plan had been thrown into disarray when the seventy-seven-year-old composer, Rafik Jelassi, called from Tunis to confide that he'd been undergoing treatment for a glioblastoma.

She'd taken the call in the Counterpoint kitchen during one of the final Debussy sessions. Ben was there to see her blanch at the news, to help her think through the vexing implications if Jelassi could not deliver, to field her anger over not having been told sooner. The Pearson Center for the Performing Arts—a gleaming postmodern fever dream whose angular concert hall hovered over the lake like a famished praying mantis—had been booked for a year. The orchestra had been engaged, critics and luminaries invited. A good deal of her sponsors' money had already been spent.

But the missed opportunity for Ana would be the greater loss. Rafik Jelassi had shot to fame for a symphony dedicated to his countryman, Mohamed Bouazizi, the street vendor whose self-immolation had launched the Arab Spring. To present the world début of a piece by such a composer would be a dramatic step up for Ana, a savvy move that would vault her to an even more rarefied plane of the music world while extending her reputation far beyond it. She was already hailed as a brilliant player; with the Jelassi gig she'd prove her political bona fides too. Her manager was already in negotiations for a joint TED Talk, composer and performer in dialogue in Paris on the ninth anniversary of Bouazizi's suicide. They'd pulled out all the stops. Ben had been in the classical music world long enough to understand exactly how much it meant for her career. For Ana the stakes couldn't be higher.

But now, as for the status of the promised concerto, the ailing composer would give only elliptical answers. Perhaps the piece was nearly done; perhaps he had miles to go. She couldn't tell. So far Jelassi had sent along nothing but the first movement, an Andante that disappointed her. She would have to find something else to play if the new piece fell through. Canceling the concert at this late stage was out of the question, though inventing a new program and securing the necessary talent might well be out of the question too. As the Debussy sessions wound down, Ben could see how it was weighing on her. The Jelassi matter was always in the back of her mind.

NEVERTHELESS, on the very night she arrived home from the Canadian tour, she'd called to ask him to dinner. The last Debussy sessions were far behind them. He could hear the clamor of an airplane cabin in the background, the harsh crackle of an announcement, the ding of the seatbelt light, the clunk of luggage being hauled down. Apparently it couldn't wait until she was off the tarmac.

He took the call in the nude, having just stepped out of the shower after a chilly evening jog. He'd been feeling better, a bit, his body more under his control. Before working her way round to her topic Ana made sure to complain about the freezing rain in Toronto, the rude Edmonton audience, the dry-as-dust tarte Tatin she'd endured in a Montreal airport café. She didn't ask him a single question. Tucking a towel around his waist he let her talk on, wandering through the house, her voice in his ear.

The sonata manuscript lay spread across the dining room table. With the workload finally easing up at Counterpoint he'd thrown himself back into transcribing the Allegro, making slow but steady progress. He couldn't believe he was on the phone with Ana Clara Matta, listening to her wend her way, through a dozen detours, toward the moment of asking him to dinner. Under the towel, to his amusement, a bashful erection made its presence known.

Only in hindsight would he see what had happened. The idea that Ben Weil was the composer of the sonata must have flourished within her as she trudged from Montreal to Toronto, Edmonton to Vancouver, the tacit lie shooting deeper and deeper roots into her heart for the simple reason that he wasn't there to renounce it. She'd been caught off guard, this woman who prided herself on always being a step ahead of everyone else. He'd surprised her profoundly. In hotel beds she'd have lain awake with the remembered music playing in her head, the riddle of Ben Weil's apparent genius hovering in the background. During sound checks, sitting at strange pianos, she'd have recalled snippets of the sonata, testing it out under her fingers, thinking hard and subtly about it, interrogating it with all her musical intelligence. He'd not been there to stop her, to muster his courage and simply tell the truth. And so she'd drawn her own conclusions.

By the time they met for dinner on a Thursday evening, the first wet snow of the season clumped on the windows of the bistro—winter having come suddenly, in the best Chicago fashion, with barely a whisper of fall—any doubts she may have harbored were gone. The manager hurried over to greet them, fawning as a czarina's courtier. They hadn't even ordered the wine before a woman nervously approached her for an autograph. In the candlelight Ana Clara Matta glowed like the diva she was. For two hours she leaned in to ply him with questions about his life, his family, even Robin, shifting her chair closer and closer as the place filled up and the clamor rose. Not once did she mention the sonata. Perhaps she was waiting for him to bring it up. In the flood of her attention, in the exhilaration of arms and legs grazing under the table, he couldn't find his footing. In such a heated scrum it wouldn't be possible to have the more serious conversation they needed to have. The nervous energy of the moment wouldn't permit it. When she ordered a second bottle of wine he knew he was lost. He was far too excited to talk sense into her now.

The conversation over dinner was a beginning, not an ending—this is what Ben told himself as they shared a plate of profiteroles. Confessions could come later. After paying the bill she'd kissed him across the table and taken his hand and walked him straight to her townhouse door as if it were all foreordained, never looking back.

ONLY AFTER THAT FIRST KISS was swamped by countless others did the question of the sonata begin rising to the surface, churned up from below like the debris of a shipwreck he'd hoped was forgotten. Her feelings for him were no longer a secret. The magical evening sitting together at the Studio A piano had already taken its place in their shared story. The coast was clear. The embargo had been lifted.

She broached the topic while they sat chatting on her bed on their first Saturday night as lovers, a plate of hummus and tiny purple carrots tucked between them. Their blood was still thrumming with her good whiskey. They'd been lovers for only a few days, but he was already more accustomed to seeing her in her kimono, as now, than in street clothes. In the late afternoon, after he returned from his Counterpoint session, they'd made love and then showered together, Ben furtively gripping the hot water tap to steady himself as she scrubbed his back, the vertigo careening in, his lover oblivious to his frailties. Two fingers of Lagavulin had done nothing to right the ship. Now that they'd decamped to the bed, the carnival ride in his head had at last begun to slow down.

In a casual way she asked him what had ever happened with his piano piece, where things stood with the composition.

The question roared in his chest but he held steady, dipping out hummus to buy time. He rued the Lagavulin in his blood.

What he should have said was: *It's not what you think—that sonata's not mine.*

Instead he told her, "Work's been so unbelievably busy. . . . These Takács sessions, then this huge remastering job for EMI, twenty Toscanini NBCs from the Angel backlist. Which is taking way, way longer than I bid. I haven't had two minutes to work on anything for myself. Literally."

She squeezed his hand. "Ben—you need to *make* time for this. Give it all your heart." He must have frowned; she stroked it away. "It's a brilliant piece, *amor*. I don't think you realize."

He glared at himself in the mirror at the foot of the bed. Aslant, unnerved. Her enthusiasm left him mute as a stone. But she only warmed to her idea.

"Look," she said, "the way I hear your sonata, the way I understand it as a player, is that this is an entire century of piano music distilled into a single piece. Not as an *hommage*, which would be deadly boring . . . more a *bricolage*, with a unifying vision. A point of view. You choose the sonata form as your vehicle just to be provocative, I think, because then you bend it like crazy. Starting with the fact that the first movement is *andante*—who does that? Then you really break glass. The development isn't anything like what a classical player expects. You follow the mood and the musical history, ignoring the canonical structure. . . . Your structure is *evolutionary*, I think. It's about the evolution of piano music. A dialogue between past and present, am I right? That may not be your architectural concept, I don't know, but it's what I heard that night in the studio. I've thought about it quite a lot since then."

"Obviously," he says, though little of what she's saying registers.

"You start with a mystery, right? A disruption. The opening arpeggio and then that weird, seven-beat rest—seven beats passing into 5/4 time, Ben? Really? Then this Impressionist motif, I'd call it, and that lovely descending minor sequence. Very neo-Romantic. Which bridges to the first modernist bits—modal, discordant, a hint of serialism in there. I need to hear it again. Really tear that passage apart. After which you segue into a folk melody. Bravo. Then—then! Your bloody *jazz* stuff, right out of nowhere. These block chords, color chords, the rootless voicings. The way you weave in these contrapuntal inner voices . . . mad smart. Brilliant. And it fits together perfectly, like lock and key. Amazing range you have— *so* creative. What an ambition."

She sat up straighter in bed. "Do you know what really impressed me about your piece, Ben, the more I thought about it? I said to myself, *Only an outsider could have written this.* No academically trained composer would have come up with this. It breaks too many rules. Which is exactly its genius."

Her praise was unbearable. He was responsible for none of the genius she'd detected. Hunching forward to grip his knees, he said, "Ana, there's something—" But at this moment her phone buzzed on the nightstand. She glanced at the incoming number and frowned by way of saying, *I have to take this.*

"Rafik!" she said and twirled to her feet like a dancer. "*Comment ça va? La chimiothérapie—c'est supportable?*"

It was Jelassi, the composer in Tunisia. Ben listened distractedly as she paced the floor and gently questioned the old man about his health, her French fluent and familiar. Gradually she steered the conversation toward the concerto she'd commissioned, sinking into the armchair by the window as she talked. Ben heard her struggling to find a tactful way to say that she'd found the first movement dull, then to ask him how the rest was coming along. He wondered what time it was in Tunisia—the middle of the night, if he wasn't wrong. Perhaps the man was on steroids for his cancer, unable to sleep.

"*D'accord, Rafik,*" Ana finally told Jelassi, rolling her eyes at Ben. "*On travaillera dessus quand vous vous sentirez mieux, Maestro.* You concentrate on getting well." Ben was surprised to hear her give the composer a pass, but she had. As they were signing off she rose from the armchair and laid a palm across her forehead as if to stave off a migraine, eyes shut tight.

When she came back to bed she sighed and said, "He claims he's almost done. He claims he'll make the deadline." She began massaging her fingers one by one, the same way she did before every performance. "I think he's lying, unfortunately. At the very least being overly optimistic. Maybe he's too drugged to think straight. I wish I knew the bloody man well enough to read him." She nibbled one of the tiny carrots, discarded it. "All I'm asking for is a bit of transparency, you know? I *despise* dishonesty. It'd help if he'd send more of the score."

"You need a backup plan."

"We're working on one, believe me. The problem is, we've already hyped this thing to death. It's an event. It's righteous politics. Minor *royals* are flying in for this, Ben. Bono is coming. Salman fucking Rushdie. It has its own Instagram feed. If the commission suddenly falls out of bed we'd better be ready with something equally grand."

"What does Sir Anthony think? This seems like just his kind of challenge." Sir Anthony Wooten, her storied manager, was known for his skill at turning disaster to profit.

"Ant thinks we'd need to come up with a real A-lister, a guest soloist who'd make everyone forget Jelassi. I promise you, Perlman playing Bach partitas is a hotter ticket than Rafik Jelassi ever will be, though of course we'd never get him on such short notice. Not to mention that it will be January in Chicago. When you're at that level you pick and choose—who would choose to come here in winter? Ant thinks we could approach Esa-Pekka to bring in one of his robotic things. The Pearson's all set up for high-tech, of course, which would appeal to him. A spectacle may be what's needed. Shock and awe. And Esa-Pekka is his client." She leaned forward and grasped her toes in a long stretch, then fell back against the pillow with a grunt.

Ben said, "What would *you* want?"

"Me? I'd rather scale it down radically. Convert it to a chamber program . . . maybe just violin-piano. But only if we could perform a piece that raised eyebrows, something really cutting-edge. A Cheryl Frances-Hoad, say. That sort. And only if we could get a top-flight violinist. One of the bright young things, maybe. Ant's already called Alma Deutscher's manager. I played with her in Vienna last year and she was superb. Still in braces, but superb. Of course there's the problem of the ridiculously short notice. . . . Anyone worth getting is probably already booked. And we can't commit until Rafik falls through, unless we cancel the commission ourselves, which the investors won't like. Frankly it's all been worrying me to death."

She met his eyes in the mirror at the foot of the bed. At the sight of him her sharp features brightened. She swiveled on the mattress to face him and crossed her legs yoga-style. "But enough of that. I didn't mean to load you down with my shite. We'll get it sorted. Ant's a miracle worker, of course." She took Ben's hands in hers. "Look—what I really want to say about your sonata, the really important thing, is that you need to finish it. You know that, *amor*. You know it in your heart. You're an artist, Ben, full stop. You can't compromise on this."

His mouth went dry. "It's not mine to finish," he said under his breath, but she was too busy lecturing him to listen.

"You know, don't you, that I'm going to take it to the world the instant it's ready? I'm going to make sure everyone knows who Ben Weil is. What beauty he's capable of producing. What brilliance! I promise you that."

At this Ben's mind went entirely blank. The half-smile he gave her cost him too much self-respect.

"So modest," she said and kissed him. "I love that about you. A quality I'll never have."

Late that night, as he lay with a pounding heart in the darkness of her bedroom, he heard her slip off into the living room and sit down at the piano to play a passage from the third movement—the little folk melody dancing down the hallway toward him, Garnier's ghost on the prowl. She wasn't going to let it go.

XXV.

JUST ASK

Now, NINE HOURS LATER, his heart is pounding again. The long march from her place takes him up to Diversey Harbor where the cold off the lake is suddenly too punishing, too much. He clutches Ana's bag of bagels to his chest like a shivering child. Early November and it might as well be February, when not a month ago it was ninety degrees. He turns west and heads for the bizarrely muscle-bound Goethe statue at the top of the park—imagine, the sovereign soul of German literature with the body of a philandering café owner—and a shudder goes through him, the wind thumping his back. His lips are chapped, his head throbbing. At a curb he stumbles over a scrap of snow and nearly falls to the salty pavement, his body defying him yet again.

The sensible thing would be to hail a taxi, but he needs to be alone. A conversation with a cabbie would be beyond him. The buses are almost empty on this early Sunday morning; he decides to walk to Clark and catch the 22. Ben trudges on, putting the lake behind him, the stores mostly closed, the bright cafés too full of people to lure him in.

At the bus stop he takes a call from Nikki.

"Remind me what time tomorrow," she says without preamble. He imagines her in her overheated kitchen, dog at her feet, *Heavily Meditated* mug at hand. "Should I pick you up?"

"You don't need to come, Nik."

"Too late, friend. I've already moved all my clients."

"I mean it. It's not necessary."

"Ben! This is important. Definitely a second-set-of-ears situation. Robin would have gone. Let me do this for you. Or do it for me, if that's easier in your head for whatever reason."

He hesitates, the snow blowing up into a tiny cyclone, the wintry air rank with exhaust.

Nikki insists. "I'm *going*, okay? We're going to hear this news together, whatever it is. Tell me where to meet you."

On the bus he feels nauseous again, all the world a choppy sea. When the driver swings around a stalled van, the great trundling chassis creaks like a ship rounding Cape Horn. For several blocks he feels he might be sick and considers getting off. His hand is poised to pull the signal cord. But none of it, this time, is real. The streets are quiet and smooth, the driving careful and unhurried. The spinning in his head has spun down. No: the tempest is in his heart.

ON THE FLOOR OF HIS FOYER lies a hill of mail, shoved through the door slot. He hasn't been home since Thursday morning, having gone to the dinner at Mon Ami Gabi directly from Counterpoint and then straight back to Ana's place after his Friday and Saturday sessions, feverish as a teenager. Rather than stop home for a clean change of clothes, he'd thrown his lived-in jeans and shirt and underwear in with a load of her laundry. How swiftly he'd become addicted to her. Or perhaps it was only that he didn't want to be alone, dangerous as his time with her felt. There isn't an addict alive who doesn't fear a grueling withdrawal. For Ben it was no different.

After sorting through the junk he comes to a reminder letter from Northwestern Memorial Hospital confirming his appointment in the neurosurgery department. A routine communication, though really nothing is routine at this moment of his life. He tears the notice in half smartly and pitches it in the trash as if it were a Dear John letter, wanting it out of his sight.

His neurologist has assured him that the chances of a malignancy are slight, but even so. His mother's excruciating death by cancer is a fact he can't ignore. The disabling back pain, the stumbling that became staggering and eventually outright paralysis, the opioid blanket that made Sylvia Weil ever more distant, like a ship pulling away from its berth—all this he remembers too well. In the face of it, especially at night, his doctor's assurances go only so far.

Dr. Eastman's preliminary diagnosis, to be confirmed by MRI—*studies* was the word she used—points to an acoustic neuroma, a benign growth on the cochlear nerve that affects balance and hearing but rarely goes beyond that. He's researched it obsessively, of course; everything he's read backs her up. The thing may be a brain tumor, technically—are there two more frightening words in the language?—but not the sort to kill you. Not usually.

The scan had been done early Tuesday morning, two days before the fateful dinner at Mon Ami Gabi. By nine it was over; he'd retreated to the hospital cafeteria for a bland breakfast and then caught the El up to Counterpoint, a sense of lopsided gravity about his body as he reeled up the steps, his balance worse than ever. The idea of his data—his brain—flashing onto some radiologist's screen was cause for vertigo in itself.

In the late afternoon the doctor had called to say that the scan had confirmed her diagnosis: he did indeed have an acoustic neuroma, though one of modest size. The next visit would be not with her but with a neurosurgeon who'd review his studies and explain the treatment options. Ben had the distinct sense that she was relieved to be handing his case off. When he asked about edema, and about impingement on nearby parts of the brain—he'd educated himself—she deferred to Dr. Lisle. He would explain it all. She seemed in a hurry to get him off the phone.

Then came the unbearable wait. The neurosurgeon was booked until the following Monday. Thank God for the distraction of Ana, for the freshness and surprise of his nights with her. If he'd been left alone to stew all week he wouldn't have slept an hour. To doze against her narrow back after making love was enough. She didn't need to know more.

Ben inspects the refrigerator and evicts two cartons of suspect leftovers and a jug of sour milk, innocent victims of his erotic distraction. He's ravenous. After toasting one of Ana's sesame bagels and making coffee he sits down at the table to eat his solitary breakfast. There's mail to be gone through but he doesn't have the patience for it. What he needs is to be still and think, to let the juggernaut of the week come to a halt so that he can understand where in the world it's landed him.

IT ALL SEEMS SO IMPROBABLE—the hours and hours in her bed, the metastasizing lie about the sonata, the MRI and what it might mean. He can't remember a stretch of days so overloaded with emotion, with developments of such moment, unless it was the week he discovered Robin's affair with Alan Hurwitz. No wonder he's exhausted.

There's no denying that Ana stands at the exact, geometric center of it all. She's set the tempo, made the passion swell with the simplest gesture, given him his silent cues. The smallest twitch of her baton has made him jump to attention. Though his anxiety about the doctor's visit has been rising all week, and though it's taken every ounce of his patience to get through the workday at Counterpoint, it's Ana who's kept forcing her way into his head. Even when they're apart he can't escape her. Now, for example: who's he thinking of, alone in his house?

In any new love there is an element of obsession—this he knows. Each love creates a sudden universe. But this has more edge to it. There's something invasive about her, a way she has of breaching his defenses, engulfing him. Sitting alone in his kitchen he feels it physically, as a constriction in his chest, an ache in his loins, a faint stutter in his heartbeat. It's anything but pleasant.

Ben can't catch a breath. He shifts in the chair to open his chest, to give the air a pathway. The mere thought of her has scrubbed the oxygen from the room. He's not sure how long he can sustain this.

SOMETHING NIKKI TOLD HIM when he first fell in love with Robin comes back to him.

"Don't be deluded by all the fucking," she said, deadly serious. "Fucking makes the brain go soft. Especially the male brain. That's just science. You have to think past it, Ben. When you fall in love with someone, you have to try and see through to the end. All the way through, no matter how ugly it gets."

It had infuriated him. Flush with new love, he was in no mood for a nihilistic lecture. But on this wintry morning his cousin's stark advice has never seemed more urgent.

Ben pushes the plate away and folds his hands on the tabletop. Out on the street a siren sounds. Sparrows dart away, flashing past the windows.

"You need to end it," he declares to the empty kitchen. "Now, before it gets dangerous."

No! a voice spits back. *Don't be an idiot.*

"Something's not right," Ben insists. "It shouldn't feel this way."

Don't overreact. Give it time.

"But I can already see through to the end."

No one can do that.

Perhaps he's just deluded by all the fucking, but the fact is, he's not sure he can give his lover up. Not yet. To let go of her intimacies is the last thing he wants. She's already begun to fill a void he's carried since Alan Hurwitz stole his wife away. It's been so long since a woman has even touched him, long enough that he'd almost forgotten how it felt. Almost forgotten how to give pleasure, too. On the floor of her living room that first night, his clumsiness had embarrassed him as much as it had amused her. The way she'd had to relocate his hands, shift his limbs, guide him like a virgin. But in a few short days with her he's begun to find his bearings again as a lover and a man. All this feels right and important. Why, then, does he find himself bolting into snowstorms when he could be making love to a famous musician in her cozy apartment?

Perhaps it's a failure of imagination. At this moment he can't picture any sort of future for them. Ana Clara Matta is an international sensation: at any given moment, somewhere in the world, someone is listening to her music. Strangers approach her for autographs. Her love affairs are keenly dissected. She certainly has far more money than he ever will. On the dove-gray wall opposite her piano hangs a Chuck Close portrait of a woman who looks very much like her—is it? Over her bed hangs a Matisse line drawing of a buxom nude. In her kitchen one of Banksy's peevish rats holds up a *Because I'm Worthless* placard. This is the world she inhabits.

Nor is he anything like her usual lovers. The men in her life are flamboyant, sui generis, citizens of the world with outsized personalities to match her own—virtuosi on cello or canvas, artists of every stripe. A guerrilla filmmaker from Johannesburg; a French Socialist politician turned crime novelist. Men hungry for the spotlight and completely at home in it. Ben Weil will never be this. At his core he's a quiet man who's happiest in the chapel-like solitude of the engineer's booth. Over the years he's scaled his life precisely to his modest ambitions, having no desire to be dragged onto a larger stage.

Her fame doesn't mean anything to him, really. Fame has never impressed him as much as kindness among the famous, the rarer thing by far. He'll never admire her simply for being the Ana Clara Matta the rest of the world admires; he'll expect more. Which will be another black mark against him, once she realizes it, regardless of her fleeting little bouts of self-deprecation.

Soon enough, he suspects, she'll see who he is and who he isn't, what he's willing to give her and what he isn't. Soon enough she'll lose interest and abandon him without a second thought.

In the frank morning light Ben sees all too clearly how it's likely to play out. He sees straight through to the end. Perhaps it's better to walk away before she does, to salvage a bit of dignity at whatever cost.

BUT THERE'S ANOTHER EMERGENCY in play. With something growing inside his skull, with his health and perhaps even his life hanging in the balance, he'd be a fool to blow things up with Ana now. She'd read it as a humiliation, he's sure, an unforgivable insult. Having deigned to sleep with him, she'd never stand for being kicked to the curb. She'd turn on him, find some lurid way to punish him before his peers and betters. God knows, she's done it often enough to be known for it—her public acts of revenge are legendary. Ben can barely imagine the hell she'd put him through. If the medical news were to prove dire at the same moment . . . and, through some perverse bad luck, his silent lie about the sonata were to emerge . . . the firestorm, roaring in from all sides at once, would engulf him. Ben's plenty old enough to know how much he can carry without breaking his back. This would be too much.

Thankfully, she's leaving for Europe the day after tomorrow, a gift of time should he want it. On Tuesday she takes the overnight flight to Paris for a kickoff concert at the Théâtre des Champs-Élysées, to be followed by a solemn recital at the Palais de Compiègne for diplomats assembled to commemorate the hundredth anniversary of the signing of the Armistice. After that she's on the road nonstop. The tour will take her up to Brussels,

Amsterdam and Antwerp, then down to Lyon and Marseille and on to Monte Carlo, Milan, Rome. Coining money all the way, as she's told him without embarrassment.

"But what bloody bad *timing*," she complained last night, snaking her legs through his and flowing up his chest for a kiss. "You'll forget about me. I know it. Out of sight, out of mind."

To Ben the timing feels exactly right. Between spending every day at Counterpoint and every other minute of his life with her, he hasn't had one quiet hour to get his bearings, much less consider next steps. The lie has been sitting in his gut, going about its silent business like a cancer, growing in him dangerously. He needs peace and quiet, away from her, to work out how to extricate himself from it. He knows only that he can't reveal it now. Too much is in frenetic motion, too much beyond his control. Better to get through the doctor's appointment, if nothing else, and see where that leads. . . .

"Shit!" he says in exasperation, setting his plate in the sink with a clank. "Enough, already." He wishes someone would just tell him what to do.

As HE STEPS INTO THE BATHROOM a swipe of vertigo passes through his head. It's hard not to blame it on Ana: apparently she's not done meddling with him. But this time, as it happens, there's something he might do to take control of the situation.

His gaze falls on three blister packs of pale blue pills the neurologist sent him home with after their sole visit, free samples of an anti-vertigo drug. He'd tucked them behind the toothbrush mug and forgotten about them, wary of the doctor's warning that they might make him drowsy or depressed. Just a little life raft, Dr. Eastman had called it, to be deployed if he found himself in deep water. How he could have used that raft at Ana's—but he'd never imagined, leaving for Counterpoint on the morning of the Mon Ami Gabi dinner, that he'd be away from home for three days and nights. And so the blue pills had languished here, out of reach when he needed them most.

Ben rinses his hands slowly, another tremor passing through his head. It isn't severe, especially, but he doesn't want any part of it. Not now. There are decisions to be made. He needs his fickle body to get out of the way. The blister pack gives him some trouble, but after fumbling with it he manages to extricate a pill and take it, slurping water from his cupped hand like a parched wanderer at a mountain stream.

"Alright," he says, studying his haggard face in the mirror, "done." Though what exactly he's done remains to be seen.

XXVI.

FAIR COPY

HE FEELS THE NEED TO PLAY. After a lazy shower he wanders into the living room, into a world of kind and familiar things. From the mantel Willa Blount's wax cylinders keep watch over the stillness, the hawk-eyed Edisons no doubt wondering what's become of him. On the Bösendorfer's music stand the score awaits his return, the Garnier recording transcribed now but for the final, outrageously difficult passage of the Allegro and the last minute or so of the fourth movement. His private world, unadulterated by the confusions of love.

Calm and balanced, without a trace of dizziness now, Ben sits down at the piano and closes his eyes. Modulates his breathing, casts about for his center. Lets the music come up slowly through the seasoned wood of his instrument, the faint vibration of thousands of hours of playing seeping gently into him.

Surely his own modest playing is the least of what the piano remembers. How many pianists played the Bösendorfer in the sixty-four years before he and Robin brought it home? What Austrian craftsman first tested the keyboard after it was bolted to the frame in the Vienna factory? Vienna, 1936. One couldn't help but wonder about that first player's fate. So many of the great European players were Jews. The piano was born into a maelstrom. And what were the first notes played on the keys? A bit of Bach? A simple scale? Some Nazi anthem? (Impossible.) All this the old Bösendorfer prefers to keep to itself. All this is unknowable. Its discretion is absolute.

Ben concentrates. Listens more closely still. An even earlier music lives in the wood: the wind through the Black Forest, soughing through the leaves of the spruce tree that was to become the elegant instrument before him. A tree born with the century, perhaps, singled out by some Bavarian woodcutter long since dead . . . a tree felled, cured, sawn, planed, sanded, varnished, polished, refined into this thing of beauty. How far it's traveled, that spruce, in space and time and artistry.

By the time Ben lays his fingertips on the keys, the confusing week has almost let go of him. Even Ana has relaxed her grip. Dr. Eastman's medical report stands in abeyance. Music is what he's needed all along: now he sees it. When the opening notes of the French sonata ring out, it's as if someone else's hands are playing them.

HE KNOWS WHOLE SWATHS by heart now. Though the project has languished over the past weeks, derailed by a flood of studio work and lately his immersion in Ana, it seems the work has continued in his unconscious mind. With no special effort on his part the music has imprinted itself ever more deeply within him. He plays through the opening movement almost flawlessly, glancing at the music only once, the muscle memory solid, his fingers knowing just where to go. The room reverberates, the sound of the Bösendorfer lush and coffee dark. As he comes to the descending left-hand passage at the close of the first movement—the Lili Boulanger passage, as he thinks of it now—he hovers low over the keys and sings along to his own playing, the hammers gently palpating his chest, the bass strings resonating in his breastbone. When he reaches the waystation of the E-major chord he smiles, knowing it's just a feint, the unsuspecting listener lulled into believing that solid ground has been reached at last. Ben holds the chord with plenty of pedal then launches into the final descent, confident of every step.

The Allegro is next but he skips it, not up to its demands, and flows straight into the third movement's folk song. Ben lets the tempo rise slightly, the music lilting through him. He feels his energy shift from head to heart, doors opening, a breeze shuffling inside him, an ease loosening his diaphragm. Again he starts to sing, unconsciously at first and then with happy intention, his voice following the melody his fingers are coaxing from the old spruce box. If he wanders into a few moments of improvisation, riffing on the composer's theme, it's only from an excess of fellow feeling. Only from happiness.

After playing through the closing fanfare Ben lets the Bösendorfer fade like a bell. He sits motionless on the bench, knowing that if he moves it will creak and ruin the perfect stillness. The living room has filled with light as he's played. The sun's slipped out of the clouds, spotlighting the city with wintry clarity, snow glowing white-hot on the cars parked outside. A sheen of ice on the leaded window above the front door throws prismatic bands of color against the cream wall. For once Ben's head is utterly still, the errant spinning quelled. He takes a deep breath and lets it coast from his lungs slowly, happy to be alone with his century-old muse in his century-old house.

IN THE SUNLIGHT he notices how dusty the room's gotten. It looks as if no one's lived in the place for months. In a quiet mood he gathers cleaning supplies and goes to work, the sonata still playing in his head. After moving the Edisons aside to dust the mantel he turns his attention to the piano, working from the pedals up. With brass cleaner and elbow grease he brings them to a high shine, then moves on to the wooden legs, fastidious as a collector polishing an antique car. With a soft cloth he buffs each key, the whisper of a note sounding when he presses down. On the middle E-flat, soured by the forced-air heat, he decides that it's time to call the tuner in.

When he comes to the music stand he gathers up the sheaf of manuscript pages so that he can clean the carved scrollwork. But then he pauses, the sonata clutched in his hand, something troubling him. Perhaps it's the urge to tidy up, to take control of his small world, but he notices how ragged the pages have gotten, how thumbed-over and dog-eared and defaced by crossouts and second thoughts and wedged-in accidentals. His struggle to accurately transcribe Garnier's playing sprawls across the page like a welter of battle scars. The Allegro is a particular sort of mess, a morass of tied thirty-second notes and dense arpeggios written far too close together. Whole stretches of it are nearly indecipherable.

He's had no special plan for the day—a trip to the Greek market, perhaps, catching up on bills, trying not to read anything more on acoustic neuroma. Now it's clear to him how he should spend his afternoon. He'll put his musical house in order, clear the decks for the next phase of work. The mechanical aspect of it appeals to him, the fastidious craft of making a clean copy of the music in a careful hand. It's just what he needs to take his mind off things.

Ben takes the manuscript pages to the dining room table and lays them out like an outsized hand of solitaire, each movement arranged in its own vertical file. For some reason this seems clearer. After scrounging about for manuscript paper and a functioning pen he arranges his workspace like a medieval scribe arranging his lectern, rough transcription above, clean pages below. When all is in readiness he brews a pot of green tea and sits down to work, the sonata playing lightly in his mind, the city cold but the house snug and warm. The afternoon stretches before him as placidly as an alpine lake. There is no place he'd rather be, nothing he'd rather be doing.

By five he has his immaculate copy, spacious and carefully done. The Allegro and the final movement are still incomplete but the rest of the sonata is in good shape now. He's squaring the pages when his phone rattles on the kitchen table.

"I know I promised I wouldn't bother you," Ana says, not as an apology but strictly for the record. "Don't even say it. But I'm dying to know how it's going over there."

He can't keep the exasperation from his voice. "It's going just fine."

"You're angry with me."

"Just in the middle of something."

"That's good. That's good to hear. Will you play it for me? Into the phone? You're at the piano?" When he doesn't respond she takes a step back. "I'm sorry, *amor*, it's just that I can't wait to hear what comes next. I'm excitable that way. Excited for *you*. Forgive me?"

"Nothing to forgive."

"And love—I was also calling because I'm bursting with news."

Ben rocks back in his chair and crosses his arms over his chest. "What's that?"

"I've just had the most wonderful call from a little bird I knew in London, an Indian girl called Vidula who worked for the MacArthur people in Delhi. Worked, you know, because they sacked her last week, poor thing. She's gutted. And furious. We talked for an hour, Ben. She said things she shouldn't have." Ana drew a tight breath. "Are you ready for this, love? They've made me a finalist for the Genius grant! Isn't it brilliant? Of course I'm not meant to know any of it. It's all handled like the nuclear launch codes. But I do know, and now you know too. Obviously you'll keep it between us."

The news gives him pause. It's impressive.

"That's really fantastic. Who nominated you? Did she tell you?"

"She did, but best you don't know." She gives it a beat. "Let's just say someone who's highly acquainted with my unique talents. *Musical* talents, to be clear."

He doesn't care to play her guessing game. "Can we talk later?" he says, though he needs a night off from her, needs to compose himself for what's soon to come.

"*Claro*. But look: come for dinner tomorrow, will you? See me off before I go. I have something to give you. A wee parting gift so you won't forget me."

He'd assumed they'd see each other again before she went, for a last tumble in bed, at least, but right now nothing could interest him less. After four days of running on adrenaline he needs a deeper sort of gratification. He needs time to himself.

"I'm not sure I can," he says, trying to sound disappointed. "I have my old college roommate in town, just for the night. . . . I really should see him. He's lost his wife. Cancer." All this is an invention. The truth is that he needs a break from her, and wants to hold the evening open for Nikki in case he needs company after seeing the neurosurgeon on Monday morning.

But there's something more: the last thing he needs is to be cornered into another talk about the sonata. At this delicate moment he's too exhausted to carry on with the lie and far too exhausted to tell the truth. He can count the hours till she'll be in the air to Europe, at which point the whole tangled mess will, he hopes, have a chance to cool off.

"So," she counters, "have a drink with your friend at Gabi and come see me afterward. I don't care how late it is."

"I need to play it by ear, Ana."

There is a long silence at the other end of the line. He's used her name to move her back a step; she's heard it. "I'm pushing too hard," she says. "I apologize. It's a problem I have. It gets me into trouble all the time." She does sound genuinely sorry. "But I'd like to see you again before I climb on that plane. It's a red-eye—I could meet you for lunch Tuesday, somewhere near Counterpoint. Though I'd rather see you in my bed."

By the time they hang up he's already decided he'll beg off. With the neurosurgeon appointment looming he can't let her crowd him. At this moment he has more pressing concerns.

Ben stares for a long moment at his fresh copy of the score, then arranges it across the table as if laying out giant tarot cards, pleased with the care he's taken to get it right. He's not finished; the remaining bars of the Allegro stretch before him as an honorable project, far more important than making love to Ana one last time. There is good work to be done and he is glad for the chance to do it. Glad, too, to be alone tonight.

XXVII.

STUDIES

"SORRY TO BE LATE—well, almost late," Nikki says as she gusts into the clinic waiting room and glances at the clock on the wall. "Fucking Red Line. Track work. Which is code for another suicide, I always think." She sits down next to Ben and nudges his arm. "How are you doing? Feeling ready for this?"

Ben shrugs.

"It must have been weighing on you. It would anyone."

"I've had plenty to distract me. More than you can possibly imagine."

Nikki's eyes narrow. "Oh?"

Before he can answer, the door to the back hallway opens.

"Tell you later."

"You'd better, mister."

"Mr. Weil," calls a young man in purple scrubs. Ben wonders if this could be the surgeon. *Too young*, he thinks. *Way too young!*

As he and Nikki step through the door, the man introduces himself as Dr. Lisle's nurse—a relief. They're ushered into an expensively furnished exam room where he takes Ben's vitals in silence. No small talk, no chatter. Perhaps this is how it is in the offices of neurosurgeons. The nurse's tight-lipped efficiency is unnerving. When he's done he shuts the door behind him with exaggerated care, like a father shutting the door on a sleeping child.

While they wait for the doctor, Nikki digs in her purse and pulls out a Rapidograph pen and a small red notebook which she spreads flat on her thigh. Ben sees that it's blank, brand new.

"So," he says, "is that going to be the book of Ben's brain tumor?"

She uncaps her pen. "I just needed something for notes. This was lying around, looking lonely."

"I know, sorry. Hey—switch places?"

She regards him blankly, then realizes what he means. "Because of the tinnitus," she says, and moves to his left side so he can hear the doctor. "Soon to be a thing of the past."

"I'm so done with it, Nik."

Nikki nods and smooths the first page of her notebook. "So— what questions do we have for this man of science?"

As if on cue the door opens on a balding, substantial man with a ruler-straight white mustache and a monogrammed lab coat. Something in the avuncular face sets Ben at ease immediately.

"Dr. Lisle," the surgeon says with a dry handshake, and sits down on a rolling stool too small for him. "My patients call me Dr. Walt, but I answer to any number of names. As my wife will tell you." A brief self-deprecating smile, mostly in the calm gray eyes. "You go by Ben?"

"Sure."

The doctor turns to Nikki. "And are you Ms. Weil?"

"Yes, actually. But the cousin, not the wife."

This too registers in the placid eyes. "So, Ben," Dr. Lisle says, "I hear you've not been feeling your best lately."

"Not hardly."

"Dr. Eastman's notes say your symptoms have accelerated over the past few weeks."

"Especially the balance stuff. Stumbling, bumping into things. Vertigo. And the tinnitus."

The doctor nods. "Which is why your neurologist suspected an acoustic neuroma. A good call." Swiveling toward the built-in computer desk, the doctor taps at the keyboard and studies the screen, his expression unreadable. "Care to have a look?"

Ben's aware of Nikki's eyes on him.

Dr. Lisle says, "Of course, it's up to you. Some people want to get a visual fix on things."

Ben hasn't prepared for this. In his research he's seen plenty of images of neuromas but has never considered, somehow, what it would be like to see his own.

"Want me to look for you?" Nikki asks.

Ben shakes his head and leans forward with elbows on knees. "Show me."

The doctor turns the monitor around and there it is: bright white on the left side of his cracked-walnut brain, an irregular blot that clearly doesn't belong there. Lisle spins his mouse wheel and the viewer descends through it, excavating, the white blob pulsating like a heart.

Shocking as it is, Ben feels some relief. The thing is certainly smaller than some of the neuromas he's seen online. Lisle coasts over on his stool and points to the screen with a pen, calmly explaining the anatomy. Vestibular nerve, cochlear nerve, impingement on the pons. . . . Ben can only look on dumbly, registering little of it, aware of Nikki scratching notes beside him.

"I know it's a lot to take in," the doctor says, pushing off from the desk. "Any questions about what we're seeing in your studies?"

Ben frowns, eyes fixed stupidly on the screen.

Nikki says, "What about the size, relatively speaking?"

"I like it. If it were bigger we'd have fewer options. And I see no evidence of malignancy here. Which is no surprise, because it's very rare for these to misbehave—only a handful of cases in the literature. So, all options are open." Nikki notes this down. "Except one, actually—the option of doing nothing. Sometimes observation's the right plan for a small neuroma, but we're past that. With the pressure on the pons it will need to come out soon."

"How soon?" Nikki asks.

"How's your Thursday look, Ben?"

A silence fills the room. Ben hears someone slip paperwork into the rack on the door and stride off down the hallway. Dr. Lisle will have other patients in the waiting room, patients with diagnoses far more grave, but he seems content to let the silence ripen.

Ben says, "Can we talk about what's involved?"

"I'd love to," the doctor says. The carpentry, the surgeon's craft, must be where it gets interesting for him. Nikki starts a new page in her notebook and the doctor launches in, Ben listening carefully now, his research having told him where the discussion is likely to lead. In an odd way he feels as if he's on familiar ground.

It's a relief to have a plan taking shape, even if the timeline is a shock. In the back of his mind he's already visualizing his schedule for Thursday and Friday, shifting recording slots and meetings, finding a way to make it work. Better to be done with it and move on.

"THE GOOD NEWS," Nikki says while they sit over plates of falafel afterward, "is that they don't need to go *in*. I mean, he made it sound pretty routine. All in a day's work."

The doctor's recommendation was clear: the safest way to remove the tumor would be with the Gamma Knife. Ben's tumor is just small enough to qualify. He's long since educated himself on the technique, which despite the outlandish name is just a computer-guided radiation treatment. According to Lisle, it should be a single session with a quick recovery and a high chance of success, all of which is hard to argue with.

"Can you be there?" Ben asks Nikki.

"Are you really asking me that?"

"I guess I'm supposed to have someone with me."

"Ben! Jesus. I'll not only be there, I'll stay over at your place after, like he said. For as long as you need me to. Know that."

The nurse has laid out his week for him. A preoperative consultation with the surgical nurse on Wednesday. Fasting and a last hair-washing that night. CT and PET scans early Thursday, followed by a pause of two or three hours while the doctors plot their attack. Then the mounting of a metal harness which will remain screwed to his head for the duration. The procedure itself will take little more than an hour; he can listen to music or take a nap if he feels so inclined. Afterward, a headache, perhaps some nausea, a few days to recover, then on with his life. By Monday or Tuesday he should be back at Counterpoint. A week later, a follow-up MRI to assess results. If all goes well, he should notice an improvement in his symptoms within weeks.

It all sounds so easy, as long as everything goes as planned. If it doesn't, it could leave him deaf in one ear, or with permanent balance issues, or damaged in some other way. The doctor had run through the possible complications dismissively. "What's the real risk of deafness?" Ben had asked, because this above all else frightened him. "Only seen it a few times," Lisle assured him. "And I've done more than a thousand of these. Of course there's a possibility, but my advice is not to worry about it for one second. This is a straightforward case. You've got a benign tumor we'll send packing without a fuss."

After lunch he and Nikki stroll down Michigan Avenue, Christmas lights swirled up all the light poles, the sun taking the edge off the cold. "So, what about the other thing?" she asks, slipping a leather-jacketed arm through his.

"What thing is that?"

"You said you'd had plenty to distract you from the tumor. More than I could possibly imagine, apparently, though yet again you underestimate my imagination. You were annoyingly cryptic. What's up?"

There's so much to tell. He'd meant Ana, but now he feels a sudden urge to confess the lie about the sonata, to come clean with Nikki. With Robin gone she's the person he most trusts in the world. What a relief it would be to unburden himself. But he's not ready.

"I'm seeing someone. I guess I am."

She squeezes his arm. "As in a new honey? Ben! Mazel tov. Do you know how I've wished that for you? Now I can say it. You deserve that. Who's the lucky girl?"

"You wouldn't believe me if I told you."

Her eyes bloom up at him. "Who?"

"Ana Clara Matta."

He watches the name register. Nikki's still close enough to the classical music world to recognize it. It may be that Ben's told her she's a client.

Something fraught enters his cousin's gaze, pushing aside the forthright happiness of a moment before. She stops in front of Cartier and turns to face him, a mittened hand still gripping his arm. She's debating with herself, he can see. Choosing her words, knowing she holds his heart in her hand.

"Ben, I don't know what to say. I want to be happy for you."

"But she has a certain reputation."

"Which is concerning to me, yes. I won't lie."

"It's concerning to me too, if that helps."

She inclines her head. "Say more?"

"I'm aware of the dangers. But I might need this."

"*This* as in the intimacy, or *this* as in Ana Clara Matta specifically?"

"That's exactly what I've been asking myself."

"Ben, can I just say something?"

"Always."

"This is not the woman to choose for a rebound relationship. She's trouble."

He needs to keep moving. Covering her hand with his he swings them around and resumes strolling. "I won't say you're wrong. But there's more to it than that."

"There always is. But she's ruined people. This is not news."

As they wait for a light to change he feels himself rising to defend his lover but doesn't trust the reflex. "Do you remember," he asks Nikki, "how years ago you told me that whenever you start a relationship you need to try and see all the way through to the end of it? That you can't let yourself be deceived by the sex?"

"I believe I used a different word, but yes. You owe it to yourself to imagine the worst. Words I live by. Which is why I'm still single, no doubt."

"Though you did slip at least once." This was true: she'd once been engaged to Peter Roth, a sound man who ran the board at the Pearson Center. Though it hadn't ended well, they'd managed to salvage a friendship from the wreckage. "You certainly didn't see through to the end with Peter."

"Look, my point is, I hope you've thought through where this could lead. I've never met the woman, but we both know you're playing with fire."

They walk on in silence for a long block and cross the bridge under the pale white cliffs of the Wrigley Building, the city noisy and festive and planed with sunlight. Nikki has his arm locked in both of hers, protective of him, affectionate in a way that moves him nearly to tears. Being with her on this eventful morning has peeled away his defenses.

Without exchanging a word they both feel a change in topic coming. It's surely the fact that they're about to walk past the Carbon and Carbide Building, through whose glass façade passersby can peer into Alan Hurwitz's latest concept café. This one is modeled on some patîsserie on the Champs-Elysées, Ben recalls reading. The two of them look straight ahead, shunning the place.

"Ben?"

"Yeah?"

"Do you want me to tell Robin about the surgery? No wrong answer here. Just asking."

It would never have occurred to him. "Why? Do you think she'd want to know?"

"I'm sure she would. The fact that you're not together anymore doesn't mean she doesn't care about you."

"It might be awkward for her, right? Do you think she'd feel obliged to reach out?"

"Why would that be a bad thing?"

"Because of Alan! Doesn't she have other things to worry about?"

"Let her be the judge of that. Though personally I don't agree with you. It's an artificial separation you're making. You're saying she should burn down the past, ignore all your years together. If I were her therapist, which thank God I'm not, I'd caution against that. Anyway, one thing you could say to me is: Tell her, but ask her not to contact me. If you wanted that."

Ben feels an unexpected warmth in his chest. When he's thought of Robin lately it's been in contrast to Ana. Thinking of her now calms him somehow, despite all that's happened between them.

"Tell her. If she wants to reach out, that's fine."

"Consider it done."

With a quick turn they reach the steps up to the El platform. Though they're heading to different lines Nikki climbs the stairs with him, not letting go.

"Hey," she says at the turnstiles, embracing him, the scent of her leather jacket lending a seriousness to the moment. "Just ask."

"For?"

"For what you need. I think you're not so good at that. Just know that you're not going through this alone." With a kiss on his cheek she's gone, his train trundling in, the afternoon stretching wide before him.

HE SHOULD HEAD UP TO COUNTERPOINT and work the rest of the day, especially as he'll soon be out for the radiation treatment. As the El skims past low rooftops and graffiti-covered brick walls, swaying atop its trestle, wheels screeching on the curves, he begins to make a mental list of all that needs to get done before Thursday. But when the Counterpoint stop arrives he stays in his seat, continuing on toward home. A few minutes later, while the train stops at Damen, he calls Eliza to say he's been dragged into a meeting downtown. She takes the news in stride, juggling another call. He's free.

Standing in his sunny living room, the Edisons tracking him from their lookout on the mantel, he texts Ana to say:

Can't come tonight. Friend is a wreck. Touch base tomorrow xoxo

Minutes pass before she answers. He imagines her at the piano, rehearsing. He knows she switches her phone off when working. When she finally replies, he's relieved to see that she's dropped her crusade to have him visit.

ok. take care of ur friend

Thanks for understanding, he taps back.

lunch tomorrow by cpoint?

This seems a fair enough trade for an evening to himself. And he would like to see her before she goes, if only to take the measure of his feelings. He has no idea whether her absence will feel like a loss or a relief.

He types: *Crazy day but will try. Text me mid AM*

ok good

Another long pause on her end, then:

amor send me ur address in case we dont see each other. can fedex u my little parting gift

Ben hesitates, which tells him something. But it's not as if he's inviting her over, and it gives him an out if he decides tomorrow that he'd rather not see her. He texts back his address with an *xo* and they're off the air.

The afternoon and evening liberated, he breathes a sigh of relief and sits down at the Bösendorfer and pages through the sonata to the second movement. For some moments he sits erect and perfectly still at the keyboard, reentering the music, calming his heart, letting Ana's fickle energy seep from his body. Then he begins to play the Allegro at half speed, coasting along its steep hills and plunging valleys, managing its terrain better than before, until the score gives out in mid-arpeggio—his scribal labors having simply collapsed one night when sleep overtook him. Twice more Ben plays it through, faster each time, his confidence growing with every measure.

Afterward he goes back to the dining room table, wakes the laptop and sits down to finish transcribing the Garnier recording, first the Allegro and then the final minute with its jazz progressions and regal fanfare.

It's time, at last, to make the sonata whole.

XXVIII.

MISSING

LATE IN THE AFTERNOON, moments after Ben's finished cross-checking the completed score against the recording, Eva Farahani calls to invite him to dinner. Feeling buoyant, his toil concluded, he accepts without hesitation. The timing is perfect. His rumbling stomach reminds him that he's entirely forgotten lunch. Between pots of green tea and the work, it's not occurred to him to eat. An evening with the Farahanis, who know nothing of demanding Brazilian lovers or French sonatas or acoustic neuromas, sounds like just what he needs.

After hanging up with Eva he scans the completed score into the computer. As an afterthought he prints a copy to take to Counterpoint for safekeeping, leaving it on the foyer table so he won't forget it in the morning. The new manuscript feels precious in a way the first crude draft did not. At some point he'll take on the chore of keying it into scoring software that can produce a publishable version, but that can wait.

Behrouz Farahani meets him at the door with a kiss on each cheek, a Persian habit he claims not to be able to break. Ben's certain he's never tried.

"Welcome, my friend!" his neighbor says, the natural affection a little wild in his eyes. "It's so kind of you to come, Ben-joon!" As always his host treats him as the most honored of guests. When Ben presents him with a bottle of plodding, grocery-store cabernet, his wine inventory sadly depleted, Behrouz cradles it as if it were a rare and precious find. "Chile!" he exclaims, "the best!"

Eva's set dinner up in the large kitchen, a trio of scratch-made pizzas laid out on the countertop. Young Oliver's ferrying the salad to the table when Ben goes in to greet her. "You have no idea what perfect timing this is," he confides, though he's not inclined to say why. She must read it in his face, this need for privacy. With a smile she lets it go.

Over dinner the talk is of the kids' coming school break, a Christmas ski trip, the tense midterm elections. Ben interviews the handsome and mannerly children, delighted to inhabit their world for a while. He hasn't felt so relaxed in weeks. Only when Behrouz describes the dire situation back home in Isfahan, where his elderly father has barely survived a stroke, does the mood change. A rare flash of anger passes through his friend's eyes; a sharp vertical crease appears on his forehead. When he cranes forward across the table, Eva lays a calming hand on his leg. Though he's been an American citizen for decades, Behrouz is afraid to go back and see his ailing father lest he be barred from returning. "Thirty years in this country and now they want to lock me out!" he says with disgust. "Keep me away from my own father! I never thought this country would. . . ." He can't continue. His eyes are burning with tears. Oliver and his sister watch their father as if watching a wild-fire creep closer and closer. "Behru," Eva tells him, "enough politics. I want to hear what's new with Ben." Chastened, Behrouz slumps back in his chair, Oliver taking his father's hand with a kindness Ben finds moving beyond words.

After saying his goodnights Ben walks home with slices of warm, foil-wrapped pizza in hand, the city having plunged back into glacial cold. When he steps onto his stoop he's startled to hear music coming from within.

It makes no sense. He hasn't played a CD in days; there's no way he's left the stereo on. Stranger still, it's the Allegro he's hearing.

In the early days of his acquaintance with the French sonata he'd sometimes have the feeling that Garnier's ghost was at large in the house. In bed, after long hours studying the music and trying to work it out on the piano, he'd hear the soft Andante playing through the ducts, or a quick triplet from the Allegro, or the dou-bled A that anchored the Lili passage. It was impossible, of course, but he'd heard what he'd heard. He'd come to accept the oddity of it, which he suspected was only an oddity in his brain—something mildly out of whack, some side effect of the secrecy in which he'd wrapped the whole project.

At this moment it's impossible to believe that it's all in his head. This performance is real. As he presses his ear to the door and listens, his heart wavering, he hears the player move commandingly through not just a few scattered notes but a run of the most technically difficult measures in the entire piece, the arresting, final passage of the Allegro that he's spent a good deal of the afternoon transcribing.

Ben slips in quietly, easing the door shut behind him. The music fills the house, the foyer reverberating now with the folk melody that opens the third movement. The playing is lyrical and free, the pianist's touch lighter than Garnier's, the spirit innocent and trusting.

Once he's inside the house Ben understands exactly what's happened.

When Ana reaches to turn the page he slips in beside her. She pauses in mid-phrase but betrays no surprise at his sudden appearance.

"It's daft to leave your door unlocked in the city, don't you think?" she says calmly, as if they've been talking all along. "You never know who might let herself in."

He should never have texted her his address. Should never have left the door unlocked in his absentminded way, the exhilaration of finishing the score making him careless.

"I can't believe you came here. You knew I'd be out."

She swivels to face him. "But not out all night, Ben. I was all set to kill time at the café on the corner till you got home, but then I found the door open." She checks her watch. "It's just half seven. I guess your friend must be feeling better." She turns back to the piano abruptly, pretending to consult the score, trying out a phrase on the keyboard, then glares up at him with glistening eyes. "You didn't have to lie to me, *amor*. If you don't want to see me anymore, just say so."

He's not going down this road. "You can't just show up unannounced and let yourself in."

"Do you know what I detest more than anything in a man, Ben?" She plays a dissonant chord and stops it. "Lying. It's the one thing I will not tolerate."

On the stand before her sits the French sonata, a lie from start to finish as far as the two of them are concerned. But she's already changed course. With a fluid caress of the keys she continues on with the third movement, picking up where she left off, the playing passionate and perceptive until she turns the page to discover the long slash and question mark indicating the gap in the wax recording.

Pivoting on the bench she says, "What's this? Suddenly you ran out of ideas? The Allegro left you too knackered to carry on?"

"Maybe, yeah."

"But why would you stop just there? It wouldn't be so hard to finish that variation, would it?" To prove her point she plays up to the break and keeps going, improvising a completely credible transition. "Voilà. Easy."

"Ana—"

He can see the music in her eyes again, the way it's overtaken her hurt. The white lie about his troubled friend is nothing next to the pleasures of the sonata. "But the Allegro . . . Ben! It's brilliant. I would never have guessed you'd take it in that direction." She plays the first long run of thirty-second notes from memory, blisteringly fast. "What fun it is to play." She plays a bit more, then stops to search his face. "Can *you* play this? I'm just curious."

"Not at tempo."

"It's *so* good, Ben. I'm glad you took time to get it right." She turns on the bench and wraps her arms around his hips, gazing up at him with a teasing smile in her eyes.

"Just tell me one thing, *amor.*"

He drops a hand to her head, threads his fingers into her curls despite himself. With everything weighing on his mind, simple human touch is worth more than ever.

She says, "Have I been inspirational?"

He smiles to deflect the question, looks past her at the Edisons on the mantel.

She presses her lips hard against his zipper. Then: "Maybe you have to get some things out of your system before you can finish?"

He says nothing, conflicted, but it doesn't faze Ana. She turns back to the piano and gathers the score into a neat stack. A part of him needs her to leave: he cannot have her in his house. She's violated his privacy just when he needs it most. But the scent of her rosemary lotion is on the air, and then her fine, narrow shoulder is under his fingers. She takes his hand and presses the palm to her lips, rocking gently against him, her high forehead tipping back in its nest of dark curls. If he bends to kiss her it's beyond his control. Once again the music's seduced them both.

In the morning she slips out before dawn, not waking him. When he stumbles from bed later it takes him some moments to recall exactly what's happened. Her stealthy visit feels dreamlike, less than real. But there in the wastebasket is a used condom, and on the edge of the sink a small wrapped gift with a card twice its size. While he brushes his teeth he eyes it warily. He doesn't want any gifts from her. After slipping on a robe he takes it to the kitchen and sets it on the table. Not until he has a mug of strong coffee in front of him does he open the envelope.

Inside is an ivory card embossed with her initials. In a scrupulous hand she's written:

Amor,

So, here's the state of play: I'll be out of your life for almost a month now, touring sad old Europe when I'd much rather be in your arms, where I belong. I don't think you know how much you've rattled my world—your music, your love, your quiet way, your kisses. I have trouble admitting these things, which is probably why I'm writing this instead of telling you to your face, but it's true. This is everything to me.

Maybe it seems too soon for me to say something like that. But just remember how long we've known each other, and remember that music reveals everything important about the soul. I know who you are, Ben, because I've played your music and taken it to heart, the same way I know who Debussy and Chopin and Beethoven were. It's the deepest kind of knowledge you can have of another person. Deeper even than sexual knowledge. I believe that.

I'm going to give you a little gift to keep you safe while I'm gone. It's what we call in Brasil a figa—it literally means "fig" but it's much more than that. This is how we Brasilians keep away the evil eye. (Even the Catholics, I promise you.) This figa was given me by my granny when I was a baby. Her granny gave it to her. It must be a century and a half old, Ben. I'm giving it to you now because I need you to be safe while I'm gone. Maybe you think it's primitive to believe in this stuff, and maybe I do too, but it can't hurt, can it? Besides, I want you to have something of mine that is irreplaceable. Keep it next to you, on your body, touching your skin, until we see each other again.

Don't forget me, Ben Weil. And know that there's more to Ana Clara Matta than what you read in the papers. She has a heart, too.

A bientôt, mon amour,

A.

The card surprises him in every way—the humility, the forthrightness, the tenderness. The hard-nosed Ana is nowhere to be found in what she's written. She has opened her heart in a way he never knew she could.

As Ben rereads her words he feels his anxiety rising. He does not need her to fall in love with him, least of all on account of the sonata. As he opens the gift he feels a catastrophe building in his chest. How could he have read her so poorly? He never saw this coming.

In a white jewelry box, nestled in a bed of cotton wool, is her small wooden talisman—a burnished-red, gold-banded forearm ending in a clenched fist. A defiant little thumb pushes up between the index and middle fingers. There is something unabashedly sexual about it, a suggestion of nether parts. The nails of the tiny fingers are painted with flaking gold leaf. The grain of the wood draws a pair of veins down the length of the arm, giving it a powerful look.

The little amulet is obviously old, just as she said. Despite the wan winter light the lacquered wood all but glows. There's a powerful dignity about it. The gift reminds him of something, but it's not until he's had his breakfast that he realizes what it is: Ana's *figa* reminds him of Willa Blount's wax cylinders. Like them, it vibrates with a past beyond living memory. Like them, it's precious in its singularity and its very survival. Later, as Ben passes through the living room, he'll set the box carefully on the mantel with the five Edisons clustered around it protectively, certain they belong together. He'd be afraid to wear it against his skin, though this is what she's asked him to do.

But now it's time to get to Counterpoint. With the shortened week there's much to be done. After slipping the laptop and a packet of the vertigo pills into his bag he walks to the foyer and lifts his heavy jacket from the rack, setting his travel mug on the table to zip it on. While donning his gloves he has the distinct feeling that he's forgetting something. For a long moment he stands at the door, trying to put his finger on it, but it won't come. He's late; there's no time to fret about it further. It couldn't have been that important. He steps through the door and locks it behind him, the air bracing on his cheeks, a blade of sunlight inserted neatly between the two flats across the street.

It isn't until he's halfway down the block that he realizes he's forgotten his travel mug on the foyer table. He considers leaving it behind but a gust of frigid wind changes his mind. Counterpoint will survive fine if he's a few more minutes late. And so he doubles back, pounding up the stairs and back into his warm house. The mug is waiting for him just where he left it, metal fluxing dully in the cold draft.

Ben pauses to take a sip of coffee before heading back outside. The odd feeling lingers: the sense that something is still missing, out of place. . . . The thought comes to him absently at first, harmlessly, then returns in a bolt of panic. Now he realizes that it wasn't only the coffee he left behind. He's forgotten something incalculably more important.

Just before leaving for dinner at the Farahanis, an hour or two before Ana's unannounced visit, he'd printed a copy of the completed sonata score and placed it on the foyer table, intending to take it to Counterpoint with him in the morning. He knows exactly where he set it down, right under the La Scala etching. It's no longer there. Slinging the bag off his shoulder Ben rifles through it on the off chance he's stashed it away and forgotten, but it's nowhere to be found. The sonata is gone.

Livid, he fumbles for his phone and texts Ana:

Did you steal my score???

He waits, and waits, biting his lip like a boy caught in a lie. The phone glows up at him stupidly, hot in his hand, useless as a chunk of wood. He stifles the urge to hurl it at the wall.

You there?? he texts. *ANSWER ME.*

Nothing.

In a matter of hours she'll be on a plane to Paris, easing into her wide leather seat with a glass of champagne, the French sonata tucked in her bag, no doubt—on its way home to France after a century's silent exile in the New World. If he thought he'd begun to understand Ana Clara Matta's heart—if he'd really been so foolish as that—he certainly doesn't understand it now. All he knows is that the sonata is no longer his to love alone.

AIGREMONT

NOVEMBER 10, 1918

XXIX.

THE LOST BROTHERS OF VERDUN

THEIR ARRANGEMENT is to meet in the shadows under the sycamore tree where she first stood listening to him play the *Clair de lune*. It was a fat harvest moon that night, saffron orange concentrating into marigold and then losing color as the hours passed. By the time Elisabeth left the carriage house at midnight it was high and bright in the sky, a crisp amber pearl set out on black velvet.

As she hurried back to the main house she was sure she'd be spotted. How could she not be? Under the steady glow from above, the gravel driveway and manicured grounds were laid out in full before the mansion's tall windows, stark as a tintype. Her louis heels crunched up the drive like rifle shots. In the morning she skipped her usual breakfast with Rena, fearful that word might have reached her, but by the end of the day there was no sign that it had. The delicious hour sitting with Charlie Westerlake at the carriage house piano, the chilly walk together up High Street dodging from one pool of shadow to the next, most of all the warming kiss in the neighbor's copse, Elisabeth standing on tiptoes to reach the Captain's moist lips—none of this, thankfully, had come to the notice of the lady of the house.

Elisabeth doesn't know what she'd say if her patroness were to confront her. It's hard to imagine Rena treating such a transgression lightly. Whatever her private affection for her daughter's friend—and Elisabeth knows there is a soft heart beating beneath that formidable breast—there would be questions of propriety that even she couldn't afford to ignore. This Elisabeth understands perfectly. It would be Elisabeth who paid the price, not the Captain. Perhaps she'd be expelled from the house, whereupon Rena would cease to cover her rent on the Roxbury apartment. Nor had it occurred to her that things should be otherwise. It was the way of the world; it would have been the same in France. And so she was relieved beyond words that the full moon had not exposed her.

Since that first astonishing night—eight days ago, a lifetime ago—the moon has been a more trustworthy accomplice. As she and Charlie take their nightly walks along the lanes that lead down to the twin lakes, hands brushing in the darkness, there is hardly a moon at all, just a shy crescent, nacreous or whey-colored depending on the cast of the sky. It will have set long before Elisabeth slips back through the heavy door, unlaces her boots on the landing, and pads upstairs to her room. After changing into her nightgown she'll be carried off to sleep on a cloudbank of darkness, her skin and hair smelling faintly of her lover, pale breasts chafed pink, long neck flushed from his mouth—her body given over to him a little more each night, their curiosity satisfied by slow degrees. As she drifts off and her modesty retires, she'll imagine his presence inside her, not so much in body as in spirit, the Captain navigating gently, taking her inner measure: it will be as if he's in Caleb's little bed too, half-folded behind her like a deck chair, rocking her gently in the moonless night. It will be as if they'd never parted.

NEVER DID ELISABETH SUSPECT that her turn through Aigremont would lead to this. Never would she have guessed she'd fall in love so easily. She's sure that only Charlie Westerlake could have drawn her out of herself in this way, could have made her laugh again and sincerely mean it. No ordinary man could have made her step so decisively out of her grief. There is something singular about Charlie, a quiet power he possesses—he is, after all, a healer. All through this extraordinary week, in every minute, she's felt his healing touch.

BUT IT IS THE TIMES, TOO, not only the man. Elisabeth has been honest with herself about this. Every sensation has been heightened, not just in these last few days but for two years or more, between the Bell Company and her wanderings through Helen Sanborn's world, the horrible war, her father's disappearance, now the epidemic—the whole dizzying downrush of events, the engine of the world shuddering and speeding and threatening to run right off the rails. Everything has conspired to make her heart susceptible.

Even her skin has felt more alive. It's for the best that she's had no time to read the newspapers, the petty tales of fisticuffs between warring neighbors counterposed against bleakly riveting tales from the front. The brute force of it all would knock her down. What news she gets is mostly from talks with Rena over breakfast or snatches of chatter from the wireless in the bustling kitchen. Even the patients in their misery are better informed than she is.

Still, she senses that something momentous is happening. Germany, she hears, is collapsing, the Kaiser shown the door by his own people, the Italians rallying . . . the general opinion seems to be that the war is finally on its last legs. Just today, after returning from Sunday services, one of the nurses had mentioned excitedly that it could all be over within days. Reverend Chidley had said so from the pulpit before offering up a prayer for the young soldiers on both sides—a generous Christian sentiment that did not land well with certain parishioners who stalked out of the chapel, the nurse said, while other heads were bowed.

Elisabeth would like to believe it's true, of course, but she wishes her tender-hearted papa could have lived to see it. On the day he left her it still seemed as though the war might go on forever, an incurable, virulent infection in the very heart of France. If only the cruel fighting had ended before Jacques Garnier, a man of forty-nine, an artist who'd never once raised a hand in anger, became obsessed with the absurd idea of sailing home to take up arms. If only peace had been made before he boarded HMS *Kentish Town* and steamed straight into the path of a U-boat on the prowl. But he would not be dissuaded, and now her gentle, foolish genius of a papa lies entombed in the cold Atlantic, having left his beloved daughter to make her way alone. Were it not for Charlie Westerlake she might have joined him in death long ago. It hasn't been easy to be alone in the world.

THE ONLY CONSOLATION—cold comfort at best—is that something of her papa's wonderful music has outlived him. Thanks to the genius of Bell and his Graphophone, and the generosity of the Sanborns in offering him a private recital, Jacques Garnier's masterful playing and visionary sonata have been preserved in wax.

Elisabeth smiles sadly whenever this word *visionary* comes back to her, recalling the moment when her papa's violinist friend, Martin, first bestowed it upon him.

The last fanfare of the sonata had died out in the Sanborn music room; Elisabeth rushed to her father impulsively and hugged him from behind, unable to hold back her emotions. *"Oh, Papa! C'est si beau!"* she said with tears in her eyes, unaware that Tom Shea was still recording. It was the first time she'd heard the sonata. He'd kept its very existence secret until a few moments before Tom dropped the needle onto the cylinder. He must have composed it on the battered parlor grand at Latin in the evenings, alone in the deserted building. When he'd started to play at Aigremont the room was transported, and not a little baffled—Rena and Helen standing like Roman statues with identical looks of mild alarm, as if gazing across the water at a smoking Vesuvius; fidgety Caleb and Jimmy abruptly becalmed on their velvet-covered chairs; Rena's rented photographer perched on a stool behind his tripod, mystified; the Sanborns' artistic friend Mary Kellogg breathing as softly as rain under her whalebone so as not to miss a single note.

And, of course, tall, austere Martin Loeffler with his impeccable Van Dyke and dove-gray waistcoat, standing by the windows with an expression that somehow combined supreme serenity with absolute concentration. German by birth but French in every fiber of his sensibility, it was Martin, she knew, who'd encouraged her papa to go back to composing. She well remembered strolling with the two men in the Public Garden the summer before, Martin having bought them all ice creams at a stand near the swans. As they walked with their cones he described a new piece for cello and piano he'd been wrestling with, then asked whether her papa might want to accompany a visiting Spanish cellist in an informal recital he was organizing at Mrs. Gardner's museum. There would be only Donna Isabella, as he solemnly called his friend the heiress, and a few of her most favored Brahmins, all of whom would be sworn to secrecy about the piece until he deemed it ready for a full public début.

Elisabeth knew from the way her father suddenly devoured the stub of his ice cream cone that he was thrilled with the offer.

Loeffler knew it too. He laughed his chesty laugh and nodded toward the stand. "Another ice cream, Jacques? You'll need to build up your strength for this, you know."

The afternoon was abruptly hotter. When they came to a bench they sat, Elisabeth perched between the two musicians, who gossiped about the changing fortunes of Fauré's former Conservatoire students. As a girl she'd been doted on by many of them, but now they all seemed to be struggling. Loeffler brought news of Debussy's grave colostomy operation; Ravel's foolhardy decision to enlist as a driver for an artillery regiment; young Lili Boulanger's great promise as a composer despite failing health.

"Lili!" Her father smiled with surprise at the mention of her name, stealing a glance at Elisabeth. "*Quel prodige elle était.* She was only a girl when I left, but what talent she had. Everyone knew it. Fauré was the one who discovered she had perfect pitch, you know. I performed with her once, at a dinner party Proust hosted at the Ritz. Lili couldn't have been more than nine or ten—it was long past her bedtime, I can tell you. Proust, you know, was *assez bizarre*, but he paid well. Pale as milk but a real bon vivant. Excellent manners. Anyway, that party made a splash in the papers, and not because of me, I assure you." Loeffler nodded amiably. "What you may not know, Martin, is that Lili and my Elisabeth were the best of friends. Isn't that true, *ma chère?*"

It was at least halfway true. For a single summer in their tenth year, the two girls had fallen in together, roller-skating in the park across the street from the Garniers' in Saint-Cloud or just across the river in the Bois de Boulogne. She remembered linden-flower tea and a many-tiered stand of fine pâtisserie in the Boulanger parlor one rainy afternoon, and photos everywhere of Lili's late, ancient father, and her bossy sister Nadia who hammered at the piano the whole time she was there. On another afternoon, sitting on the rug in her own room, she taught an eager Lili to play piquet, noticing how swiftly the sharp black eyes grasped the game and learned to count cards. Hours spent in Elisabeth's company seemed to set the serious-minded Lili at ease. For a few months they were all but inseparable—except that her friend was constantly being called away, her mother postponing their meetings because Lili had to practice for a coming recital, or play for some musical luminary passing through, or see the doctor yet again for an illness that was never explained. Even then Elisabeth sensed there was more of the adult than the child in Lili Boulanger, that she carried the weight of obligations and troubles beyond her years.

"She's creating beautiful work, Jacques," Martin said. "Brilliant work, some of it. She has a gift." His ringing blue eyes followed a passing swan boat. "My worry is that she won't live long enough to say everything she has to say. She's always sick, poor girl. Something intestinal. Something quite serious. She and Debussy with their digestive troubles—Beethoven too, for that matter. Poets die of consumption, composers of bowel trouble. It's almost de rigueur."

With this a pall fell over the conversation, until her papa said, "Do you have scores? I'd love to see what she's been producing."

"I'll bring you her latest, the *Trois morceaux*. It will tell you all you need to know. It's uneven in places, conventional—she's young, it's as you'd expect. But parts of it are so very good. So modern. You'll see." Martin stood to stretch his long legs. "And what about you, *mon ami*? I remember that lovely C-minor concerto you brought to Medfield. Just student work, you said in your modest way, something you wrote at the Conservatoire. Though in my opinion it was already the work of a mature composer. You must go back to writing music, Jacques. You owe it to the rest of us."

Again her papa fell silent. Elisabeth saw the way he turned inward, the shadow of a tree dappling his face. What mattered most, as usual, remained unspoken. But Martin was not one to insist. "Shall we walk?" he said, and they set off on the path around the pond again, the subject closed for now.

A year later, in the Sanborns' sun-washed music room on an unseasonably warm autumn afternoon, faraway France stricken to its knees, Elisabeth understood that this brave new sonata was the result of that brief chat beside the swans. From the very start of the recital they all had the sense that they were privileged to be present for a grand unveiling, that something extraordinary was unfolding for them and them alone—a feeling that had been building since they arrived to find a photographer waiting near the piano, ready to capture the moment. It wasn't going too far, perhaps, to say there was a sacred mood in the room.

As FOR ELISABETH, the strangeness of the sonata stole her breath away from the first few notes. Not the notes themselves, actually, but the impossibly long silence that followed them, a passage of empty air in which she worried that her papa's memory had suddenly frozen, that some paralyzing emotion had come over him, that he would not be able to continue. He'd been on edge all week. It wasn't impossible that he'd simply panicked, that stage fright had overcome him. It had been a very long time since he'd given a recital, and certainly not with a photographer standing by. All her heart was with her papa in that moment.

But then he began to play again. As the piece unfolded Elisabeth saw that the long rest was only the first of its countless surprises— the sonata a shapeshifter, her father a Merlin of the keyboard, the music moving through dangerous, enchanted forests she'd never known existed. The room was spellbound from the first note to the last. When it was over and she rushed to wrap her arms around him, she felt him shaking with emotion. If only her mother were there to witness the moment. "*Papa,*" she said quietly, "*j'aurais voulu que Maman puisse voir cela . . . un présent du cœur.*" Leaning his head back against her he replied, "*C'est pour toi, ma douce. Quelque chose pour se souvenir de moi, Elisabeth.*"

Something to remember me by. The words chilled her, the thought that one day he'd be gone. She straightened and put her hands on his hunched shoulders, massaging them until they began to release under her touch. The photographer caught the moment, the click of the shutter brisk as a conductor's baton rapping on the stand.

Now Elisabeth understood the late evenings when he wouldn't come home till long after she went to bed. Evenings that had made her wonder whether he'd met a woman, or had been swept into some unsavory political movement. He'd been composing on the humdrum piano at Latin, inventing what sounded to her like an entirely new kind of music, hauling it up from the depths of his suffering over the loss of his beloved Sylvie and the desecration of his beloved France . . . perhaps, too, over the derailment of his career as a rising young concert pianist lured to America by a promise that was immediately broken. All this seemed to well up through the music. Yet in certain passages Elisabeth heard a lightheartedness, too, a playfulness that was also her papa, an earlier Papa she so missed.

At one point, she was certain of it, a children's song from Normandy flitted through. Every little girl knew the words by heart, but she'd been the only girl whose papa kept dreaming up hilarious new verses. It became their private song. As she leaned down to embrace him at Aigremont, her cheek against his whiskers, Elisabeth felt the accumulating tragedies of his life flow into her, yes, but also his deep capacity for happiness, his memories of times happier than these.

The spell was broken when Martin Loeffler stepped up to the white piano. He was shaking his head in wonderment. "Bravo, maestro!" he told her father, and clapped gently, three times, in the echoing music room. "*C'est inspiré—c'est formidable.*" Then, turning to the room at large, his bright gaze singling out Elisabeth: "The man before you is a visionary, my friends. There is no other word for it. We're so very fortunate to have witnessed this moment! To attend a private début of such a piece—what an honor. Jacques: I thank you sincerely."

She'd shifted her hands back to her father's shoulders. She felt them tense and then relax.

"My dear friend," Martin continued, "will you share the name of this marvelous piece?"

Elisabeth felt her father hesitate. For a long moment he didn't breathe. But then he said: "I'm calling it *Élégie pour les frères perdus.* For the boys lost at Verdun."

A silence settled over the room as this was considered by all. Noticing her mother's puzzled look, Helen translated: "Elegy for the Lost Brothers."

"So, then," Martin said, "*un hommage. Et quel hommage tu as rendu à ton chère patrie, mon ami.*"

Dutifully Helen translated again: "What a gift you've given your mother country."

Elisabeth remembered how Verdun had devastated her papa: the late nights scouring the newspaper for every detail of the ruthless battle, his sorrow and disgust played out before her at the kitchen table month after month as the two sides pummeled each other in a deadly stalemate. It was this battle, more than any other, that had gutted him. It had gone on for ten months. When at last the Germans retreated he'd hammered at the fact again and again, shaking his head in disbelief. *Dix mois—c'est une abomination!* A disgrace. He couldn't absorb it.

"Would I be wrong," Martin continued in a more confidential tone, speaking directly to her father now, "in hearing another little *hommage* tucked into that early descending passage? *Un hommage* to an old friend of your daughter's? Perhaps even a bit of a requiem?"

This made no sense to Elisabeth—what friend would that be? And a requiem! She'd lost no friends to death.

Her papa shook his head in fond disbelief. "What an ear you have, Martin. . . . You're right, of course. It's in honor of Lili. What a terrible loss."

Elisabeth faltered, her hand still on her father's shoulder. She squeezed gently. "Papa. Lili Boulanger? She's *died?*"

He covered her hand with his. "In March. Just ten days before Debussy, if you can imagine. I'm so sorry, my dear. I couldn't think how to tell you."

Martin said, "A devastating double loss. Almost impossible to believe, isn't it? And the nearness in time . . . so strange. Fated, you might say."

"But she was my age!"

"And always in fragile health."

It was true, of course. Lili had always been in poor health, but Elisabeth couldn't conceive that her friend was gone. Between the astonishing sonata and this terrible news, she felt tears streaming down her cheeks. Martin Loeffler offered his folded handkerchief.

"How kind of you to honor her in this way," he told her papa with emotion. "How generous. And you chose your passage well, Jacques, if you'd like my opinion. The darkness suits the hour." Turning to the others he explained, "The passage in question is a variation on one from Lili Boulanger's *Trois morceaux*, her *Three fragments.* An *hommage* in the best tradition, ladies and gentlemen, the living composer in dialogue with the dead."

Afterward, in the little pavilion attached to the house, the Sanborns hosted a luncheon of squab and salmon terrine during which no one discussed the strange sonata. Perhaps it was because the music had sailed right over the heads of everyone but Loeffler; no one understood it well enough to comment. Or perhaps it was the connection to the bloodshed of Verdun. Clearly the music had come from the darkest recesses of the composer's heart, a place where solitude should be respected. The special agony for a Frenchman could only be imagined. Rena steered the conversation through warmer latitudes, asking her friend Mary Kellogg about her latest dance recital, chattering on about a hospital fundraiser in which various masterpieces of taxidermy from the private collection of Colonel Smith would be auctioned off, prodding Loeffler rather transparently about his friend Mrs. Gardner, whose glittering social circle Rena plainly longed to penetrate. All this Jacques Garnier seemed to take in stride, relieved that the recital was behind him and that he was no longer the center of attention.

Even with Elisabeth he held his tongue. Later, in the back of the Sanborns' Silver Cloud on the way home to Roxbury, he'd talk to the chauffeur the whole time about Ty Cobb's base stealing, as if to speak to his own daughter of his elegy for the lost brothers of Verdun would be to render their sacrifice somehow common. The music said all he had to say on the matter.

XXX.

Nowhere to Be Seen

IT ALL SEEMS AGES AGO NOW, that day when the sonata was committed to wax. Helen was still living in Winchester, engaged to marry H. E. Rollins. Aigremont was still a grand, pleasant house filled with servants and flowers and fine furniture, not the miasma of the dead and dying. Rena Sanborn had shown Oren the door, packing him off to the Parker House while her attorney drew up divorce papers—no one, including Oren, thinking this a particularly bad idea. The only wonder was that it hadn't happened sooner. As always, Elisabeth had been impressed with Rena's pluck.

As for Papa, he was still very much alive, though his days on earth were dwindling fast. Elisabeth still made his breakfast each weekday morning before he walked the twenty minutes over to Latin; afterward she headed off to the Bell Company where she'd long since made herself indispensable. On the surface, at least, life resumed its familiar shape. With the sonata completed, her papa no longer disappeared in the evenings, and they fell back into their old routines of reading to one another, playing cards, talking the hours away. His conversation turned more and more to the family home in Honfleur—the place of her earliest memories, before the move to Paris—and his childhood friends, his cousins, the neighbor who owned a Calvados shop in one of the old timbered houses tucked into the rue Haute. He seemed to be going back in time, deeper by the hour.

Despite the comfort of old routines, in the days after the recording session Jacques Garnier's mood was unpredictable, relaxed one minute then gloomy the next. The bad news about the war kept coming. The U-boat that would kill him was likely making its crisscrossing rounds a few hundred miles west of Le Havre. If his decision to join the French army was a secret that he kept from his daughter until the very last, his fast-approaching death was a secret the world kept from them both. For a brief time Elisabeth was permitted to believe that all was as well as it could be, considering a war was on, and was glad to have her papa back—a *visionary* now, if Martin Loeffler was to be believed, a wonderful father who also happened to be a genius. In time his *Élégie* might open a new horizon for them both, but for now she took comfort in the ordinary closeness between them. Something relaxed in her deeply. A knot was untied.

But there was no Charlie Westerlake then. Elisabeth's body was as dormant as a seed in the ground, waiting for spring rains to awaken it. She would not want to trade one sort of happiness for another, her last days with her papa for her first days with Charlie, but she's grateful now for the sudden happiness he's brought her. She's certain her papa would be happy for her too.

At times it's hard not to imagine a future with Charlie on the family farm in the countryside west of Chicago, where he plans to return after the war. He's told her a little bit about his small town, sketching in random details as they come to him, the rest supplied by her imagination. She can easily picture the vast golden wheat fields ringing the main street, the homely shops with American-style grain elevators looming behind them, the good-hearted neighbors. When the war's over he plans to set up his surgery next to the Wells Fargo bank building, exactly where his late father practiced medicine for thirty years. It's already been arranged. The town will welcome him back with open arms. And she, Elisabeth . . . but here she stops herself, knowing it's dangerous to let the fantasy run further. To say more, even in the silence of her heart, would be to risk a disappointment she can't bear.

She and the Captain—she calls him this teasingly now, when he takes the helm—have never discussed what will become of them after the war. Their world is more immediate. It's no exaggeration to say that they're comrades in arms, fighting in the trenches against a deadly disease—and as anyone knows, there is no love like the love of comrades who've stared death in the face together. No wonder they've fallen for each other. No wonder they can't bear to be apart.

It's all she can do not to run to him on the wards and throw her arms around his neck. As the grueling afternoons wear on and the suffering around her takes its toll, the thought of meeting her Charlie in the darkness is her sustenance and her salvation. She looks forward to it the way she'd look forward to setting off on a glorious trip to the South Seas, her grim Boston life collapsing into the horizon as she steams off for the equator. Perhaps the journey is a honeymoon . . . but again she hushes her imagination, giggling at her own girlish fancies.

WHEREVER HIS FINGERS BRUSH HER SKIN they set off tiny explosions: her body is a battlefield glimpsed from a Zeppelin. After evenings with him she lies in Caleb's bed and maps his remembered scents like a bloodhound on a trail. The English soap with which he tries to scrub away the odors of the wards. The chalky scent of a daub of shaving powder left behind his ear, a groggy morning's oversight. The laundered scent of the cotton drawers he's changed into before going out to meet her. The musk of his private parts nestled within them, carried invisibly to her hand. Most of all the scent of his breath, a bounty that is never exhausted.

And a last scent, of course, forever unexpected: the scent of herself on his skin.

TWICE NOW she's had to wait for her lover under the sycamore for more than an hour, some emergency in the wards detaining him, some inarguable matter of life and death. Since the outbreak of typhus in the town—its first victim the raving, bespectacled old man whose diarrhea had so repelled Elisabeth—the situation has turned even more perilous. Though the flu has been easing, this new disease stands ready to take its place. The war in Europe may be ending, but the one in Winchester has opened a new and chilling front.

So far they've seen nine cases. If they're to stop it in its tracks, immediate measures must be taken. Influenza has taught the world a hard lesson about decisive action. The hospital has no space for the isolation of such patients; reluctantly Rena has answered an appeal from the chairman of the board. And so the Aigremont stables have been turned into a typhoid ward, patients relegated there for fear they'll spread the contagion to the staff or the other patients. Amid leather tackle and horseshoes and the smells of hay and manure and human diarrhea, the new arrivals are dying in solitary misery, their struggles unseen by those in the main house. All this Charlie's tersely described to her, keen to change the subject to something lighter. She can see how it's undermining him. It's the only time she's seen fear in his eyes.

Though Elisabeth is terrified for her lover, she's resisted the urge to plead with him not to attend the stables, to assign Lazar or LeBlanc to oversee the typhus cases. Doctoring is his calling, and besides he'd never do it. He'd never abandon his patients nor put his colleagues at greater risk than himself. There would be no point in asking. She knows this instinctively. The three men have been to war together, have entrusted their lives to one another. Charlie's loyalties are ironclad. And so Elisabeth keeps her fears to herself as best she can, waiting for her lover to find her under the sycamore tree. She'll wait here forever if need be.

But just now she's tired of standing. Despite the chilly weather she spreads her skirts and sits on the turf with her back against the tree, knees drawn up, fingertips fussing with the hooks and laces of her boots, the blood skittish in her veins. To pass the time she's been watching the planets and stars and playing music in her head. First Ravel, then *Eine kleine Nachtmusik*, and in these last minutes a showtune she's picked up from Charlie's wide and catholic repertoire while lying in her bed and listening to him play.

Now it's a different and more serious music she hears. Perhaps it's the act of sitting on the ground, connected to the earth, that's shifted her mood. Looking up, she sees the first inkling of the crescent moon, hung on a branch like a Christmas ornament. The air is cold on her cheeks and hands but not unpleasantly so. With no warning at all she hears the opening phrase of her papa's masterpiece, his *Élégie pour les frères perdus*. As she waits out the long rest that follows she feels tears welling in her eyes. She plays haltingly through the opening movement in her mind, descends through the passage her father dedicated to Lili, makes her way soberly toward the explosive Allegro . . . then stops, shuts the music off at the tap, the rapid-fire second movement vague in her memory and not in tune with her mood anyway.

She wishes she could recall more of the sonata, which she's heard only her father play, and only a few times at that. What she remembers of it comes mostly from a Sunday, not long after the Aigremont recital, when she accompanied him to Martin Loeffler's house down in Medfield. With a glass of lemonade in hand she settled herself in her host's music room to listen, two miniature Chinese junks caught in mid-sail on the wall over her head, the windows open to the scent of lilac from Mrs. Loeffler's ample garden. After two hours of rehearsing Loeffler's new cello sonata with the Spanish cellist—who, to their astonishment, turned out to be not just any cellist but the famous Casals—their host had prevailed upon him to play his elegy for the war dead, then play it again, more slowly this time, so they could better understand it. In the course of the afternoon, her father played it four times through, the other two men listening raptly to its every twist and turn, and Elisabeth too. She saw how their minds raced, trying to decipher what they were hearing. When the music paused, the discussion that ensued was mostly over her head. The men delved excitedly into every nuance of the piece, shifts of time signature and Oriental-sounding harmonies, tone colors and radical chord voicings in the final movement, a hundred nuances of composition and performance. Loeffler and Casals threw questions at her papa almost faster than he could field them. Now and then one of them would play a few measures to illustrate a point, working from memory, violinist and cellist transposing snippets for their instruments by ear. They were enthralled.

Elisabeth recalls well the moment when, during a break for coffee, Casals shifted in his chair, lit his stubby pipe, and in his insistent English asked a question that drove the conversation into darker waters. What, he was keen to know, was the meaning of the odd seven-beat rest after the opening arpeggio? What a brave artistic statement it was—but what on earth did Jacques have in mind?

On its face it was another purely musical question. The truth was otherwise. Her papa answered by retelling a story he'd read in the newspaper in a grave voice whose flatness, Elisabeth sees now, belied the grief he felt for France. As the other men listened with frozen expressions, he described a German attack, some months into the Battle of Verdun, on a tiny village near the front lines, in the aftermath of which a local farmer, his wife, and their five sons were executed by machine-gun fire against the stone wall of the family barn—their crime being only that they were French, as far as anyone could tell. This was the meaning of the seven-beat rest, her papa explained: it was the tolling of a silent funeral bell for those five innocent farm boys and their parents. "*C'est bouleversant . . . si poignant,*" Loeffler said after a long silence, and Elisabeth agreed: a shattering and harrowing valedictory it was. The tiny Casals let his chair swallow him, devastated by the sad tale. Had the other men not been there Elisabeth would have run to her papa and taken him in her arms. It was some time before the mood began to lift and the men went back to their instruments, the music more passionate for the grim story. None of them spoke of it again.

As they were leaving—Mrs. Loeffler having fed them a wonderful sauerbraten, then an apricot strudel which the men ruined with cigars—Martin Loeffler asked discreetly for a copy of the score. "Only if you are comfortable with the idea, my friend," he said, touching her papa's sleeve. The composer demurred; he had only the original. He would make a clean copy when he could and send it by post. None of them could have known that only weeks later he'd be dead, the sole copy of the score almost certainly sent to the bottom of the sea in the oxblood leather portfolio where he'd kept his sheet music since Elisabeth was a girl.

SHE STRETCHES HER LEGS OUT BEFORE HER on the close-cut Sanborn turf, the cold stiffening her hips and knees, her lover still nowhere to be seen. On the air there's a scent of woodsmoke. The night is deeply quiet, somnolent, emptied out by the human urge to retire early when the temperature falls.

"Charlie," she says aloud. "Come *on.*"

She's on the brink of shivering now. She should get up and walk, shake the cold off. The truly sensible thing, of course, would be to abandon the wait and go up to her room, perhaps exchanging a glance with him if he's in the wards when she passes by. He must have his reasons, his important work. She's confident that he wants nothing more than to break free and hurry out to meet her. He knows what she has in store for him tonight—everything has been building to it. She's not breathed a word of it but her body has spoken for her.

She's timed it to the day, in fact, waiting for the precise middle of her cycle when, according to a school friend of hers, the chance of a mishap is lowest. Not that she would mind, especially. It would bind Charlie to her, launch them forward. They'd marry quickly, secretly; she'd make some excuse and withdraw from Aigremont the moment she began to show. Once the war was over they'd leave for Illinois where it could all be finessed, the exact date of the marriage, the circumstances of their acquaintance, everything.

But she'd never make such a decision without him. She's not that sort of woman. It's possible, too, that he'll come prepared, which would be a decision in itself. The important thing is that it happen tonight. And so she will go on waiting for him—in part because this is the night Mother Nature has chosen for them, in part because she can't bear the thought of his disappointment were he to rush to the sycamore and find her gone.

IN HER RESTLESS DISTRACTION her mind wanders back to her father, and a familiar worry: how is his masterpiece to be preserved? With the score almost certainly lost, it lives on only in the imperfect memories of those few who were lucky enough to have heard it and, of course, in the wax cylinders from the Sanborn recital. But even these have slipped from her hands.

The cylinders are as precious a gift as any she's ever been given. If she entrusted them to Helen Sanborn—how hard it was to let them go!—it was only so that they might find their way to the right ears.

After only a month in New York Helen had written to say, incredibly, that she'd met Arturo Toscanini, through Caruso. H. E. thought the maestro would give the recording a hearing if Elisabeth would send it down. Elisabeth hadn't known what to do with the cylinders in their fragile cardboard tubes, torn between asking her papa's friend Martin to hold them and keeping them close to her as talismans. The thought of shipping them through the post was terrifying. But it was *Toscanini* Helen was talking about—for the sake of her father's future renown, the opportunity could not be ignored. In America the famous conductor's word was law. When a friend of Mrs. Sanborn's offered to hand-carry the cylinders on her next trip down, the matter was quickly settled.

Helen had asked Elisabeth to include a note about the piece and the composer, to pique Toscanini's interest. But her courier's travel schedule left little time. The woman was leaving for New York on the next morning's train. Rather than send slapdash notes, Elisabeth decided to give the request the attention it deserved and follow up by post. She sat down to write Helen as soon as Mrs. Sanborn's friend left with the precious parcel.

The more Elisabeth worked on her letter, the more important it seemed to get down on paper not just the basic facts but everything she could recall, because Jacques Garnier could no longer speak for himself. The page she'd planned to write sprawled into four and then five and then six. She began with the sonata's essentials: composer and title, approximate dates of composition, the dedication to the lost soldiers of Verdun, the date of its private début in Winchester. Next she ventured into a bit of musical background: the story of the peasant family's murder and the meaning of the strange seven-beat rest; the *hommage* to Lili Boulanger. All this seemed suitable. But then Elisabeth found herself writing about her papa in the most direct terms, pouring love and grief onto the page. To really understand the sonata, after all, one had to know something of Jacques Garnier. There was his musical awakening in Honfleur, his matriculation at the Paris Conservatoire at the age of sixteen, his friendship with the young Debussy. His marriage to Sylvie Burnouf, soon followed by the birth of a daughter, Elisabeth Amélie, and twelve years later by a bold move to America. And finally, inescapably, the war: his passionate attention to its every twist and turn, the slow burn of his sorrow as events unfolded—a sorrow that led, through an intensely private process of the heart, to the creation of the *Élégie pour les frères perdus*, and soon after to his tragic death at the hands of the Germans. Now and then Elisabeth would pause to review what she'd written, imagining how it might sound to Toscanini, but by the fifth page her invisible reader's opinion no longer mattered. She blazed through the writing, in tears at her kitchen table. She needed the world to know what a kind, gifted, admirable man it had lost in Jacques Garnier.

By the time she'd finished she had ten dense pages before her. She was exhausted in every way. She considered keeping the letter rather than mailing it to Helen, but decided instead to make a copy for herself, which she did at once. She'd like her friend to understand her papa as she did. Never before had she found such clear words to express her reverence for him. She'd leave it to Helen to decide what to share with Toscanini. This she was in no position to know, and by now it seemed almost beside the point.

As it happened, the Toscanini plan failed almost at once. The link to the maestro was deftly severed by H. E.'s infidelity. The girl Rollins had run off with was a member of the conductor's orchestra at the Metropolitan Opera; in the wake of the scandal Toscanini wanted nothing to do with H. E. or anyone connected to him, including Helen. It was certainly not the time to ask him to listen to the recording. Helen counseled patience: things would blow over. Another opportunity would present itself. It was New York, after all, and she and Caruso were still on good terms. She'd hold the cylinders until the right moment came. But then the influenza descended, and Helen's unexpected pregnancy, and Elisabeth heard nothing more on the matter.

She could only hope that her friend, quarantined in her posh hotel room, was keeping the cylinders as safe as her stupendous jewelry. More than once she'd had nightmares of a distraught Helen drinking too much and setting them on a hot radiator. Or perhaps some dishonest housekeeper would pocket them, thinking they held popular songs. . . . Elisabeth imagined a dozen calamities. She weighed the idea of asking Helen to mail them back, thinking even the post might be safer than Helen's chaotic world.

But the Roxbury apartment was surely less safe than the Knickerbocker. With war hysteria at its peak, the streets below were more dangerous by the day. There had been murders nearby—including, shockingly, a mob assault on Helmut Buchmann, the German playboy who'd given Elisabeth her first sale for the Bell Company. They'd staved his head in when he asked an Italian worker for directions, his Prussian accent impossible to conceal. The address in question belonged to a drab walkup Elisabeth thought housed a brothel. On another night a drunken Latvian had kicked in the door of her building and charged up to the second-floor landing before a neighbor confronted him with a pistol. Roxbury was inflamed like an angry wound. For the moment, Elisabeth concluded, the cylinders were probably safer in Helen's hands.

Now she wishes that Charlie knew the piece—that he could play it for her whenever she asked, could share in its genius. To bring together the memory of her sweet father and the hands of her sweet lover would be a pleasure beyond any she can imagine. What a way it would be to keep the music alive . . . but they've never had time to talk about the sonata, have never gotten that far in exploring each other's pasts. What a gift she'll give him one day.

XXXI.

MYSTIC LAKE

SHE'S FREEZING NOW—there's no pretending she's not. She needs to walk, to get the blood flowing. Clambering to her feet, she smooths her skirt and pulls her wrap tighter against the New England cold, scanning High Street, deciding where to go.

"You waited for me," a voice says behind her. "What a sweet girl you are."

When she whirls around it's him: Charlie with dark circles under his eyes, hair tousled as if he's just rolled out of bed. She throws herself against him and presses her lips to his warm neck. As they stand under the sycamore a light goes out in the carriage house: LeBlanc or Lazar turning in. Reflexively they come apart, Charlie stepping back and affecting a disinterested pose as if they'd crossed paths by chance.

"Don't you know what time it is?" he says with a mischievous smile.

"Time just stopped," she laughs.

"Shall we?"

They slip away, taking their usual path through the sheltering trees. Lights still blaze in the main house, much to their advantage. After a long detour they cross High Street and make for the tight-knit darkness that lurks among the houses leading to the lakes.

Once Aigremont is out of sight Charlie stops and takes her in his arms with an urgency that startles her. She looks up at him but he's averted his eyes. Though they've shifted away she distinctly sees a sadness in them.

"What's wrong, my love?" she says, squeezing his big hand. "You've lost a patient?"

He shakes his head but still won't look at her.

"Come on," he says a little roughly, "we're running out of time."

Charlie Westerlake takes her by the arm and steers her down the lane that leads to their hideaway, the place of their love.

How KIND OF RENA to lend the Captain the key to the Sanborn boathouse, though how misguided—as if he'd had the leisure, back before the weather turned, to sail for pleasure, or fish, or canoe on the twin Mystic Lakes. A man of leisure he was not, and even less so now. Not with an infirmary to run. But perhaps she was just looking for small ways to repay him for his many sacrifices, or to rope him in tighter lest he put in for a change of post. Surely Rena Sanborn is not above a bit of strategy. Whatever the case, the key languished on his dresser until he kissed a certain French nurse-assistant and its true purpose made itself known. Now he slips it in his pocket every night on his way to meet his lover, the boathouse their sanctuary, the only place they can be truly alone.

In the darkness they leave the road and wend their way down a gravel path to the docks near the Boat Club, the spongy planks softening their steps. Near the water the damp makes the cold more cutting. Elisabeth hugs herself tightly as she watches her lover fumble with the padlock, the clumsiness so unlike him, his surgeon's hands suddenly awkward as dog's paws. Since the moment of his arrival under the sycamore tree she's felt a nervousness in him, an anxiety she'd like to believe is excitement over what's soon to come—though there's a tense edge to his mood that seems to come from far outside the world the two of them have created. It isn't simple, whatever it is that's troubling him.

They're in at last. In the murky light she can just make out the racks of canoes and kayaks, the life vests, the shellacked trout and lobster pot mounted to the clapboard wall. It's chilly but not nearly as chilly as outside. Stooping in the corner Charlie strikes a match and lights the kerosene camp heater, then nudges the grimy window open to vent the fumes. She, meanwhile, unfolds the heavy woolen blanket and lays it out under shelves with fishing tackle and oars and nautical paraphernalia. This is their ritual. Every night they set up camp only to strike it a few hours later. They leave no trace of their temporary bivouac amidst the stowed summer gear. When he turns to take her in his arms their tiny world is complete.

They might as well be on a raft floating in a warm southern sea, terra firma and all its worries left far behind.

It's past midnight when it happens, when her long wait comes to an end. The Allegro is playing in her head despite her best efforts to stop it. Her papa is here—a strange feeling that should make her uncomfortable but urges her on instead.

There is pain, at first, but not as much as she'd feared. He draws back to let her catch her breath, waiting for her to squeeze his shoulders again, his signal to continue. With a surgeon's delicacy he probes and explores, intimately familiar with the relevant anatomy, his own passion controlled for the sake of her comfort and perhaps, if all goes well, her pleasure. It's frightening but it's the only thing she wants. The kerosene heater hisses and sputters when a moth bumbles into the burner. Out on the lake an owl hoots mournfully. They are profoundly alone, profoundly together.

Afterward he kisses her more tenderly than he ever has before and drops straight into sleep, rolling onto his back and breathing noisily, his complete collapse making her giggle like a schoolgirl in the stillness of the little boathouse.

Elisabeth's not watched him sleep before. For a long while she studies him in the blurry glow of the kerosene flame and decides that she could spend the rest of her years watching this man fall asleep and awaken again, exiting and entering each day at her side. She can no longer hold her imagination back. She imagines the bed she'll make for him, the exact duvet, the embroidered sheets from Normandy, the smartly tucked corners . . . the Westerlake homestead in Illinois, on a rolling hill overlooking Blackberry Creek, the sturdy white house she'll decorate with a woman's touch, fit out with French flourishes. With children, too—how many, she can't say—children she'll teach to speak French, children who'll play the piano as seriously as their grandfather and grow up to be doctors like their father. Elisabeth knows exactly what she wants, in fine and copious detail. She sees the road ahead clearly.

She must have drifted off, because when the church bells awaken her she doesn't know where she is. Charlie is on his feet in an instant, oriented and sharp. As a soldier he knows to hit the ground running.

"What the hell," he says, ear to the fogged window.

"What is it?" she says hazily from the blanket on the floor.

Even in the few seconds they've been awake, the clamor has risen. A cacophony of pealing church bells breaks out in all directions, some close by, some quite far away. In the remote distance a ship's horn blares. She pictures an ocean liner lit up in Boston Harbor, the sound rumbling across the miles like thunder. But why at this late hour? Elisabeth feels for her Red Cross pocket watch and consults it: three o'clock in the morning! Never have she and Charlie dared stay out so late. Never, for that matter, has she been awakened by such clamor in the dead of night. Not in Winchester, anyway, where there's barely a light to be seen after ten. None of it makes sense.

Charlie throws the doors of the boathouse open and the pandemonium surges. She hears gunshots in the night, or perhaps they're firecrackers, a calamity of sharp reports, a fracas breaking out in every precinct.

"Holy Christ," Charlie says at last, taking her in his arms. "It's over!"

"What's over?"

His eyes shine down on her. "Don't you know?"

"No—"

"The war, Liz—the damned war!"

XXXII.

HOME

This changes everything.

Elisabeth should be exhausted when she steps into the breakfast room on the first day of peace, having slept only a few hours, but she's bursting with energy. Rena is elsewhere; it isn't hard to imagine that she has more important things to do on this particular morning, breakfast giving way to more pressing concerns. Elisabeth imagines the lady of the house dictating telegrams, placing telephone calls, discussing the monumental news with her friends. For a doyenne of Winchester there will be civic duties to discharge, celebratory plans to be laid. Elisabeth wonders what it all will mean for her patients at Aigremont.

Though the flu has hardly been conquered, the tide is turning. There is a smattering of empty cots now, the hospital shipping fewer and fewer cases to the mansion on High Street. Charlie confided the other night, during the walk down to the lake, that the typhus patients in the stables would soon be transferred to a Boston hospital, another great relief. Soon the waves of sickness will pass. For the first time it seems possible to say this.

Mrs. Sanborn's help has been invaluable. Her generosity in opening Aigremont has saved lives. The naked bravery of it continues to astound Elisabeth. But surely Rena must be longing for the day when the patients will be gone and her grand home will be put back to rights. Perhaps she's already laying plans for her peacetime life. Perhaps she's planning her own glittering victory celebration in the carefully disinfected, redecorated rooms of Aigremont, an all-stops-pulled affair with Champagne fountains and an oyster bar and the best dance band in Boston. Perhaps she's already contacting caterers, florists. It's only seven in the morning, but the early hour surely doesn't matter. Elisabeth supposes that few in Winchester or Boston, in the whole vast country, are still in their beds.

On this particular morning Elisabeth is happy to take her breakfast alone. No doubt Mrs. Sanborn would want to talk of the German surrender, but Elisabeth has other things on her mind. The precious hours spent with Charlie Westerlake, the gift she's just given him. The flood of new sensations, the fullness of her heart. Most of all the ache she already feels, the need to touch his skin again, to feel his body pressing down on hers . . . she can't discuss these things with anyone, yet she'd be hard-pressed not to blurt them out. It's for the best that Mrs. Sanborn hasn't turned up.

She fills her cup from the silver urn on the sideboard, then sits down to await breakfast. It's always Rena who rings the bell for the servants. Elisabeth hesitates, then tugs the cord herself. Breakfast will not come otherwise. But who is she to act the duchess and order servants about? Her parents never once considered the idea of having them. For a family of three modest souls to keep servants was just the sort of idiocy they mocked in the petite bourgeoisie of Honfleur.

In Illinois she'll have no servants. She will be mistress of her own home. She'll do the marketing and cooking and cleaning with pleasure, content to manage Charlie's house while he does his own good work. When the children come she'll have help aplenty. After chores she'll let them romp down the hill to Blackberry Creek and splash in the water on hot July days, playing with the tenant farmer's children and teaching them bits of French, furthering their education with none of them the wiser. She smiles at the thought, too tired to stop her imagination from running out ahead. Charlie's told her just enough about his life back home to give her all the raw material she needs.

When the maid enters with her breakfast on a tray Elisabeth makes a point of gazing warmly into her eyes and wishing her a good morning. The maid's name is Anja. She's a shy, sweet girl— Swedish, Elisabeth's heard, with the tangled English of a recent immigrant. But poor Anja is caught entirely off guard by her guest's unaccustomed friendliness. This is certainly not how Mrs. Sanborn greets her. On the contrary, Mrs. Sanborn looks directly at Anja only when something is not to her liking. Elisabeth means only to express her equality, her solidarity. It takes a moment but Anja seems to grasp this. With a smile she curtsies, an afterthought that makes both of them give up a little laugh.

As Anja sets the tray on the sideboard Elisabeth has a sudden urge to confess everything to her. How can she hold within herself the excitement of all that's happened in the last twelve hours? She must tell someone—she'll burst if she doesn't—but there's been no one to hear her story. Helen is far away; her father and mother are dead. Her acquaintances from school have fallen out of touch, not least because she's always preferred the company of her parents. Rena Sanborn is out of the question, obviously. So, perhaps it will be Anja. As the girl lays out her plate of eggs and sausages and pots of jam and clotted cream Elisabeth takes note of the wedding ring on her lean finger, the thinnest band of cheap gold.

"You're married," she says.

The girl looks at her in surprise. She can't be more than twenty-one or twenty-two. There's a skittish bird fluttering inside her, constantly on the qui vive as a matter of survival. She could so easily fly away.

"Yes?" Anja says uncertainly.

"For how long now?"

"Three years, ma'am."

"Happy years?"

The girl blushes and looks away. "Yes, ma'am."

"What's his name?"

Again Anja hesitates, gauging the risk, the danger in allowing the interview to go on. "Egil. Egil Hermansson," she says carefully.

Elisabeth nods at this formidable name, then blurts out: "Anja, did you and he—before you married, I mean. . . ." But the moment the words are out of her mouth she's horrified by them. She is too embarrassed to complete the thought. Now she's the one to blush. "I'm sorry. I shouldn't have. It's not my place."

The girl steals a frightened look at her. To answer such a question in the wrong way could be disastrous. It's hard to read one's betters in America, and there is the problem of language—could the pretty Frenchwoman really have been asking what she seemed to be?

Elisabeth sees her panic and touches her hand, filled with guilt for putting the poor girl in such a position. The fact is, if only she'd slept a few hours more . . . if only she weren't feeling so emotional . . . but really there is no excuse for her behavior.

"Please accept my apology," she pleads, but the damage is done. Anja won't return to clear the dishes until long after her guest has left the room.

CHASTENED, Elisabeth walks down the hall toward the library, only to run straight into an exhausted Charlie Westerlake. To her surprise he's just come down the children's staircase. For a brief moment they're alone in the sunny corridor.

"Where were *you*?" she whispers loudly, giving him a teasing smile. She reaches for his big hand but he tucks it into his pocket and jingles loose change. She knows exactly what he's up to. He is sending her a silent warning. *Careful!* she chides herself. *Don't take foolish risks.* They aren't in the darkness of the lane anymore. They aren't tucked away in the boathouse. Here they're easily spotted.

It's so difficult to keep from touching him. He, meanwhile, won't meet her eager gaze. She's not the only one afraid of losing control. Only hours ago they were skin-to-skin, not a scrap of clothing between them.

"I was upstairs," he says dully, as if she'd not just seen him come down off the bottom step. His voice is very tired, a bit remote. For an instant she imagines him stealing into her room, going through her things, his hands plunged in her dresser drawers, fingers touching her silks, remembering. Reliving. The thought thrills her. But then he explains, keeping his voice low: "Meeting with the Queen of Sheba in her room. She had the maid fetch me before I'd had one sip of her nasty coffee. Couldn't wait ten minutes, apparently." Elisabeth recoils a bit at his irritation with Rena, but lets it pass. He's entitled to his opinion.

Charlie draws a deep breath and sighs it out, annoyed. "With the war over, she's worried I'll go."

A flicker of panic passes through Elisabeth. "Go where?"

"Home. It'll be officers first, starting with wounded officers. My set. We're being demobbed."

She doesn't know this word. "*Que signifie ce mot, amour*—'demobbed'?"

"Just a matter of the papers coming through. A few weeks, maybe sooner."

But he still hasn't explained. "Charlie—what does this mean, demobbed?"

"Demobilized. Discharged. Free to go home."

Now he meets her eyes, but only for an instant. His gaze is a flashing hummingbird.

"Charlie, I—"

"The old gal wants me to stay and ride this out, whether I'm enlisted or not. She's offering good money." He scowls at the sunlit floorboards, plucking at his lower lip as if to retrieve a shred of tobacco that isn't there. "Jesus. As if I work for *her*." Charlie grips the doorknob. "Well, I'll tell you something right now—I don't."

Elisabeth's stopped breathing. It's almost too much to take in, after all that's just happened. Life drags on for months without anything very important happening, only to explode in a day.

"What will you do?" she manages, but at the same moment the door of the kitchen flies open and the hallway is abruptly full of clattering noise and foot traffic, three of the other nurse-assistants charging toward them with trays of broth. Charlie retreats partway up the children's staircase to clear the way. Elisabeth withdraws into the library a pace. As the nurses pass by, they nod their greetings, smirking at each other the moment they've passed, the bowls jangling on the trays. The hallway is filled with the cloying scent of bouillon.

Elisabeth realizes in this moment that she's been the subject of gossip and speculation. Perhaps one of the others has caught a glimpse of her and Charlie meeting under the sycamore, or slipping back onto the property after one of their nocturnal rambles. Perhaps she and the Captain are no secret at all. But it doesn't matter, because it's soon to end. Charlie will be leaving Aigremont with her beside him. Their love will shine out proudly. As they step back into the corridor she has a vision of riding next to him on the train to Chicago, the rails clopping monotonously down below, the car rocking them gently against each other as the boundless countryside slides past. The scent of his shaving powder and masculine skin brings her the most private sort of peace. Never has she felt so contented. So loved.

"Well," he says with a grudging look, "time to get to it, I guess."

"I guess so."

"Oh, by the way, Liz . . . not tonight. I can't."

She stares at him blankly. For nine days now they've spent every free moment together. Just last night she gave herself to him in an act of perfect devotion. She needs to see him again in the boathouse, as soon as possible. She wants more. She wants everything he can give her.

"Sorry," he says, looking away. "Just too much to attend to, with the surrender and all. Since I said no to staying on, Rena wants to sit down over dinner and work out what it'll take to wind things down here. I'm the medical director—I have to do it, Liz. You understand."

She does not understand. No. Such dull work could wait another day, or two, or three, whereas she needs Charlie's touch right away. Being in his presence brings it home even more clearly. But before she can say another word he turns and walks away, his limp making a syncopated music as he hurries off.

XXXIII.

RING

THE MORNING IS SO BUSY that she has little time to reflect on the brief encounter in the corridor. It lingers in her chest like the ghost of a cough as she goes about her duties. Four patients are being discharged; Dr. Lazar has directed the staff to consolidate two of the wards, moving the library patients into the dining room and stowing the beds away. The tide really has turned. Soon the infirmary at Aigremont will fold up. Which pleases Elisabeth immensely, for reasons having nothing to do with the patients' suffering. There will be nothing to keep Charlie here, nothing to tempt him to reconsider Rena's offer in the event she sweetens it.

The ridiculous thought passes through Elisabeth's mind that Rena is in love with Charlie too, despite the difference in years. Perhaps she wants him to stay on for more personal reasons. Elisabeth feels guilty for thinking of Rena in this way, but the idea sticks to her like a bramble. For some minutes she can't get it out of her mind. But then the outlandishness of the notion strikes her, and she's overcome with a laughter she can't tamp down, laughter that overtakes her and subsides and overtakes her again. At one point she actually flees to a corner of the ward and bends over to clutch her knees, overcome, trying to get a grip on herself. The head nurse sends her a barrage of sharp looks. Patients smile up from their beds, sharing in her amusement though they can't possibly guess what's behind it. When Rena darkens the doorway on some officious errand it all starts again, a fresh gale of hilarity driving Elisabeth from the room. She hasn't laughed so hard in ages.

Through the morning she contrives to cross paths with her lover whenever she can, hoping to catch his eye. She knows his body well enough now to see how very tired he is. When he leans over a patient he braces himself on the bedstead, or sits heavily on the edge of the bed, taking weight off his bad leg. Again she wonders what pain he carries from the shrapnel still embedded next to the bone. Not once has he complained about it.

At lunch in the kitchen the lively talk is all about the boys coming home. Nearly every girl has a beau or brother in the service. Some are overseas, others stationed at bases in American towns Elisabeth's never heard of. One of the nurses reminds the table that the absent head nurse, Mrs. Scott, has a husband who's been stuck at a run-down hospital in Paris for six months, recovering from injuries whose nature was at one point the subject of much catty speculation. Nurse Scott is not well-liked despite the unfortunate situation with her husband. For some minutes her unlikability is dissected in detail, forks and knives clanking away on the plain dishes, the Portuguese cook humming to himself as he brews an enormous cauldron of broth for the hospital. Elisabeth listens to all the talk but doesn't say much, keeping her eyes on her beef and gravy—beef in celebration of the day, beef of victory. What's on her mind is not to be shared with a table of flighty girls. When lunch is over she steps outside for a few minutes to take the crisp November air and clear her head of all the banter. She has no patience for it now.

A GRAND CHANGE is coming, she can feel it. It's like a wave in the ocean, vaulting her forward on its broad back. The force beneath her is not of human scale. There's danger in it. And as her papa used to say, there's danger in anything worth doing, but a greater danger in doing nothing at all.

She must stay alert and be ready to move quickly when the time comes, to leap into the dance like a ballerina at her cue. There will be only one chance to get it right. Illinois depends upon her quick thinking, her readiness to give herself fully and without hesitation to Captain Westerlake. She must seize the day: something else her father used to say, though he followed his own advice only rarely.

Carpe diem, ma chère! she hears him say in her head. *Saisis ta chance!*

I will, Papa. I will!

Elisabeth smiles to herself, not caring if the others wonder what she's thinking.

All it needs, she adds, yawning into her hand, *is one good night's sleep. I'll be ready.*

At DINNER her body finally collapses under her. The fractured sleep of the night before, the long day on the wards, the low rumble of worry over Charlie's remoteness—all of it pulls her down at last. At some point, as the banter sails over her head, she realizes she's half-slumped over her plate of chicken and potatoes. From across the table one of the other girls gently squeezes her arm and says, "Go to bed, honey. Go to bed."

There's no point in fighting it, especially since Charlie's tied up, presumably, in his dinner meeting with Mrs. Sanborn. In Caleb's room she changes out of her things and slips on her robe to pay a last visit to the lavatory, across the hall from Rena's bedroom. She's asleep on her feet, the pull of clean sheets and duvet irresistible. But as she opens her door she hears Rena's door open, too.

Charlie steps out into the hallway with a light, good-natured laugh, in a better mood now. Elisabeth ducks back into her room, peering around the doorjamb at him. In the glow ushering from Rena's open door he appears godlike to her, more vividly alive than an ordinary man. Cast against the wall behind him, his shadow apes his every move. She still can't believe he's hers.

"You'll do just fine here," he tells Rena. "But you don't need me to tell you that."

"As I said, Captain, we owe you an enormous debt of gratitude. All of us. I can't begin to put words to it. If you happen to pass through Boston again you must come out and visit. I'll be offended if you don't."

"I appreciate that very much."

"I'll give you Oren's room. He certainly won't be needing it again."

There's a brief drift in the conversation. Someone in the wards downstairs begins to snore faintly. Elisabeth pulls back from the doorway, worried she'll be spotted. At the moment it's better to listen quietly.

Unable to see Charlie and Rena, she wonders if they're perhaps shaking hands. Then Rena says, "When do you plan to leave?"

"Nothing set in stone yet. The proper thing would be to wait for my discharge papers to come through. But the word is they're looking the other way, letting officers head home ad lib. I may take advantage once things are buttoned up here. Especially since Lazar's going to stay on for a while. You won't be without help."

"Well, I certainly can't keep you here. You've done more than your fair share, goodness knows."

"All in the line of duty, Mrs. Sanborn."

Another lull. Elisabeth tries to imagine the looks on their faces, wonders if they're exchanging an unspoken message with their eyes. The spells of quiet are odd. As the seconds pass Elisabeth finds she needs to know exactly what's happening in the corridor. Carefully she leans forward, peering around the doorjamb until Charlie comes into view.

In the dim light he stands at ease, hands clasped behind him, the bad leg bent slightly at the knee. He's looking at Rena, but the movement from down the corridor has caught his eye. With a slight turn of his head he spots Elisabeth and straightens, refusing to meet her urgent gaze. Without the slightest flicker of acknowledgment he turns back toward Rena, his stiffened back the only sign he's noticed his lover at all.

Then Rena says: "I expect your wife's on tenterhooks, waiting for you to come home. Your son and daughter, too, my goodness. No one would fault you for leaving on the next train west. Least of all myself."

At first the words don't register in Elisabeth's mind. It's her body that responds, her pulse breaking into a sprint. Paralyzed, she's distantly aware of Charlie wavering, the injured leg giving way slightly, but he steadies himself immediately. She's desperate for him to look back at her and desperate for him not to.

Meanwhile Rena's words hang in the silent corridor, demanding a reply. Elisabeth waits for Charlie's response like an animal quivering in its burrow, waiting for some predator to make a second, deadlier strike. But Charlie says nothing. If Rena's information is wrong he doesn't correct her. For an infinitely long moment the corridor is utterly silent. It's as if the grand house and all its inhabitants have drifted off to sleep, etherized.

Elisabeth clutches the doorknob, feeling she might faint. After bearing the airless stillness of the corridor for what seems an eternity she withdraws into her room and closes the door and falls against it, ear pressed to the wood, bile curling around the root of her tongue.

When Rena speaks again her voice is sharp, its edge unmistakable even through the door.

"I believe it's time you put your wedding ring back on, Captain Westerlake. Don't you?"

IT'S THE LAST THING ELISABETH HEARS until she awakes on the floor of Caleb's room, head throbbing, mouth foul with vomit.

She has no idea how much time has passed. She's fallen out of time. Rolling onto her back, the cold floor beneath her, she stares at the ceiling and feels tears sliding down her face, indifferent as rain. She's almost too stunned, too shocked, to be angry. The brief conversation in the corridor roars through her mind like the war chant of some exotic tribe, incomprehensible but incalculably perilous. The day she decodes it, perhaps, will be the day she dies.

Eventually the window begins to gray with morning light.

The question now is what to do.

FOURTH MOVEMENT

Appassionato

CHICAGO

DECEMBER 2018

XXXIV.

THE BODY'S OWN BUSINESS

IT'S ASTONISHING, BIRDSONG—Ben's deep into the wonder of it this afternoon, sitting on his stone bench in the botanic garden's tropical conservatory, the peeps and squawks and bell-clear melodies of the colorful denizens lively on the air. He's come here in pursuit of the simplest of pleasures. With the Gamma Knife behind him and the dogged tinnitus all but gone, it's the unadulterated song of the natural world he's after, a reunion with elemental acoustics. In the dead of a Chicago winter, there is no better place to really hear.

He's been here more than an hour, having absconded from Counterpoint and all the rest, convinced in some way that's new to him that he can't go on with his work without making time for this. Birdsong is the music behind the music. Before the piano came the wren; before the violin the lark. The history of musicmaking overflows with avian mimicry, Prokofiev's quacking duck and Vivaldi's flocking songbirds, then Messiaen and Bartók and Sibelius right up to Bird's *Ornithology*, but none of it rivals the real thing. The plain sparrows who slip through the exhaust louvers behind the palm trees put them all to shame.

The place was swarming with raucous schoolchildren when he arrived, but now it's just him. He closes his eyes to orient himself to the soundscape. A rustling and burbling from above and to the right, a tropical squawk to the left. A fast whistling melody directly ahead in the maze of ferns. There must be dozens of birds, the parrots and toucans installed here to round out the fantasy habitat, the drab intrepid city birds lured inside by the humidity and warmth. Ben wonders what they talk about. As a mourning dove coos from a strut near the arched glass ceiling he smiles, letting it all flow through him, delighting in the newfound acuity of his hearing.

It's not that his hearing is perfect. At night, in the quiet of his bedroom, he can still detect a faint whine in his left ear, a high signal somewhere around ten kilohertz, but in this place, in this moment, it hardly matters. If anything, it's a reminder of how far he's come. Here in the faux tropics he couldn't care less about it. The music of the birds is a thousand times stronger.

When he rises to go, another gaggle of children mustering noisily in the Orchid House next door, it's with the effortless balance of a much younger man. The vertigo is simply gone. He is absolutely steady on his feet. With an easy stride he walks to the ornate front door and steps back out into the December day, the bracing cold nothing to him, the blare of a car horn glancing off his fine mood like a falling leaf.

It was a late lunch with his old friend Peter Roth, the concert sound engineer and Nikki's long-ago fiancé, that brought him down to Lincoln Park. They met at a Greek place on Clark, drinking retsina and sharing a platter of souvlaki, having fallen out of each other's orbit for far too long. It had been a difficult year for Peter. A raging divorce after his wife left him for another attorney at her firm; a custody battle; a kid with an anxiety disorder. The latest scorching email from his ex arrived just as the souvlaki did, Peter having made the apparently unforgiveable error of introducing their son to his girlfriend of seven months.

"Never divorce a fucking lawyer, man," Peter said, slapping the phone across the table like a flat little hockey puck. "Never *marry* a fucking lawyer. After the way she screwed me over she has no right to complain about anything I do. Am I right?" He finished his retsina and refilled his glass to the brim. "I *am* right." Then: "Hey, sorry, man. I don't mean to lay all this on you. I lose my shit every time I talk about it."

Ben knew the feeling. It had taken most of a year to burn through his anger over Robin and Hurwitz. The first shocking sting of betrayal had pierced ever deeper as she set up housekeeping with her lover and the divorce played out, releasing venom all the way. It wasn't until the legalities were concluded that the fury began giving way to a tangle of quieter, more elusive emotions, some of which he could barely put a name to. Sorrow was one strand, surely—but not, he thought, the main one. There was more to it than that. All

Ben knew for certain, in those strange early days as a divorcé, was that the anger he'd endured for the past year no longer interested him. He didn't know how to hold a grudge; not really. It wasn't in his nature. This much he did understand about himself.

With the anger cleared, he'd come to see his own part in their unraveling. Certain hard truths came into focus. The way he'd come to treat Robin more as roommate than lover; the way cooking elaborate meals together had edged out the sex. The way he'd let Counterpoint, always hungry for his love, overtake the marriage. Though the repellent business with Hurwitz had hurt him as he'd never been hurt before, eventually it had ceased to surprise him. The logic behind Robin's betrayal was as lucid as algebra.

After nearly two hours, the lunch with Peter Roth collapsed under its own weight. They squabbled over the check in a perfunctory way until Ben snatched it up and headed to the cashier's station with its sticky counter and yellowed photos of the Acropolis. The squat owner scowled as he ran the card, never once looking at his customer. Ben was ready to be on his way.

It was while he was standing at the cash register that the idea of wandering over to the conservatory occurred to him. He needed to drain off some of his friend's high amperage. After dropping Peter at his car he continued on to the park, fighting a bit of guilt at not returning to Counterpoint but telling himself not to be a slave to work. It was Friday afternoon; most people in his position wouldn't think twice about knocking off early. He'd earned the right to throttle back. In his head he heard Nikki insist that there was no shame in self-care. Soon he was sitting quietly on his stone bench, ensconced in a humid fantasia of ferns and huge shining leaves and a chorus of birds who sang their hearts out for their audience of one, content as could be.

BACK OUT ON STOCKTON Ben waits for a cab, acutely aware of Ana's building hunkered just across the street. Were she in town she could easily look down and spot him standing there, arm jutting in the air in the taxi-hailer's universal Sieg Heil. But she's not due back from Europe for some weeks yet. For now the city is his; the city is safe. He smiles over at her building as it if it's an old adversary glaring at him from the other side of a prison fence. Just down the street is Mon Ami Gabi, the place of their first excitable rendezvous, but this too fails to move him.

Since Ana's left town he's largely managed to put her out of his mind, the fury over her theft of the sonata score shoved aside by the surgery and his body's triumphal return. It isn't that he's free of her—hardly that. On the contrary, Ben feels her lurking just below the surface of his life, her capricious energy held in taut reserve, the missing score clutched in her greedy fist. But for now he's relishing a break from her drama. A reckoning can wait. He needs this time to heal.

When a cab pulls up he gives the driver his home address rather than Counterpoint's. His head is too full of birdsong, his mood too serene for work. Perhaps he'll go in after dinner and wrap up a thing or two. The cabdriver catches green lights all the way up to Ravenswood, muttering into his phone in Arabic while Ben slumps in his seat and watches the neighborhoods fly by, the dry cleaners and bank branches and clumps of shivering Chicagoans huddled at bus stops, the familiar anatomy of his city laid out block by block, nerve by nerve. It's a city he loves, a city that's been good to him despite its perverse weathers and moods, a city perfectly scaled to his heart and imagination. He's never seriously considered living anywhere else.

By the time they pull up at his place the idea of going into Counterpoint after dinner has slipped away. Three forty-five and already the light's failing, the short December day closing up shop, the cold coming right up through his boots as he stands in the street waiting for the driver to hand his card back. Once darkness falls it would take a monumental act of will to budge him from the house. He knows perfectly well that he'll be in for the night.

After shedding his coat he heads straight for the wine fridge Nikki had him buy while he was renovating the house. Since his dinner at the Farahanis', when he couldn't lay hands on a decent bottle to present to his hosts, he's replenished his stocks amply. He stoops before the dimly lit shelves and slides out one bottle after another, pondering his options. Ever the miser at heart, he steers clear of the few high-end bottles the people at Binny's flattered him into buying, then chooses an eighty-dollar Napa cab anyway, proud of himself for breaking his own rule. He's been saving the pricey bottles for a special occasion. Why not a celebration of his restored health, even if he'll be raising a glass alone? To be alone is a comfort.

As he cuts the foil and eases out the cork, the late afternoon and evening unfold before him lazily, empty of commitments to anyone but himself. He settles into the soft leather couch with his wine and takes up the remote control, thinking he'll poke around for a good movie, but then sets it back on the coffee table, the birds of the afternoon still roosting in his head, the silence of his home soothing. Even the Bösendorfer, poised elegantly in the next room with the sonata score waiting on its music stand, knows better than to tamper with such a mood.

HE MUST HAVE DOZED OFF. He awakes with a start and then a laugh, struck yet again by how easily sleep comes now. It's Nikki's doing: the moment they arrived back at his place after the long day at the hospital she insisted he curl up on the couch or crawl into bed whenever he felt the urge. He was to follow his body's dictates without argument. In that first day or two his thirst for sleep was unquenchable. He'd awake to find an afghan spread over him, tucked in by invisible hands, feeling cosseted and cozy and safe. Nearby would be a glass of water, or a pot of herbal tea, or a plate of Italian wedding cookies, his caregiver self-effacing to a fault. It was succor, pure and simple; he didn't know when or where Nikki slept, unless it was in one of the deep living room chairs while he slept, too. He only knew that she was there whenever he needed her.

In return for her many kindnesses she got to share the moment when he donned headphones, cued up a quiet Ravel piece and hooted with joy, the signal clean and pure for the first time in many months, the scream in his ear silenced. The two of them understood full well what it meant. It meant he was back.

Though they wouldn't talk about it until some days after the procedure, they'd each been thinking of their fathers—of Nate and Arne Weil, felled by strokes at seventy-seven. They'd both lost their mothers, too: Sylvia Weil a decade ago, Nikki's mother Helena some years before. Ben's tumor had brought with it some inevitable reckonings. It seemed important to say out loud what they were both thinking. Nikki was the one to broach it.

"Ben? We're getting to the age when things start to break down, when it all goes to hell physically. You know what I mean? Diseases, stupid accidents, all manner of agita. If you live long enough, it happens to people you love, it happens to you. One day in the shower, there's a lump. One day you piss blood. You can't predict what it'll be or when, but you know something's coming. It's going to happen. We're going to need each other for that, okay?"

This was simple: he took his cousin in his arms, too emotional to put words to his gratitude. What was there to say? He held her for a lingering minute, feeling her breathing accelerate and then subside, a profound calm coming over them both.

"I'm here," he said, and it was enough.

XXXV.

THE BIRTH OF VENUS

NIKKI HAD KEPT HIM WHOLE in other ways. Soon after their initial meeting with the surgeon, for example, she'd called Robin in Boston to tell her about the impending surgery. Ben had given her leave to do so and then promptly forgotten about it. While riding downtown in her car on the morning of the procedure, he was surprised to see an email from his ex pop up on his phone.

> Nikki told me what's going on. I had no idea, Ben. Hope you're feeling good about the surgery. I'll be thinking of you today. I'm sure it will go fine. Be strong. R.

"Robin emailed," he told Nikki, who was navigating irritably through rush hour traffic on Lake Shore Drive. The sun wasn't yet up over the lake. "Nice enough note." In fact he felt quite moved by it. He read it aloud.

"She cares about you, Ben."

"Imagine that. But okay."

He began to write a reply but sent a text instead. *Thx for your email. That was kind of you. How's Boston?*

She'd been there since late summer. Hurwitz's café venture must be well underway by now. Perhaps she'd already auditioned for the cello chair at the BSO; perhaps she'd taken on students. And her life with Alan? It was hard to picture this with any clarity.

Delivered, the phone reported with a whoosh.

Minutes passed with no reply. Ben's text dangled in the ether, abandoned just as she'd abandoned its sender.

As they veered off onto Michigan Avenue, slowing for the first light, Nikki said, "No answer? What exactly did you say to her?"

"I just thanked her. Asked her how Boston was."

"Ben."

"What?"

"Needling. Provoking. Don't fall into that. Hate to say it, but she was right not to answer. The Boston bit was gratuitous, and you know it."

Which was true, of course. How fortunate he was to have Nikki Weil in his life.

ROBIN ISN'T THE ONLY ONE who's broken off communication. He hasn't heard a word from Ana since sending his furious text on the eve of her departure, demanding to know whether she'd stolen the score from his foyer table. Of course she had; there was no other explanation. Her silence proved it beyond the shadow of a doubt.

By now she'll have played her Armistice Day concert and done her gigs up in Belgium and Amsterdam. She must be in Lyon or Marseille. Not once has she reached out to the man who made love to her for four nights running before her departure. Perhaps this is her standard procedure with lovers. Perhaps she's been sleeping her way across Europe, meandering through old sexual byways, making the rounds among the countless musicians and fans who desire her. Weeks and weeks of sex, Ben imagines, sex in ornate hotel rooms and Paris apartments and green rooms minutes before walking on stage. Sex on the move, sex at all hours of day and night, sex in various languages and flavors and weathers. It seems entirely likely. Or perhaps she has other reasons for staying incommunicado, though shame, he's sure, isn't among them.

Ben is startled, then, when on a frigid Saturday afternoon his phone trills and he sees her face fill the screen. He knows the photo: it's cropped from the come-hither shot on the cover of her Chopin CD. His fingers can feel the nest of soft, dark curls, the warm scalp under his fingertips. She wants to start a video call.

Anxiety flares in him. He's been chopping tomatoes for a ratatouille; as he washes his hands he notes that they're shaking. He wills himself to slow down. He does not rush. An ambush is not what he needs. When he reaches for the dish towel, the phone stops trilling and he leans over the sink, head down, angry with himself for letting her get under his skin yet again.

The trilling starts again. Against his better judgment he touches the button to answer the call, leaving the phone on the counter.

"Uh!" she snaps, the static photo of her face swapped for a live, grimacing one. "Are you trying to bloody *blind* me?"

He realizes that the phone is pointed straight at one of the overhead lights.

"Sorry," he says, and takes it up.

She scowls back at him. "Apols for reacting," she says, with no detectable remorse. "It's just not how I imagined our brilliant re-union. A bit too brilliant. But alright. How are you?"

There are beads of sweat on her forehead. She might be calling in from the Amazon. He finds himself tongue-tied, torn between reviving his complaint about the stolen score and keeping his powder dry.

"Ben? Is everything quite alright?"

"Everything's fine."

"Even without me?"

"You've shut me out, Ana."

The plucked brows rise as if this has not occurred to her. "I can't tell you how awful it's been here, *amor*. The bad pianos, the deadly receptions, the *trains*. . . . You can't imagine how unglamorous it all is. It's enough to make a girl drink herself stupid. Why should I bore you with it all? Besides, it's seemed like you might need time to think."

"Why would you say that?"

He hears the sound of splashing and realizes she's in the bath. Hence the flushed face, the sheen of sweat on her forehead, the gold-veined marble tile behind her. When she props the phone against the wall he sees that the tub is scalloped like a giant clam.

She says, "I mean, it's a lot to digest, what happened with us. Thought I'd give you space."

"You never answered my text about stealing the score."

The face on the phone looks away, distracted by something outside the camera's range. He wonders if she has company. Is some lover of hers perched naked on the edge of the tub, just out of view, smirking at the American dupe on the other end of the call?

"I only want what's best for you and the music. You know that."

"That score wasn't intended for you."

"No? You left it right on the table. Forgive me for making reasonable assumptions."

"How could I have left it for you? I didn't know you were coming! You stole it."

She smiles, showing him her long throat. Again a splash from outside the picture. He pictures her toes flicking water at the unseen lover, carrying on a teasing little game with him.

"Think of it as an exchange of precious gifts," she says coolly.

"What's that supposed to mean?"

"I left you my *figa*—you left me your sonata."

"How is that in any way the same? What bullshit! I assume you've kept the music to yourself, at least."

A slender hand comes into view, streaked with suds. She appraises it while he waits. Runs her thumb over the carefully trimmed nail of her middle finger. "Mostly."

"What are you saying?"

"You worry too much. You know I'd never betray your trust."

"Then why 'mostly'?"

The brown eyes flick back to him then flick away, zeroing in on something at the far end of the tub. The unseen lover again, or a shapely foot. Her distraction is infuriating. If they were together he'd take her by the shoulders, make her focus.

"I may have played the odd bit for a few people."

"Which people?"

"No one you'd know. Well, except for Jérôme and his daughter, I suppose. They're touring their four-hand program over here. Stravinsky's piano reduction of the *Rite*—have you heard it? Brilliant. Anyway, we keep turning up at the same hotels. It's daft. I appear out of nowhere and Eulalie says, 'The Animal's stalking us!' I did play a bit of you for them, I'll admit. Couldn't resist. There'd been prosecco. There was an awful piano in the hotel lobby. Can you imagine the look on all those faces, in this shitty little hotel in Amsterdam? The three of us, at the top of our game . . . Jérôme and me, anyway . . . playing our hearts out for free. Urged along by a bit of Dutch courage, you know."

"Jérôme *Assouline*?"

"There can be no other."

A biting little pulse starts up in Ben's right temple. Ana can't possibly know the place that Jérôme Assouline holds in his heart. The idea of her telling the maestro that the sonata is his work is unthinkable—terrifying, in fact. Not the telling, but the shame that would suffocate him later, when the truth comes out. The thought of it nearly stops his heart in his chest.

But Ana hasn't stopped talking. "Had I known we were going to overlap like this, I'd have tried to arrange something with him, you know, a double bill, at least, or a duet—Debussy's *Petite suite*, maybe. He's played it with Argerich. But the main thing is this, Ben: they were gobsmacked by your sonata. By the Allegro especially. Jérôme begged me to lend him the score overnight. He wanted to take it upstairs and *study* it. That's the kind of impression you're making with the work, Ben. You're turning the heads of the greatest pianists in the world. They're dying to get their hands on the thing. What do you think of that?"

"Tell me you didn't give him the score, Ana."

"Are you saying I should have refused Assouline? What's wrong with you?"

"Ana! It wasn't yours to give. You can't pull this shit."

"But he's completely trustworthy! All he cares about is the work—and you, Ben. He's *amazed* by your talent, especially since he never suspected, in all the years he's known you, that you composed. He'll be quiet as a church mouse about it, utterly discreet. It hardly needs saying, though in your case it apparently does. You know what a sterling man Jérôme is." In a confidential tone she adds: "By the way, between us—he's going to make a call and see if he can get me a residency at the Berlin Staatskapelle, with Barenboim. They're mates from who knows how far back. Though of course I'd miss you, love. Anyway, he's keen to raise a glass to you. I promised to arrange it."

"I assume he returned the score to you."

She gives the camera a sour frown. "What do you think? It's called integrity, Ben. But I can tell you, when I came down to breakfast in the morning he had it spread across the table, taking it apart measure by measure. You know he doesn't see well, poor thing . . . Maestro was floored by your piece, love. It's the same for everyone who hears it."

Ben grips the edge of the counter. "Who else?"

"Oh, relax. Bits and bobs of people. A little Chinese girl at the Ritz in Paris. Is she a threat to you, too? And some hideous little *Le Monde* reporter at the Armistice show—couldn't take his eyes off my neck while I was playing, like some kind of vampire. I quite doubt he heard the music. What he wanted was a snog. If he mentions your piece in the paper I'm sure Ant will clip it, but I'd be truly surprised if he did. What he was after wasn't to do with music." A slender foot comes before the camera, clutched apelike in one hand, the painted nails submitted to inspection. "In Antwerp there was a radio host who had me record a few bars of the Adagio to use as the theme for her show. It'll be played every weeknight at eight. Not such bad exposure for an unpublished piece, wouldn't you say? Not that Antwerp counts for anything. I was sure to pitch you during the interview, don't worry. She promised she'd credit you on their website. You see? Nothing sinister at all. It's all good. You should be absolutely chuffed, love. Your first reviews are brilliant."

"Ana! Stop this right now. You do *not* have my permission to play the piece for anyone. Understood?"

She waits for his words to echo back at him.

Then she says, "I won't be spoken to in that manner, Ben."

"I mean it. I'm serious."

"Really? Are you, now. What's so wrong with your sonata enjoying her first little tour of Europe? Let her spread her wings a bit. Once people hear the piece, the name *Ben Weil* will be everywhere. In the press, on marquees. Everywhere! I've been in this business long enough to say that for a certainty. And this girl is doing everything she can to make it happen." Her face moves in closer. "What I don't get, Ben, is how you can be so bloody ungrateful."

"Ana—listen to me carefully."

"I always listen to you carefully."

"Destroy the score. Right now."

For a moment she's taken aback, but then she dissolves into laughter. "You think I haven't learnt every note of it? The paper's nothing. I don't need paper."

Somehow this has not occurred to him. It strikes him like a blow. She's indeed famous for her ability to memorize a piece on first reading. Of course the score doesn't matter. What's in her head is the dangerous thing.

"Then I forbid you to play it for anyone else," he snaps. "Respect my wishes on this. Promise me right now."

She smiles to herself and suddenly the video jerks into violent motion, accompanied by a noisier splashing. It seems that bath time is over. After a wild ride the camera ends up staring at a golden chandelier. The thought flies through Ben's head that she's not in a hotel but in the château of some French aristocrat. What sort of hotel would put a chandelier in the bathroom? Even in Europe this seems farfetched.

As she clatters about, water swilling down the drain, he gropes for something he can threaten her with, some kind of leverage, but there's nothing. She's thousands of miles away. He can't touch her. Can't prevent her from spreading his lie to Jérôme Assouline and who knows how many other luminaries of the music world, which is his world. Can't keep her from injecting it into *Le Monde* and broadcasting his name over the Belgian airwaves. And even if she were in Chicago, would he really attempt to sue her over a sonata that wasn't his? On what grounds? He's powerless to stop her.

"Ana!" he shouts, the commotion at the other end of the call blotting out his words. "Pick up the phone."

With another juddering motion the camera is shifted away from the ceiling and propped against the wall—and there is Ana Clara Matta in all her nakedness, slick with water, head inclined in a suggestion of nebulous tristesse. One hand covers her pubis; the other is poised artfully over her breasts, fingers splayed. The scalloped bathtub has disgorged her like a pearl.

The sight of her body freezes him. The nights of lovemaking come back in a concentrated injection, titrated down to their essence. But as seconds pass and she doesn't move a muscle he realizes that the vision isn't sexual at all. It's as if she's posing for a portrait . . . and then he sees it. The miniature tableau on his phone is Ana's version of Botticelli's Venus, mollusk and all.

"So?" she says with a laugh, dropping her hands. "Have you missed me, Ben? Have you missed *this*? Just try and tell me you haven't. I won't believe it for an instant."

If she didn't disgust him before, she disgusts him now. With a sharp tap he disconnects the call and shoves the phone across the kitchen counter with anger pounding in his veins, wondering how in the world he's let himself be taken in so easily. He wants desperately to be done with her, to cut the cord and be rid of her forever, but with the sonata in her head he can't just walk away. She's in his life whether he wants her there or not.

THERE IS ONE THING he can do. Ben goes to the living room, the house cautiously on guard as he makes his way through it, his anger over Ana and Assouline, in particular, eating away at him. The Bösendorfer holds its tongue as he passes. From the mantle the five Edisons eye him with concern. Nickering in the grate is the fire he built after shopping for the ratatouille. He crouches to lay a birch log on the coals and the papery bark flares up in seconds, stoking the embers back into flame.

Ben lays a hand on the mantle. There, ensconced in its small box next to the Edison cylinders, sits Ana's Brazilian *figa*—her great-grandmother's talisman, the charm Ana says has kept her family safe from the evil eye for generations. Without ceremony he slips the box open to expose the little forearm and clenched fist, carved and filigreed more than a century ago, the marks of time upon it. The totem is obviously well-traveled. It's made the rounds. Seen it all. Like the wax cylinders, it must have a thousand stories to tell. But while the little talisman may have protected Ana Clara Matta's family from evil, nothing can protect it from Ben Weil.

With only a moment's hesitation—a final pause of grace in honor of the *figa*, not its inheritor—he bends to toss it into the flames.

XXXVI.

GOD WILL RECEIVE HER

IN THE DAYS THAT FOLLOW, Ben realizes how completely he's lost control of the sonata. Unleashed by his fleeting lie, it's out in the wild now, crashing through its own perilous adventures, beyond calling back. Propagating, reduplicating, ravenous as a virus awakened after a century's slumber. There's no telling where the winds of music will carry it—and with it the name Benjamin Weil, a name rushing headlong toward a disgrace he can barely imagine.

As he goes about his familiar life—walking the salt-stained streets, plodding through the long days at Counterpoint with their intermittent consolations of music and craft, cooking dinners for his dear cousin and chatting with neighbors when they cross paths—the profound danger of his situation begins to hit home. Everything that gives him joy, everything that anchors and defines him, could be swept away at any moment, yet he can't see how to stop the coming deluge.

He wonders if there's a way to tell Ana the truth. But how? Over a shaky video connection while she's distracted by a hundred other things, not least her star-struck hobnobbing with the likes of Jérôme Assouline? And what would she say to the maestro about Ben Weil, thousands of miles outside his hearing, if he were to make some kind of long-distance confession? Surely not that she'd been had—that despite all her hardnosed savvy she'd allowed him to deceive her. She'd betray him in a heartbeat. She'd make it his fault and his alone.

He can see no way to tell her the truth. Not while she's away, and certainly not while she's within range of people like Assouline. If it's to happen, it will have to happen once she's back in the States, when he can explain himself in person, read her reaction, somehow make peace with her. Even then it will be a high-wire act. He can't imagine her simply forgiving him—not when she's already appointed herself ambassador for the undiscovered, brilliant Benjamin Weil. It isn't only about his reputation now, but hers too. This, it seems to him, is where the real danger lies.

HE TRIES TO IMAGINE how Maestro Assouline would react if the lie were to come to his attention. As the chilly days wear on, it's this thought that pains Ben the most—not because of the man's immense influence in the classical music world, but because of a simple kindness he bestowed upon Ben a decade ago, a gesture of musical compassion he'll never forget.

Assouline had come to Chicago to record his favorite composer, Chopin, on the sidelines of a three-concert series with the CSO. He was in his late sixties then; the imposing head was covered in steely curls, the gifted hands faintly liver-spotted but as powerful as ever. He stepped off the Counterpoint elevator wearing the famous glasses with the thick, round, electric-blue frames, an updated Stravinsky look that had long been his signature.

Ben emerged from his office to find one of the interns, a boyish Loyola music major, hurrying toward him with an ashen face.

"Mr. *Assouline*," he said in a whisper, "here to see you."

Ben laughed and squeezed his arm. "And you!"

Maestro Assouline was a consummate professional, of course. The morning session went without a hitch, both of them in fine spirits, the collaboration effortless, the Chopin exquisite. At noon they broke for lunch in the conference room, where Counterpoint treated the maestro to a spread of local ethnic specialties—lasagna from the oldest restaurant on Taylor Street, Thai beef salad from the Bangkok, borscht and pierogi from Staropolska. The menu was schizophrenic, but it was exactly what he'd asked for; wherever he traveled, Jérôme Assouline made a point of eating the local offerings. Whisked from Marseille as a babe in arms on the eve of the Nazi occupation and then raised in Havana, where his parents waited out the war, he'd been a citizen of the world since before he could speak. For some years now he'd been based in Barcelona.

Over lunch, napkin tucked in his collar, the maestro asked Ben a string of questions about himself, nodding encouragingly as he sampled the odd feast before him. Though they'd met only that morning, and though he was one of the truly great names of classical piano, often mentioned in the same breath as Horowitz, he felt as familiar as a beloved uncle. Eventually, as Ben popped open a container to reveal a lopsided tiramisu, the maestro came round to the subject of the Weil family.

At that moment Ben's mother was in a Skokie hospice, on the downslope toward death, her bones brittle with cancer. Robin was in Latvia, her agent moving heaven and earth to ensure that she'd be within reach of a major airport should she have to get home quickly. Ben had considered rescheduling Assouline, but it was impossible to know when the end would actually come, and the maestro's schedule for the balance of the year was locked in tight. At Robin's urging he'd decided to forge ahead, keeping his phone always at his side.

When his guest asked whether his parents were still living, Ben fingered his phone where it lay on the table and hesitated—but then the sad facts spilled from his lips before he knew what he was saying, the pent-up pain of the last months pouring out. The older man's unassuming manner had lowered his guard. Ben stopped talking only when it became necessary to wipe his eyes and blow his nose. The maestro sat across from him with a look of profound concern, saying nothing, waiting for Ben to break the silence.

"I'm sorry, Maestro," Ben managed after some moments, "you didn't come here for this."

"Not at all, Benjamin. This is life. This is death. This is real. I'm honored you would share it with me."

Ben nodded, at once embarrassed and grateful. He didn't know what to say. He fluttered his hand pointlessly and hid it in his lap, at a loss for words.

"My friend," the maestro said kindly, leaning across the table to squeeze his other hand, "I'll pray for your dear *muter*. I'm praying for her right now. She has a rabbi seeing to her?"

"She's not so Jewish since my father died."

"She was raised how?"

"Catholic. She converted for him. Not that it was well received, especially."

Assouline sat back in his chair and took off the Stravinsky glasses to rub his eyes, then folded them carefully and set them on the table. Ben had never seen the maestro without glasses. The brown eyes were smaller but somehow warmer, too, perhaps because the bright blue frames tended to electrify them. There was something undefended about the man now, Ben thought, and it moved him to see it. He didn't doubt that it was a response to his own moment of vulnerability, a way of leveling the playing field.

With a resigned sigh the maestro said: "So, there was ugliness when this nice Catholic girl ran off with a Jew."

Ben hesitated, then decided he had nothing to hide. The man before him was all heart. At the moment the world-renowned pianist was nowhere to be found.

Ben said, "At first there was ugliness. Yes. For sure. My mother only recently confessed this to me. It was horrible for her, hearing her parents toss off these casual antisemitic remarks and then lecture her on how mixed marriages never worked. But what really threw her was that my father wasn't shocked at all. He grew up a Jew in the forties and fifties, you know, in a Chicago neighborhood that was mainly Poles and Ukrainians. . . . He'd expected worse, actually. He went into that marriage with eyes wide open. I think my mother didn't understand until that moment what it meant to be a Jew in America."

Assouline laced his fingers under his chin. "But you imply that the family got through it. How?"

"The usual way: a grandchild. Me. When my mother told her parents she was pregnant they drove straight to Chicago to plead for forgiveness. They really humbled themselves—in particular to my dad, who was completely caught off guard.

"My mother says at first he didn't believe a word of it. He just dismissed it, you know . . . didn't trust them one bit. But they kept at it until he had no choice but to believe them. He forgave them because their remorse was sincere. He found them honorable because they'd admitted their mistake." Assouline nodded approvingly. "When we'd visit them in Brookline my father and grandfather would go off on their own and talk for hours about who knows what, like they were childhood buddies. I remember that so well.

My grandfather actually got my dad to play *golf*—though always at public courses, because my grandfather had quit his private club over their refusal to admit Jews. Later my parents found out he'd actually sued the club over it. It was a matter of principle for him."

"Or atonement."

"You could be right."

"It's an encouraging story you tell, Ben. There aren't enough of them."

After lunch they went back into the studio to record three more Chopin nocturnes, Eliza joining Ben in the control booth, as Assouline had long been her favorite pianist. "Friends," the maestro said calmly before beginning, "would you be kind enough to dim the lights?" It was an unusual request for him, but Eliza stepped into the studio and at the maestro's bidding dropped the lights lower and lower, until Studio A was as dark as a moonless night.

With Eliza back in her chair Ben cued the maestro and started recording. But when Assouline began to play it wasn't Chopin that flowed from the monitors. Bent over the keyboard, eyes closed, the maestro walked lovingly into Ravel's *Kaddish*, the playing stately yet free, the ancient Jewish prayer for the dead filling the booth with the inevitability of an incoming tide.

It took Ben a moment to realize what was happening. But then he felt something collapse within him, a dam of self-control yielding suddenly, all his careful vigilance washed away by grief. A few miles away, his mother lay dying; here, in the studio where he'd passed many of the most emotional moments of his life, Jérôme Assouline was giving him permission to let her go. The stark, searching melody of the Kaddish wove and swooped through him like a black swallow, deeply familiar but elusive. Halfway through the piece Ben turned the controls over to Eliza and slipped out of the booth, unable to carry on, the rush of emotion too much to bear. In his office it took him fifteen minutes to get control of himself. Assouline's kindness and wisdom were entirely beyond him.

"Benjamin?" the maestro said, rapping softly at the door.

"I don't know what to say."

Assouline raised a palm to quell the thought.

"It will be okay, Ben. God will receive her."

Eight days later, when Sylvia Weil passed quietly away with her son holding one of her hands and her daughter-in-law the other, Ben heard the Kaddish in his heart and remembered the maestro's promise: *God will receive her*. Ben was anything but a believer, but it mattered little. What mattered was Assouline's kindness. There was something inconceivable about it, this intimacy he'd felt with one of the world's greatest musicians, but he didn't doubt that it was genuine. Jérôme Assouline was above all a man. His sort of decency wasn't easy to find.

The thought that Ana might shatter the bond he and Assouline forged that afternoon leaves Ben utterly bereft now. She knows nothing of the Kaddish story, of course; surely the maestro would never repeat it. But she and Jérôme Assouline do have this in common: they believe, without question, that the French sonata is the work of Benjamin Weil. Nothing could terrify Ben more.

SHE'S LEACHING AWAY at his sleep again, but this time for all the wrong reasons. It isn't her soft mouth and skillful hands that keep him up now, but his own racing thoughts. Since the video call he's lain awake every night until three in the morning or worse, adrenaline seeping into his blood on the back of a growing anger toward her. Fatigue is making him erratic: twice now he's slept through the alarm clock, his exhausted body plowing him deep underground, burying him in the sleep he so desperately needs, Counterpoint be damned. Through the endless somnolent afternoons he's had to lean on espressos just to stay awake in the dusky womb of the control booth, the caffeine setting him up for yet more misery after nightfall.

The more Ben's mulled things over, the more he's felt outraged by the sheer arrogance of Ana's behavior. The way she's refused to take his concerns seriously, scoffing at his demand that she stop playing the sonata for others, the brash audacity of her self-regard. The fact that she'd leave the score with Assouline overnight, amplifying the lie immeasurably. The blithe way she provoked him with her nakedness. Late at night, sprawled across his mattress in bitterness with all of Chicago seeming to sleep soundly around him, Ben rehashes his charges against her to the point of collapse, feeling nothing but disgust.

With Robin he could always count on a fundamental decency, an even-handed spirit. She would not knowingly hurt him, or if she had to hurt him would take no pleasure in it. For months, it was true, Hurwitz's poaching made Ben wonder if he'd ever really known his wife at all—but in time he saw that the injury she'd inflicted on him had cost her dearly. Some part of her hated what her selfishness had done to him. He'd noticed it in subtle ways: downcast eyes on the few occasions when they met, tears that were better explained by a sense of guilt than of loss. Even her sporadic bursts of self-righteousness betrayed her true feelings—the way she'd defend the affair with Hurwitz so half-heartedly, damning her new life with such faint praise. Neither of them was persuaded by a word of it. She knew perfectly well what pain she'd unleashed, and she was by no means at peace with it. But that was a different life; that was Robin. If there's any such decency in Ana, Ben's yet to detect it.

Playing jazz is the only thing that seems to cut through the anxiety. Night after night Ben goes to the piano, craving its solace, hoping it will help him unwind enough to sleep. Often he'll start with some phrase from the sonata and then flow into a free improvisation, stretching out, scattering blue notes and color chords in the air, playing off the original with complete freedom. For an hour at a time he can disappear into the music. Nothing is better for his soul.

There are moments when he's so pleased with the results that he has to stop and record the ideas on his phone. The best of them stay with him, resurfacing later, gradually cohering into longer passages, their ambitions growing. It's occurred to Ben that little by little, phrase by phrase, he may be writing an *hommage* of his own, if only as a kind of therapy. Sometimes a searching conversation with the sonata is the only thing that enables him to sleep at all.

XXXVII.

NATHALIE

ONE FRIGID MORNING not long before Christmas, sitting at his sunny desk at Counterpoint, he slices into his favorite apple strudel. It's a peace offering from Eliza, who's shown up late, without explanation or apology, three days in a row. To complement the pastry she's fixed him a French press pot with coffee thick as oil. She herself is a Lapsang-Souchong drinker; though he appreciates the overture, her coffee's execrable. His nose picks up its depravity easily. Even Hurwitz's would appeal to him more.

It's as he's savoring his first bite of strudel that Beethoven drifts into his head. In particular, the maestro's obsessive relationship with coffee—his bizarre insistence on counting out exactly sixty beans for his morning dose, day after day with metronomic precision. Through some elliptical connection this makes Ben think of the unknown composer of the French sonata. Perhaps it's the caffeinated Allegro, who knows. Before he's halfway through his strudel he finds himself lost in a daydream as rich as any memory, pulled irresistibly into the past. Bemused, he lets his mind wander down its own path, curious where it will take him.

He's always pictured the faceless genius sitting at the piano, scrawling notes on a sheet of manuscript paper. Now he imagines the composer's hand lifting a china coffee cup, *Le Figaro* neatly folded beside a breakfast plate. Perhaps there is a meandering conversation with a child, conducted across a tablecloth littered with pots of jam and flakes of croissant. Perhaps a touch of gas or indigestion, too, or a more concerning pang elsewhere. The day's work bearing down as breakfast is finished—are students expected? Is teaching what pays the bills? Perhaps there are money worries, a dwindling bank account, loans that can't be repaid. Sleep-addling bills and chits. Sharp words between husband and wife over some purchase that wouldn't have been extravagant in better times but

266

could break the bank now. Yet there is still breakfast. This newspaper, this cup of tepid coffee. There is still time for this ritual, this illusion of leisure. In the vividness of his daydream, Ben feels he's a guest at the table, the composer an old friend. If he were there he'd offer to help with the money troubles, to free his host to focus on the really important work. There could be no better use for his money. But he is not there. The money worries crowd in and sink their hooks deep.

The composing work may be part of the problem. Perhaps the project waiting on the music stand is a commission from some wealthy patron, worryingly overdue—the deadline long gone, payment withheld, the composer driven to greater heights of inventiveness mostly to justify an abject failure to deliver. Perhaps a grand début is looming in a matter of days, the prospect of a spectacular public embarrassment bearing down. Beethoven, Ben recalls, faced such pressures but redeemed himself through the brilliant work he delivered time after time. Those storied performances of his own creations, made poignant by the steady fade of his ability to hear them, Vienna evenings charged with pathos and originality. . . .

Ben stops chewing, a realization dawning on him.

Who's to say that J. Garnier, like Beethoven, wasn't performing *his own* work? All along he's assumed that Garnier was a virtuoso pianist performing someone else's masterpiece. Why not his own?

Ben swallows his strudel and washes it down with a bolt of Eliza's bad coffee. The picture may be much simpler than he thought. The idea opens within him like a rose.

SHOVING THE PLATE ASIDE he starts an email to Artigue, the acoustician in Paris. It's come to him that Jean's wife is a musicologist at the Sorbonne. He'd mentioned it in passing during their long afternoon together in Studio A.

Jean -

Great meeting you here in Chicago. I hope this finds you well.

I wonder if you'd be willing to help with a little side project I'm doing. I need to establish a provenance for an antique wax cylinder recording of an unidentified piano piece. I'm trying to hunt down the performer, who may also be the composer, but the only name I have is J. Garnier. Garnier would have been active

Ben pauses, forgetting the precise dates of the recording session. Late 1917, he thinks—he's always pictured autumn colors in the trees. He'll confirm it against Willa's letter at home tonight. He continues typing:

around 1917, which would make him (or her) a contemporary of Ravel, Debussy, etc. The name sounds French and the piece is identified as "Fr. sonata," but the recording was made in Boston.

The piece itself is just amazing—Ana Clara Matta agrees. Far ahead of its time, really visionary. So I'd like to identify the composer, and the sonata too. I've searched every source I have and have listened to hours of piano music, but I can't pin it down.

I thought your wife might be familiar with Garnier or have access to resources there that I don't have here. I wouldn't want her to spend time on it unless it interests her. I certainly understand if she's too busy—please, no pressure at all.

Again Ben hesitates, pulling back from the computer and folding his hands in his lap. Something flashes outside his window but it's gone by the time he turns his head to look. A bus waits at the stop across the street, exhaust snapping behind it like a white flag. Through the half-open door of his office come the familiar sounds of morning at Counterpoint: the staff arriving through the frosted glass door, the low-key greetings, the coat closet sliding open, a phone already bleeping at the reception desk. In Studio B Eliza will be setting up for the latest wunderkind, a Korean boy who's already in command of some very arduous Chopin études.

Ben could leave the email as it is or he could push it a step further. For Garnier's sake he adds:

I could send along the score if that would help.

Let me know what's possible, and in the meantime all the best from Chicago.

Ben Weil

He hits Send and eases back in his chair, letting go of a long breath. It's a small step but a good one. If nothing else, perhaps he can do right by the composer, by Garnier, by Willa and the Sanborns and all the rest who've touched the French sonata over the years, who've lent it their love. What he'll do about Ana is another matter entirely.

He's still working on the strudel when Artigue replies.

Ben, my friend, how good to hear from you. I happen to be sitting here with Nathalie when your email comes and she is very excited about your project. Puzzles like this are a passion of hers. She asks that you send the score. Can you send the recording, also?

And you are right, she has access to excellent resources through the Sorbonne. One of the top Debussy scholars in the world is her tennis partner, in fact. She's on the telephone with Geneviève right now.

Let us hear from you soon, *cher ami.* I copy Nathalie here.

J/A

So, here it is: the sonata's next foray into the world, its next adventure. As Ben clicks through folders to locate the recording and scanned transcription, he feels something let go in his chest, a release of trapped energy. It was never right for him to keep the piece to himself. Now, with Ana sowing it all across Europe, it's no longer an option. To put the sonata in Nathalie Artigue's hands is the right thing to do. He writes to her immediately.

Nathalie - Thank you for taking this on. I so appreciate it. Although the audio is problematic, I think you'll see that this is an unusual piece of music. It's certainly a virtuoso performance. I can't wait to hear what you think of it.

I'm no expert, but one idea I'll pass along is that there is a passage in the first movement, starting at about the two-minute mark, that seems to me to quote Lili Boulanger's Trois morceaux. The corresponding Boulanger passage is in the first morceau, D'un vieux jardin, starting at the "p grave et doux" marking ten measures from the end. But I could be completely wrong about this. It's not a direct quotation of the Boulanger. Maybe it's unconscious plagiarism. Maybe the entire sonata is Lili's, quoting from herself. Or maybe it's coincidence. That's why I need someone like you to listen to it.

Again, many, many thanks to you and also to Jean.

Ben Weil

It occurs to him some minutes later, while scrolling through emails before going in for the Korean kid's session, that Ana has spent substantial time in Paris over the years. She was there just a few weeks ago and will likely circle back through for the flight home. It seems unlikely that she knows the Artigues, but the thought gives him pause. She and Nathalie are both specialists in the early twentieth-century French repertoire, after all.

He plays it out nervously. As far as Ana knows, the composer of the piece is the same Ben Weil who's just asked the Artigues to hunt down the actual composer. Now they have a hundred-year-old recording in hand, proof positive that the work is not contemporary. Were they all to cross paths . . . but the idea is ridiculous.

"Come on!" Ben says aloud, thumping his armrest. "That's really over the top."

It is. The idea that Ana would meet up with the Artigues in Paris, then somehow stumble over their mutual interest in Ben Weil's sonata, is absurd. The odds are just too long. Yet it reminds him once again that his world and hers overlap in countless ways.

When he turns back to his strudel it's gone tasteless, and Eliza's bad coffee's cold. With a heavy step Ben walks to the kitchen to brew a proper espresso, Ana dogging him all the way.

THOUGH FEW CASUAL LISTENERS would recognize the name Ben Weil, within his professional tribe he's nearly as well-known as she is. As respected, too, for what he does: only two years ago he won *Gramophone*'s Outstanding Producer of the Year award for the third time, the first in the magazine's hundred-year history to pull off such a trifecta. Virtuosi from Yo Yo Ma to Anne Sofie von Otter have made a point of thanking him in liner notes and interviews. No less a maestro than Itzhak Perlman has called him the George Martin of the classical music world. His work has appeared on twenty-three Grammy-winning recordings. What he's built over his thirty years in the business—each recording another granite block in the edifice of his career—could never be replaced. It sickens him to think how easily Ana could blow it up. A few words whispered to the wrong people, a passing remark in a magazine interview, a public defrocking at some cocktail reception . . . this is all it would take.

It's no secret that Ana's proud to be notorious. It's an image she cultivates, deftly supported by Ant Wooten's whisper campaigns. She is, after all, known on the circuit as The Animal, a moniker that clearly pleases her. And so his confession, whenever it comes— because in the end, he's increasingly convinced, he'll have to tell her the truth—must be handled with extreme care. On this quiet morning, sealed into Studio B, Ben fears it will backfire horribly no matter how he frames it. The only real question is how viciously she'll attack once he's bared his flank. She can be a raging Valkyrie when she wants to be. Just ask the cellist Lörber: when people speak of him now, it's not his musicianship they talk about, but the way Ana savaged him on a Munich stage. In a matter of minutes she could drive Ben Weil from his profession for good.

And not only from his profession. There is his private life to consider, too. He's been on the cover of *Chicago Magazine*, after all. The Farahanis proudly keep a copy of the issue on their coffee table. *That's our neighbor, right next door!* How humiliating it would be to see that magazine discreetly vanish. How could he show his face in the neighborhood if news of his casual deceit, shouted from the rooftops through Ana's megaphone, were to hit the *Trib*? He could no longer meet friends for coffee at Café Selmarie, or queue up for his beloved knackwurst at Meyer's. A shadow of infamy would always lurk behind him.

He'd have no one to blame but himself, of course: he lied to Ana and then let the sex confound him. A handful of nights in her bed was all it took to make him a fool. Nikki's words come stinging back: *Don't be deluded by all the fucking. Fucking makes the brain go soft.*

Yes. This.

XXXVIII.

ATONEMENT

IT WON'T BE LONG before she's back in Chicago. By now the tour will be winding down, the last of the concerts soon to be played. As the days trudge by and the winter light grows weaker, Ana's impending return presses in on Ben like silence from a jury room. To have her running loose in Europe is one thing. To have her showing up at his door is quite another.

In the midst of a long night, as he lies in bed with worries swarming in his head and a blizzard gusting in, he admits to himself that he may not be able to think it through alone. The secrecy's worn him down. Driven him to an impasse. He needs the good counsel of someone who knows him well, who loves him. He needs, perhaps, a confessor.

Robin's the first to come to mind, a reflex born of long habit but out of the question now. Then there's Nikki: since the tumor they've been closer than ever. Yet their very closeness gives him pause. He can't risk losing her. She's a therapist, it's true, trained to hear every sort of confession without judgment, but he's not her client. He's her cousin, as good as a brother. He could never forgive himself for disappointing her.

Then her voice comes into his head: *Don't underestimate me, Ben. Give me a chance here. I can help you with this.*

He knows it's true. In the hopeless muddle of the night he's let his fears chase him down a blind alley. There's no reason to think Nikki wouldn't forgive him if she knew the truth. She knows who he is, knows his character. Knows he's not a liar at heart.

Stumbling through the darkness to the bathroom where his phone sits charging, he taps out an email, afraid he'll wake her if he sends a text. *Nik— need to talk something through. When can I see you?*

With this he falls asleep at last, the house creaking quietly, the cold digging deeper.

WHEN HE GETS UP in the morning her answer is waiting. *You ok? Sounds serious. Slammed all day but drinks after work at Guthrie's? xoxo*

Perfect, he writes back, already feeling some relief.

He meets her just after five, wanting to have their talk before the dinner crowd filters in. She's waiting for him at the bar but he waves her to a booth. After they've ordered whiskeys and a cheese plate she touches his hand and says, "So?"

She makes it much easier than it might have been. As he tells the story of the sonata and the lie she listens thoughtfully, nodding now and then, not a hint of censure about her. Not a hint of the therapist, either; he's expected her to listen at a slight remove, with professional detachment, but the woman before him is kindness itself.

When he comes to the end, capping off the story with Ana's distressing call from the bath, he slumps back in his seat and takes a deep breath.

"So," he says, "now you know what a fool your cousin is."

"Not at all. This took courage, Ben. How can I not admire that?"

"Courage? It's not like I've had the courage to tell Ana. Courage is easy when it's you."

"She's a loose cannon. You can't risk it. I get it, believe me."

The drinks and cheeses arrive. Ben cuts a wedge of Stilton and takes a bracing sip of whiskey, considering her words.

"The thing is," he says, "I owe it to the composer to come clean. Ana's spreading this bullshit of mine all over Europe without even knowing it's bullshit. She's told Jérôme Assouline, played it for him—think how many people *he* knows. How many he's already mentioned it to, not realizing, of course, just in the spirit of helping me, of getting my name out there. Being supportive. I can't let it go on, Nik. It's not just about me. It's about giving credit where credit is due. Otherwise it's just theft. No other word for it."

"The composer's dead. You're not."

"Doesn't matter. I can't live with it."

"Then you'll have to tell her. You'll have to step up. But you've got to be smart about this, Ben. You certainly don't need to go off charging into a hail of bullets. The ethics are important to you, and they should be, but this is not worth ruining your career over. Think how long you've spent building your reputation. Think of the beauty you've helped bring into the world. Guard that. It's precious."

He frowns, wanting to be persuaded but still skeptical.

Nikki says, "Maybe you need someone to say this to you before the guilt clouds your judgment: Don't do anything rash. We'll think it through together. Strategize. Look, the one thing I know is that Ms. Matta can't be trusted to do the right thing. Do you think she'll just forgive you and move on? No way. Even I know that much. Her cruelty is a matter of public record."

He can't disagree with this. They occupy themselves with their drinks and cheeses, the tavern gradually filling up, a slap of cold air hitting them whenever someone opens the door. Gradually Ben begins to relax, having spoken his piece at last.

They call for menus. After the waiter goes Nikki smiles across the table.

"You know what else, Ben Weil? You're more of a Jew than you think."

"Where did that come from?"

"There was this little thing you did, when you were telling your story earlier. I happened to notice . . . professional habit, I guess. Right when you got to the part where you were sitting with her at the piano, when she asked if you were the composer, know what you did?"

"I hesitate to ask."

"This." Nikki sits up straighter and thumps her chest with a fist. "Did you even realize? I thought you'd swallowed wrong, maybe, but that wasn't it. It was atonement, Ben. Like you were in shul on Yom Kippur, confessing your sins. An unconscious gesture, I'm guessing."

"You think?"

"It's interesting, where we turn for consolation. This stuff runs so deep."

Ben thinks of his well-meaning mother, standing in shul every year pounding her chest with surprising violence, as if to drive the thorn of Judaism ever deeper into her Catholic heart. As a boy it frightened him, this annual episode of self-abuse, for that is what it seemed to him then. Only later did he understand her striving. Adopted as an infant by the Monaghans of Brookline, a dutiful daughter of St. Aidan's until she met her beloved Nate in college and converted to marry him, Sylvia Weil did her level best to be a good Jew until nearly the end, when cancer made her ask for a priest. Ben remembers tenderly now her faltering Shabbat Hebrew and clunky seders, her tendency to sprinkle Yiddish into conversation as if she'd grown up immersed in it. She was, in her way, a more committed Jew than he'll ever be. Yet now, at this crossroads in his life, Ben's the one thumping his chest with remorse.

"Hey," Nikki says, "I have a thought question for you, if you want to hear it."

"Fire away."

"What was it that silenced you in that moment at the piano, when she asked if you were the composer? What was it really?"

For all the times he's asked himself this question, he's never broken through to an answer that rings true. The obvious explanation seems deeply inadequate. Shameful, even.

He says, "The only excuse I've come up with is pretty thin."

"Let me guess: you think it was just because you wanted to sleep with her. A kind of musical foreplay. All the elements are there, right? Alone in this dark studio, hip to hip with this sexy woman, hearing her play this fabulous music, then she looks at you and asks this incredibly flattering question . . .what a setup. You keep quiet, you don't say a word, and she fucking *kisses* you. The reward, straight to your limbic system. Soon enough you wind up in her bed. Once that happens it's basically impossible to backtrack. To admit the truth."

"Deluded by all the fucking, to quote a favorite psychologist of mine."

"Except that I doubt it was only that. Give yourself more credit, Ben. As you were telling the story, it seemed to me that it was actually her playing that confounded you. The music—the immediacy of it. The energy. Those few moments of spontaneous performance, the famous Matta sitting right there next to you, channeling the sonata through her body. Literally! Putting all her heart into it on the very first take, the way only an evolved player can."

"She was brilliant, Nik. The way she picked it up off the page, the feeling she had for it right out of the gate, without even hearing the original—you can't imagine. And it's one complex piece of music, let me tell you. To be sitting right there with our thighs touching, actually feeling her work the pedals, the muscles going. . . ."

"You two were already making love through the music."

"I suppose so. Though I wouldn't have believed it at the time."

"Here's what I think. You were literally touching genius at the instant of creation. The composer's genius fused with her genius, transmitted through touch. What could be more erotic? Musical energy is sexual energy, doesn't matter if it's Beethoven or Hendrix. So *of course* you kept quiet. You let her believe what she wanted to believe. You wanted the moment to last forever. Who wouldn't have?"

He'd like to think it's true. For decades he's been fortunate to live in the magnetic field of genius, but until that night he'd never touched genius quite so literally. For a few moments, with his leg pressed against Ana Clara Matta's, he'd felt the electricity of creation as a virtuoso felt it, had merged with her as the music raced thrillingly through her body. He'd felt the sonata sing through her nerves and muscles in real time, the music sweeping them both away. It was exactly what he himself had never been able to achieve in his days as an aspiring pianist, this ability to open oneself fully and unashamedly to passion, to play with naked emotion. At the critical moment her passion had left him tongue-tied, unable to answer a simple question.

Or perhaps he's just looking for reasons to forgive himself. The man sitting at the piano that evening was a lonely soul, God knows, ejected from his long marriage and celibate ever since. His motives may have been far more primitive.

"Even if you're right," he tells Nikki, "it's no excuse. And it doesn't change anything."

"But it's important to know the *why*, Ben. Because this episode is part of your life now and forever. And because it will help you decide what to do next. You're thinking this is all just therapist talk, but I happen to know it's true. Trust me on this. I've worked with liars far more craven than you." She finishes her whiskey with a wry squint. Dinner is making its way toward them. "Like I said, we'll figure it out together. It's so important that you told me."

"I put it off for a long time, you know. Kept it to myself."

"As hermits do."

"So cruel."

"But largely true, since Robin left." She looks past him into the restaurant, distracted. "Speaking of which, she's coming back."

"What?"

"She left Hurwitz. She's done. He fucked up royally out there—used investor money to buy himself a waterfront condo rather than a café space, a fraud right out of the gate. What a loser. Of course they hit him with a fat lawsuit as soon as this little unpleasantness came to their attention. At which point Hurwitz actually took a *swing* at Robin . . . then picked up her hundred thousand dollar cello and held it out the open window of said condo, threatening to drop it if she left him. Held it outside in a *snowstorm*, Ben . . . Boston in December, right? That cello is two hundred years old. Anyway, she told him whatever she had to tell him and got her ass out of there the very next day."

"Where is she now?"

"Staying at a friend's in Cambridge. She's buying a car to drive back here and move into my guest room. She'll be here next weekish."

Ben sits completely still, immobilized by the news, unable to say a word. The thought of having Robin back in town is one thing, but the thought of her moving in with Nikki feels threatening in ways that surprise him. Of course she'd stay with Nikki while she got on her feet; there's no one in Chicago she's closer to. But since his diagnosis Nikki has been as dear to him as any lover, any wife—this he can't bear to see threatened. He's jealous of his ex. Strange to say, but it's true.

"So, she's crashing with you till she finds a place?" he asks as neutrally as he can.

"Not sure how it'll play out, really," Nikki replies, watching over his shoulder as the server approaches. "Maybe longer-term than that. I'd be open to it. We'll see how it goes." She meets his eyes, a hint of defiance in hers. "Would that be a problem for you?"

"Of course not."

"I love you both, you know. And I'm perfectly capable of holding two people I love in my heart simultaneously." She squeezes his hands where they sit clenched on the tabletop. "Robin's still in my life, Ben. It doesn't mean you'll lose me. You never will. And she won't lose me, either."

XXXIX.

GOLD DUST

THEY'RE WAITING FOR CABS just inside the entrance when his phone jangles in his pocket.

Ana, the screen reads.

"Jesus," he says, and shows the phone to Nikki.

"No way."

Ben grits his teeth and touches the Decline button. Now is not the time. There may never be a time. But a few seconds later she's back, this time requesting a video call. Again he shows the phone to Nikki.

"Tell her to fuck off," she says. "Want me to?"

Something makes Ben touch the Accept button, and there she is, angular features lit with stark lamplight against a gray brocade wallpaper. She's tied her curls back tightly, making her face taut and severe. She seems to be in distress.

"Ben, don't hang up," she says curtly. "I need to talk to you right now. Where are you?"

"In a restaurant."

"Alone?"

Nikki ducks back a step.

"Why do you care?"

"Don't be clever with me, Benjamin. This is important."

"I'm listening."

Ana leans closer into the phone, eyes looming. "Rafik Jelassi's dead. I got the call from Tunis yesterday. The cancer. And now I'm fucked. It's cut me dead."

"What are you talking about?"

"My bloody commission! He left nothing, no score, not a trace of any further work on it. He was lying to me when he said it was nearly done. I have one movement, Ben, that's all, and it's shite. And now I've got this show to do in January, this grand début of a thing that doesn't actually exist. We've promoted the hell out of it—people are flying in from all over. Minor Windsors. Tilson Thomas. Amal Clooney, who was a big supporter of Jelassi's. Michelle Obama was supposed to give the man a peace award. Are you tracking, Ben? This was going to be the righteous event of the year. Bigger than the music. And now what? I'm a lamb to the slaughter."

She looks away in despair. For a moment he feels for her. Then the dark eyes pivot back, locking onto his. "But Ben, listen to me— I'm trying to see this as an opportunity. For us both."

Ben turns the phone toward the window to shift himself out of view. In the dim light of the restaurant Nikki's eyes widen.

"Are you there? Come back on," Ana pleads. "Why are you do-ing this to me?"

"I've got to go," he says, off-camera. "Cab's here."

"Oh for fucksake, Ben Weil, look at me."

Still he holds the phone away. She forges on regardless. "Alright, fine if you want to act the child. I'm going to tell you anyway, be-cause it's very exciting and you need to know." She gathers herself. "I'm going to use that show to début *your* work, Ben. Not Jelassi's— yours. And you'll be there as the guest of honor. You'll be my pièce de résistance."

Ben's mind goes blank. Ana's words leave a field of pure red alarm behind them.

The face on the phone talks on, the words coming faster and faster, the exasperation cresting. "Look, Ant's already pitched it to Oprah. He's proposing an audience talkback after the show, you and me together with her, but focusing on your work. Focusing on you. O loves the idea."

Even in his alarm Ben knows this is ridiculous. It's pure fabri-cation. The sort who'd brave a January evening in Chicago to hear classical music are not Oprah's demographic. But Oprah is beside the point. A cab swerves in and Nikki waves it off.

He's a long way from having any coherent words to say. From her distant perch Ana bristles at his silence. "Bloody Oprah, Ben! Do you have any idea what this means for your career? It's gold dust." After a little snort of exasperation she changes tack, softening her tone. "Look, I know it's the music you care about, love. You know I'll do the work justice. Having Matta début you will make your reputation—you know that, too. We'll leave the stage blazing, you and I. We'll kill. I just know it."

Nikki clutches his wrist. The phone weighs in his hand like a grenade. He feels Nikki ease it away, watches her raise it and speak to the caller.

"None of that's going to happen," she tells Ana flatly.

"Who the hell are you?"

"Someone who doesn't care to see my Ben made a fool of."

"*My* Ben? This is strictly between him and me. Put him back on the phone."

"He says no. No to the whole idea. Cease and desist. Stop."

"What is wrong with you people? I'm doing him a brilliant fucking favor here! If he doesn't understand that—"

"You want to use him to save your skin. Make him your discovery. You said so."

"Who the fuck *are* you? Are you sleeping with him? Were you all along?"

Nikki looks at Ben, a flicker of enjoyment in her gaze, a bit of mischief. Without taking her eyes off him she says, "I've known Ben longer than you've been alive, girl."

"Then you should be thrilled I'm going to make him famous. You should be thanking me. Do you realize the platform I have? I don't know who you are, but you're a fool. I can make this happen for him. Or I can walk away. But I'm doing this. If he cares to show up for it, wonderful. I'll put him on the world stage. And ask for nothing in return."

"The answer is no."

"Piss off."

"It's his work. His permission to give. He's not giving it."

"Put him on the phone."

Without an instant's forethought Ben takes the phone and looks Ana straight in the eye.

"Ana? Just *no*."

"Then fuck off, Ben. I'm doing this. With or without you."

With this she disconnects the call, leaving the phone hot in his hand.

IN THE CAB, when he's nearly to his house, the phone rings again, this time with a New York number he doesn't recognize.

"Mr. Weil," comes a cloying British baritone, "Anthony Wooten here. Maestra Matta's manager. I hope I'm catching you at a decent hour. I believe you've just spoken with her."

Ben says nothing. Ant Wooten takes it in stride.

"Mr. Weil, Maestra's asked me to have a chat with you about arrangements for the January show. Program, permissions, so on. Publicity—I'll need a bio and headshot post-haste, tomorrow if you can manage it. We also need to discuss the Oprah interview, schedule some rehearsal time for that. I have the ideal coach, a Miss Gonzalez. She's brilliant at this. A real taskmistress in the event, but you'll thank her when it's all over. And we should give some thought to wardrobe, styling . . . we have logistics to attend to."

Still Ben keeps quiet.

"Mr. Weil, I understand there's been heat between you two, but this is just business. There needn't be any heat between you and me. I'm certain we can work together on this."

Ben says, "She doesn't have my permission to perform the sonata. In any form. Anywhere."

"If it's a question of compensation—"

"It has nothing to do with money."

"Then let's talk about professional reputation, Mr. Weil."

"Whose?"

"Yours, mainly."

"Are you threatening me?"

Wooten demurs. "Both of you have an opportunity to burnish your reputations here, but especially you. You have only to take it up. To premier a Jelassi work would have been a special privilege for Maestra Matta, but it's not to be. Mr. Jelassi could not deliver and now he's dead. Our challenge, and I'm certain you can appreciate this, is that we've already lined up *tout le monde* for that special evening. Chicago royalty, British royalty, Hollywood royalty, musical royalty . . . a brilliant list. Unfortunately we can no longer offer them what they signed up for. So, what to do? If we can't give them the début of a new Jelassi, we must give them something exciting after a different fashion—for example, the chance to be present at the unveiling of a brilliant new American composer, unknown to all save Ms. Matta. Years from now, people will be proud to say they were there when Ana Clara Matta launched Benjamin Weil into the world. Do you understand what a gift has landed in your lap? You could hardly ask for a better audience than this. These are the gatekeepers. The palace guards. Which is why Maestra's offer is so very generous." He adds in a confiding tone: "Candidly, Mr. Weil, the work of an unknown composer would never get such exposure otherwise, whatever its excellence. To have Ana perform your sonata for that audience . . . well, you know perfectly well what it means."

"She's not to do it. We'll sue if necessary."

The instant the words are out of his mouth Ben realizes what a mistake he's made. There is a long pause from Sir Anthony's side of the call. Then comes the chilly reply: "I certainly hope it won't come to that, Mr. Weil, really I do, for your sake. The work is unpublished and unfinished; I think you'll find you have no copyright claim whatever. Ms. Matta could just as easily put her own name to it. But if you were to insist on pressing your case, I can assure you you'd be badly outgunned. We have access to the best legal talent in the business, as you'd expect, and the means to keep them fully employed on our behalf."

Wooten is bluffing on the merits, Ben's almost sure. He knows enough about copyright law to suspect that such a lawsuit would be thrown out regardless of whether the sonata's been published. Though of course it isn't his property in the first place—this Sir Anthony does not know. But the legal nuances don't matter. What matters is that Wooten is surely right about outgunning him in court. They'd drown him in legal bills. In sheer anxiety. It would be a disaster from every angle. But there's nothing to be done in the heat of the moment. He needs to think things through.

As the driver pulls up to his house he tells Wooten, "You have my answer." He disconnects the call without awaiting a reply and climbs from the cab, wavering on his feet for the first time since the surgery, the world wobbling on its axis in the Chicago cold.

XL.

FWD: PEARSON CENTER
FOR THE PERFORMING ARTS

For three endless days Ana and her manager are silent. Not a call, not an email, not even a text. It's hard not to wonder what they're plotting. In the evenings, tinkering restlessly with his jazz variations on the sonata, Ben can't concentrate, the good energy of the music failing him. He's only waiting for the phone to ring.

Not until the fourth day does he have his answer. It comes not from Ana or Wooten but from Robin, of all people.

On Sunday morning, as he sits scrolling through his phone while waiting for the coffee to brew, he comes upon a forwarded email from his ex-wife with the subject line: *Fwd: Pearson Center for the Performing Arts: Important Program Change, Ana Clara Matta 1/11/2019*

Robin's message, above the forwarded text, reads simply: *Ben, WTF??? Is this some OTHER Chicago Ben Weil, or have you been hiding something from me all these years?*

Ben hunkers low over the phone, barely breathing, and skims the announcement.

Dear Robin Weil,

We're writing with an important program update for Ana Clara Matta's piano recital on Friday, January 11, 2019. You're receiving this email because you've subscribed to receive news from the Pearson Center Concert Series.

Due to the untimely passing of renowned Tunisian composer Rafik Jelassi, the program will no longer feature the world premiere of his Kasserine Suite, commissioned by Ana Clara Matta but unfinished at the time of his death. In place of the

Jelassi work, Ms. Matta will perform a solo piano arrangement of excerpts from the composer's award-winning Arab Spring Symphony and then will début exciting new work by Chicago-based composer Benjamin Weil. Mr. Weil's French Sonata will be offered in its entirety in a world premiere, broadcast live on WFMT 98.7.

We look forward to having you join us as we honor the memory of a beloved composer and herald the arrival of a thrilling new voice on the classical music scene!

Yours musically,

Constanza Barrows, Artistic Director
Pearson Center Concert Series

Ben is aghast. Ana's defied him outright—did she and Wooten think word wouldn't reach him, and quickly? Now his name's been spread far and wide, to the outermost reaches of the Pearson Center mailing list. He can't imagine how many thousand classical music aficionados received the announcement. How many have already Googled *Benjamin Weil* and found his bio on the Counterpoint website, which mentions nothing of his supposed work as a composer yet proves his embeddedness in the classical music world? Questions will be raised; questions have already been raised, without a doubt. He's furious and terrified in equal measure.

The coffee is ready and he needs it badly. Standing at the sink with mug in hand he looks absently over at the Farahanis' kitchen window, lined up perfectly with his own. Eva is standing at her sink too, lost in thought as she works away at something. Ben watches her emptily, needing someone to confide in but knowing she's not the one. A sympathetic listener she'd no doubt be, but how could he possibly explain what's happened? It's Nikki he needs to talk to.

Snatching up the phone he begins to forward the Pearson Center email to her, but rereads Robin's message first: *Ben, WTF???* He'll need to tell Robin something. To explain himself somehow. He owes it to her. It's her world, too, after all, and she shares his last name. Questions will come flying at her. It's his duty to arm her in advance. But where to begin?

When he looks back at the Farahanis' window Eva is smiling his way, tipping a platter of cookies toward him invitingly. He recognizes them: they're the Scandinavian ginger cookies she serves at the lively Swedish-Persian solstice celebration she and Behrouz host every year. Ben has the fondest memories of these convivial evenings—ginger cookies and glögg from the Minnesota Swedish side of the marriage, pomegranates and nuts and boisterous readings of Farsi poetry from the other, each poem followed by Behrouz's impassioned, baffling translation. With a pang Ben realizes he's completely ignored this year's invitation. His constant distraction has made him an unreliable friend.

With hand over heart he mouths the words *Can't wait!* to Eva, envying her family rituals, her steady world of cookies and ancestral traditions and settled marriage. Ben would give anything to inhabit her world for a week or two, to forget the sonata and Garnier and Ana Clara Matta and the Pearson Center mailing list and drop into the loving little world next door with its basil pots and home cooking, its soccer games and debate tournaments . . . the straightforward, companionable family life he'll never have.

Instead he's to be disgraced before his own tribe. Held up for ridicule before all those who matter to him—most of whom will feel it their duty to abandon him. There can be no question of attending the concert, of course, assuming he fails to stop it, but his downfall will surely come soon after. The ruse will be exposed in no time.

And who will be to blame but Ben Weil? Like a panther, Ana Clara Matta is only doing what nature commands. Her ferocity should have sent him fleeing the moment she pressed her thigh against his.

After forwarding Robin's email to Nikki without comment—she'll understand its significance just as quickly as he did—he writes the briefest of replies to Robin.

Long story. Are you back in town? We should talk.

When he refreshes his inbox it's flooded with messages, all with the same subject line: *Fwd: Pearson Center for the Performing Arts: Important Program Change, Ana Clara Matta 1/11/2019.* The senders range far and wide across his professional network, from Peter Roth to Riccardo Muti, every one of them demanding to know the same thing: *Is this you, Ben? How could you have kept this under wraps all this time?*

Buried somewhere in the avalanche is the most alarming message of all, this one from Jérôme Assouline.

Mazel tov, Ben, this is wonderful news! I can hardly wait to hear Ana play your beautiful piece again. As she may have told you, she gave Eulalie and me a lovely private recital a few weeks ago in Amsterdam, the whole sonata from start to finish. It's truly inspired, my friend. The effects you achieve, the jazz elements, that unhurried Satie/Ravel delicacy in certain passages, then that muscular Allegro. . . . It's all so very good, Ben. And what a surprise, needless to say. In all the years I've known you, you never once hinted that you were composing on the side. You're a man of many talents. And many secrets! I hope there's much, much more where this piece came from. You have a gift, and it's obvious you've put in the work.

You know, as I was listening to your sonata I kept thinking about orchestration. Have you considered orchestrating it? If it's not something you feel able to take on, I could put you on to people who'd jump at the chance. I'd be happy to consider an orchestral version, Ben, for the Orquesta Sinfónica in Madrid, who for some wrongheaded reason have made me artistic director. We're just putting together our 2021 season and I could hold a slot for you if you think you might have something ready in time. Of course we'd need to hear the end product before committing, but I'm confident that the right collaborator could help your wonderful sonata find an even wider audience.

Let's talk about it over a nice dinner. I'm going to try to make it there for your January debut. Ana's begged me to come, and there are friends there I'd like to see. You know how I miss Chicago, even in January, and you know just how persuasive the Animal can be.

With a sweep of his arm Ben sends the phone flying. The day's barely begun and already the earth has given way under him. His stomach in freefall, he bolts from the kitchen and runs to the bathroom where he gets to his knees and vomits his shame into the toilet, certain beyond the shadow of a doubt that the real misery has only begun.

Roxbury

November 1919

XLI.

ALL FOR SYLVIE

ELISABETH SEES what she sees, the image as sharp as a thorn on a rose cane. And what mother could ignore such a thing, once having seen it?

The blood crashes to a halt in her veins then breaks loose in a torrent, propelling her across the workshop floor like some new invention of Mr. Bell's, her limbs awkward as a sideshow automaton's. For some seconds she's a stranger to her body. She's carried off by a force beyond her control. Thinking, thinking as her feet move her away, her brain hot with logic, her heart hot with love. . . .

She shouldn't be surprised at this latest development. Signs of trouble abound. All one need do is count the empty stools at the workbenches, each occupied not so long ago by a Macauley or Ricci or Kowalczyk, all of them dead now or dying, sent back to the tenements to infect their kin and neighbors. Pride keeps them from the new sanitorium over in Mattapan, which is packed with the truly destitute; home is where Bell men and women go to die their fevered deaths, coughing up blood day and night until the coughing falls silent forever. Elisabeth can hardly imagine the racket and misery in the packed West End flats, the suffering. It's no wonder they die in droves. For the working man there is no escape.

Yet still Cyril Jones refuses to let in fresh air. Perhaps he's right to worry that briny summer breezes might corrode the delicate workings of the half-assembled Graphophones, but now the bay is jigsawed with ice, the harbor stink smothered by cold. Even a little fresh air could help dispel the trouble that lurks in the workers' lungs. But the foreman won't have it. He is strict on the matter. And so the high chicken-wired windows stay shut, an ashen winter light bleeding through the Boston grime. The assemblers hunch over their work in close, overheated air, dim Edison lamps buzzing above, the smells of cigarette smoke and unwashed clothes and pungent cooking assaulting Elisabeth when she alights at the top of the iron stairs. At eight forty-five each morning, punctual as a train conductor, fat Sean O'Malley hurries to the spartan lavatory to do his explosive matutinal business, adding to the general stench. The offense lingers for hours. Lately the building smells as rancid as a rotting chop. Elisabeth dreads the moment of arrival, the bile playing in her throat. But what she dreads most is being the next to go home coughing, the next to leave and never come back.

The consumption germ may be invisible but its effect is plain to see. It's become a reflex, the way her gaze sweeps over the workbenches looking for another station left suddenly empty, another soul snatched away. Hardly a week passes without another worker lost. She can't understand how she herself has somehow dodged it. On days when she feels especially tired or has a touch of winter cough she fears it's come for her at last. The onslaught is so frightening and heartbreaking—far too reminiscent of mornings at Aigremont when she'd walk through the wards and find a familiar face abruptly gone, stolen by death sometime in the night. First the German war, then influenza and typhoid; now this. When will the chain of misery end? It's gotten very hard to believe in goodness at all.

THIS MORNING IT'S AUGUST SPEYER who worries Elisabeth, though panic would be the better word. As she makes her way toward the sales office, anxious to get past the workbenches, Augie is seized by a cough that crumples his chest and shoves his broad shoulders forward, a cough so violent that the man has to grip the workbench to keep from falling off his stool. As Elisabeth watches from the corner of her eye he swivels away and spits up hugely into a handkerchief. Augie does his best to hide his distress but there is no one who isn't watching, listening, waiting, vigilance being second nature now. When the cough subsides Augie swivels back and peers down into his handkerchief. The alarm in his bloodshot eyes tells Elisabeth everything she needs to know. The scarlet blot only confirms what is already as plain as a newspaper headline. She's done enough nursing to know exactly what she's seeing—there is no doubt that Augie Speyer is infectious, and a fair chance he's dying.

Elisabeth flies into the sales office and locks the door. She paces back and forth with coat still buttoned, trying to think what to do, more frantic with every pass. Augie Speyer isn't just another sick Bell man. His case strikes at the heart of her life.

When she hugs herself she can feel little Sylvie in her arms. The wriggle, the dogged little yawns after she's suckled her fill; the featherweight, fragile being of her baby girl. A fluttering little bird of a child, her *poulette*. Her treasure.

By the grace of God she looks nothing like her father. The resemblance is to her grandmother—her namesake—and to Elisabeth, yes, in the forehead and brow line, the proportion of waist to leg, of mouth to cheek. Even at four months she has her mother's smile, the one that only Sylvie, in all the world, is permitted to see. There was a time when Elisabeth still smiled for others, a time when other sorts of love still made sense, but when she smiles now it's for Sylvie and Sylvie alone.

The trouble in Augie Speyer's lungs cannot be allowed to pass to her little girl. This is all she knows. She needs to get home as quickly as possible. Flinging the door open she strides to the manager's office and raps at the glass window, preparing to make her excuses.

Tom Shea spins around in his chair and starts to launch himself from it, furious at the interruption and ready to deliver one of his filthy Irish tongue-lashings—but then sinks down again, deflated, when he sees it's Elisabeth.

"C'mere to me," he says wearily, waving her in. The stink of last night's liquor, or perhaps it's this morning's, sloshes toward her.

Elisabeth stays put, hands sunk in her coat pockets. "I've got to go back home."

"What's your trouble?"

"It's about Sylvie. I'll come back once it's settled."

Tom smiles tartly. "You'll need to say more, love. You know I can't let you go on just that wee bit. Not on a Friday—it doesn't take a Harvard man to know when a girl's looking to get a leg up on the weekend. Don't take me for a fool, Liz."

He infuriates her in this manner regularly. If it were still Jack Rimes in the manager's chair she'd never be treated so rudely. Jack

295

would never question a mother's judgment. Jack would show real human feeling. But Jack's gone, his throat slit by a fleeing German soldier at Amiens, a sorry death for a good man. It's Tom Shea who's taken his place, outrageously, Mr. Bell too removed from the operation to recall anything but Tom's bald flattery and a ridiculous jingle he'd once sung out to the old man: *All's well in the Land of Bell, sir!* Elisabeth could do a far better job in the position, as Tom himself's admitted, but the idea seems never to have entered the old man's mind. So it is that she finds herself begging a knock-toothed, snag-haired, whiskey-besotted young Irishman to let her go so that she can save her child's life. Just now he smells like a tramp snoring on a bench. If Mr. Bell were to walk in unannounced, she has no doubt that the fool would be out on the street in an instant.

"Just give a fella something to bank on here, Liz. A hint is all."

"I don't care to say more."

Shea gives her a brazen going-over. Up and down his eyes go, tiny mice scurrying over her. "Come on, now, Liz," he says, "drop the awful puss and tell your Tommy the truth."

This is too much. Elisabeth spins on her heel and leaves the place, storming down the rusty stairs and out onto the snowy, clamoring street, making for the streetcar stop as fast as her feet will carry her. Tom can say what he likes. They can't do without her, with the ranks hollowed out by tuberculosis and Victor's round records mounting an all-out assault on the cylinder. Elisabeth Garner's skill at selling the Imperial Graphophone and the new Emerald Dictaphone to Boston's wealthy set is a good part of what's keeping her branch of the Company afloat. Tom may be warming Jack Rimes' chair for the time being, but she's the one in the driver's seat.

The streetcar can't go fast enough. As it rattles along toward Roxbury she tries to rein in her disorganized thoughts, to devise a plan, to find the words she'll need to say to Augie Speyer's wife. The sudden loss of income, Augie's and Greta's at a blow, may sink the Speyers, but there's nothing she can do about it. Her daughter comes first. There is more than enough misery to go around. She's in no position to take on charity cases.

As the conductor clangs for her stop a terrible image comes to her. Greta Speyer is sitting at the kitchen table, striped blouse open to give little Sylvie her enormous, mole-freckled breast. The tiny lips tug at the swollen nipple; the sweet blue eyes are glazed over with the warm sorcery of it. But then with a terrific cough Greta spits blood across the tabletop, a gross eruption of sickness that spatters over Sylvie's mottled head as it rockets past, a red rain of disease and death. In the trolley car Elisabeth's head jerks back as if the woman's blood is coming straight for her.

The pretty young woman in the hand-me-down mohair coat draws looks from all around. She clutches the pole tightly to bolster her resolve, then steps down into the street the instant the trolley stops. If the pavers weren't so slick and her heels not so in need of mending, she'd sprint the two blocks home to her daughter.

Elisabeth feels a window closing: she on the one side, little Sylvie on the other. By the time she lets herself into the apartment the window is nearly shut, her daughter out of reach forever. But she's arrived just in time.

HER EYES FIND SYLVIE instantly.

Her daughter lies bundled in her rose blanket on the old sagging sofa, alone. A kitchen chair has been shoved up against the cushion to keep her from falling to the floor—a shaky scheme that any fool could see is pure trouble. Thankfully Sylvie is sleeping, still as a stone. For the moment she's not in danger, but with an instant's restlessness she might knock the chair back and plunge to the floor. Greta Speyer is nowhere to be found.

In a fury Elisabeth runs to the sofa and throws the chair aside and takes her daughter in her snow-dusted arms, rousing her from sleep into a piercing cry. Elisabeth dips her gently and smiles, nose to nose, and in an instant her good-natured girl is burbling with laughter. "*Ma princesse*," Elisabeth whispers to her, her embrace perhaps a little too tight, "*ma tendre*." Everything in Elisabeth eases, everything melts: this is all she's wanted, and all her daughter's wanted, too. For some moments the two of them sway together in the quiet room, the confusing world falling away around them, the winter morning simplified.

But there is Mrs. Speyer to be dealt with. And here she is: with a look of panic the stout woman wavers at the door into the kitchen, knowing she's been caught out.

"Miss Garner, I just. . . ." she says in her heavy German accent, groping for the English expression, ". . . answer the calling of nature."

This is a lie. Elisabeth can see it in her eyes. Looking past the rounded shoulders she spots wet footprints on the kitchen floor. She storms past the woman to the back door and flings it open on the falling snow, the spindrift on the rear stairs quite plainly disheveled by heavy footsteps. There, smoldering in its own little pool of snowmelt, Elisabeth discovers the stub of a cheap cigarette, proof positive of Greta Speyer's dishonesty.

It's just the excuse she needs. She needn't bring up the husband's bloody cough at all. Slamming the door shut and latching it behind her she confronts the woman.

"You leave my daughter on the sofa, from which she can easily *fall*, so you can smoke on the stairs? Is this how you conduct yourself, Mrs. Speyer? How you've raised your own children? Do I pay you to *smoke*?"

Greta Speyer is almost a head taller than Elisabeth and twice her weight, but under her employer's righteous attack she withers like a child, heavy cheeks flushing.

"This is not how it looks like, Fräulein! You come at the wrong moment."

"No, Mrs. Speyer. I came at exactly the right moment."

The woman creeps toward Elisabeth in supplication but Elisabeth steps away, mindful of the infectious Augie. There is no telling what contagion she's brought into the flat. "Miss," Greta pleads, "this never again happens! This I promise."

Another lie. Even little Sylvie can smell it this time. Elisabeth feels the bundle in her arms fidget and gather itself for a piercing scream. Greta Speyer cringes at the cry, guilt written on her red face. For a passing moment Elisabeth again feels sorry for her and Augie, whose situation will turn dire when Augie's sent home ill and Greta loses the little bit she earns from nursing Sylvie—but what she's done is unforgiveable, with or without the cloud of illness hanging over her. Elisabeth only hopes it's not too late. The cough gathering deep in her own chest, she's sure, is a product of her rattled imagination. Reaching into her coat pocket she finds two bits, a day's wage, and tosses the coin onto the table between them.

"Mrs. Speyer, I'm sorry, but this is the end of our arrangement. I believe this compensates you for the morning. I thank you for your help." As Greta Speyer lugs herself downstairs in a maelstrom of hot German, Elisabeth lays Sylvie in her bassinet and moves through the apartment opening every window, snow wafting in to scrub the Speyers' dangerous germs from the air. Boston cold is preferable to consumption. She pauses by a window just to drink it in. But the freezing air, in an ironical turn, throws her into a fit of coughing, her lungs complaining sharply. It's only the world's perverse sense of humor; she's seen it before. She'd laugh but there's nothing funny about the moment.

Afterward Elisabeth goes to her dozing daughter and bends to listen to her tiny lungs, the little puffs of air slipping in and out as soft and small as sparrows' breaths, not a trace of the Speyer trouble to be heard in them. *Mon Dieu, je t'en supplie,* Elisabeth whispers in silent prayer, *protège ma fille.* . . . She hasn't believed in anything like a god since her father was lost to a U-boat, but at times like this a little prayer can comfort her. It certainly does no harm. With Sylvie down for her nap she lies down herself, suddenly bone-tired, the confrontation with Greta Speyer finding its way into her joints. In a few moments she's out, the day barely on its feet, the flat filling with the sounds of Sylvie's sleep and hers too.

XLII.

THROUGH THE GOOD OFFICES OF
A WILD BEAST

SYLVIE IS WHY SHE'S STILL HERE—not only at Bell, earning her pittance to keep the wolf from the door, but on this cold earth, pinned like a captive moth to a place she no longer loves. Her mother gone, her papa gone, the father of her child a liar . . . on her worst mornings Elisabeth has sometimes felt it would be easier to throw herself under a streetcar than ride it back to Bell. But it's not just her life to be considered now. Sylvie needs her. There's nothing she wouldn't do for her daughter. Weighed against her little girl's innocence, her own fits of sadness are of no account. And so she's soldiered on, dutifully seeing to her daughter's needs and letting motherhood soften her heart whenever it turns hard.

She hasn't always cared much for Sylvie—an angular, indigestible fact she can't make sense of, a shameful truth of which she can never speak. For weeks after her daughter came into the world Elisabeth felt only nagging irritation at the squalling little creature's constant demands. Nothing, certainly, that could be called love. In the face of her own indifference she wondered if she was losing her reason. What was happening to her? What had she become?

Certainly the moment of Sylvie's arrival, on a hot summer midnight under the glare of the flat's electric lights, had brought no joy at all. The labor had ground on for twenty-one hours, the heat stifling even after sunset, the unsmiling Portuguese midwife, Mrs. Ferreira, eating plates of cod at her bedside though the smell of it sickened the mother-to-be. By the time Elisabeth started pushing she'd begun to wonder whether the ordeal would ever end. Though the birth itself should have been a wonderful moment, her daughter's first squeal a marvel, what Elisabeth actually felt was defeat, the army mule's collapse at the end of a long march. Her newborn child, toweled clean and swaddled and presented to her like a pink Christmas ham, did not move her at all. Mrs. Ferreira had to prod her to take the bundle in her arms. The sad, alarming truth was that Elisabeth couldn't find it in her heart to welcome into the world the life that she and Charlie Westerlake had created.

She soon realized that she neither loved nor hated the child, a horrible, unforgiveable failure. Her neutrality was a disgrace. What was wrong with her? This was not the Elisabeth she knew, the warm and intelligent girl raised by Jacques and Sylvie Garnier to be kind to all creatures, to be a loving friend and companion. Had they been alive, of course, things would have been far different. She could so easily imagine her mother's glowing happiness at meeting her granddaughter for the first time, her father's beaming pride as he walked little Sylvie around the apartment after a feeding, a cloth folded on his shoulder such as a violinist might have. . . he'd have adored her. As she grew into a girl and eventually a young woman he'd have been the best sort of grandfather. But Elisabeth was on her own now, with no one but the crude Mrs. Ferreira to witness Sylvie's arrival. Even in her exhaustion she knew something was deeply wrong.

Nor did the situation improve in the days that followed. Feedings, changings, the milky blue eyes that tried to bring their mother's face into focus—all of it weighed on Elisabeth like a death sentence. She was tired, so tired. She barely ate; her clothes hung off her like a man's. Had her kindly downstairs neighbor, Ella Montgomery, not taken it upon herself to launder the bloody towels from the birth, she'd have simply thrown them out, such basic chores beyond her. She could barely see to her own needs, much less a child's. Her broken sleep brought no relief. When she awoke to another hungry squall, the tiny being who'd come into her life was still a complete stranger to her. Worse than a stranger, in fact, because Elisabeth, through some compact to which she'd never subscribed, was its sole support.

What kind of woman, she wondered, would turn such a stony heart toward her own daughter? And yet this is exactly what she did, hour after hour, unable to find in herself the slightest love for the girl. She had no right to be a mother, none at all.

Elisabeth wondered if it was all because of her fury toward Charlie Westerlake, which hadn't dimmed in the year since their final evening together—the evening when both she and the Germans surrendered. But little Sylvie, the innocent product of those hours in the Sanborn boathouse, had played no part in the Captain's betrayal. When it came to assigning blame, Elisabeth would be next in line after Westerlake himself. She'd been the naïve one. No wonder she was alone, left to deal with the devouring needs of a being she'd never invited into her life.

THEN, THROUGH THE GOOD OFFICES OF A WILD BEAST, the fog lifted. One late September morning there was a rap at the door: her neighbor Ella in housecoat and hairnet, freckled American face turned up inquiringly. Ella was never without a smile. Elisabeth answered the door with Sylvie squirming in her arms, her daughter overdue for a changing.

"How's the little princess?" Ella asked, tweaking Sylvie's nose. "And how's Mama?"

"Well, you know," was all Elisabeth could manage, her weary smile fleeting but honest.

"Women's work is so much harder than men's. Though there isn't a man alive who'd admit it."

Elisabeth saw that Ella had brought a gift. Perched on the landing sat a dented stroller, undoubtedly used by all her four children.

"I thought this might come in handy," Ella said, "if you haven't got one already. Keep it for as long as you like. I've told Frank I'm good and done with the tender arts, if you know what I mean. Four's enough!" With a sly smile her neighbor rolled the stroller forward for inspection. "It's an old jalopy but it's in perfect working order."

For the hundredth time Elisabeth went cold with shame over her failures as a mother, so starkly exposed in the presence of this mother of four. She should have bought a stroller long ago, of course, but in her malaise she'd never managed to. As it was, she'd barely taken Sylvie out of the apartment, and always bundled in her arms. The humble stroller in the dimly lit hallway felt like an accusation.

Ella Montgomery seemed to sense what was going through her mind. In a sisterly tone she said, "It's alright, hon—to feel at sea, I mean. I can tell you in all honesty, as God is my witness, that after the twins came I could hardly get myself out of bed. And you being a single gal, forced to work for a living . . . I can only imagine. At least I had Frank."

A silence opened in the hallway. Elisabeth couldn't sort her embarrassment from her gratitude. Ella squeezed her arm lightly. "You'll get in the swing of this soon enough, I promise. Don't be blue." With a slippered foot she nudged the stroller. "Shall we try it on for size?"

Not an hour later, the three of them—Ella and Elisabeth, with Sylvie tucked into her new stroller between them—were standing in a pool of sunlight before the zebra pen at the Franklin Park Zoo. Ella had bought a candy apple from a cart near the great apes, its scent mingling oddly with the musk from the zebras. Sylvie squealed with delight as one of the big animals wandered over to greet them, huge jaws working at a wad of hay. Nearby stood a miniature version of the animal, watching the other's progress with wide black eyes.

"Funny horse!" Elisabeth teased her little girl diffidently, stooping down to point out the striped neck and bristly mane, stiff as a hat brush.

"What a pretty little one you have, Mama," Ella said to the zebra, nodding toward the smaller animal watching intently from behind.

In reply the zebra tossed its head and spat out its chaw and made a queer barking sound. Sylvie squealed again. The smaller animal meanwhile made its way toward them at a trot, as if to meet its mother's new friend. Again the zebra barked, and again Sylvie squealed. The big animal rubbed its flank against the fence, drawing closer, making a chuffing noise to which its little human friend replied with a gurgling cackle. The two of them, girl and zebra, seemed to be engaged in amiable conversation. Ella began to laugh, and all at once Elisabeth found herself laughing too, a laugh that came straight from the heart, Sylvie's joy irresistible, the round pink cheeks and the animal's striped neck lovely in the autumnal sunlight, the moment so simple and yet so complete.

This she'd not felt before. Later she tried to put a word to the sensation. What came to mind, unexpectedly, was the word *liberté*. To take pleasure in her daughter's pleasure—this was a kind of freedom. It would take days for Elisabeth to make sense of it, but the simple fact was that in a glade of morning sunlight, with Ella and a grand African beast looking on, she'd at last broken through her despair. From that day forward, as the mercury dropped by slow degrees and the leaves along the path turned to scarlet and gold, she and Sylvie spent every Saturday at the zoo, content in each other's company, Elisabeth's heart unfolding into adoration as it should have long ago.

By the time she witnessed Augie Speyer coughing blood into his handkerchief she was fiercely in love with her child. She couldn't imagine ever speaking to anyone of what had happened in Sylvie's first weeks, of her own heedless indifference. It made no more sense to her than had the insanity of the war. Thankfully no one was calling her to account—though Ella Montgomery, just downstairs, seemed to understand perfectly well what she'd been through.

Now that Greta Speyer's been sent packing she'll have to find another wet nurse, and quickly. She has only the weekend to arrange something. But perhaps it's time to consider a more American solution.

The idea has actually been in her mind for some time. When Mrs. Speyer began coming to the flat, it was Ella who'd pointed out with gentle amusement that a *modern mother* ought to feed her baby in a *modern way*. To have a wet nurse come in was so old-fashioned, though she'd grant that perhaps France was different. The bottle was how mothers did it here in America. Elisabeth had brushed the comment off; in the France of her youth such an idea was un-heard of. Much as she disliked the idea, it was her duty to nurse Sylvie herself, and to bring in another woman to help out when she couldn't. There was no substitute for the breast. Besides, it was easi-er to give a nipple than to wrangle bottles and evaporated milk and whatever else would be required. Elisabeth didn't have the patience for it. And so when the time came to go back to work she'd engaged a nurse, the stout wife of a coworker, just as any good Honfleur bourgeoise would have done. It wasn't only the nursing, after all. She needed someone to watch over her little girl while she went to work. No bottle could do that.

Now, though, with Greta Speyer gone, perhaps the bottle is the sensible thing. There must be any number of women who could watch over little Sylvie and manage a few feedings while she's calling on customers. The question is, how does a mother know whom to trust? At least Greta was no stranger, or Augie anyway.

As she sits nursing Sylvie, dry snow sifting across the kitchen window, Elisabeth draws a blank. She'd certainly not risk another woman from the tenements. Nor would she trust anyone who'd advertise her services in the newspaper. The fact is, she knows so few people, between keeping to her parents when they were alive and then losing herself in Aigremont and the Company later. In the end there is really only one candidate. After burping Sylvie and working up her courage she swaddles her drowsy daughter in a blanket and makes her way downstairs to knock at Ella Montgomery's door.

She has barely a chance to say the words she's rehearsed. Her neighbor makes it effortless. "Oh, I'd be delighted!" Ella exclaims with an endearing smile, laying a palm against the dozy Sylvie's cheek. "I miss having a little one around, though don't tell Frank. There's such a sweetness to them, especially this one. We'll be great pals, won't we, Sylvie?" When Elisabeth mentions payment she won't hear of it. It's the only time she's seen the woman frown.

With no further ado Ella ushers Elisabeth into her impeccable kitchen and wrangles baby bottles and tins of Horlock's from the curtained shelves, setting them out on the table for the young mother's approval. But what does Elisabeth know? She trusts Ella to do a better job of it than she ever could. After pressing a dollar on her friend for supplies she carries her little girl back upstairs with a feeling of immense relief. She should have done this long ago, before ever bringing on Greta Speyer and whatever sickness she carried into the flat. But the important thing is that she's done it now.

XLIII.

FROM YOUR LIPS TO GOD'S EARS

OVER THE WEEKEND, as a fickle snow paints the windows and the radiator hisses and clanks, Elisabeth realizes that she must make a deeper change in her life. The blot of red blood in Augie Speyer's handkerchief haunts her. How close she's come to putting herself in grave danger, and thus endangering Sylvie. To bring the sickness home to her daughter—to leave her motherless, even, if she herself were to fall sick—is unthinkable. She can't go on tempting fate. She's stayed at Bell, risking everything, only because it sometimes seems that half the city has been turned out onto the street. But lately the papers say that jobs are coming back. Somewhere there must be a safer berth for a woman of her talents. She must find a better situation.

Yet there's something beyond tuberculosis on her mind. The Bell Company has enabled her to keep body and soul together, and thank goodness for it, but was she really meant to sell novelties to the rich? Even before the war, the excitement of calling on Boston's grand houses had worn thin. After the horrors of Aigremont it seemed idiotic. And now the business itself is slipping away, Victor's and Edison's disc records crowding out wax cylinders and Bell's machines right along with them. She can see which way the wind is blowing. Soon enough she'll be reduced to selling Dictaphones to stenographers.

But what to do? Perhaps, she considers, something more suited to her training. She didn't earn a degree in social work, after all, only to squander it as a hawker of expensive gewgaws—a temporary position she'd never have taken seriously had she not proved so good at it, and had her papa not died and left her in dire need of money. But to be a social worker would mean going into the tenements. She can't risk it.

As she's putting Sylvie down for her nap an idea strikes her, or rather a name: Mrs. Porter Dunleavy. "Well! What would you say to that, *ma douce*?" she asks her baby girl, intrigued. After humming Sylvie to sleep she makes herself a methodical cup of tea and sits down to think through the possibilities, a small window opening in her heart.

Mrs. Dunleavy—the former Violet Madigan—is the mousy young wife of Mr. Porter Dunleavy, a Boston stock broker who made his name by briefly cornering the market in bridge rivets. Elisabeth had read about his exploits in the *Globe* one Sunday morning in early summer, her belly huge and uncomfortable with Sylvie. Immediately she'd had the idea of angling for an invitation to the Dunleavy home, a prize she was quickly able to finesse through her customers the James Prestons, who summered near the Dunleavys up in Swampscott. It was to the Dunleavy beach house on Little's Point that she was invited on a humid August day a few weeks after Sylvie's arrival, the shoreline crowded with plovers, the salt air and the sound of combers setting her at ease as she was driven in from the station. At the grand house she was shown through a cool foyer to a patio that overlooked the shimmering flank of the Atlantic, and here she awaited the lady of the house, relieved to be out of the city and in the fresh sea air. Relieved, too, to have left her infant daughter in the hands of Greta Speyer, who understood a mother's duties better than she did. What a mercy it was to have a few hours of distraction from the scolding voices in her head.

"I'm so glad you've come!" Mrs. Dunleavy exclaimed when she arrived, clutching her hand with unnerving fervor. To Elisabeth's surprise her hostess was done up in a dotted orange dress and stylish cloche hat. She dandled a matching orange parasol on her shoulder as if for a leisurely excursion into the city. Elisabeth quickly sensed that Mrs. Dunleavy had dressed for her, and a warning bell sounded in the back of her mind. Her apprehension was not misplaced. Soon enough it became clear that the petite, freckled woman, still childlike at thirty or so, was ravenously hungry for companionship, though a confessor was perhaps what she really needed.

As they sat on the limestone terrace overlooking a frothy green tidal pool she talked in an endless stream, boasting of her eleven-year-old daughter's high intelligence and her husband's prowess at money-making—and then, with some agitation, of her brother-in-law's astonishing accomplishments as a surgeon at Mass General, especially (she confided *sotto voce*) his pioneering work on maladies of the female parts. A genius, she called him, and such a *humble* man. Handsome, too . . . like a dashing young Wilson with his aristocrat's nose and pince-nez. By the third cup of tea it was clear to Elisabeth that Mrs. Dunleavy's relations with her sister's husband went considerably beyond the familial bond. Elisabeth further suspected that the maid had covertly fortified her employer's cup with each refilling. The depravity of her betters never ceased to astonish her. So many of the society wives seemed to teeter constantly on the brink of nervous collapse.

While the woman prattled on, one wearisome hour dissolving into the next as the skies clouded over and the sea turned gray, Elisabeth listened for an opening into which she might introduce the topic of the Bell Company's wares. But eventually her hostess removed the need. "I hope you'll excuse my jabbering on like this, Elisabeth," she said abruptly, "but it's how God made me. You're the soul of patience! But look, now, I know you're here on business, and a girl certainly can't be Porter Dunleavy's wife without understanding a bit about business. I'll gladly order up two of everything you've got, one for here and one for the Beacon Street house. How does that sound?" With a sodden smile Mrs. Dunleavy congratulated herself. "Well, now that I've put that matter to rest, perhaps you'd like to meet my daughter?"

When the maid brought the homely Suzanne Dunleavy to the table for inspection, the girl's mother commanded her to speak French for her guest. "Miss Garner's from Parrris! Be sure you get it right." Unfortunately someone had taught the girl to speak like a Parisian guttersnipe. The French that came from her mouth was so fractured and vile as to suggest that her teacher meant to exact some kind of revenge upon the unsuspecting Dunleavys. But the only thing to do was compliment mother and daughter. Elisabeth duly did so. As soon as the girl was sent off, Mrs. Dunleavy leaned across the table with a watery gaze.

"Do you know what, Elisabeth? I've just had a fantastic idea! You should come work for us as Suzanne's governess. You could teach her perfect French. You could turn her into a cultured lady like yourself. What I wouldn't give! Of course my husband would pay you far more than you make at this . . . job." She warmed quickly to her own idea. "The timing couldn't be better! We sail for Europe in May, so you'll have plenty of time to get Suzie polished up. And of course you'll make the crossing with us! Paris is our very first stop. You can show us the sights. I can hardly wait to see the Louver."

Nothing could have appealed less to Elisabeth than being Violet Dunleavy's traveling companion. She thanked her hostess civilly, saying that she'd made certain commitments to Mr. Alexander Graham Bell himself—this seemed unassailable—but would surely keep the offer in mind. The main thing, clearly, was to slip away before Porter Dunleavy arrived and was cornered into the arrangement by his tipsy wife.

Thunder had begun to rumble threateningly out over the water, giving Elisabeth an excuse to be on her way. Her hostess insisted she stay for dinner; she demurred. With a pout Mrs. Dunleavy walked her to the waiting car, locking arms with her guest to keep herself from toppling down the grand steps. The woman was as crestfallen as a jilted schoolgirl. Elisabeth wondered what she would be like without alcohol in her blood, or Dunleavy's money in her life. Perhaps not unlikeable, but there was no telling. As it was, Elisabeth was happy to drive off with orders for six Bell products in her bag, the rain coming in flat slapping drops as the driver pulled into the tiny Swampscott station. She didn't give Mrs. Porter Dunleavy another thought except to vaguely plot a second visit, before summer was up, just to sit by the sea. The sea in its grandeur made up for a great deal of Dunleavy nonsense.

Now, perhaps, it's time to reconsider. It's three months since Mrs. Dunleavy made her excited offer; perhaps she hasn't yet found the governess she wanted. More likely, she hasn't thought to look, since the idea seemed to have had more to do with her attraction to her poised French visitor than with any real interest in her daughter's improvement. Elisabeth's fairly sure the post could be hers for the asking, assuming her hostess remembers making the offer.

The prospect of working for Violet Dunleavy holds no more appeal than it did in August, but to spend her days in a Beacon Street mansion would surely be safer than stewing in the bad air of the Bell factory. She can tolerate nearly anything if it keeps little Sylvie safe. It seems worth a conversation, if nothing else. Perhaps Mrs. Dunleavy will be steadier in Boston, less of a wild card with summer's relaxed ways behind her.

Elisabeth finds pen and paper and sits down to compose a letter of inquiry. Almost immediately there is a problem: how should she address the woman? A few minutes into their meeting at Little's Point she'd insisted Elisabeth call her Violet, but in writing it seems too familiar. *Mrs. Dunleavy* is safer. After a cordial thank-you for her confidence in Bell products and in her personally, Elisabeth gets straight to the point.

> I believe I mentioned, Mrs. Dunleavy, that I would be very interested in your kind offer of employment as Suzanne's governess were it not for certain prior commitments I'd made to Mr. Bell. As those commitments have now been satisfied, I write to inquire whether you are still, by chance, in search of help. I suppose that by now you've engaged someone for the role, but if not I'd be grateful for an opportunity to discuss it with you. I am available at your convenience.

Elisabeth sets her papa's fountain pen down. Another problem has occurred to her: Sylvie. Mrs. Dunleavy's offer, she assumes, was for a live-in post. How could she manage it now? Surely no society woman would welcome an unwed mother into her home, much less as governess. How unjust it would be if Sylvie's very existence stood in the way of her mother's efforts to protect her!

She goes in to check on her daughter, as if Sylvie herself might offer advice. She's sleeping soundly, the picture of contentment. Feeling lightheaded, Elisabeth sits back down at the kitchen table and writes,

I'm not certain you know it, Madame, but I am recently widowed and have sole care of Sylvie, my daughter. Perhaps this disqualifies me from consideration as a live-in governess, in which case I could come and work with Suzanne during the day, leaving Sylvie in the care of my neighbor.

Again Elisabeth hesitates, remembering Violet Dunleavy's idea of taking her to Europe. This seems impossible too. She decides to pass over it in silence, and winds up the letter by offering her telephone number should Violet prefer to call. The telephone supplied to her as a benefit of employment at Bell hasn't rung more than three times since it came into her life, but she's glad to have it now. Elisabeth fetches her address book and seals the letter, eager to settle Sylvie into her stroller and walk to the mailbox the moment she awakes.

It's long past breakfast time. She should eat, though she isn't hungry. Rummaging in the icebox she finds an egg and a bit of cheese and mustard and fries up a child's omelet, pleased with the step she's taken. The lie about widowhood tugs at her only weakly. The truth is that Charlie Westerlake has been dead to her for a year now. She might as well be a widow. Late in the pregnancy she'd considered hunting him down in Illinois to demand that he support his child, had imagined in spiteful detail the look on his face when she surprised him at the door of his tidy farmhouse, the fruit of his betrayal cradled in her arms. But how would she ever locate him? He'd never told her the name of his town—now she understood why. And a trip across the country would be a trial with a babe in arms, even if she could take the time off from Bell.

All this pushed against the idea. But what finally settled the matter was the fact that when she pictured the door of the Westerlake home swinging open, it wasn't Charlie's startled face she saw before her but the hazy face of his poor wife. Whoever she was, she surely knew nothing of her husband's wartime infidelities. And their children! What if they were playing in the yard when the visitor blew in, with not a care in the world now that their papa was back from the war? Elisabeth's anger toward Charlie Westerlake did not give her the right to ruin the lives of his wife and children. Of this she was absolutely certain. She'd not been raised to inflict pain upon the innocent, and she wouldn't do it now. Perhaps in time she'd find a way to confront him properly, to make the man stand up and face what he'd done, but it certainly hadn't been revealed to her yet.

When Sylvie awakes, Elisabeth changes her, bounces her on her knee for a few minutes and bundles her up for the walk to the corner, the letter to Violet Dunleavy tucked in her pocket, her heart full of hope. The snow's paused again, teasingly; perhaps the weather will clear in earnest. She's more than ready for a change.

VIOLET DUNLEAVY'S CALL comes on Tuesday evening, just as Elisabeth is sitting down to chicken soup and the last of her Exton crackers. Since sending the letter she's had almost no appetite, nor has she slept well. She's been literally feverish with anticipation, waking up in the dead of night sticky with perspiration, her dreams veering into strange waters. The toll of waiting for Violet's reply has flattened her. When the telephone jangles she nearly upends her soup bowl.

"Elisabeth! There you are!" the caller shouts through the earpiece.

"Mrs. Dunleavy!"

"How pleased I was to get your letter. You've been very much on my mind."

"Yes?"

"I was just saying to Mr. Dunleavy that I needed a helping hand with Suzie, and what should I find sitting in the letterbox but a sweet note from just the person I'd choose. I was so excited that I called Mr. Dunleavy at the office, something he *hates* for me to do. Let me tell you, Elisabeth, it was worth his vinegar this time. When I gave him the news he could hear how happy you'd made me."

Again Elisabeth feels the woman's awkward familiarity, her loneliness. But never mind: what Violet Dunleavy has to tell her is grand.

"I'm so happy to hear all this, Mrs. Dunleavy."

"Violet!"

"Violet."

"May I call you Liz? What do you prefer?"

"Anything you like, Violet."

"Then Liz. When can you start? Porter and Suzie and I are about to shove off for the holidays, Christmas with my husband's people up in New Hampshire. Dull as dishwater, I can tell you. But we'll be back on New Year's Day. Could you come on the second of January?"

Before Elisabeth can answer, Sylvie lets out a great squalling cry from the bassinet in the bedroom, as if having just now heard the telephone ring. Elisabeth can only wait it out. She'd go to her but the telephone keeps her tethered to the kitchen. Thankfully her daughter falls quiet again almost at once.

Mrs. Dunleavy is laughing. "Please thank your daughter for introducing herself. I meant to say, *of course* you must bring her with you, Liz. We're very modern here. The staff will tend to her while you're with Suzie. Honestly, I had no idea, *no* idea, you were a mother yourself, and, well. . . ."

"A widow?"

"Yes, that. I'm so sorry, dear. You mustn't feel the need to tell me what happened. In fact, please don't. My heart might break."

"Thank you, Violet. And thank you for allowing Sylvie to come."

"Sylvie?"

"My daughter. But Violet . . . is this a live-in position? Or would you prefer I come days?"

"I'd hoped you'd stay with us so that we could get to know one another that much better. We have the loveliest upstairs bedroom for you, with its own little parlor and a splendid view of the Frog Pond. You can bring your ice skates. How does that sound?"

Elisabeth can almost believe it would be alright. She'll learn to manage Violet Dunleavy; she'll have to. "Wonderful, yes," she says, her chest tightening with excitement. She'd not hoped for such a windfall.

"Mrs. Dunleavy?"

"Really, Liz! Enough of that, now."

"I'm sorry—Violet. I just want to thank you for the opportunity." The next words are out of her mouth before she can stop them. "You've answered my prayers, you know."

This is far too much. But Mrs. Dunleavy is unfazed.

"From your lips to God's ears. Mine, anyway."

Elisabeth has to laugh. There's something clumsily charming about the woman.

"Expect a call soon from Port," Mrs. Dunleavy says. "He insists on talking to you personally about the business end of things. But don't be concerned, dear. I'll make sure he goes easy. Sometimes these men forget that not everything in life is a battle to the death. In the meantime, just between us girls, let's consider our arrangement done and dusted."

After the call, Elisabeth goes straight to her daughter and sweeps her up in her arms, unable to believe her good fortune. For once something's broken her way. The sun has just burst through the windows to set the bedroom ablaze, marking the moment like a shaft of heavenly light in a Renaissance painting. This too makes her want to laugh, the sky's silly theatrical gesture.

"*Mon petit trésor*," Elisabeth coos, dancing her daughter around the room, "*ne t'en fais pas, tout se passera bien maintenant, tout se passera bien. . . .*" Even she believes it: all, indeed, will be well.

XLIV.
To Stand Apart from Men

With Violet Dunleavy's offer in hand she brazenly avoids the Bell factory, inventing sales calls in great houses in order to stay away. None of it matters now. A better future is within reach. Shea can think what he likes. She'll take no unnecessary risks. Twelve days before Christmas she gives her notice—Tom dumbfounded by the note she slides under his blotched nose—and flies down the iron stairs, putting the dank place behind her as fast as she can. Out on the street she falls back against a brick wall, the exultation taking her breath away.

Now the waiting comes: it's nearly three weeks before she's to move to Beacon Street. In the meantime, she nervously awaits Porter Dunleavy's call. Violet's words echo in her mind constantly. *He insists on talking to you personally. . . . Sometimes these men forget that not everything in life is a battle to the death.* How neatly the words sketch the man. Elisabeth recalls the photo of him alongside the *Globe* article: a heavyset, aggressively whiskered bourgeois with a snub nose, unsmiling as a matter of personal principle. It's all too easy to imagine his bluster. Elisabeth dreads his call like the extraction of a rotten tooth.

But no call comes. After three days of panic at the idea of negotiating a wage with such a personage, her nerves shift to the vexing matter of his silence. She'd simply like to know why he hasn't rung. Perhaps it's a way of throwing her back on her heels, as if she were some business adversary from whom he means to extract a concession . . . in which case it's ridiculous. Perhaps he's simply forgotten—or worse still, talked Violet out of the idea entirely. Whatever the reason, the new position won't seem real until she talks to Dunleavy. It's getting harder to convince herself that the impetuous decision to quit Bell was a wise one. But she certainly has no intention of throwing herself at Tom Shea's feet to plead for her old job back.

The strain of it is making her genuinely sick: joints aching, chest tight with worry, exhaustion overtaking her at odd moments. For hours at a time she can't get a single good breath in. Sometimes the worry will press so hard on her chest that it sets her to coughing, her lungs trying to eject the whole notion of Porter Dunleavy and his wheeling and dealing. One wet cough breeds another, and soon enough she sounds like one of the consumptive Bell men, though her case is, of course, quite different. Her misery is the fault of a man, not a germ. If only she knew a way to bring it to a close.

ELISABETH IS DOZING at dusk one late afternoon when the telephone in the kitchen finally jangles. She bumbles from the sofa and hurries to the kitchen to take up the receiver, trying to sharpen her drowsy wits for the conversation she's been dreading. But it's a woman's voice that crackles through the static.

"Liz! Can you hear me on that end? It's Helen."

Relief vies with disappointment in Elisabeth's heart. She drops wearily into the chair beside the telephone to hear what Helen Sanborn has to say.

"Helen, how good to hear your voice. How are you?"

"Oh . . . wonderful, actually. Though of course I miss Boston terribly. And Mother. And you."

She must still be in Maine. Sometime in the spring, after returning from her disastrous sojourn in New York, Helen had gone up for her brother Jimmy's wedding at the Sanborn horse farm and stayed on at the invitation of some man from the wedding party. She'd written to say she was falling in love. Elisabeth reaches for the name and somehow finds it. "You're still in Maine? How are things with Beck Turner?"

"Beck! Oh, goodness. Ancient history. But Liz, Maine is glorious, even in winter. I've been hibernating like a she-bear. It's just me, myself and I up here, if you don't count the caretakers and three beautiful Arabians, all from the line of my grandfather's stallion, Gemare. They're excellent company. I ride in all weathers, like a Cossack." Helen took a breath. "But how's your little one?"

Your little one—something tells Elisabeth that Helen doesn't recall her daughter's name. How far apart they've grown since the war.

"Sylvie's a treasure," she says, trying to put some enthusiasm in her voice. "I'd love for you to meet her."

"Oh, I will, I will. I already have a little gift for her, something very Maine. I'll be down for a visit in the spring, I'm sure."

Too late, Elisabeth says to herself.

There was a time, during her pregnancy with Sylvie, when she'd foolishly hoped Helen would come and be at her side for the birth, but Helen never offered. Her friend's own life was in upheaval, it was true, between the divorce from Rollins and the escalating divorce battle between her parents which featured regularly in the society pages. But was this any reason not to give a few days to a friend in need? For weeks Elisabeth was furious over it.

But in time it occurred to her that there might be a good explanation. Helen's own pregnancy had ended disastrously. A dangerous miscarriage in her Knickerbocker lavatory; a serious concussion when she cracked her head against the sink pedestal afterward, having fainted while trying to haul herself to the telephone. As Helen put it, she'd lost enough blood to fill a bordello bathtub. She'd spent a week in the hospital where she was told she was lucky to have survived at all. All this had left Helen deeply shaken. The more Elisabeth considered matters, the more she understood that for Helen to come and sit by her side while she gave birth, so soon after her own ordeal, was simply too much to expect. The selfishness wasn't on Helen's part but her own. She'd forgiven her friend. But now Helen couldn't even recall her daughter's name.

"And how is your mother?" Elisabeth asks, stifling a cough.

"You've not heard from her? I'm surprised. She's so fond of you."

"I've had no word." Elisabeth hesitates, wondering how much to share. "I didn't leave Aigremont in the most gracious manner, you know. It could be that she's angry with me."

"I can tell you she's not. She knew perfectly well that you had to get away from that awful man. She told me so. She's had no truck with him since his doctoring stint ended, exactly because of the way he lured you in. Mother's no fool."

This is surprising and welcome news. After overhearing Rena ask Westerlake about his wife and children on that final night—peace having been declared everywhere but in Elisabeth's heart—she'd bolted from the place, finding a ride into town with some revelers and sleeping on a station bench until morning when she caught the first train back to the city. In the fury of the moment she'd fled Aigremont as if it were a house afire, never thinking to tell the lady of the house that she was leaving. She's always assumed that Rena must be furious with her for her abrupt departure, all the more so because she suspected she knew perfectly well about her and Westerlake. To hear that Rena's been firmly in her camp is a relief indeed. There is much a young woman might learn from her generosity.

"I'm glad to know it. She was very kind to me, you know."

As Elisabeth says these words, she hears a tightness in her own voice. Perhaps she has Porter Dunleavy's stubborn silence to thank for it.

Helen says, "Between you and me, Liz, Mother's hit a rough patch."

"How do you mean?"

"What's wrong with your voice, Liz?"

"I'm just a little tired."

"Sounds more like you're under the weather. I hope not. Anyway, Mother's soldiering on, as she does. This divorce has turned into a god-awful stink. Apparently my father really has squandered all the money. Or hidden it. I never realized how dire things were. And Liz?"

"Yes?"

"She's had to sell the house. It's been snapped up by some shyster who appeared out of nowhere and made an insulting offer Mother had no choice but to accept. The man saw her flank exposed and went in for the kill. He'll sell it for twice what he paid. Barefaced extortion, if you want my opinion. He has absolutely no intention of living there. As a condition of the offer he gave her exactly five days to vacate—can you imagine? She's had to consign most of our things . . . furniture, Persian rugs, paintings, you name it, to an auction house. She's selling the *wallpaper*. And the entire library! An embarrassment, so heartbreaking for her. She claims she's put it behind her, but she can't have."

Even in Elisabeth's distraction, the news deals a blow. It's unimaginable that the Sanborns would lose Aigremont.

"Oh, Helen," she says in a hush. "Your childhood home."

"The least she could have done is tell her children, so we could say goodbye to the place. And collect our things!"

"I'm sure she made certain all your personal things were spared."

"Not everything. Remember the hiding place in my room, the little cubbyhole in the wall? Well, Mother never knew about that. Whatever was there is still there."

"Oh! The love letters from Rollins when he was courting you. . . . I remember you showing me. Other irreplaceable things, I'm sure. You must be beside yourself."

"I don't give a jot about old love letters from Rollins. Burn them! But there are other things I'd like to have back. Kind letters from you, for example, when I was so miserable in New York. I saved every one of them, then stashed them at the house when Mother ordered me home. I certainly wasn't going to leave them lying around for prying eyes. You and I were quite frank with one another, weren't we? Imagine the maids' glee if they'd found them."

An unnerving thought flashes through Elisabeth's mind. "Helen—where are the Edison cylinders now? They weren't there in your hiding place, were they?"

"No! Goodness, no. Just some of the photos from that day. The cylinders are safe with me, under lock and key in a case I've kept with me for . . . what has it been? Almost four years now. They're as precious as anything I own. Where I go, they go. I'm just sorry I couldn't get them in front of Toscanini. Blame Rollins and his chorus girl for that. But Liz—say the word when you want them back. They're yours, of course."

Something like a hunger flares in Elisabeth: the urgent need to hear the sonata again, to hear her father play. Like birdsong the opening arpeggio sings teasingly in her head. She'd give anything to hear the rest. It would give her strength. But under the circumstances she'd best let Helen keep the cylinders. They wouldn't be safe in the cyclone of her own life.

"What will your mother do now?" she asks quietly.

"She's moved to a flat in Brookline. She's cooking for herself, if you can imagine. Not that the kitchen's terra incognita to her. But at least a colored woman comes in to clean. You should hear the strain in Mother's voice. I told her I'd take the Flying Yankee down in a few weeks to help out, poor girl. Not that I fancy traveling down there in winter, but my awful brothers haven't lifted a finger for her."

Another distressing thought comes to Elisabeth. "Helen, did she sell the white piano?"

"The piano your father played that day? I'll confess I haven't inquired. Shame on me. If he were alive, I know Mother would have gifted it to him, no matter what dire straits she was in. I'll ask what's become of it. Would you want it for yourself?"

"Me? I can har—"

A coughing spell cuts her off. Elisabeth bends over in her chair, heaving heroically, trying to master it, but it overtakes her completely. She can't drag a teaspoonful of air past the phlegm.

"My lord, Liz!" Helen cries when she puts the telephone back to her ear. "What is that dreadful *hacking*? You sound wretched. Sick as a dog! How frightening."

Elisabeth has no chance to answer. Another attack comes, crueler than the last.

"Liz," Helen says sternly when the crisis subsides, "tell me you've seen a doctor about this. We both know that's a dangerous cough. Not an ordinary cough at all. Dangerous for your daughter, too. You must see to it."

Elisabeth is too shaken to continue the conversation. "I will," she says in a narrow voice, "but I need to go look in on Sylvie. I'll say goodbye now, Helen." Without awaiting a reply she hangs the earpiece on the hook and hurries to the lavatory where she spits a thick gout of phlegm into the toilet, relieved to see no blood in it.

EXHAUSTED, ELISABETH CHANGES INTO A NIGHTGOWN and goes to bed at seven-fifteen after putting Sylvie down in the bassinet beside her. She's tired of the wintry day, tired of her racing thoughts about Porter Dunleavy, tired most of all of the miserable, dogged coughing. Even the conversation with Helen has taken something vital out of her. But sleep doesn't come. For what seems hours she lies awake on her lumpy mattress, listening to her daughter's taut little breaths and feeling alternately hot and cold, her whole body rebelling against Dunleavy's mulishness. She can't stop worrying about what it means. Can't help feeling angry toward the man. Something is building in her chest like a war cry.

When Sylvie rouses and begins to wail, she gets up and tends to her wearily. Only the breast will comfort her little girl. She keeps her breath shallow, afraid the cough will return. When she's put Sylvie back down to nap she washes her face, the water ice-cold in the pipes, the electric light in the lavatory glaring, the toilet loud as a steam engine when she pulls the chain. She abandons sleep and makes a cup of tea instead. She must behave sensibly if she expects sensible results.

It's not even eight-thirty. She could swear it's been hours since she collapsed on the bed. Along with everything else, the constant worry over Dunleavy has meddled with her sense of time. To keep dangling this way, like Houdini twisting over Niagara Falls, will be the end of her. When the man finally does call she'll have to use every power at her disposal to keep the anger from her voice.

She needs to calm down. With teacup in hand Elisabeth stands at the parlor window, the heat of the radiator lapping against her thighs, and plays through the *Clair de lune* in her head, just as she used to do while waiting for Charlie Westerlake under the sycamore at Aigremont. For some reason the thought of Charlie comforts her just now. Or not Charlie, really, but the recollection of feeling so much happiness despite the misery all around her. Dozens were dying in the wards of the lit-up mansion, thousands more in French trenches, but still she could wait contentedly in the moonlight with Monsieur Debussy playing in her head, knowing that soon—in a minute, in an hour—everything would change for her, if only for an evening. In those sweet moments she could feel life quietly preparing a wonderful surprise for her, like a girl listening at the door while her mother wraps a birthday gift. In this knowledge her heart was serene. She was the tree that sank its tap root and held its ground, unwavering and solitary. Now, too, gazing out into the white streets, the night skies clear after days of snow, Debussy playing in her weary head, Elisabeth feels she's slowed to a halt, the world carrying on without her.

It isn't a lover she's waiting for this time, of course. It's a hard-looking mogul from the newspaper. But what did love teach her, in the end? Only to stand apart from men and not give ground. If one couldn't trust a Charlie Westerlake, whom could one trust? Perhaps his betrayal had prepared her, in some way, for the talk to come.

By the time the telephone jolts her from her reverie she feels ever so slightly saner. She does not hurry to answer the call. Setting her cup and saucer on the wide windowsill she goes to the telephone and lifts the receiver calmly. "Yes?" she says.

"Is this Miss Garner?" asks a basso voice.

"This is she."

"Miss Garner, it's Porter Dunleavy, Mrs. Dunleavy's husband. How do you do?"

It isn't, in the end, anything she'll say wrong. Nor is it Porter Dunleavy, who, contrary to her suspicions, turns out to be a man of warmth and charm. What defeats her is her own body. After an agreeable few minutes talking about French wines, of which Dunleavy is as fond as she is ignorant, and after a somber moment in which her future employer makes it clear that he disagrees strongly with Wilson's unconscionable delay in sending troops to the aid of her countrymen, he finally comes round to his wife's offer of employment.

"You have no idea how pleased Violet is that you're coming on board, Miss Garner. I've not seen her this gay in as long as I can recall. I owe you a debt of gratitude for that." The matter of her salary is settled effortlessly, and astonishingly. "I propose to compensate you at the same rate my friend Ellery Sedgwick, over at the *Atlantic*, compensates his daughter's governess. That would be thirty-five dollars per week, plus room and board, of course. Would that suit?" Elisabeth quickly does the math: she'll earn nearly three times what Bell's paid in the best of months, with room and board into the bargain. There is nothing to be negotiated. It's beyond belief. At a word the dam has burst: all the anxiety of the preceding days is released in a torrent.

Mr. Dunleavy is awaiting her answer.

"Why, of course that—" she says, but then a painful spasm cuts her short. With a wheezing heave she tries to get oxygen into her lungs but they're as turgid as setting concrete. When she tries to finish her interrupted sentence the cough digs even deeper, dredging up mucous and making her bend over double just to eke out air to breathe.

Desperate to conceal what can't possibly be concealed, Elisabeth covers her mouth with her forearm and spits phlegm into the sleeve of her nightshirt. She senses Mr. Dunleavy listening acutely on the other end of the line. Cupping the mouthpiece she manages to draw a half-breath with a groan, hoping he hasn't heard, and swallows hard.

"Excuse me," she rasps out. "I—" But again her lungs seize up, stopping her cold. Another explosion goes off in her aching chest. Again she covers the mouthpiece, hoping against hope that Dunleavy won't hear. But of course he does, and someone else too: through the floor beneath her feet she hears Ella Montgomery call her name to see if she is alright. In another moment Ella will be at the door.

"Miss Garner," Port Dunleavy says quietly, "I believe you need to see a doctor. Immediately."

"It's no—"

Elisabeth stops, feeling another convulsive wave coming, staving it off with silence. Something begins to scream in her head but she has no idea how to stop it.

"You know," Mr. Dunleavy says in a guarded tone, "I think we'd best postpone our arrangement until you're feeling better. It seems to me that what you need to attend to right now is your health."

"I—"

"Please call us when you've got the all-clear from your doctor. And Miss Garner? Do see a doctor. I don't like the sound of that cough at all. With consumption going round one has to be exceptionally careful. Not saying you'd find yourself around the class of people who catch this thing, but it's no time to take chances. Take care, now."

With a solid click the line goes dead.

Elisabeth slides down the wall to the cold kitchen floor and closes her eyes. Having wreaked its havoc, the cough dies in her chest with convulsive little shudders. Her face is awash in tears. It's horrible, all of it, and now Sylvie is crying in the bedroom, sensing in her own way that everything has collapsed at once.

Ella knocks at the door. "Elisabeth, are you alright?"

When Elisabeth opens her eyes, both daughter and neighbor in need of her attention, she faints dead away at what she sees.

First came Porter Dunleavy, then Sylvie, then Ella—then nothing at all.

XLV.
WITH SWIFT CLARITY

IF TIME WAS AT A STANDSTILL before Dunleavy's call, now it hurtles out of control.

Elisabeth awakes on the kitchen floor with her head in Ella Montgomery's lap, a cool cloth folded on her forehead. Somewhere in the background a child is squalling. . . . It's a moment before she realizes it's Sylvie. She tries to sit up, a mother's instinct setting her muscles in motion, her whole body driven toward her daughter. Ella eases her back.

"Lie still, now," she says, stroking her hair. "You're alright."

Elisabeth starts to speak her daughter's name but her *Sylvie* is lost when a spasm seizes her. An arrow of pain shoots down her ribs, piercing everything in its path.

"Turn to your right, sweetie," Ella says, covering her mouth lightly with the cloth. Obediently Elisabeth rolls onto her side, something metallic-tasting draining into the cotton. "That's alright, then," Ella says, and pulls the cloth away when the coughing subsides. "Take a breath."

When Elisabeth manages to sit up, she says, "Sylvie needs me."

Together they make their way to the bedroom, Ella supporting her, her chest quiet now but for a gurgling deep in her lungs. In the bassinet her daughter is tetchy, restless. Like a magnet she draws her mother to her. But in passing by the mirror, Elisabeth catches a glimpse of her own ashen face and her knees fail her.

A vision comes screaming back from the instant before she fainted in the kitchen: the rumpled sleeve of her cotton nightshirt, stained garishly with blood. In the mirror the stain shouts at her like a motorman's warning flag.

"*Mon Dieu!*" Elisabeth says under her breath. The woman in the mirror sinks down to sit on the edge of the bed, Ella sitting down beside her and pulling her head gently onto her shoulder. For a moment the two of them breathe in unison. But then the barrage begins again. Again Elisabeth covers her mouth with her sleeve, and again looks down to find it glistening with bloody sputum.

"No," she sobs under her breath, "no, no, *no*. . . . I can't let. . . . I can't. . . ."

Ella rocks her like a child with night terrors.

"Get away," Elisabeth tells her friend, slipping out from under her comforting arm. "You can't be near me now."

"I'm not afraid, sweetie. But we need to get you some help."

"What about Sylvie?"

"You know I'll take care of her. Don't you worry about that."

"But is she alright? She's not sick, too?"

"She's perfectly fine. You're a good mother, Elisabeth. You've kept her safe."

Elisabeth shakes her head slowly, the cruelty of the situation bewildering. She reminds herself to breathe slowly and carefully, demanding as little as possible from her body. The feeling of suffocation is terrifying. Ella takes her clammy hand.

She must go to her daughter. With Ella's help she gets to her feet and casts about for something to cover her face, stripping the pillowcase and improvising a mask from it. At the bassinet she gazes down on her beautiful girl, desperate to take her in her arms. But her arms are covered in blood, her very breath polluted. Sylvie is as untouchable as the risen Christ. And now Elisabeth feels another fit coming on, starting in the muddy riverbed of her lungs and clawing its way toward the light.

If she's infected her daughter she'll take her own life. She accepts this simple truth without argument or confusion. Still, at the sight of her mother Sylvie calms instantly, and with a relaxed little chortle Sylvie smiles.

Elisabeth is hardly aware of Ella's hands when they come to rest on her shoulders.

"I'm calling for a doctor," her friend says. "Frank has a line on one through the mill."

Elisabeth's first instinct is to refuse. But when Sylvie cackles from the bassinet she nods, for her daughter's sake.

"Good girl," Ella says, and goes back downstairs.

ELISABETH MOVES to the kitchen floor, needing its solidity. As explosions detonate between her ribs she sobs openly, craving her daughter's touch but afraid to go to her.

She is both surprised and not surprised by what's happened. For months it's seemed inevitable that the sickness would catch up with her. The wonder is that she's evaded it for so long, though she sees now that the signs have been accumulating for some while. Her mystifying tiredness, the ache in her joints. Fevers in the dead of night. The way her clothes have hung looser by the week. The brutal coughing, of course, and tonight, for the first time, the blood. Yet despite the mounting evidence she's managed to keep herself completely in the dark. The larger pattern has eluded her. For a week now she's blamed her indisposition on Porter Dunleavy's silence, on the frigid air, on everything but the obvious culprit. How foolish she's been.

She has no idea what she'll do when the doctor confirms what she already knows. She's far too unnerved to devise a plan. As the minutes crawl by she feels the usual nighttime fever come on, a shiver rattling her bones, her forehead already damp with sweat. Soon there will be even less hope of thinking clearly. All she knows, and she knows it as unshakably as a law of nature, is that she must keep Sylvie from harm.

Ella lets herself back in, a look of distress on her face.

"I've talked with the doctor and he'll see you at City Hospital in the morning. He won't set foot in this building if there's a chance of tuberculosis. Can you imagine? A doctor! If we had a better address he'd step lively, I'm sure."

Perhaps it's the doctor's hesitation that causes Ella to linger in the bedroom doorway rather than go to Elisabeth where she sits. The world is beginning to pull away.

Ella says, "Shall I take Sylvie for tonight? So you can rest?"

Both of them know the real reason but neither is brave enough to speak it aloud. All Elisabeth can do is nod, trying not to look over at the bassinet where her daughter lies mewling.

"I'll be just downstairs," Ella says, and steps around her to take her child away.

ELISABETH KNOWS she won't be able to sleep. She's at the kitchen table, inhaling steam from a saucepan with a dishtowel tented around her head, when the telephone rings again. It's all she can do to get over to it and lift the earpiece from the hook.

"Elisabeth?" says a husky-voiced woman. "It's Rena Sanborn."

Elisabeth falls back against the wall. Rena might be one complication too many, whatever her good intentions.

"Mrs. Sanborn. What a surprise."

"Please forgive my calling like this, but I've just gotten off the telephone with Helen, who says you're quite ill. She's beside herself with worry. Since we disconnected I haven't been able to think of anything else. How are you feeling, dear?"

"I'm quite tired."

"I can hear it in your voice. I wonder, is anyone there with you? Have you seen a doctor? Helen thought you hadn't. Frankly, she thought you *wouldn't*. I can help with that, Elisabeth. As you're aware, I know many fine doctors."

"I'm not so sick as that," Elisabeth protests, but the lie is exposed by a violent cough that tells Rena Sanborn all she needs to know. The conversation is halted for nearly a minute as Elisabeth struggles to breathe. When the attack subsides, Rena is waiting.

"Elisabeth, I've heard this sort of cough before and I know exactly what it means. I suspect you do, too. Don't trifle with this, dear. If you'll allow me, I'd like to make arrangements for your care. Would that be alright?"

"I'm meeting a doctor at the hospital tomorrow."

"Listen to me very carefully, young lady. You are not to set foot in any hospital. I don't care if it's Massachusetts General. Chances are good you'd never leave. What you need is a sanitorium, and I don't mean Boston Consumptives."

"But I couldn't possibly—"

"There would be no question of you paying, my dear. Not after you gave so generously of yourself at Aigremont."

Elisabeth feels tears coming on, the older woman speaking directly to her heart. She's needed such kindness more than she knew. Needed someone to take her part like this. But then she thinks of Rena's own reduced circumstances—selling Aigremont, auctioning off the furniture, cooking for herself. While Rena's flavor of poverty might be luxury compared to her own, she can't possibly accept her charity.

"I'm so grateful, Mrs. Sanborn, but I couldn't ask you to pay my way."

"Oh, I won't be paying. I sit on the board of a new sanitorium up on Plum Island. Without my knack for raising funds they'd never have opened their doors. There are certain perquisites."

Elisabeth hardly knows what to say. The evening's relentless tide of circumstance is sweeping her into ever deeper waters. Lightheaded with fever, exhausted from hours of coughing, it's hard to take it all in.

"Is it very far?"

"Far enough to be safe from city air. It's just off Newburyport."

"But—my daughter?" Elisabeth asks, more as a plea than a question. The idea of leaving Sylvie behind tears at her heart. Only a few minutes ago she could hardly bear to watch Ella carry her downstairs.

"Where is your daughter now?"

"With the downstairs neighbor. But she has four children of her own. Could I take Sylvie with me to this place?"

"Sylvie needs to be somewhere safe, not in a place where she's surrounded by the sick."

The sick and the dying is the phrase, Elisabeth's well aware. It stings in her ears even if Rena won't say the words.

"Of course," she says faintly, "you're right."

"Let me get to work on this, Elisabeth. We'll get you a berth at Plum Island Hygienic, for tomorrow night if at all possible, and I'll find a safe place for Sylvie until such time as you're able to care for her again. Helen's idea was that we move her up to Maine where she could look after her with the help of the caretaker's wife. Her brother's in-laws are there to keep an eye on things, too. Lovely English people, close by. Your daughter would certainly be safe from consumption up there. It's quite good thinking on Helen's part, actually."

"I couldn't ask her to do that," Elisabeth protests, though in truth she simply can't imagine Helen caring for an infant.

"Helen would do anything for you," Rena insists. "She'll throw herself into it if you say the word. Or I could call Frank and Lily Monaghan, here in Brookline. Good friends who'd adore having a little one in their home, being childless themselves. We'll find a wonderful place for little Sylvie while you're on the mend, don't you worry." Elisabeth hears Rena get to her feet. "Let me get to work, dear. It may be nearly ten but it's not too late to start making calls. God knows, I've never shied away from rousting people out of bed when I need to. It gets their attention. And Elisabeth? You'd best have your things ready for a morning departure. Sylvie's, too. We're not letting grass grow under our feet."

When they've said their goodbyes Elisabeth sinks back to the floor and curls into a ball, clutching her knees to her chest. She is shivering with fever and fear. Gratitude, too. What would she do without Rena Sanborn and her power to set things right?

Through the floorboards she can hear Ella working industriously in her kitchen, clinking baby bottles, preparing the last feeding of the day . . . Sylvie in good and competent hands, oblivious to her mother's suffering. She pictures her friend filling a bottle while gently bouncing Sylvie on her hip, well-practiced at juggling household chores with motherly affection, all of it coming so easily to her. The fever etches the vision into Elisabeth's brain. But Ella isn't her only recourse. Others hover near. Behind Ella stands Helen Sanborn, arms outstretched to receive little Sylvie, and behind her the caretaker and the English in-laws, and behind them the couple in Brookline, Rena's friends, a chain of kind souls ready and willing to help. Should the worst come to pass, Sylvie will be in good hands. Rena and Helen will make sure of it.

But it means saying goodbye. At this moment, trembling on the hard floor in her empty flat, Elisabeth mourns her daughter's absence as a soldier mourns a fallen comrade or a missing limb. Though Sylvie is only downstairs, she might as well be an ocean away. Never have Elisabeth's arms felt so empty. They clutch her knees in misery when they should be cradling her daughter at her breast.

How, how, how will she ever say goodbye to her little girl? There isn't time to make peace with the idea. Tomorrow morning Sylvie will be taken from her. Tomorrow she'll watch someone walk away with her daughter in her arms. Tomorrow she'll be left behind, to live or die as the Lord and her lungs see fit. The thought of it sends her into a fit of coughing as vicious as any that's come before.

When the crisis ebbs, it leaves a spatter of blood on the floor and a stark truth in her heart: it's possible that she's already held her daughter for the last time. Elisabeth sees with swift clarity that Ella will not let her take Sylvie in her arms tomorrow morning, will not let her kiss the soft little cheek goodbye. Surely Ella won't allow Sylvie into the upstairs flat. She will protect her fiercely, as if she were one of her own, even if it means keeping her from her own mother.

From downstairs comes the sound of a chair scraping across the floor, then the sound of a sharp little cough. Ella murmurs something she can't make out; the cough comes again. Elisabeth begins to sob and then coughs in reply, her precious daughter just below but as unreachable as any star.

CHICAGO

JANUARY 2019

XLVI.

ATTENTION AUX DENTS

ONLY A WEEK INTO THE NEW YEAR and the earth is barely hanging on, Ben sees, skimming the headlines on his phone while onions soften in the pan. The Pacific is warming like water in a kettle. Monarch butterflies are dying off in droves along their flyways, gusting down like autumn leaves. Eighty thousand are dead of influenza in sub-Saharan Africa. But the Chinese have landed on the far side of the moon; extragalactic radio bursts have been detected by the Canadians. The Americans have flown past a snowman-shaped planetesimal out beyond Neptune. Whether any of this is cause for hope Ben can't say—but at least there is a world beyond this one, if only he could find his way back to it.

It's all too easy, lately, to feel that his own world is imploding. In exactly five days and five hours, on the second Friday evening of the new year, Ana Clara Matta will take the stage at the Pearson Center for the Performing Arts and sit down to play a sonata he had no hand in composing, contrary to what the program will say—the whole disaster broadcast live on public radio for an audience of who knows how many. Much of his professional world and a good deal of his private one will be present to witness this opening act of his humiliation. Because the truth, in the end, will out: he can't say how or when, but the lie will show itself, bursting into view when he least expects it. He can well imagine the stinging rebukes, then the silence that will descend as everyone he knows draws away. And after this . . . well, a life after this he cannot imagine.

He hasn't slept well, not a single night, since the Pearson Center announcement hit his inbox. As the calendar has counted relentlessly down toward the eleventh of January he's turned in earlier and earlier, only to lie awake imagining various humiliations, caustic emails and stinging exposés and stilted conversations with famous maestros and ordinary neighbors, canceled recording dates and the ruin of Counterpoint . . . all the while feeling for a way out, some deft turn that would enable him to escape the trap he's blundered into.

More than once he's toyed with the loaded gun of revenge. Perhaps there would be a way to expose and humiliate Ana Clara Matta before she does the same to him. She, after all, was the one who stole the sonata, in the most literal sense. By the time she resurfaced, lolling in her French bathtub, the chain reaction was already past halting. But this too is a dead end. The inescapable fact is that he's not without blame in the situation. It was he who led her to believe that the sonata was his. He who was too addled by sex and vertigo to tell the truth before she disappeared into Europe, taking his lie with her. So, no: he will not disgrace her before her peers. It would only backfire. More importantly, it's not the Ben Weil he's tried so hard to be.

As for Ana, she and Wooten haven't stopped hectoring him. They refuse to take his stubborn silence for an answer. After pressing him relentlessly in the first days after the concert was announced—Wooten brazening through the question of performance rights, threatening to sue if Ben didn't honor some bogus verbal contract, then Ana with her righteous accusations of ingratitude—they've pivoted to a charm offensive, leaving genial messages on his voice-mail, name-checking celebrities and famous players as they relay the buzz that's building around the enigmatic Weil sonata. They assume, for the sake of argument or sly persuasion, that he'll be there. They act as if he hasn't already spat his refusal in their faces. If it's some kind of strategy, it's not working—unless making him thrash in his cold bed, night after night, is their measure of success.

But Ana and Ant aren't the only callers. Other unwelcome messages have been rolling in, adding to the sense of unreality. Nearly every day he receives a voicemail from some arts reporter angling for an interview. Ian Haycock from BBC Music; Larry Lourenço from *Classical Music Digest*. Joanna Cutler from *International Piano*. Some basement blogger with reggae playing in the background. All they want is a brief call, ten minutes out of his busy schedule . . . the pitch is always the same. Then the tedious spelling-out of an email address and the slow enunciation, twice for good measure, of a telephone number. They're doggedly reachable, these people. And every one of them has obtained Ben's unpublished number from Ant Wooten. This he hasn't doubted for a minute.

Ben's not returned any of their calls, because what could he possibly say? Unless, of course, he decides to use some lucky critic to correct the record, to seize control of his fate like a condemned man hanging himself in his cell the night before he's to be frog-marched to the gallows. He hasn't ruled it out. It's not a time to close off options, however reckless they might seem.

Very soon it will be decision time. With every insistent message he feels the bleak sky lower itself another notch, descending upon him as the eleventh of January looms closer and closer.

IT'S TEMPTING TO SIMPLY FLEE. Just this morning, after reading Nathalie Artigue's arresting email about Jacques Garnier, he found himself searching for flights to Paris, plotting an escape. Perhaps it was time to accept Jean Artigue's invitation to dinner there, to lose himself in a good meal while disaster played its hand on the other side of the Atlantic. For once he might allow himself to drink to excess.

For twenty minutes, as he perused flights, it seemed an option no worse than any other. To remove himself from the situation, to be a no-show, to let events run their course without having to face the congratulatory words, the admiring smiles, the praise that would soon turn to poison—this had real appeal. But the fact was, he'd have to fly back eventually, because Chicago was home. And Paris was no refuge; word would reach there within hours. After lining up a one-way flight he abandoned it without paying, the futility of the notion obvious to him. There would be no running away from what he'd done. Not now.

Besides, he's already set something else in motion that requires his presence in Chicago. To his utter consternation, Willa Blount has decided to fly in for the début of the French sonata. In their last phone call he'd blurted out the news that a famous pianist had taken up the cause, meaning only to prove, really, that his vaunted connections had finally borne fruit. There seemed no reason to add that the pianist believed Ben Weil to be the composer of the sonata.

While he may have been on the downswing from a wine-soaked lunch with his cousin when Willa called, he wasn't as stupid as that. Though she didn't recognize the name Ana Clara Matta, thankfully, Willa did sound genuinely impressed, pleased that the sonata was getting such high-octane attention.

It should have ended there. His point had been neatly made. But something possessed him to keep talking about it, to babble on compulsively until he worked his way around, like a spider circling a drain, to the coming show. Not only had Ms. Matta taken an interest in the sonata; she was going to present it to the world. "Tremendous!" crowed Willa, usually so phlegmatic. It was her enthusiasm that fatally disarmed him. In a final blast of self-sabotage he offered to send her a ticket to the show—a bit of unhinged largesse he knew was idiotic even as the words were coming out of his mouth. Afterward he literally tore at his hair, unable to believe what he'd just said. His reflexive honesty had made him a fool.

He could excuse himself for telling Willa that interest in the sonata was rising. She'd hoped his labors would bear fruit in just this way. But to reveal the concert and then *offer her a ticket*—this Ben could understand only as a reckless fit of forthrightness, guilt having borne down hard on him in the course of two glasses of midday wine and a frank talk with Nikki. He'd liked the feel of Willa Blount's approval, too, her obvious regard for his brilliant connections; this was a fact. By the time he hung up the phone he was disgusted with himself in more ways than he could count.

Later that evening, soaking in a tepid bath, he wondered whether he'd been laying a trap for his own conscience. Perhaps he was daring himself to tell Willa the fuller truth. Which by no means would make him a man of integrity; he'd thrown the offer of tickets out never dreaming she'd take him up on it. (Did she still fly, even, at her age?) Hence his shocked surprise when he received an email from a travel agent in Maine with her itinerary attached. She was booked to arrive two days before the show, then would take a limo to the Knickerbocker Hotel where she'd settle in for a week's stay. Ben read the news with an acid stomach. What on earth had he done?

Willa's fucking coming! he texted Nikki in panic.

To which she replied: *You'll know what to do.*

Perhaps she was right, but he's still waiting for inspiration to strike. At this moment, sweating onions in a pan, he can't imagine facing Willa, can't imagine how he'll explain himself. She lands in Chicago in just three days' time. But Willa Blount is just one more spark to light the fuse of his undoing. There are uglier problems to solve before he gets to hers, beginning with the problem of his rattled, profoundly baffled conscience.

IT COMES DOWN TO THIS, he's decided: above all else, he owes it to *Garnier* to set the record straight, to tell the truth to anyone who might be at risk of falling in love with the sonata. This feels irreducibly right. For all the mistakes he's made in his life, for all his frailties and foibles, he's never once taken credit for work he didn't do. Nate and Sylvia Weil didn't raise him to be a liar, much less a thief. If anything violates his personal sense of right and wrong, it's this.

The sonata is brilliant. He can't possibly claim it as his own. What he should do instead—it's clearer by the hour—is move heaven and earth to prepare Jacques Garnier for his grand début. He needs to put flesh on the man's bones before Ana Clara Matta takes the stage. However and whenever the truth finally emerges, the real composer must be fully prepared to step into the light, to take up his rightful legacy. Garnier must be far more than just a name. Whatever personal humiliation awaits him, Ben is determined to do justice to the man.

And now, it seems, Nathalie Artigue has carried him a good part of the way there. Turning the burner off, Ben opens the laptop and rereads her email from last night. The subject line still carries a charge: GARNIER: FOUND.

Ben, I think I know exactly who your Garnier is.

When Debussy returns to Paris after his Prix de Rome residency, there is in his circle a young pianist from Normandy named Jacques Garnier. The two men were students together at the Conservatoire, studying composition under Ernest Guiraud. From the few notices we find, we know that Garnier

339

is admired for his pianism, especially for strong performances of his own work. His compositions are considered very avant-garde, very *à la mode*. In one notice Debussy calls his friend's work *"étrange et stupéfiant comme un masque kabuki"*— strange and stunning as a kabuki mask. High praise.

The provenance of the sonata is more obscure. While I find reference to a Garnier concerto for piano and violin in C minor, there is no mention of a sonata. The concerto is perhaps a student work. It seems that Jacques Garnier continues to compose fascinating music for some years. So, why the world has never heard of him?

A 1903 letter of his to Debussy, from a private collection of Debussy papers, gives us a clue. (See the attachement.) In effect Garnier is offered a teaching position at Harvard and an opportunity to play with the Boston Symphony. We don't have Debussy's letter, but it seems that he tries to dissuade Jacques, because in this response Jacques makes defense of his decision. "I know you say America is full of dangerous musical beasts, but I won't forget your advice: Beware of the teeth!" (Perhaps my English version isn't quite right; *"Attention aux dents!"* are his words.) He thanks Debussy for letters of introduction to the oboist Longy and violinists Franz Kneisel and Charles Martin Loeffler. They are fellow Europeans who can make the introductions. From all this one thinks that Jacques Garnier sails to America circa 1903–04. This gives more than enough time for him to compose the sonata before your recording date.

One more item. You point me to the descending passage that you feel might quote Lili Boulanger's *'Trois morceaux.'* A comparison of the two scores does expose similarities, I agree. This alone, of course, proves nothing of the composer's intent, and the passage is too short to build a reasoned case upon. There can be other explanations for the echoes we hear.

But I believe your instinct is exactly right. I passed some pleasant hours searching back issues of l'Écho de Paris, a quotidien newspaper of the day with good coverage of Parisian culture. And what do I find there? A *morceau* of evidence that supports your idea of a Boulanger connexion.

According to a notice on December 1, 1902, the writer Marcel Proust hosts a dinner party at the Ritz which includes a recital by Jacques Garnier and his special guest, the nine years old 'demoiselle éblouissante et hors du commun' Mlle Lili Boulanger. Lili plays a Fauré piece in honour of the composer, who is present. What Garnier plays, we don't know. According to l'Écho, Proust is so charmed by Lili that he spontaneously gives her his fountain pen. (Don't you wonder where that pen is now?)

Does this prove that the passage in your sonata is a quotation of Lili's morceau? Not to the standards of the music historian. But it does say that they knew each other well enough to perform together. And there is Fauré, who taught both Boulanger girls at the Conservatoire, where he most likely also taught Jacques Garnier and Claude Debussy. We may never know the full truth about that passage, but my sense is that you are correct. I say this informally, in my role as music lover rather than scholar.

I hope this is of help, Ben. I believe that if Garnier had stayed in Europe and continued to compose at this level he would have made lasting fame here. It is a fateful decision that he takes. On the evidence of this sonata alone, even if no other work turns up, he deserves a place of honour in the great European-American musical diaspora. When we speak of Dvorak, Rachmaninov and Toscanini, we must also speak of Jacques Garnier. It is my firm conviction. Perhaps you can finally bring attention to his work.

Amitiés,

Nathalie

Ben has to catch his breath. Nathalie Artigue's words are every bit as galvanizing now as they were over breakfast. In a single email she's confirmed so much of what he's long suspected but been unable to prove. How could this not be the Garnier he's been searching for?

After perusing the fascinating attachment—Garnier's handwriting in the Debussy letter elegant in a way that somehow puts him in mind of the Adagio—Ben forwards the email to Nikki.

Found him! he writes. *My Paris contact nailed it.*

His cousin is still his only confidante, the only one who knows the truth—though in a few hours, if he has the nerve to carry through with his plan, she'll be joined by another. He'll proceed one confession at a time, hoping that each will make the next easier. If only he could confess to Jacques Garnier himself—apologize to him, ask his forgiveness for letting a small circle of the musical world believe, for a time, that his genius belonged to someone else. If anything might bring him a measure of peace, it's surely this. But the maestro, alas, is unable to hear his plea. Ben Weil will have to find his peace closer to home.

XLVII.

REGRETS

BY FIVE THIRTY he's nearly done with the paella and is well into an even-tempered Rioja, Robin's old favorite accompaniment for her old favorite dish. He's made countless paellas for her over the years, classing up the recipe with homemade chorizo, imported Valencia tomatoes, smoky Extremadura paprika, saffron from Khorasan, braised rabbit in place of chicken. . . . It's evolved into his best dish, without question. He's always made it for her with love. He's surprised to find that tonight is no exception. As nervous as he is about the conversation to come, he's looking forward to having her in his kitchen. Cooking for her, caring for her.

By the time the doorbell rings he has the mussels steaming and is setting the kitchen table, hoping the informality of eating there might ease any awkwardness. The Rioja awaits her; a crusty baguette sits on the bread board with a saucer of Spanish olive oil beside it. Keith Jarrett flows from invisible speakers, a neutral enough choice, the improvisational energy right. Ben's as ready as he'll ever be.

When he opens the door it's to find a nervous smile awaiting him, a pair of pale green eyes turned shyly upward. She's wearing the Peruvian alpaca hat he gave her years ago. He wonders whether she's chosen it on purpose.

"Hey," she says. "Not early, am I?"

She knows she isn't. She's timed her arrival to the minute.

"Not a bit. And even if you were, it's only me."

She slips her jacket off and hangs it on the coat tree as she did for years, this much, at least, unchanged. But once she steps into the living room her eyes widen at the upgrades he's made. The house she left was humbler, messier, badly dated. Even the recessed lighting seems to catch her off guard.

Under the jacket she's wearing an Irish knit cardigan he's never seen. She hides her hands in its pockets and surveys the room with wonderment.

"Wow, Ben. Nikki said you'd renovated, but I had no idea."

"Couldn't have done it without her."

"That's exactly what she said."

Soon she's sitting in his kitchen, cradling a glass of wine in her lap, taking it all in—the high-tech range and hood, the Sub-Zero fridge, the luminous floors, the knockout into the dining room. He notices a drift in her eyes, her thoughts wandering elsewhere, but he needs to tend to the mussels. With tongs he plucks them from the steamer and arranges them atop the golden paella, the artful finishing touch, then delivers his offering to the table.

"I can't believe you did all this, Ben," she says. "It's a ton of work."

"Special occasion."

She studies the stem of her wineglass. When he's settled at the table she looks over and says, "Is it?"

"I think so."

"I wasn't sure we were ready."

"Let's find out." He lifts his glass. "You know . . . to friendship. Whatever that turns out to mean."

For a while they content themselves with eating, letting the hearty food settle their nerves. Despite the familiar menu and familiar company, the meal feels entirely different from the thousands they've eaten together at the same table. The kitchen overhaul is part of it, the newness of the space screening out the past, but it's not only that. When Ben tops off her wineglass she sets her fork down and sends him a nervous glance.

"So, I guess we should talk about the elephant in the room."

Ben abandons the twist of bread he's torn from the loaf. It occurs to him that she could be referring to any number of elephants. Hurwitz . . . the concert . . . even Ana, if she's caught wind of their fleeting affair. He wonders what Nikki's told her.

"Which elephant in particular?"

"*Alan.* If you need me to say it."

Actually Ben could care less about Hurwitz, now that he's off the playing field. There's something more urgent he needs to discuss. But perhaps this is a way in.

He says, "I'm sorry you had to go through what you did. Not that I know details, really."

"What would you like to know?"

"Just . . . whether you're at peace with what's happened. Whether you're alright."

A skeptical look crosses Robin's face. "I appreciate that. I really do. But look, I feel horrible about how it all played out. I feel like I owe you answers. Isn't there anything you want to ask me?"

This he's not prepared for. A jolt of anger tenses his shoulders— an unwelcome surprise. He feels a fat dose of adrenaline dispensed into his veins. The next heartbeat comes with an odd jab.

"Like what?" he asks. "Like how you could have left your husband of twenty years for a loser like Alan Hurwitz?"

She blanches. "I guess. Among other things."

"Though maybe it would have stung even more if you'd slept with someone in your own league. Another player. A conductor. What do you think?"

"You know I would never have done that."

"Actually, I don't know that," he says, though he never doubted her fidelity until Hurwitz appeared. "You can't blame me for wondering. It's not like you didn't have opportunities on tour. I'm sure there are men all over the world who'd love to drink you into bed. Can you really sit here and tell me I'm wrong?"

Ben hates the words even as he's speaking them. Hates the ugly lashing-out, the pettiness, the lightning-strike of anger he's so carefully bled off. The swerve into malice is as shocking to him as it must be to Robin. He has absolutely no reason to suspect she was unfaithful to him before Hurwitz. It's baseless and cruel and beneath him, and they both know it.

Head careening and heart thundering, he scrambles to throttle back, to take control. He needs to find his way back to a Ben he respects. Robin is staring across the table in open disbelief, as if a kidnapper's thrown her ex-husband from his chair and sat down in his place.

"Ben, where's this coming from? I thought we were talking about Alan."

He takes a yogic breath and slowly siphons it off. She looks on, head tilted as if to dodge a glancing blow. The adrenaline is still charging through his veins, an unworthy but formidable adversary.

"I'm sorry, Robs. Jesus . . . that was way off base."

"No kidding."

A lull descends over the table. The paella before them, all his hard work, appears in a new and dismal light. He spoons another mussel from the platter but makes no move to eat it. Robin sips her wine tensely, scrutinizing the cherrywood cabinets, then helps herself to more Rioja without topping off his glass. When he steals a glance at her he finds her expression hard to read, the old familiarity gone. There is hurt, yes, but also toughness, a defiance that's new to him. If he's to save the evening he'll need to break the silence somehow. She certainly isn't going to.

"There's something I want to say to you," he tells her quietly.

She pins her glass to the tabletop as if on a ship that's made a sudden lurch. "Something more constructive, I hope."

"I think so."

"I'm listening."

Ben takes a deep breath, having decided to err on the side of generosity. "It's that I don't think Alan's what blew us up. All Alan did was light the fuse."

"Oh?"

"The problem wasn't Alan. The problem was that I wasn't giving you what you needed. I wish I'd seen it in time to make it right. I'm so sorry I didn't, Robs."

Robin's eyes widen with surprise, touch his for an instant, and then flit away. It's her turn to be caught off guard. He sees a thought germinate in her, then push its way toward the light. She takes a prodigious gulp of wine. Girds herself.

"No way is this all on you, Ben. I wasn't giving you what you needed, either. It took a long time for me to admit that to myself."

"I hear you. It took me almost a year to face up to my part in it. Gallingly."

A flicker of sympathy darts across her features. Something softens in her mouth, her pale cheeks. He's attuned to her like an intricate piece of music.

"Really?"

"Really. I was angry. Righteous. I couldn't see straight until I burned some of that energy off." He smiles sadly. "Though apparently I still have work to do."

"Hey—seeing me . . . having me here . . . I get it. It's bound to trigger things. I halfway expected it."

"I didn't mean to say all of that. *Any* of it. I don't know where it came from."

"Let go of it. I have. It doesn't matter."

Another lull comes over the table. Her eyes shift away, scanning back and forth as if reading something inscribed on the refrigerator door. When they find his again there is a new urgency in them.

"Ben? I'm glad we're both doing the work. That's good. But look, what *I* want to say is that what I did with Alan was shameful, no matter what issues there might have been in the marriage." She falters. "I was awful, Ben. To both of you."

"Why to him?"

"I used Alan. And I think he realized it. It probably explains some of his craziness at the end there. Which is not your concern, obviously. The point is, I used him to try to break through to you, because I was too confused or stupid to find a better way. Maybe just too exhausted. I slept with Alan to send you a message."

She looks away. "Maybe at first I just needed affection. Sexual attention from a man. Excitement. But the longer it went on, the sloppier I got about hiding it, because unconsciously I must have wanted you to find out. I think I wanted to save us, weird as that sounds. I wanted you to *notice* me. I've thought long and hard about this, Ben." She shakes her head, just once. "So unbelievably banal. But like many banal things, it happens to be true."

He can't help but hear Nikki behind Robin's words. No doubt they've talked for hours about all this, unraveled it thread by thread. But of all she's said, only one word truly stings: *excitement*. This is something Hurwitz gave her that he no longer could. After twenty years of marriage, the first electrifying thrill was most certainly gone—how could it be otherwise? At this moment, fairly or not, it feels to Ben like a failure of character. He sets his glass down without taking the sip he'd meant to.

Robin's not slowing down. The tide of confession rushes on. A scant second after she takes another deep swallow of wine, he sees it surface in her eyes.

She says, "Maybe I wanted you to fight for me. Be jealous. That's the real message I was sending. But by the time you got it, it was too late." Under the heavy sweater her shoulders sink. "I could have just talked to you. . . . I know you would have heard me. I am so sure of that, Ben."

There are tears in her eyes. With a deft move she brushes them away but they come back in force. "And then—then—to keep going with it! Jesus. Right on through to *divorce*. . . . I don't know what the hell was wrong with me. It's a blur, like after a car crash. I just know that I hurt you, and I'm sorry, Ben, I really am. You didn't deserve it. I need you to know that."

He nods. She smiles back ruefully, cheeks shining with tears. "I'm a mess," she says, blowing her nose into the napkin. All at once the kitchen feels tight and airless. Though she's within easy reach he hesitates to touch her, to soothe her distress. The urge to comfort her is reflexive, all but automatic, but he smells danger.

It occurs to him that if she feels so driven to apologize to him for her betrayal, perhaps she'll need to apologize to Hurwitz, too. If the whole affair was nothing but a way to get her distracted husband's attention, she may have unfinished business with her lover as well. Perhaps tonight's visit is only the first stop on her apology tour. And so Ben stays just where he is, giving her space to compose herself, then rises to clear the half-finished plates.

XLVIII.

THE FULL TRUTH
AS HE KNOWS IT

ONCE AN APPLE CRISP is in front of her Robin seems inclined to change the subject. Having said what she came to say, she eases into another sort of evening.

"Hey," she says, animated by the Rioja, "I wanted to tell you: I'm so glad you're back into making music. *So* glad. And in such a big way. It's amazing. I was just floored when I heard about this Matta show. Literally speechless. The Animal playing your grand début—that's rich." She takes up her fork then lays it back down. "But when in the world did you write this sonata, Ben? After I left? I mean, I guess you had time on your hands. And things to work through."

He shrugs, having no answer for her. They take their first bites of dessert.

"This is amazing," she says, blotting her mouth with her napkin. "But honestly, in all the years we've known each other, I never had an inkling that you were a composer in the making." Her eyes smile over at him. "Did you even know it yourself?"

So, here it is.

He's prepared no words for this moment. As a younger man he'd have spent hours plotting it out ahead of time, honing his speech, trying to guess her reaction and weigh how various explanations might be received, but he's old enough now to trust his intuition. Authenticity matters so much more than control. Sincerity is everything. And though the evening's already strayed into dangerous waters, the matter of Hurwitz has nothing to do with why he's invited her here. Hurwitz is the least of his worries.

As Robin takes another bite of apple crisp Ben sits quietly and waits for the right words to come, falling into his ex-wife's expectant gaze, knowing that this is the very last moment, for them, of tonight's innocence.

He says, "I'm going to tell you something only Nikki knows. I'm going to tell you because I may need your help in thinking it through. Okay?"

Robin sets her fork down with care, searching his eyes. "Ben, you're scaring me. Is the tumor back?"

"No, not that. Maybe worse, in a way. I don't know."

"What are you saying?"

"I'm telling you because I trust you, and because you know me better than anyone else in the world."

She's watching him very closely now. She parts her lips to speak but closes them again, thinking better of it. With an unreadable frown she pushes the plates aside so she can cover his hand with hers. At the same moment her phone rings in her back pocket, the ringtone something from deep inside a Bach cello suite. Her face tenses as she reaches back to squelch it.

"Sorry. Such timing."

"Modern life."

To his surprise he feels no nervousness at all. "Has Nikki told you anything about the concert at the Pearson? About the sonata?"

"Nothing. She's been weirdly evasive about it. Why are you asking?"

And so he tells her—omitting nothing, excusing nothing—the full truth as he knows it. The drawn-out Debussy sessions in Studio A. The gradual build between Ana and him all through the spring and hot summer, his head buzzing with tinnitus and vertigo. Her attentions irresistible in the face of his loneliness, of the constant temptation to burn away evenings at Counterpoint rather than go home to an empty house. And then, with no warning whatsoever, the ruinous moment sitting with her at the Steinway, the studio deserted, her thigh against his as she played through the score on the music stand, the rippling legwork arousing him as she plied the pedals.

"Too much information?" he asks Robin, worried he's gone too far.

"It's all part of the story," she replies, looking a bit jarred but willing to take it on. She's still leaning forward on her elbows, covering his hand with hers, completely focused. Lights snap on across the way: a Farahani entering the kitchen. From a certain angle the neighbors would be able to catch a glimpse of Ben and his guest, hands touching across the tabletop. It doesn't matter. They'd only be happy for him.

"So," Robin says, "she ambushed you and was blown away by your sonata. She didn't know you composed. Just like I didn't."

"She didn't know it because it wasn't true. I didn't compose. I *don't* compose."

"I'm not sure what you mean."

"It's not my piece, Robs. Not my sonata. She assumed it was when she saw a handwritten score, an obviously unfinished score, but she was wrong. And I didn't set her straight, to my great shame. There's no excuse for my silence in that moment."

Robin cocks her head, trying to make sense of it. "But . . . you've lost me. Whose work is it? Why was the score unfinished? Help me out here."

Ben rises. "Come with me."

Together they walk into the living room, Robin touching the Bösendorfer as she passes. "*Cher ami,*" she says to it, letting Ben lead her. At the mantle he takes down one of the Edison cylinders and gives it to her to hold.

"I believe the sonata's the work of a French pianist, this guy named Jacques Garnier who emigrated to Boston around the turn of the century." Robin looks from the cylinder in her hand to him and then back again, no less confused. "Almost nothing is known about Garnier's time in America, except that by 1915 he'd composed the sonata Ana played in the studio that night. It was my hand transcription she saw on the music stand." He taps the cylindrical box. "You're holding in your hand the only known recording of it. It's all that's survived of Garnier's work."

"Whoa." Gingerly Robin turns the box in her hand, studying the Edison cameo, the timeworn label. "I've heard about these but never actually seen one." She touches the cardboard cap. "May I?"

"Sure," he says, and turns a light on.

She eases out the cylinder, holding it with her fingertips, and turns it under the sharp light, the tiny ridges faintly visible, the ghostly imprint of Garnier's spectacular performance so ephemeral and modest. The cylinder might just as easily hold a recording of a dancehall tune as a groundbreaking piece of avant-garde music.

"It's beautiful," she says.

"It is."

"Like a fine old instrument. And how is it that Ben Weil happens to possess this?"

He sits her down on the sofa with an apple brandy to hear the rest of the story. The inquiry from Willa Blount, followed by his first awestruck listening session in the Studio A booth. His struggle to transcribe the recording and to unearth something—anything— about a J. Garnier. The way he'd sometimes hear the sonata playing faintly in the house while drifting off to sleep, his constant and inscrutable companion . . . and the way the serenade deserted him, in time, drowned out by the roar of events. He mentions nothing of the exhausting nights as Ana Clara Matta's lover, because there's no need to put Robin through it—only that she stole the score out from under him on her way to Paris, setting in motion a disastrous chain of events he's been powerless to stop.

Robin sits cross-legged at the other end of the sofa, transfixed. He can see she's having trouble processing it all after three glasses of Rioja and now the apple brandy. When her phone rings again it's only a faint vibration from her back pocket, the ringtone muted. She purses her lips for an instant and lets it go.

"One question," she says. "Why don't you just tell Matta? She'd have to cancel the show. Walk it back."

"It's already gone too far. She's told too many people. She just grabbed the wheel and took off, Robs. Never looked back. By the time I realized what was happening she'd already outmaneuvered me. She's lined up all the major critics, celebrities . . . everyone who matters. She wants to throw me at their feet like a fresh kill. Her personal conquest. Her brilliant discovery. It's a disaster." Ben frowns at his brandy. "And now her reputation is on the line too. She'd turn on me in a heartbeat. Remember what she did to Lörber in Munich? That could be me. Or worse."

"You really think she'd go after you like that?" Robin asks, then answers her own question. "Of course she would. It's who she is. She's absolutely cutthroat when it comes to her public image. I know—I follow her on Twitter just for the sick entertainment value of watching her shred people. Nikki follows her too. And you're right, she'd never admit she was duped."

"Exactly. Especially to certain people she can't afford to disappoint."

"Who are we talking about?"

"Jérôme Assouline, for one, who's offered to wangle her a residency in Berlin, with Barenboim. She played the sonata for him in Amsterdam—he emailed me about it. He was impressed enough to borrow the score and study it. Which is absolutely horrifying to me, terrifying, really. . . . I love that man. You remember how he played the *Kaddish* for my mother? It makes me physically ill to think of disappointing him like this."

"Totally understand that. What a lovely man. What a great soul. And so fatherly to you, exactly when you needed it."

"But he's not the only one she's told, Robs. There are any number of marquee names she's trying to shake down for one thing or another. Then you have the MacArthur people: she's a finalist for a Genius Grant. She wants that one badly. Not so much for the money, I suspect, but because she wants the word *genius* attached to her name. So, yeah—I'm dead sure she'd throw me under the bus to save her own skin."

"And now you have the Pearson concert to deal with."

"I didn't even know about that show until you forwarded me the announcement."

"Come again? You know what? Fuck her."

At the far end of the sofa Robin pulls an afghan around her shoulders, the heat stepping down as they cross the threshold of nine o'clock. He senses her playing out the implications in her mind, mapping out his professional peril just as he's been doing for weeks now.

"This is just unbelievable," she says quietly. "What in the world are you going to do?"

"I have to come clean somehow."

"With Matta? I thought you said—"

"Not with her. I mean publicly. Even if there's a way to stop the concert, the lie's already out there. Think how many people got that Pearson Center email. Thousands. Damage has already been done. I don't know how or when, but it has to be faced. And I have to introduce Garnier—that much I'm clear on. I was hoping . . . well, maybe you and Nikki and I could figure it out together. There's no one else I'd trust with it."

The faintest hint of a smile plays across her lips. He sends a hand her way along the back of the sofa. She takes it with a bittersweet look.

"Hey," he says, "I completely trust you with this. I mean it. I've been thinking about it ever since you got back."

"I'll help in any way I can. Of course I will. Just say the word."

"I really—"

"But you know, I should go. Early start tomorrow. I'm meeting a friend for breakfast at a ridiculous hour." And with this she's on her feet, seeming to put the evening's careful conversation behind her. All Ben can do is watch from the couch, not knowing what to make of the abrupt move. His heart sinks slowly as she buttons her sweater, avoiding his eyes. Though she's standing before him, she's already left the room.

WHILE SHE USES THE BATHROOM he ferries the glasses and brandy bottle into the kitchen. When he comes back he spots her leaning against the wall in the shadows by the bedroom door, phone to her ear, the screen throwing a blue glow against her cheek. She's frowning severely, unaware that he's watching.

The situation comes clear in an instant. For a long moment Ben wrestles with a surge of anger and hurt, a feeling of having been betrayed yet again. He debates whether to speak up and risk turning the evening sour. It's the last thing he wants. But when she comes back into the living room, slipping the phone into her back pocket, the words are out of his mouth before he can stop them.

"So, was that Alan calling?"

"What do you mean?" she says, flushing instantly.

"Your phone kept ringing tonight. Was it him?"

"Ben, you don't have any—"

"No, I don't. But I wouldn't mind if you told me."

She hugs herself tightly and sways in the quiet room, grimacing at the floor. "He's back in Chicago. I guess you should know that."

"Is he the one you're meeting for breakfast?"

Robin steals a glance at him, something frantic in her eyes. "He's in deep trouble, Ben. They're suing the shit out of him. There's a good chance he'll lose everything, the Chicago stores too. I'm worried he might kill himself, actually. He's tried it before. He owns seven guns, you know. Seven. Including an AR-15."

"Shit. I had no idea."

"Nikki's furious with me for having any contact with him at all."

"So, why are you?"

"Because he has literally no one else. He's pushed everyone away. But I just texted him and canceled breakfast. I told him I wouldn't see him again. More drama with Alan is the last thing I need right now."

"What do you think he'll do?"

"Tonight? I really don't know. For all I know, he has a gun to his head right now. It scares the hell out of me to think about it. But it can't be my problem. I'm clear on that."

"I'm glad to hear it."

"I may be crazy, but I'm not stupid crazy. Typically."

At the front door she bundles up and gives him her cheek, then changes her mind and wraps her arms around him, burying her face in the crook of his neck. For a long moment they stand in the foyer of what was once their home, and then she's gone, striding off into the cold without a backward glance.

Ben rinses the dishes and loads the dishwasher slowly, retracing the evening's conversation, the surprising revelations on both sides. He feels both wrung out and exhilarated by Robin's visit. The evening has been a long time coming.

When he shuts the kitchen lights off and collects his phone from the coffee table he finds two messages from her:

Thanks for tonight, you. I needed that. A lot.

Then, a few minutes later:

We can't let the Animal ruin your life, Ben. Send me everything you have so I can start thinking about this. I'm in.

XLVIX.

A Pro Bono Matter

Monday leaves him little time to think further about Robin, the coming concert or anything else, because all his attention is absorbed by the multidimensional chess problem of recording a gamelan orchestra. He and Eliza have to call upon every engineering skill they have, and every microphone in the safe, to set up for gongs, bamboo flutes, xylophone, rebabs, drums, voices. After six hours of setup, the tedious recording session goes late into the evening. For one blessed day the sonata barely enters Ben's mind. At home he bolts down a whiskey, tinkers at the piano for a bit, and falls into a heavy sleep.

But by mid-morning Tuesday Robin has news for him. As he sits through an interminable meeting with the Counterpoint accountant, bored beyond words, a message flashes up on his phone: *Call me.*

"So," she says brightly, "I may have something on Garnier's stint in Boston."

"Do tell."

"After reading that email from the woman at the Sorbonne—Nathalie?—I called this friend of mine at the BSO to see what kind of archives they have from that era. Turns out they've got tons of stuff. She referred me to the archivist. I got him right away."

"And?"

"You know those two BSO violinists Debussy put Garnier in touch with? Well, Kneisel was concertmaster for years, so there's all kinds of material. There isn't much on Loeffler—*but* the archivist happens to know Loeffler's biographer, who spent months over there while researching her book. He wouldn't give me her number, but he promised to call and ask if she knows anything about a Jacques Garnier. In the meantime he's taking a spin through the Kneisel papers. Of course I couldn't let on how urgent this all was.

But I'm hoping the Loeffler connection will bear fruit. Apparently Dr. Ellen Knight is the world authority."

"Robs, thanks for this."

"May go nowhere, but who knows. Maybe we can put some flesh on the bones. Any more thoughts on what you're going to do Friday evening?"

Ben pauses, consults his gut. "If you ask me right now, I'd say I certainly won't be attending any concerts. Maybe stay home and watch a movie."

"No grand confession before a cast of thousands?"

"A hanging in the town square doesn't appeal, somehow."

"So, how are you going to get the word out there?"

For this he has no answer. "Haven't solved that one yet."

"Ben? Come to Nikki's for dinner tonight. Let's the three of us put our heads together on this. We'll order in and we'll figure this out. We won't quit until we do. Okay?"

EACH OF THEM comes away from the long evening with an assignment. Ben wastes no time in tackling his. The moment he returns home from Nikki's—it's after midnight but he's wide awake—he sits down at the computer and finds, as promised, an email from Robin's brother, a corporate litigator with a Loop firm. Midway through the evening Robin put Dave Masters on speakerphone to help them strategize, Ben's former brother-in-law warming to the fight immediately. To watch Dave's mind work was a revelation: the rapid-fire tactical thinking, the matter-of-fact dismissal of their half-baked schemes, the clear grasp of how various gambits would play out. For Dave it wasn't a particularly difficult puzzle to solve. They watched each other in bafflement as he thought out loud. In ten minutes a plan was on the table.

When Ben jotted $$$ on a scrap of paper and shoved it across the table to Robin she only smirked. *He's got plenty*, she mouthed silently, rubbing her fingertips together. Ben knew this but felt obliged to offer.

Seeing his discomfort, Robin told her brother, "So, Ben's worried about your fee. I said no way would you take his shekels."

"You said right. You're still family to me, bro. Don't tell my little sister." When Ben didn't answer, he said: "Okay, so it's an arts thing, right? Call it a pro bono matter. I'm way behind on my pro bono hours. Done." He'd run the obligatory conflict check in the morning and send an engagement letter, but in the meantime Ben was to consider himself represented by counsel.

It came time for Dave Masters to put his kids to bed. Before signing off he offered to draft the note that Ben now copies into a fresh email message.

Ms. Matta and Mr. Wooten:

This is to provide you with formal notice, to be followed by a letter from my attorney identical in substance, that I deny permission for Ms. Matta to give a public performance of my "French Sonata" at the Pearson Center for the Performing Arts, located at 1 Northerly Island in Chicago, Illinois, on January 11, 2019, or at any point thereafter. As you know, I denied your verbal request for performance rights in December, but you have nevertheless proceeded with plans to present the piece, undertaking no due diligence to obtain my written consent. Any such presentation would constitute an unauthorized public performance of an original work to which I hold sole and exclusive copyright.

Furthermore, I assume that you will be compensated for your performance. You have tendered no offer, written or verbal, to share the proceeds with me or to pay a fair royalty for the privilege of performing my work and profiting thereby.

As a final matter, any representation, implied or otherwise, to the Pearson Center for the Performing Arts that you are entitled to perform my sonata is or was predicated upon your prior familiarity with the score. As you admitted in a video call between us on December 6, 2018, you removed a copy of the original score from my home after entering the premises without permission on the evening of November 9, 2018. This illegal entry and theft constitute further cause for potential legal action against you and/or the Pearson Center for the Performing Arts should the concert proceed as planned.

In view of the above considerations, I demand that you remove my piece from the January 11, 2019 program and communicate this change immediately to Ms. Constanza Barrows, Artistic Director of the Pearson Center Concert Series, as well as in any public notices that may be issued in connection with the event.

Be advised that we are prepared to seek all legal remedies to which we may be entitled, including but not limited to an emergency injunction against the venue and/or liquidated or actual damages to be paid by you and/or the Pearson Center for the Performing Arts, should you proceed with the performance.

Please expect a letter from my attorney, David Masters, Esq., tomorrow which memorializes these demands.

Sincerely,

Benjamin Weil

cc: David Masters, Esq. – Boone, Peters LLC

It's a bluff but not an empty one. Dave Masters has advised them that an emergency injunction may indeed be possible, that a judge might be persuaded to bring the show to an unseemly halt. But much of the damage has already been done. No injunction can undo the announcement by the Pearson, or the publicity spots on the radio, or the inbox full of congratulatory messages from all across Ben's professional network. Stopping the concert will not stop the bleeding.

And stopping the concert, Ben's come to realize in the course of this long evening, is actually the last thing he wants to do. His email has another objective entirely. No: Garnier will have his moment in the spotlight, if not exactly in the way Ana Clara Matta intends.

It isn't long before the trap is sprung. At ten-thirty on Wednesday morning Ben checks email and finds a screaming reply from Ana Clara Matta. Not a word of it surprises him. He skims through it with mounting satisfaction.

FOR FUCKSAKE!!! You wait until NOW to bring this up? I'm doing you a HUGE FAVOR, in case you haven't figured that out. Look at who's coming to see this. You think you could have gotten that kind of attention without me? You're an idiot if you think so, full stop.

I took that score from your house because I loved the piece and I wanted to help you. That's all. If I'd waited for your permission you'd still be sweating out every little note. You'd never be done with the thing. It would never see the light of day. So I took it, OK, but for your own good. I guess you don't see that either.

Don't be a child, Ben. You can't win against us. We have the best lawyers in the business. They'll sue you to within an inch of your life.

I'm giving you until 5:00 this afternoon to grant us rights. After that, no promises. Don't underestimate me.

And Ben? Fuck you.

ACM

It's everything they've hoped for and more. No doubt there will be a less hotheaded response from Ant Wooten or their lawyers, but Ben's email has done exactly what it was intended to do. The brief thread is all the evidence he needs. He forwards the furious note to Nikki, Robin and Dave Masters, then gets back to work.

As he sits in the control booth recording a mediocre guitarist, he keeps an eye on his phone. Nikki is the first to respond:

Nailed her! Checking for Constanza's email address.

Then Robin:

ha! the bitch!

And not long afterward, Dave Masters:

Nice. At 5:01 sharp you forward that chain to your
Pearson Center contact with my covering text. Will send
verbiage after this meeting.

Ben wraps up the guitar session and dives back into his office, latching the door behind him. The promised email from Robin's brother is ready and waiting. Pulling up Ana's furious note from the morning he attaches it to a fresh email, pastes in Dave's text and then reads the thread through from top to bottom, starting with the covering note and proceeding through Ana's unhinged message and his original cease-and-desist email to her. He plugs in the Pearson Center email address Nikki's tracked down and then saves the whole thing to his Drafts folder where it will sit until five o'clock, ticking like a bomb.

Ready, he texts to Nikki, Robin and Dave Masters, and flies out of Counterpoint into the bright winter day to walk off his excitement, the shape of the coming days far from clear but a degree less cloudy than before.

L.

WAR ROOM

WAITING FOR CONSTANZA BARROWS to show herself, Ben, Nikki and Robin hunker down in the Counterpoint conference room with a spinach pizza, stress-eating. Ben keeps a close eye on the laptop before him. Robin wonders aloud if Ms. Barrows is the type to check email after hours. It's hard to imagine, they decide, that an urgent message arriving at 5:01 for the Artistic Director of the Pearson Center Concert Series would escape notice. They imagine the poor woman frantically mobilizing colleagues, hopping on the phone with lawyers, scrambling for a response. Perhaps it will be a lawyer, in fact, who replies. Dave Masters has prepared them for this contingency and is on call should the need arise.

For a time the little war room falls into a lull, the pizza plundered, Ben's email and phone eerily quiet. There is nothing to do but wait. Nikki peruses her laptop, Robin and Ben their phones. At some point Robin hands her phone to Ben and says, "Looks like congratulations are in order."

"How so?"

"You're a hashtag now. Look what Missy tweeted right after the Pearson announcement went out."

Opposite a stern little headshot of Ana, Ben reads @ACMaestra's tweet:

Truly honored to be introducing the brilliant Chgo composer Benjamin Weil to the world on 1/11 at the beautiful @PearsonCenter. Come hear me debut his "French Sonata" – it's genius! #frenchsonata #benjaminweil

Ben sees that the tweet's garnered more than three thousand likes and twenty-seven retweets. "No pressure," he says, handing the phone back. "I mean, now that she's got everyone all amped up."

"She's got almost seventy thousand followers."

"No wonder she's freaking out."

Nikki says, "Which doesn't mean you have to freak out too, hashtag benjaminweil."

Ben doesn't like the feel of it at all. The conversation trails off, the minutes crawl by. Constanza Barrows remains stubbornly silent. The three of them take turns stepping out for fresh air, staying close in case Constanza should suddenly surface. Robin leafs through back issues of *Gramophone*; Nikki hunkers over her laptop. Ben closes his eyes, the better to listen to the music playing in his head.

Eventually Nikki says, "Hey."

Robin and Ben regard her across the table, slow to come to order.

"So, I've been on this genealogy site, sniffing around for Boston Garniers. I wasn't finding much—some Garniers from the wrong era, also some Gar*ners*, which could be an immigration clerk taking spelling liberties, okay, but it's not like Garner isn't a common enough American name. Well, I widened the Garnier search just now to look at other kinds of documents, and bang! Up pops a ship's manifest for the SS *Bretagne*, departing Le Havre on April 20, 1903, arriving Boston on May 1. Care to guess who's on board?"

"No way."

She swivels the laptop around so they can see for themselves. On the screen is a blurry page from a *Manifest of Alien Immigrants*, inscribed in a spidery, laborious hand. Ben scans it quickly, trying to process what he's seeing—and there, quietly awaiting him halfway down the page, sits none other than Jacques Garnier, thirty-eight years old, profession *Music Teacher*.

"Jacques!" Ben crows, bringing the flat of his hand down on the table.

"Keep reading," Nikki says.

Below the entry for Jacques, indented slightly, he spots a Sylvie Garnier, age thirty-three, and below Sylvie an Elisabeth Garnier, age twelve.

"*Toute la famille*," Robin whispers over his shoulder. "Amazing."

"Send it to me," Ben tells Nikki, and at this moment his phone rings, vibrating on the table.

C Barrows, says the caller ID.

"Here we go," Ben says. Robin pulls up her brother's number on her phone, ready to dial him if he's needed.

Ben puts the call on speakerphone.

"Ms. Barrows. Thanks for getting back to me."

"Well, Mr. Weil, thank you for bringing this situation to our attention. I'm sorry we have to meet under such circumstances." The British voice is unflustered, or pretending to be, as if such situations arise with every concert. "Am I on speaker? Is someone there with you?"

"Only my assistant. Anyone with you?"

"Not as yet. In my experience with matters like this, Mr. Weil, it's usually best to have an informal conversation to start with. One sometimes resolves things simply."

"Couldn't agree more. Was everything clear from the correspondence I sent?"

"Vividly. You and Ms. Matta seem to be miles apart."

"Which is why I thought you'd better be in the loop. I didn't trust her to keep you informed, frankly. Had she even mentioned this to you?"

"Not a word of it. In fact, she's represented quite a different state of affairs."

"Meaning what, exactly?"

"As a matter of legal housekeeping, Mr. Weil, we have our guest artists sign an affidavit attesting to their unencumbered right to perform any piece that isn't in the public domain, as well as any royalty obligations they or we may be undertaking. Ms. Matta's manager provided this affidavit early on. I have it here in front of me."

"They're lying. I never gave her performance rights. I denied them."

"Which is why we do this in the form of an affidavit, Mr. Weil. The artist is representing to us, ultimately under penalty of perjury, that certain facts are true. We undertake no obligation to verify them independently. If she's later drawn into a dispute, the venue cannot be dragged into it. The lawyers call it a firewall. It helps prevent unpleasant surprises."

"But what if that dispute happens *before* the show? And you're made aware of it? Seems like your firewall might not be so fireproof."

Constanza Barrows downshifts into a harder tone. "I'm certain you realize, Mr. Weil, that I must protect the Pearson Center at all costs. I noted in your email to her, of course, your threat to involve us in litigation if she were to proceed with her performance."

"My attorney's idea. I realize it's awkward."

"May I be frank? The Pearson has no intention of involving itself in a knife fight. Ms. Matta's affidavit would help us in court, but really it's in everyone's best interest to resolve this amicably. And promptly, Mr. Weil. Cancelation at this late date would be an extremely serious matter. No one needs that trouble, surely. Or that financial loss."

"Of course not."

"You know, we've already worked very hard to recover from one major program disruption, thanks to the Rafik Jelassi situation. That hasn't been easy at all, Mr. Weil. We'd pulled out all the stops to promote the show, which we believed to be of international interest, really of global significance. We'd done Platinum Circle fundraising on the back of it. But when Ms. Matta proposed to début your piece instead, and especially when she played it for us privately and we heard its brilliance, we were quite interested indeed. It seemed an opportunity for a graceful recovery, especially as you were a Chicagoan and—forgive me—something of a blank slate as a composer. The element of mystery was intriguing. Though I won't lie to you, Mr. Weil: our advisory board wasn't exactly keen on the idea. But Ms. Matta was very persuasive indeed. She prevailed, and since the decision was made there's been full-throated support. To change course yet again, after that ordeal. . . . Well, it's hard to contemplate."

"Understandably." Ben strikes a confiding tone. "To be honest, I'd like nothing better than to see the piece début at the Pearson. But given Ms. Matta's behavior, I can't allow her to be the one to do it. It needs to be done with integrity. I'm sure you understand."

A long sigh comes from the other end of the call. Nikki raises an inquiring brow. Robin points to her phone to ask if she should call her brother, but Ben waves her off.

"Mr. Weil," Constanza says, sounding tired and beleaguered, "if you have a solution in mind, I'd like to hear it. What would you have us do? I think you understand my constraints."

Robin and Nikki nod in unison. Now is the moment.

"I did have an idea, actually," Ben says. "What if the composer himself were to present the piece?"

When Constanza says nothing, he forges ahead. "The first half of the program would stay as it is—Ana performing the Jelassi tribute. Let her have that. But after intermission you'd shift to me. The world début of the French Sonata, as promised—with the added bonus that the composer himself will play it."

Again the line falls dead. In the conference room, the three of them wait for Constanza Barrows to react.

At length she says, "May I be candid, Mr. Weil? We've never heard you play. This is a very challenging piece, and it will be a very savvy audience. Critics will be present, any of them perfectly capable of sinking you. Do you have performance experience? Sorry to be blunt."

"You won't be embarrassed. I can commit to that without reservation."

"I'm certain you play perfectly well in your own living room. Performing for fifteen hundred people is an entirely different matter. I do appreciate the picture you're painting, Mr. Weil, but you're asking me to take quite a risk here."

"You're already taking quite a risk. If you proceed as planned, my attorney will seek an emergency injunction to stop the show. Of course I'd hate for it to reach that point."

Constanza Barrows permits herself another rueful sigh.

"You really do hate Ms. Matta, don't you?"

"It's not too strong a word."

"I can't honestly say I'm surprised, though you didn't hear it from me."

"How do we get to a decision, Constanza?"

She takes her time before answering. Robin, Nikki and Ben exchange looks over the ravaged pizza box, waiting while she weighs her options.

They're all surprised when she says, "I'll take it up the chain tonight, Mr. Weil. I need two approvals. I can't promise what the response will be—I can't even guess what they'll say, to be frank with you. This is as irregular as it gets, in my business."

"I imagine so."

"One question before we ring off. If they should want to hear you play—to audition, in a way—is that a possibility?"

This, too, Dave Masters has foreseen.

"No."

"No?"

"I need you to take me at my word, Constanza. The performance won't embarrass you."

Constanza Barrows groans. "Alright! I suppose I'm only the messenger here. Is there anything else I should know?"

"Just a small request. I'd like to have Peter Roth on the sound board, if that's alright. I know he freelances for you."

"Noted."

"So, when can I expect to hear back from you with a decision?"

"I've just texted the key parties. We're talking at half six. You'll know as soon as I do."

"I appreciate your going to bat on this."

"Keep your phone close, Mr. Weil."

BEN SPRINGS TO HIS FEET, exhilarated.

"Dave Masters is a genius," he says, pacing the room. "That went exactly as he said it would. Almost word for word."

Robin's already texted her brother. "He says settle down. The next step is the tricky one."

"Yeah, yeah. I need to reach out to Peter, warn him they'll be calling."

"Already done," Nikki says.

"Ben," Robin says, "you were great on that call. A pro. Real sang-froid."

"I'm sure she saw right through to the terrified child within."

"She didn't, trust me."

"So, we wait."

And wait they do—until six-thirty, then seven, then seven-thirty, Nikki eventually making espressos just to occupy herself. It's almost eight when Constanza Barrows calls back.

"Mr. Weil," she says in a distinctly warmer tone.

"Constanza."

"I'm sorry to have kept you waiting, but it was an involved discussion, as you'd expect. We arts professionals don't like surprises, and this was quite a surprise."

"Sorry for that."

"Not at all. In any case, I have good news to report. We're on board with your general plan, subject to a few small considerations. I won't say it was easy to get there, but we are there now. The Pearson Center will be pleased to host your début of the French Sonata."

"Wonderful. What are the conditions?"

"We'll need you to sign the same affidavit Ms. Matta did, of course—I assume this won't be an issue. And we will need that affidavit to include a waiver of any performance fees. The reality, Mr. Weil, is that despite the program change we're not in a position to decrease Ms. Matta's fee, which leaves no money for you, unfortunately. I'd hope the prestige of the venue and audience will be compensation enough."

"Absolutely." Ben holds Nikki's gaze across the table. "So, you'll be talking to Ms. Matta to clarify things?"

"She is my very next call."

"Good luck with that."

"I appreciate it. My assistant will send you the affidavit tomorrow, along with our standard performance contract, which we'll need you to turn around at once. And I'll have her approach Peter Roth about handling sound board duties. He may already be on the rota for Friday, as our regular lad is away. Is there anything else I can do for you, Mr. Weil?"

"Only to accept my thanks for making this far less painful than it might have been."

"Good night, now."

In the war room Nikki hunkers over the conference table like a general over a map.

"Total fucking victory," she declares, her eyes flicking from Robin to Ben and back again.

Now it remains only to prepare for the next battle.

LI.

TO BE A WISE FOOL

BEN WITHDRAWS to prepare himself. In the morning he emails the Counterpoint staff to say he'll be out the rest of the week, offering no explanation. Surely they all know about the coming concert by now—the team is full of classical music aficionados—but only Eliza has mentioned it to him. "So, Matta's doing your big début," she said with a frown, the day after the first Pearson announcement went out. "That's so fucking dope." And that was all—a relief that she knew to leave it at this. Given the circumstances he's been happy not to answer questions.

He needs time to feel his way toward the light. To let his worst fears recede and rear up and recede again. Most of all he needs quiet in order to hear his own voice, to eavesdrop on the man speaking at the lip of the stage, the man standing at the pivot point between Jacques Garnier and the next version of Ben Weil, whoever he may be. Because he's made his decision: he will be there on Friday night after all.

The concentration of the moment will be profound. The radical distillation of everything important to him. He imagines the sea of familiar faces and imagines how acutely they'll all be listening. He pictures the spotlight raking the stage, Matta seething in the wings. There will come a moment at which time stops, the world waiting for him to speak. . . . Yet even now, with only two days to go, he has no idea what he'll say. No idea how he'll settle accounts with Jacques Garnier. With himself.

If he were true to his convictions he'd not prepare at all. He'd trust the words to find him in the moment. But never has it been harder to let go. Twice now he's been jarred awake by a nightmare in which he stands tongue-tied and dry-mouthed on a brutally spotlit stage, unable to find his voice, terrified, the audience a smear of scornful faces. A nightmare requiring no

371

interpretation whatsoever, a nightmare literal as a court order. Perhaps once it's all over, once he's done what he must do, his dreams will turn interesting again, enigmatic as dreams should be.

HE CLEANS HIS HOUSE LIKE A SAILOR, the diligence of the work keeping him calm. Lintels are finally dusted. The range hood's hidden pockets of grease are mucked out. Every bit of stainless is buffed to a high gleam. When he needs to, he stops to take care of more exigent matters: paperwork for Constanza Barrows, audiovisuals for Peter Roth, some incompetent ironing for the occasion. Through it all he denies himself the consolations of music. The stereo stays quiet, biding its time, giving him space. Even music might distract him, ironically enough. His house is as silent as it's ever been.

All the more startling, then, when the phone trills loudly on the coffee table. He stares at it like a beast of the forest, uncomprehending.

"Ben," the caller says, the voice familiar if not the greeting. "It's Willa."

They've talked on the phone four or five times now, but never has Willa Blount countenanced the use of given names. He's as startled by the *Ben* as by the *Willa*.

"Willa. Are you in Chicago?"

"All settled in at the Knickerbocker."

"Well, then, welcome."

Despite the heady brush with familiarity she's still incapable of small talk. She'd like him to visit her in her room tomorrow after lunch, if at all possible. Say, one o'clock? There's much to discuss. She'll explain when he arrives.

A chill runs through him, though he reads no anger in her tone. He wonders whether she's stumbled across an announcement for Friday's program, some reference to *Benjamin Weil's French Sonata* that's perplexed or upset her. It could be as simple as a blurb in one of those *Around Town* flyers all the tourist hotels have. Or perhaps she's found a complimentary *Tribune* or *Time Out Chicago* artfully arranged on the nightstand, within it a listing for the show. As long as Willa was in distant Maine—a woman of fountain pens rather than web browsers—the chances of detection seemed remote enough. Now that she's here, the truth could spring upon her at any moment. But it's just one more scenario Ben can't control. All he wants is a chance to talk to her in person before she finds out through other means.

She says, "Would that plan work for you? I expect you're quite a busy man."

"I'll be there. So looking forward to meeting you, finally."

"It's exactly why I've come to Chicago, Ben. Goodbye, now."

When he sets the phone back on the table he meets his own gaze in the mirror and says: "Time's up." Then laughs at his own dour expression, the heaviness in his eyes.

The important thing, he thinks, is to remember *why* he's decided to do what he's about to do. To approach the precipice, if possible, with a light heart and a righteous one. To be a wise fool. He isn't there yet, surely, but with every hour that passes he's edging closer.

Robin calls as he stands at the stove, plate in hand, dispatching a solitary omelet.

"Ben! Huge news. Are you sitting down?"

"Actually, no."

"Then sit."

She's heard from the violinist Loeffler's biographer, Ellen Knight, who's retrieved from her files a 1916 letter that appears to be from Jacques Garnier to Loeffler, one of several water-damaged documents rescued from the cellar of Loeffler's home near Boston. With the envelope long gone and nothing to go on but the signoff—*Avec toute mon amitié, Jacques*—the biographer had set it aside for future investigation, unaware of any Jacques in Loeffler's acquaintance. She's delighted to have a solid lead on the author.

"I'm emailing the PDF, but just listen to this part," Robin says.

"'*Cher ami*, you had kindly asked for a copy of the score for my *Élégie pour les frères perdus*, and I'd promised to send you one. I've been inexcusably remiss and I apologize sincerely to you, but the war has claimed all my heart. My thoughts so rarely return to music these days. A copy of the score sits on my desk half-finished, abandoned somewhere in the Allegro, but I shall do my best to get it to you in time. I say 'in time' because I'll soon be steaming for France—the other news I wanted to convey to you. Martin, I can no longer endure sitting here in Boston, turning schoolboys into mediocre pianists, while French men, women, and children are being slaughtered every day. I've decided to join the fight. You'll object that I'm too old to be useful as a soldier; you may be correct in that judgment. But I must try.'"

Robin stops reading. "Ben—we've got a title."

"Read it again?" He scrambles for a pen to write it down.

"*Élégie pour les frères perdus.* It's *Elegy for the Lost Brothers*, right? He means the war. Later on he mentions Verdun—wasn't that the bloodiest battle of all time or something? It makes total sense that an expat Frenchman of that era, pinned down in Boston, would have turned his suffering into art. Imagine the agony of watching it all from afar. Imagine the grief. And it also makes sense to me that eventually he'd realize art wasn't enough."

"I wonder if he did go back. It would probably take research in France, war records and such. Or ship manifests, like the one Nikki found."

"And I wonder if he ever got Loeffler that score."

"That would—"

"Wait—check this part out," Robin says, reading on.

"'When you asked in Medfield about my odd seven-beat rest, the 'Oriental pause' as you so interestingly called it on the wonderful afternoon we spent playing with Casals, I told you in brief of the event that inspired it: the brutal murder of a farm family near the front lines at Verdun, innocent civilians going about their lives in the midst of unthinkable violence. A terrible incident that showed yet again the depravity of the Kaiser's army. But Martin, there is a detail of the story that I left out, simply because I cannot speak it aloud. It's too horrible . . . and yet, it is what made the story so unforgettable, so heartbreaking, that I had to retell it in music. This much you already know: during a lull in the battle, in the tiny commune of Fleury, a family of seven consisting of a husband and wife and their five boys, barley farmers, were lined up against the wall and cut to pieces by a German machine gun. Barbarism. *Mal absolu*. But this was not all. What I did not tell you and Casals is that the youngest boy, Jacques, called Jacky by everyone, was feeble-minded, a sufferer from mongolism—a fact their German executioners found worthy of mockery rather than mercy. This son was singled out for special cruelty and made to undress before the entire village, then to watch his family shot down before he too was shot. The account in *Le Temps* implied other cruelties too vicious to print; one can only imagine. Martin, I could not forget this barbarity once it entered my imagination. The story haunted me. It haunts me still. With your 'Oriental pause,' my sonata tolls a silent bell for each of those seven poor souls, but most especially for poor Jacky, so defenseless, so innocent in the face of evil. Those five brothers sit behind the title of the work, too, along with the boys lost at Verdun. They are all brothers to me, Martin.'"

"This is just amazing," Ben says, thoughts racing. "What else?"

"Nothing more about the sonata, I think . . . just skimming through it here. He begs off some recital he'd committed to do at a Mrs. Gardner's, then there's a bit about his daughter.

"'My deepest sorrow in going home, Martin, is to leave my dear Elisabeth alone, motherless, and with a papa an ocean away. Fortunately, her mother and I raised her to be morally strong and intelligent and capable in all her worldly affairs, and I'm proud to say that she is all of these things. Leaving her here will be like leaving a lung or a kidney behind, something vital to me, but I know she will be well. Nevertheless it would be a comfort to me if I might have your permission to equip her with your address and telephone number, should anything or anyone stand in the way of her happiness. Sometimes in this world even an independent young lady needs the assistance of a gentleman. May I?'"

"It's like he's still alive," Robin says. "You can hear his voice. It's so immediate."

"I need him to be as alive as possible for Friday, Robs. And does this ever help."

THOUGH HE'S STEERED CLEAR OF MUSIC all day, Ben drops into an armchair and dons headphones to listen to Garnier play his *Élégie pour les frères perdus*, sinking into it more deeply than ever before, hearing things he's never heard. After the opening flourish comes the silent, seven-beat rest, pulsing with tragedy and the sins of war—not a musical statement so much as a moral one, he now knows. The ominous, thudding bass notes at the end of the Lili passage, pulsing through a fog of minor chords—are they the mortars of Verdun, thundering down through clouds of poison gas onto Frenchmen huddled in trenches? Even the little folk song anchoring the third movement—the last, unsuspecting children's dance before the shells rain down? Scattered through the Allegro, he notices only now, there is a recurring run of seven thirty-second notes followed by a rest. The tatter of German bullets, one for each member of that poor farm family, followed by an eerie silence and the stench of gunpowder?

The sonata unfolds for Ben like the map of a long-ago battlefield, Garnier's genius astonishing him anew. Until this moment he's heard the composition with a musician's ear, puzzling out its structural innovations, listening for antecedents, trying to place it in the tradition. Now he feels it with his whole heart: its strife, its exquisite agony, its melancholy beauty. Its sheer grief. At the core of the music beats the hot pulse of a man.

When it's over he plays it twice more, extracting more emotion with each hearing, the shattered composer drawing ever closer. They're arm in arm now, kinsmen, Jacques Garnier opening his heart with bravery and trust. By the time Ben slips the headphones off he's as exhausted as a man laid out by a tropical fever, his body reeling. Come Friday he'll have so much to say, so much to tell the world.

LII.

WILLA

"Ben, come in," says a familiar voice from within the hotel suite. She's left the door canted open for him. When he eases past it he sees why.

Willa Blount sits on the sofa of the suite's living room, an aluminum walker parked beside her. In her heather sweater and smart maroon scarf she seems smaller, frailer than the woman in the photos Ben's seen on the internet. Time has taken its toll. The short, practical haircut and precise wire-rimmed glasses give her a genderless look. But behind the round lenses the tenacious gaze is instantly recognizable. It's the first thing he noticed about his client when he hunted her down online.

"I'd get up and greet you properly," she says, "but this new hip's ordered me to stay put. I'm sorry to be rude."

"Please," Ben says, striding over, "no apology necessary. I imagine spending hours on a plane hasn't helped any."

When he takes Willa's hand he expects an iron grip. To his surprise she clasps his hand with delicacy, then takes it in both of hers. With a genuine smile she says, "It's such a pleasure to meet you in person, Ben Weil. Truly."

"Likewise."

A flicker passes behind the eyeglasses. "It's not the sonata I've come for, you know."

He doesn't know what to make of this. Something unspoken lurks behind the words. But she rescues him at once. With a nod toward the adjacent armchair she invites him to sit. He unslings his messenger bag and sets it beside him, rubbing his hands to chase away the lakefront chill. The frigid wind slamming through the narrows between the Drake and the Knickerbocker hit him full on the face when he turned the corner onto Walton.

Willa says, "May I order you up a refreshment? I suppose it's too early to start in on their famous martinis, but the bellhop highly recommended the tarragon lemonade. Would you share a pitcher with me? Or perhaps you'd prefer something to warm you up. Coffee?"

"Coffee would be perfect."

She nods. "You're chilled to the bone, I can see." She picks up the phone to call downstairs. "Coffee's one habit I've never acquired, oddly enough. Negative associations, I suppose." When it comes to coffee, Ben has a few negative associations of his own. "I'll try the lemonade and give you my unbiased review."

After Willa hangs up with room service they sit back and eye one another smilingly, the silence easier than it ought to be. He detects no hint of the strictness she emanates on the phone. The woman beside him is as placid as a grandmother in a rose garden. If she's stumbled across a mention of Benjamin Weil's *French Sonata* somewhere, it must not have perturbed her.

"So," she says at last, "we've had quite a journey together, haven't we?"

It seems an overstatement, but he plays along. "That we have."

"It's lovely that the sonata's getting the attention it deserves. I can't thank you enough for your efforts, Ben." When she rearranges herself in the sofa he wonders how badly the hip's troubling her. "Have you found out anything more about our elusive Garnier?"

"I have, actually. There are some late-breaking developments. Exciting ones."

"Really! So glad you've taken such an interest in our man. I was hoping you would. Fill me in."

He's happy to shift into particulars. Before he leaves today he'll have to tell her the truth about the sonata, or enough of it to get them through tomorrow night. But he's not ready for that conversation. He's still learning her manner, recalibrating his understanding of who she is. The better he knows Willa Blount, the better words he'll choose when the time comes. In the mean time he's happy to talk about Garnier.

As she watches him thoughtfully, hands folded in her lap, he fills her in on Nathalie Artigue's discoveries. The Debussy connection, the Conservatoire period. The fateful decision to come to America. From his shoulder bag he fetches a printout he's made of the letter to Debussy and hands it to Willa, who spreads it across the coffee table with an antiquarian's care.

"Such beautiful penmanship!" she says, examining the page. "What an excellent discovery, Ben. To see our man's actual words, in his own handwriting. . . . There's something thrilling about it, isn't there? Do you have more documents like this one?"

Ben produces Nikki's contribution: the immigration ledger with entries for Jacques, Sylvie and Elisabeth Garnier, a glimpse of the little French family at the very moment of their arrival. "Here's something my cousin just found."

"Cousin on which side?" Willa asks, as if this might affect the worth of the document.

"Father's. Why do you ask?"

She ignores the question. "And what have we here?" She traces the entries with a fingertip. "Ah! From an immigration register. I've had these pass through the store now and then. Years ago we sold a very special Ellis Island example for quite a lot of money—Irving Berlin's entry record, if you can imagine. Or Israel Beilin's, I should say."

"Look," Ben says, pointing out the Garniers.

Willa's crooked fingertip scans down to meet his. "Oh!" she exclaims, a girlish lilt in her voice. Her eyes glitter. "I can almost picture them, can't you? Jacques, Sylvie and Elisabeth, beginning their life in America. Imagine their excitement. And their nervousness. What a bold move to make."

She settles back into the sofa. "Ben, I'm curious—do you have a mental image of Jacques, having spent so much time with his music? How do you picture the man?" She nods toward his shoulder bag. "Or are you about to show me photos?"

He laughs. "No photos, alas. I'm not *that* good." Though he's not expended any conscious effort on trying to imagine Jacques Garnier's face, Willa's question makes him realize that an image has nonetheless formed in the back of his mind. But his version of Garnier looks far too much like Debussy, the precipitous forehead, scruffy goatee and wide-set eyes belonging to a different face entirely. Lacking a photo of the man, he's had Debussy stand in for the role.

He says, "I don't have much of a picture of him, I guess. Do you?"

"Yes, in fact." He waits for her to elaborate but she moves on briskly. "What else do you have there in your bag of wonders?"

Ben retrieves the Loeffler letter and lays it next to the manifest. Willa adjusts her glasses and hovers over the dense script, lips pursed in concentration, left hand pressing against what must be the new hip. Garnier's handwriting is smaller and tighter than in the Debussy letter, harder to decipher. The elegant penmanship is under pressure. Ben wonders if it's a mark of depression, or perhaps just the labor of writing in English. But Willa reads every word, lips set into silent motion by certain phrases. He settles back in his chair and gives her space to do it.

A knock at the door; room service. Ben has the refreshments deposited on the table and sets Willa's lemonade next to her. She barely notices, so immersed is she in Garnier's letter. He pours himself a coffee and then abandons it, worried he'll have a hard enough time sleeping tonight without caffeine in his blood.

At length she says, "So, this is the last we hear from Jacques Garnier, I suppose? Until the sonata recording?"

"The last thing we've found, anyway."

"I really wonder what became of him. God knows, you took your life in your hands steaming across to Europe back then, what with blockades and mines and U-boats. The *Lusitania* was far from the only passenger ship that went down. And even if he survived the crossing, to be a middle-aged man thrown into the trenches . . . hard to imagine he made it through. Would you agree?"

"It seems like a huge risk. A crazy risk. Which makes the sonata all the more amazing. He must have been in a state of high emotion while he wrote it. I think that comes through."

Willa nods pensively, sips her lemonade. "It's thoughtful of you to have brought all this, Ben," she says, eyeing the documents he's spread across the coffee table. Then, with an unreadable smile: "I've brought a few items of my own, actually."

"Really?"

"Would you—?" She leans forward in the sofa and gestures toward the walker. He pulls it closer for her and helps her to her feet. "We'll need some room to spread out." She nods down at the coffee table with its raft of paper. "If you'll just bring these things."

They resettle themselves at the dining table where Ben lays out his artifacts in chronological sequence. Willa reaches below and retrieves a small, timeworn briefcase that appears to be made of reptile skin.

"Uh! The key. Will you fetch it from my purse, please, on the nightstand?"

As she inserts the tiny key in the lock, arthritis slowing her down, she sees him admiring the unusual case. "It belonged to my mother, who got it who knows where. It was hidden away for many years—it's come to me only recently. One of my appraisers says it's shellacked iguana. Already an antique in my mother's day. Not exactly my style, but it does remind me of her."

The brass buckle snaps up.

"Now," she says, "let's see what we have that might interest you."

WHEN THE LID OF WILLA BLOUNT'S BRIEFCASE OPENS Ben feels something shift under him. The compartment, lined in purple felt, is packed solid with items—yellowed letters bundled with a faded pink ribbon, manila envelopes, a cardboard portfolio of the sort photographers once used for plates, a purple velvet jewelry pouch. A faintly comical vision flies through Ben's head: Willa at airport security with her shellacked iguana briefcase full of obscure documents and objets trouvés, a modern-day Mata Hari talking her way through a treacherous checkpoint.

"Let me see," she says, surveying the contents. "Where to begin?" With care she lifts out a fat packet of letters. "With a love affair, I suppose. Always a good place to start."

Ben crosses his arms impatiently—aren't they here to discuss the sonata? But he's here at her pleasure. Willa loosens the ribbon and slips a few letters from the bundle, laying them out on the table like oversized playing cards. Each of the ivory envelopes is addressed to *Miss Helen Sanborn* in a confident, masculine hand.

It takes a moment for Ben to make the connection, but he quickly does: Helen Sanborn of Aigremont, of course, the same one who sold the Wooden Arabian to Willa Blount years ago, conveying the Garnier cylinders along with it.

"Love letters," Willa says fondly, smoothing one of them against the tabletop. "From a paramour of Helen Sanborn's who put on a full-court press when she was barely nineteen. She was a Boston ingénue, no doubt quite sheltered. H. E. Rollins, on the other hand, was a carpetbagger from Savannah who married Helen for her money and promptly ran off with a singer in New York City. A rotten thing to do. The marriage failed before it even got going. Though not before Helen got pregnant and miscarried—quite alone, as best I can tell. Imagine, in those days. What a trial by fire. This was all a decade before she met my father."

"Your father knew her?"

Willa inclines her head with a wry smile. "I should say so. He married her." She touches Ben's arm gently. "Helen was my mother, you know. I never said that clearly to you, did I?"

Ben feels a connection fall into place, like an electrical relay closing.

"Definitely not. I thought you'd bought the antique shop from her."

"The Wooden Arabian was my inheritance—nearly the sum total of it. My mother moved to Maine after Rollins left her and opened the shop as a hobby project, but when the family money evaporated it's how she kept body and soul together. She sold some of the Aigremont furnishings there, in fact, things my grandmother couldn't bear to auction off when she left the house . . . though when it came down to it, my mother couldn't always part with them, either. They were the last vestiges of her childhood home, after all. She met my father when he came in and tried to buy the old Sanborn piano. She wrote up the sales ticket and then couldn't bring herself to let it go, which made such an impression on him that he invited her to dinner. And well—here I am."

For the first time Ben hears Willa Blount's laugh, a laugh freer than any he'd have imagined for her. He's charmed.

"Willa, do you think that was *the* piano?"

"I know it was. It was unusual—a white Mason and Hamlin from Drury's. My mother eventually donated it to our little town in Maine, where it was used for some years at civic events, school recitals, that sort of thing. An admirable second career in public service. I'm sorry to say it was lost right after the Second World War, when a fire destroyed the town hall." Willa fusses with an antique ring too large for her finger. "It was quite a bad year, 1947. My grandmother Rena died in January. A month later it was my uncle Cabe in Maine, who either hanged himself in his barn or fell off a ladder to his death, depending on whether you believe the family gossip or the obituary. The piano went in March."

Willa reaches back into her iguana briefcase. The second batch of letters comes out, ten or fifteen of them, yellowed envelopes bound with a cracked rubber band. Ben sees that they too are addressed to Helen Sanborn, but in a feminine hand.

"Now, Ben, we come to the more interesting thing. But let me tell you more about this briefcase for just a moment. Bear with me."

"I'm in no hurry."

True; not true. He wants to hear it all but the clock is ticking down to tomorrow night's concert. He has a story to tell, too, before it's too late.

Willa says, "I've had this case only since last spring. One day I took a call at the shop from a man I know down in Winchester, Tom Sevigny, who chairs the local historical society. Lovely people, New England preservationists like me, you know, who saved Aigremont from the wrecking ball some years back. By then it was owned by the school district, which used it for offices. They were about to demolish the place and put up something hideous when the historical society stepped in. They arranged to lease the house from the town for a song, in exchange for a promise to turn it into a cultural center. Well, Aigremont was in serious disrepair, in need of a new roof, a new boiler, a hundred other things. But these people got to work and raised the money. At some point they reached out to me to see if I'd like to donate any family heirlooms, and I did give them a few small things. The society was very appreciative. They've been wonderful at keeping me up to date, knowing I'm the sole living descendant." At Ben's look of surprise she explains:

383

"Not one of my uncles started a family. Nor I, for that matter. My late husband struggled with manic depression and was determined not to pass it on. We Sanborns haven't demonstrated much staying power, I'm afraid. When I go, we'll be extinct."

As Willa sips her lemonade Ben tries to read her mood. He sees no regret in her eyes. If she harbors any, it's not for sharing. She is a woman of exacting composure.

"Once the Aigremont renovation got going they found asbestos everywhere, which meant the walls had to be taken down to the lath. Well, lo and behold—when they got to my mother's child-hood room they pried off the baseboards and discovered a little hiding-place she'd made, clever girl. Stashed inside it was this briefcase. It must have been left behind when my grandmother sold the house, which she did under considerable duress and in a great hurry. No one but Mama would have known to go looking for it. But thanks to that asbestos it's finally come to light, all its contents intact. And how precious those contents are, Ben. May I show you?"

LIII.
A FACE TO THE NAME

FOR WHAT SEEMS HOURS, sitting spellbound in Willa Blount's suite high above a frozen Chicago side street, Ben barely takes a breath.

What Willa's brought in her bag is astonishing. There is no other word for it. As she lays out her items one by one, the story of the sonata writes itself. Willa sits beside him patiently, talking him through it in her imperturbable way, pausing now and then to let him absorb what he's hearing. He's foreseen none of it. He thought he was bringing discoveries to Willa Blount, but his modest gleanings are nothing next to hers.

She begins with one of the letters, fatter than the rest, slipping it from the bundle and laying it on the table before him.

"Who are these from?" Ben asks.

"A girlfriend of my mother's, a young Frenchwoman living in Boston in the late teens. At the time of this particular letter Mama was a newlywed—she'd married H. E. Rollins in New York and stayed on with him there. If he'd already started his affair, she wasn't aware of it. I think she was quite happy just then. They'd managed to find their way into some pretty rarefied circles. They lived right upstairs from Caruso, at the Knickerbocker."

"The *Knickerbocker*?"

"The original." Willa waves vaguely around her suite. "Of course I couldn't resist booking here. I'm not exactly sentimental, Ben, but I do have my moments."

"No shame in that."

"Anyway, my mother exchanged quite a few letters with her friend during that New York period. Liz was still in Boston, working for Alexander Graham Bell." Willa taps the briefcase. "Mama saved all her letters, luckily for us. Now, can you guess what her friend Liz did for the Bell Company?"

"I don't know . . . telephone operator?"

"Not quite. She sold Graphophones to the wealthy, Ben."

"Huh! Which is how there happened to be one at Aigremont."

"Exactly. The Sanborns were customers of hers."

Ben has the impression that Willa's building a case of some sort, step by step like a meticulous prosecutor, not revealing all her evidence at once.

"Turn the envelope over," she instructs him.

He glances at her and detects a faint amusement in her eyes. With care he flips the envelope and aligns it on the table carefully. There, written across the rear flap in ink gone iodine-brown, is the return address:

Miss Elisabeth Garner
43 Ruggles St., No. 402,
Roxbury,
Boston, Mass^tts

Ben doesn't understand what he's looking at. It simply doesn't register. Gently he pins the corner of the envelope with the tip of his index finger, as if it might flutter away. His mind is racing but strictly in circles.

He looks at Willa and says, "Elisabeth Garner? Jacques's daughter was Elisabeth *Garnier*. That's weirdly close."

Willa shifts the printout of Nikki's immigration ledger down alongside the envelope.

Pointing to the Garnier entries, she says: "Elisabeth Garnier at twelve." Then, tapping the envelope: "Elisabeth Garner at twenty-four. The very same young lady, I assure you. A slight Americanization of the name, something immigrants did all the time. They still do." Willa folds her hands on the table. "Between the two of us, my friend, we've got her nicely bookended. I propose we refer to her by her birth name, Garnier, shall we?"

"Wait—Liz was Elisabeth Garnier? Your mother *knew* her?"

"They were very close."

"So . . . you must know all about her."

"Very little, actually. She passed away more than a decade before I came along. My mother rarely spoke of her. I believe the loss still pained her terribly."

"How did she die?"

"I've no idea. I do know she had a little girl, though I know nothing about the father. A reasonable guess might be that he was a soldier killed in the war." Willa shifts in her chair to take pressure off the aching hip. "You know, I so wish I could have met Elisabeth. She was a single mother and a working woman in a position of some responsibility at a time when that combination was rare as hen's teeth. I can imagine how her courage would have impressed my mother. They were true friends, despite the class difference. When Elisabeth died, in fact, my mother and grandmother arranged for her little girl to be adopted by friends of the family. That's how close they were."

"And what about Jacques? I suppose your mother knew him, too?"

"Open the envelope. I'll wait while you read."

ELISABETH'S LETTER TO HELEN is ten compressed pages, though at first it doesn't appear to be a letter at all. In place of a salutation there is an underlined heading: *Of the late Jacques Garnier and his final Work.* The first pages recount much of what Ben already knows from the Debussy and Loeffler letters, from the sonata's title to the Lili Boulanger connection. It's all there. Ben wishes that Nikki and Robin were by his side, reading along with him. With every line their research is confirmed.

But then the writer goes deeper, shifts into a more intimate tone. With fondness she gives an account of her father Jacques, from his days as a piano prodigy in Honfleur to his matriculation at the Paris Conservatoire; his student friendship with Debussy and eventual return to Honfleur where he marries a childhood friend, Sylvie Burnouf. Then the arrival of Elisabeth Amélie, who will spend her first happy years in Normandy, their little *ville* tucked between countryside and sea, until music calls her father back to Paris. For one full, charming page the writer describes how her father teaches her to play the *Clair de lune* during a Paris snowstorm, working from a hand copy of the score given to Jacques by Debussy himself in payment of some debt. "Whoa," Ben says under his breath, and glances over at the briefcase, wondering whether Willa has the precious score with her. Nothing would surprise him now.

As the tale grows more personal, the handwriting grows less careful. It's obvious that Elisabeth is writing in a burst of passion. She comes to the offer of a post in Boston and the voyage across the Atlantic, leaving no detail out. Her seasickness during the first miserable days of the crossing. The sling chair where her father would sit practicing English with other passengers. A bold Swiss boy who wouldn't leave her alone. Her mother's excitement as the ship steamed into Boston Harbor to the cheers of motley Americans waiting on the wharves. But then, only weeks after their arrival, the collapse of the promised Harvard post, leaving Jacques to find work as a music teacher at the Latin School. The sad passing of his beloved wife some years later, and finally, of course, the war: his obsessive newspaper-reading, the agony over the news from home that led his heart to create the *Élégie* and then to make the fateful decision to sail home and join the fight.

The composer is dispatched in one stark sentence: *Jacques Garnier died at sea in December 1916, lost to a German U-boat in the North Atlantic.*

The letter ends abruptly, with no summing-up, no fond regards, no signature. Ben slumps back in his uncomfortable chair, overwhelmed and suddenly quite exhausted.

Only a few days ago, Jacques Garnier was but the outline of a man, a loose sketch in faint pencil. Now he is as real as real can be.

"YOU KNEW ALL THIS and didn't tell me?" Ben says. "All this time?"

Willa regards him unflinchingly, arms laid along the arms of her chair like stonework.

"Better you found your way to Jacques Garnier through his music. Through a language both you and he understood. I knew some elements of his story, it's true, and learned much more when this briefcase surfaced. But I didn't know enough to make sense of the work, you know, to judge how important it might be. I lacked the necessary foundation in music. I needed you for that. You may question my judgment, but it seemed important to me that you approach the sonata without preconceptions. Without the biographical element."

He says nothing, unconvinced.

"There's another thing, Ben, even more important: I'm old enough to know the value of leaving the map at home. Sometimes it takes a long wander through the forest to take full possession of one's past. It has to be earned, no matter how long it takes. You're earning it right now."

"I don't follow. This is your past," Ben says, tapping Elisabeth Garnier's letter. "Not mine."

"Are you really so sure?"

"You just told me Helen Sanborn was your mother."

Willa nods once, efficiently, then studies his face, in no hurry to respond. He'd like her to just say what she's thinking, as has always been her way. The afternoon's ellipses are becoming an annoyance. The light through the window is failing and he still needs to broach the subject of the concert.

"Ben, let me ask you something. What would you think if I told you that Elisabeth Garnier named her little girl Sylvie, in honor of her mother?"

At first the question seems irrelevant, a footnote to the larger story. But then a sort of melodic variation comes to Ben, a tiny spin on a familiar note.

Sylvie, he says to himself. *Sylvia*.

Almost without thinking he asks, "What was the name of the family who adopted Elisabeth's daughter? Do you know?"

Willa smiles. "They were the Monaghans of Brookline. Who took the liberty of rechristening Sylvie as Sylvia, to make their little girl sound more American. The Garnier connection was erased with a stroke of the pen. She became Sylvia Monaghan on that day. Perhaps the name rings a bell?"

Ben's on his feet before he realizes it, striding across the suite. Exhausted only moments ago, now his limbs pulse with energy. Willa watches him pace back and forth, a contented smile on her face.

"It's not possible," he protests.

"It's the truth."

"But that would make Elisabeth my grandmother, and Jacques Garnier—"

"Your great-grandfather. You're his direct descendant, Ben."

"But . . . you couldn't possibly have made that connection. The adoption records were sealed. My mother never knew who her real mother was. How could you?"

"I didn't need adoption records, Ben. I knew because I attended your parents' wedding."

"*What?*"

"After your mother's adoption, Mama kept in touch with the Monaghans, who were great friends of the Sanborns. Mama had known them all her life. They allowed her to keep up with Sylvia's doings from a discreet distance, knowing how devoted she'd been to Elisabeth. She was presented to little Sylvia as an old friend of the family's—true enough, if not the whole truth. Consequently my mother was able to watch her friend's daughter grow into a young lady. When Sylvia Monaghan eventually got engaged to Nathan Weil, Mama was invited to the wedding as a family friend. Sylvia wouldn't have suspected a thing.

"I was fourteen that year. Mama and I took the train out to Chicago, quite an adventure for a girl from small-town Maine. The wedding itself was memorable because it was my first Jewish one. I was terribly upset about that smashed wineglass, although I loved the chair dance. The whole trip is still so vivid to me, Ben. I recall what a lovely bride your mother was, and how charming your father was, really quite dashing, and so kind to me. But once they started a family and put stakes down in Chicago my mother fell out of touch with them. Maybe with Sylvia safely married off she felt her obligation to Elisabeth had been fulfilled. I can't say. We never discussed it, and then she passed away, a few months before Kennedy was shot.

"It was only when this briefcase surfaced and I read Elisabeth's letter that I made the connection to the cylinders. They'd been in storage since I inherited the shop. Frankly, I'm somewhat surprised I remembered them—by then they'd been packed away for forty years. It was more the ledger entry I remembered, but we finally managed to dig them out. Amazing to hold them in one's hand, the *originals*. . . . I'll never forget the moment." A quiet smile; a pause to remember. "Well, it wasn't too long before I got to wondering what had happened to Sylvia, of course, and with the help of one of my computer-smart assistants I found her on one of these genealogy websites. They knew all about Sylvia and Nathan and Benjamin Weil, of course, but you're quite right: Sylvia's birth mother was hidden in closed adoption records. She was traceable only as far back as the Monaghans.

"Which is the other reason, frankly, why I didn't share details with you. The more important reason by far. One never knows how someone will react when their past is uncovered, especially where adoption's involved. I didn't know you, Ben. We were strangers to one other. It certainly wasn't my place to divulge your mother's background. Had you not brought me the information you did today, in fact, I might not have divulged it even now. But you were getting very close on your own. You would have gotten there even without my help."

Willa leans forward across the table. "So, I kept on digging. I wanted to know about *you*. When my assistant located you on the Counterpoint website and I saw what you did for a living, and how you looked . . . well, the plan took shape very quickly in my mind. And here we are."

Overwhelmed, Ben stalks to the bathroom and locks the door behind him, not caring if it's rude. Leaning over the sink, he studies his face in the mirror with the eerie feeling that Jacques Garnier is staring back at him. The maestro has tears in his eyes. What does he think of the grand mess his great-grandson has made for himself? Stinging through Ben's astonishment is a shame so sharp and fresh he has to look away.

It's several minutes before he goes back to Willa. She sits waiting for him, a kindness in her eyes.

"It's a lot to absorb," she says when he resumes his seat. "I know that." In his absence she's taken the cardboard portfolio from the briefcase and set it on the table. "Are you ready to put a face to the name, Ben?"

He isn't ready for anything. Nevertheless he nods, lets himself be carried along. Willa slips out a sepia-toned photographic print and lays it before him.

At a white piano, in a sunny Victorian drawing room, sits a gaunt, careworn man who looks very much like Ben. The shape of the brow; the squared-off chin; the high, noncommittal hairline. And most startling of all, the eyes. Ben feels a shock of recognition but also a wave of affection, as if he and the pianist are the oldest of friends. Beneath the piano bench someone has scrawled *J Garnier*.

But Jacques is not alone. Standing behind him, her hands on his shoulders, is a pretty young woman with a high-necked collar and locket, her black eyes aglitter with what might be tears. *E G*, reads the hasty inscription below. *Elisabeth Garnier*, Ben says to himself, feeling his way gingerly along the unaccustomed family tree, instructing himself. *Grandmother*. Off to the right, meanwhile, stands an austere, goateed man leaning into the walking stick planted firmly before him: *Loeffler*.

There are two more women in the photo, and the ghost of a servant, perhaps, in a doorway half-lost in the murky emulsion, but the annotator has left them unidentified.

"Helen," Willa says, pointing to the younger of the two. "And Rena, my grandmother."

"I can't get my head around this, Willa. Really."

She slips a second print from the portfolio. Taken from a different angle, it shows Garnier in furious and blurry performance, leaning into some difficult passage with his left arm extended all the way to the far end of the keyboard, his eyes resolutely shut. And there, under the raised piano lid, dipping down toward the hammers like a hummingbird probing for nectar, is a long, slender funnel: unmistakably the intake horn of a Graphophone.

This, then, was the moment: the true début of the *Élégie*, Garnier's masterpiece captured in wax at the very moment of its revelation. Looking at the photos, touching their edges delicately as if to be sure they're real, Ben can barely breathe. His heart fills his chest alarmingly, ballooning out of control, squeezing everything out of its way. For a moment he feels he might be on the brink of real medical trouble. But by force of will he calms himself, takes on oxygen. Settles his racing thoughts. Willa's presence at his side is a great comfort to him now.

It will take him a very long while—years, surely—to fully absorb what lies before him on the table. But he must somehow digest enough of it, in the hours that remain before he takes the stage tomorrow night, to properly introduce Jacques Garnier to the world. He's been given a gift and must not waste it. First, though, he has a confession to make.

"Willa," he says, laying a hand on her forearm. "May I buy you a martini?"

LIV.

A Higher and Better Truth

Marooned in rush hour traffic with his Uber driver, Willa's iguana briefcase on his lap and her sage advice ringing in his ears, Ben calls Nikki. She puts him on speakerphone for Robin's benefit.

"How did it go?" Nikki asks.

"You can't possibly imagine."

"So, tell us."

And he does. Methodically he recounts the extraordinary afternoon at the Knickerbocker, Nikki and Robin asking hardly a question. Not until he reveals his personal connection to Jacques Garnier does Nikki stop him.

"Holy shit, Ben. For real? And she hadn't said anything, all this time?"

"Not a word."

"You're going to have a *lot* more to talk about tomorrow night. We need to get everything to Peter ASAP. Scan Willa's stuff when you get home and email it to me. I'll take it from there."

"Ben," Robin says carefully, "did you tell Willa? I mean—"

"I told her everything."

"And?"

"I wish we'd had the conversation a long time ago."

"She wasn't angry?"

"She took it in stride. She's very clear-eyed about human nature. She was more interested in helping me think my way through it."

"What did you two conclude?"

Ben pauses, not sure how to sum up the searching conversation in the hotel bar, Willa's walker parked beside the booth, martinis at hand. Talking things out had done his soul immeasurable good.

"She was quite clear about certain things. For example, that the lie about the sonata wasn't worth destroying my career over. That it was a totally understandable mistake, almost a trivial mistake. That my inability to forgive myself was the real issue."

"Wise woman," Robin says. "But the lie's already out there. What does she think you should do now?"

"First, forgive myself. Then tell a higher and better truth—that's how she put it. Forget the grand confession."

Robin says, "Because even if lying to Ana might be understandable in personal terms, it definitely won't be read that way by strangers."

"The auto-da-fé aspect being far more interesting," Nikki says.

"Can't you just picture the *New Yorker* article about this? Janet Malcolm would have a field day."

"No doubt," Ben agrees. "You know, one really interesting thing Willa said was that whereas a confession ends the conversation, genuine truth-telling starts one. It should be a dialogue. Open-ended."

"Generative," Nikki says. "Right on."

"Which gets to her idea of telling a higher and better truth."

"By which she means?"

"Starting a more interesting conversation. In this case a musical one, maybe. I think it's hugely important to her that Jacques be recognized. It's like a gift she can give. A way of honoring her mother's friendship with Elisabeth by honoring Elisabeth's father. And it's the right thing to do, plain and simple. It doesn't take a lot of ethical calculus to get there. We've dug out the truth. Now it should be spoken."

"And you're the vehicle," Nikki says, "if only all this Matta noise can be cleared away. It's got to be of secondary importance to Willa. A distraction from the bigger picture. While at the same time she clearly understands how important it is to *you* to make it right. She seems like the kind of woman who could hold both those truths at once. Who could be pulling for Jacques but for you, too."

"I think she's exactly that woman."

The driver's finally made it to Lincoln. The traffic begins to move. As they pass Montrose, Robin says, "Ben? I'm still not sure what all this means for tomorrow night. Did you two come up with a plan?"

"She wouldn't go there. She insisted it was up to me to solve it. To own it. *You're the keeper of the flame now,* is what she told me. *I can't begin to tell you how to keep it lit.*"

Ben replays the moment in their Knickerbocker booth: Willa with a faint sheen of tears in her steady eyes, passing the torch to him with a few short words and then bringing a martini to her lips. He could feel her physically letting go, releasing it all to him. The relief of that act, the way something eased in her expression; her immense trust in him, sobering and dear. Then the unexpected touch of her hand on his. *Thank you, Ben. Whatever happens tomorrow night, thank you.*

Something else comes back to him now, something important. "There was another thing she said: *If this doesn't change you somehow, you've missed the opportunity of a lifetime.* That shifted everything for me. It gives me so much bigger of a canvas to work with."

Nikki says, "She's really smart about this. Though I wouldn't agree that brainstorming with someone necessarily makes a decision less authentic."

"Says the therapist."

"Do you want to talk it through some more, Ben? Should we-slash-I come over?"

"Actually . . . no. I need to be alone with this."

"With the decision?" says Robin.

"With Jacques. It's between him and me now." The car's pulled up at his curb. "I have to go. Just got home."

Robin says, "Call if you need us, okay? We won't disturb you."

"Love you guys. I'll be fine."

IT'S TRUE: HE WILL BE FINE, strange as it seems. The long talk with Willa has finally put some solid ground under his feet. His heart has found a fragile peace. Which is surprising, because in twenty-six hours he'll be taking the stage to say . . . what? He has no idea, except that the story of Jacques Garnier must lie at the heart of it. Now, thanks to his own hard work, and Nathalie Artigue's, and Nikki's and Robin's and Willa's, that story has come into sharp and surprising focus. If he roots himself in it, all will somehow be well. This much he does understand.

As Nikki asked, he scans and emails off the key artifacts from Willa's briefcase, beginning with the photos from the Aigremont recital and Elisabeth's long letter telling the story of her father and his work. He's closing the briefcase when his eyes fall upon the velvet jewelry bag. As an afterthought he loosens the drawstring and takes his grandmother's cameo pendant in hand, closing his fingers around it. Ana had her grandmother's *figa*; he has this. When Willa showed it to him in their Knickerbocker booth, the fine gold chain looped around her crooked finger, he felt the same sort of power in it, a power of great age and history.

Elisabeth gifted it to her friend Helen on the day she died: this was the story Willa grew up with, the story her own mother told her when they came across it one day in her jewelry box. Now Ben opens the tiny latch again, and there, as before, is the forthright smile of his great-grandmother and his own mother's namesake, Sylvie Garnier—a wondrous thing. Hers was the face missing from the Aigremont recital photos, because by then she'd been dead for some years. With the cameo the Garnier family portrait is complete. Ben arranges the open locket carefully on the scanner and sends the image to Nikki. A few moments later his inbox lights up: *I can't believe we have their faces now! Amazing. Beautiful. Mazel tov.*

Ben settles down to work. He has serious thinking to do, though not of the usual sort. The puzzle of what to do tomorrow night will not be solved by words or logic. The path to Willa's higher and better truth leads straight through music. He's sure of it. After arranging the recital photos and locket on the music stand he pours a tall glass of wine and sits down to play, willing his fingers to guide him, willing his fingers to sing.

WHAT COMES FIRST and most naturally is not the sonata but the intimate music he's been improvising around it. He has a dozen recorded snippets on his phone now, turns of phrase, riffs, chord melodies, jazz-infused variations on Garnier's central themes, from the meditative first movement to Lili's descent, from the Allegro to the folk song, from the astonishingly contemporary modal section to the closing fanfare—a meandering record of his months-long journey through the sonata's inner reaches. All through the long

Chicago winter he's sat at the keyboard and created a music of his own, never thinking of it as a composition in itself but only as a loose translation, unapologetically free and personal, of Jacques Garnier's masterpiece. Tonight he sees that he's been penning a kind of love letter to his great-grandfather, feeling his way toward the truest sort of *hommage*.

Now, as he plays the sonata's opening arpeggio and waits out the seven-beat rest, Ben feels a force of inspiration surge up in him, sending blood through to his fingertips where they sit poised on the ivories. When the final beat of silence expires he closes his eyes and begins to play spontaneously, joining the dance once again, his music and his great-grandfather's twined in a graceful and affectionate pas de deux. Never have the ideas come so easily. Ben plays and plays, entirely forgetting the glass of wine poised atop the piano, the energy building, the current subtly quickening as he wends his way toward the Allegro.

The long, breakneck runs of thirty-second notes are still beyond his skills. No doubt they always will be. Rather than stumble through the Allegro he disassembles it, slicing its DNA into shorter phrases that coalesce into a variation of his own making. A different sort of beauty emerges. The ideas keep coming, making him smile and frown and laugh out loud in the privacy of his snug home, the Bösendorfer alert and eager under his touch.

The third movement's folk song whistles gaily through him, light and playful, unaware of the trap that lies just ahead—but when he reaches the spot where six seconds of the Garnier recording were obliterated by a gouge in the wax, Ben keeps playing, inventing his own music to fill the gap. With no effort at all he finds a flawless transition back into the Garnier. His muse is unstoppable.

When Ben passes into the final movement's jazz section he throttles back, giving himself even more room to experiment. He dwells here for a long while, the music carrying him along on its broad back. The ghost of Bill Evans makes a fleeting visitation; Keith Jarrett lurks in the thicket of the bass register. Monk contributes an off-balance, syncopated line. Meanwhile Ben's long-lost ancestors, posed for their group portrait, gaze at him with curiosity from their perch on the music stand, spurring him on—his grandmother Elisabeth so very beautiful, a strong young woman who dotes on her father, leaning down to say something into his ear, hands resting protectively on his hunched shoulders with the weightless touch of an angel. From the open locket his great-grand-mother smiles and smiles, transmitting her warmth to him across the gulf of years. As for Jacques—in the performance photo he's torrential, immersed, dominant, a blur of brilliance, a true artist at the very pinnacle of his powers. The shutter is too slow to capture him clearly: everything about him is in motion. Everything is on fire.

The music keeps pouring out. For a moment Ben will surface into the sonata as Jacques meant it to be played, running with a particular chromatic change or melodic line, then will dive back into the river of his own ideas, jumping off from a bit of counter-point or modulation never to look back. When finally he coasts into the closing fanfare, he chooses to play it straight, hewing to his great-grandfather's climbing melody note for note, closing out the *Élégie pour les frères perdus* just as Jacques Garnier performed it so long ago. Eventually, with gratitude, Ben Weil comes home.

His whole body is tingling with the alchemy of it all. He knows he's found his way to the higher and better truth Willa spoke of. It's fallen open for him like a seed pod, bursting with abundance. He's commended his soul to the music, given it his whole heart, and the music has graciously saved him.

THERE IS MUCH WORK TO BE DONE before tomorrow night. Good work; joyful work. Ben checks the time on his phone—almost nine—and plots out the dwindling hours, deciding that the only thing to do is keep playing. The music is helping him think, helping him see the path ahead. Like Rossini, famous for writing entire overtures the night before a show, Ben's focus must be near perfect now. Sleep would be out of the question anyway. He's too keyed up. After boldly brewing a pot of coffee he returns to the piano and closes his eyes, re-entering the flow, the opening phrase of the sonata ringing out as he shoves off for another long, unchartable journey.

SOMETIME AFTER MIDNIGHT he stops for a snack, hunger intruding on the work. He's forsaken dinner. As a bagel toasts he stands gazing out into the city's murky half-darkness, in awe of what the evening's taught him. There have been moments of ecstasy, moments of profound communion. Moments of agitation, and peace, and sly humor. He never suspected he had such music in him. It took a rendezvous with the past to uncover it, but now—he's certain of this—it belongs to him.

His wrists ache from playing. He'll have to give them a brief rest if he means to carry on. The laptop's sitting on the kitchen table and he flips it open, finding an email from Robin and Nikki wondering how things are going. They've been off the air all evening, respecting his wish to be left alone. By now they're surely asleep.

He sends them a simple message: *All is well. Higher and better truth in sight. xoxo*

Afterward Ben wanders through the dead-quiet house, icing his wrists, gauging his body's condition. Though he's physically drained, he's never felt more alert and receptive. A crash will come, no doubt, but until then he'll keep pushing forward, hoping to catch a few hours' sleep before the show.

He can't wait to begin again. Going to the piano, he takes up the photos of the Aigremont recital and studies each in turn, trying to sense the energy in the room, the living vibration of that moment a hundred years ago. The extraordinary music on the air. The austere attentiveness of Loeffler and the others. Sun pouring through the tall windows to warm the room. Scents and sounds emanating from elsewhere in the sprawling house, a celebratory meal being prepared in the kitchen, perhaps. The quiet ripple of life bearing music forward through the day, and music bearing life.

The people in the photos—his people—gaze out from their static world with such candor. What did they say to each other that afternoon? What would they say to him, if he were to step through the photo into the music room? Now that he's seen their faces, he wishes he could hear their voices. Wishes he could hear what Elisabeth is whispering to her father as she bends over him, hands on his tense shoulders, her white blouse flaring in the sun. . . .

It hits Ben like a blow to the chest. A connection is made. Setting the photos on the stand he grabs headphones and races to the kitchen. On the laptop he searches for an audio file he's long ignored, his heart in his throat, and when he finds it he dons the headphones to listen. With a click he loads the file and starts playing the last eighteen seconds of the final cylinder—the distorted, barely intelligible chatter the recordist happened to capture after the music ended. On the very first night Ben worked on the project he'd split the section out into its own file, intending to go back and make sense of it later. Now perhaps he can.

He's never gotten around to cleaning up the audio. It's in even worse shape than the sonata was, the voices garbled and faint, all the timbre leached from them. But now he knows something he didn't before: it's possible that the speakers, a man and a woman, are conversing in French. After turning the gain up and equalizing the signal he's sure of it. Even with his rusty French he can make out a few words and phrases as the woman speaks: . . . *que Maman puisse voir cela . . . un présent du cœur . . .* The male voice is easier: *C'est pour toi.* Then, ringing out like a bell: *Quelque chose pour se souvenir de moi, Elisabeth.* Something for you to remember me by.

"Elisabeth!" Ben crows, and plays the recording again, certain beyond the shadow of a doubt that he's hearing the voice of his grandmother tunneling down through the years, then the emotional baritone of Jacques Garnier himself. Her affectionate father; Ben's elusive muse. For all the surprises this singular day has brought him, there is none more moving than this.

"*Merci,*" Ben says, in tears now, hoping against hope that they can somehow hear him too. "*Merci pour tout. . . .*"

LV.

THE FRENCH SONATA

"LADIES AND GENTLEMEN," SAYS CONSTANZA BARROWS, calling for silence with a raised palm, "*Mesdames et messieurs.*" Ben waits in the wings behind a thick curtain that smells of dry cleaning fluid, the audience a murky blur beyond the stage lights. Nikki gently kneads his shoulders, a rock-solid presence beside him. Robin lingers behind them, arms crossed over a sequined green blouse he knows well. Somewhere in the semidarkness beyond the stage, in an aisle seat with her walker folded beside her, sits Willa Blount, a certain cameo locket around her neck at his request.

Constanza waits for the last of the intermission talkers and coughers to quiet down. With her sharp mulberry blazer, helmet of golden hair and flashing diamond necklace she cuts a commanding figure. Like a stern schoolmistress she will wait for however long it takes to gain the room's undivided attention. When she has it she says: "Wasn't Maestra Matta's performance just extraordinary? Let's give her another hand, shall we?"

She leads the applause drily, thin lips pursed. Across the expanse of stage, sitting on a folding chair in the wings opposite, Ben spots a smoldering Ana, who's refused to make eye contact with him all evening. Even as applause ripples through the house and an enthusiast cheers her loudly from the balcony she stares fixedly at her Punjabi slippers, turning one of them back and forth for inspection, disinterested as a bus driver at the end of a long shift.

Knitting her fingers at her waist, Constanza Barrows attempts a casual tone that is soundly defeated by her British accent. "Now, friends, we have quite a surprise for you."

From the corner of his eye Ben sees Ana abandon her chair and head backstage toward the dressing rooms, the black sheath dress making her waddle just a bit. He's not sorry to see her go.

He wonders if she'll change into street clothes and leave straight-away, or watch the second half of the concert on the dressing room monitors.

If he were a betting man, he'd bet on her staying. Her ego will need to see how the evening turns out. No doubt she expects him to go down in flames, well aware that the sonata's technical challenges far outstrip his pianistic skills. Perhaps she's already composing a cutting tweet that will take credit for discovering the brilliant new composer while disavowing all responsibility for his disastrous per-formance. After all, she's primed her 70,000 Twitter followers for a personal triumph that now will never come. . . . She'll have to get out in front of it somehow. Ben's sure she'll find a way to lay the humiliation at his feet.

"You'll note in your program," Constanza Barrows is saying, "that the second half of tonight's performance was to feature Ms. Matta in the world premiere of the Benjamin Weil *French Sonata*. Now, as some of you know, the composer is proud to call Chicago home . . . and as it happens, to our very good fortune, he was able to open his schedule and be here with us tonight." She pauses for effect, a murmur filling the house. "The Maestra has graciously stepped aside so that Mr. Weil himself can perform his *French Sonata* in its world début."

Again she pauses. It's hard to gauge the invisible audience's reaction to this unexpected development. Ben imagines some of them ostentatiously leaving, muttering about a bait-and-switch, but it doesn't matter.

In a confiding tone Constanza says, "Now, I give you my word: this is the very last program change for the evening, unless Mr. Weil knows something I don't."

Constanza will find out soon enough what he knows. With a theatrical gesture she turns toward the wings.

"So! On behalf of the Pearson Center for the Performing Arts, ladies and gentlemen, it's my great pleasure to introduce the com-poser of the *French Sonata*, Mr. Benjamin Weil. Please give him a warm, hometown Chicago welcome."

IN THE MOMENTS BEFORE HE TAKES THE STAGE Ben is filled with an unaccountable calm. Though anyone would forgive him for panicking—since his student recital days he's been on stage only to give and receive awards, never to perform—he feels only the faintest concern. Even after watching Ana charge through her solo piano arrangement of Rafik Jelassi's *Arab Spring*, her mastery of the instrument more astonishing than ever, he feels no pressure from within or without.

Perhaps it's simply fatigue. After working through the night he somehow managed to sleep four hours, then ate a late breakfast and spent another energizing hour at the piano before taking a taxi down to sit with his birds in the Conservatory. Not as much sleep as he'd have liked, but enough to feel in reasonable control of body and mind. Yet the calm that's come over him feels more profound than lingering fatigue. He's not the same man he was before hearing the tale Willa Blount had to tell. Not the same man he was before hearing the voices of his ancestors in the intimate theater of his headphones. Not the same man he was before spending the long night—months, really—raising his own music upon the deep foundation laid by his great-grandfather. All this has changed him. Tonight it's stilled him.

An instant before he steps out from behind the curtain he hears Robin whisper in his ear.

"It's a good day to die," she says, and brushes his cheek with her lips.

He laughs quietly, caught off guard in the best of ways. Since their earliest days together, Crazy Horse's immortal battle cry was Ben's way of wishing her luck before taking the stage. Though it would make no sense to anyone but them, it means everything to him now. When applause begins to ripple in he walks out into the bold stage lights, freer in his heart than he's felt in years.

"THANK YOU FOR THAT KIND INTRODUCTION, CONSTANZA," he says into the microphone at the edge of the stage. His voice is clear and steady. "And thank you, Ms. Matta, for graciously allowing me to step in."

Ben nods cordially toward the wings at stage left, knowing she's long gone. His eyes have begun to adjust to the spotlights: the house is full save for a smattering of bad seats on the outskirts of the balconies and a few of the hundred-dollar box seats up front. They're not there to hear him, of course. Ana Clara Matta was the real draw. Still, few seem to have defected.

Straight ahead is the sound board, a raft moored in a sea of faces, and behind it Peter Roth, his angular features lit by a tiny task light. Ben can just make out his impish smile. When Peter flips a switch, the huge projection screen at the back of the stage begins to lower, the machinery all but silent. Ben senses the puzzled audience looking past him, trying to guess what's coming.

He says, "I know Ms. Barrows promised there would be no more program changes, but I do have one more to announce. Apologies, Constanza." As he scans the hall for her, his eyes fall upon a more familiar face, dead center in the box seats. With a nod he greets Jérôme Assouline, who's watching him with an unreadable smile. If the occupants of the box seats are any gauge, Ana's own promised luminaries are no-shows. Bono and Michelle Obama and Princess Beatrice seem to have made other plans.

"If you'll allow me, ladies and gentlemen, I'd like to make an introduction of my own."

Ben turns to the projection screen to find an enormous blowup of the photo of Jacques Garnier at the piano, hands in frenetic, blurred motion. Nikki's cropped the image to remove everything but the maestro and his instrument. Enlarged to such titanic dimensions, the portrait is breathtaking. Clicking through Nikki's slide deck on the laptop over breakfast, Ben worried that the image might be too small, but on the vast Pearson screen Jacques might as well be Lincoln seated on his marble throne.

Ben can sense the audience struggling to put a name to the face before them, trawling through remembered portraits of pianists of the black and white era. Ravel? Dvořák? Paderewski? Rachmaninov? He lets them dangle, then nods to Peter Roth. To the right of the portrait materializes Jacques Garnier's signature, lifted from the letter to Debussy. The name does nothing to dispel the mystery.

"May I present, with great pride and the deepest respect, Maestro Jacques Garnier, of Normandy, Paris, and Boston." Then: "My great-grandfather."

Several things happen at once now, like the slow-motion skid of cars on an icy country road. To his right Ben spots Constanza Barrows standing along the wall next to one of the billionaire Pearson women, he can't recall which, resplendent in a cobalt blue jacket and gold hoop earrings—Chicago royalty, hotel money, whose largesse paid for every inch of the complex where they're standing. Arms crossed, Constanza surveys her blindsided audience with a distraught look, leaning in to whisper something to her benefactor. From the balcony a fusillade of camera flashes rains down, a dozen phones pointed at the mysterious Jacques Garnier and a few, perhaps, at Benjamin Weil. In the third row of the main floor Ben sees Larry Lourenço, the *Classical Music Digest* reviewer, lean over his girth to consult with the *Tribune*'s bespectacled critic. And in the box seats below center stage, in his pinstriped black blazer and black golf shirt and blue eyeglasses, Jérôme Assouline hunches forward, the beginnings of a smile on his broad, genial face.

Ben savors the moment, wishing only that Jacques Garnier could be present in person for his grand introduction. He's present in spirit, without a doubt: Ben feels the maestro's voice inside him, the vibration of his musical intelligence. With a nod he signals Peter to advance the slide.

Nikki has put together an artful montage of the Garnier story, with photos of the Conservatoire at the turn of the century and Debussy as a student, a snippet of the letter from Jacques to him, the immigration logbook with the Garniers highlighted . . . finally the photos of the recital at the Sanborns', of Elisabeth and Jacques Garnier, Helen and Rena Sanborn, Martin Loeffler with his Van Dyke and walking stick. But the audience hasn't come to see a slide show. Ben walks briskly through the highlights of his great-grandfather's life and comes straight to the point. At his signal Nikki slips from the wings and hands him two of the Aigremont cylinders which he holds aloft for the audience, sweeping them slowly around so that all can see. On the screen behind him, beside the recital photo, huge images of them materialize, weathered silos emblazoned with Edison's face.

"Last year, somewhat by serendipity," Ben explains, "these wax recording cylinders landed on my desk." Willa's asked him not to mention her part. "They hold the audio from a private recital my great-grandfather gave in October of 1917, in Boston—a performance of a really extraordinary piece of music, as groundbreaking and visionary as anything being written at the time. Every bit as original as Debussy, Satie, Ravel, I'd argue. More so, in some ways. But you shouldn't take my word for it—I'm related to the man. Better to judge for yourselves."

A rustle goes through the orchestra section. On the screen Peter projects the first page of Ben's transcription. Every musician in the house begins to study the music, their collective concentration reaching the stage in a warm wave.

Pointing to the title at the top of the score, Ben says: "The music Jacques Garnier played that day is an elegy, a lament for the dead. He called his piece the *Élégie pour les frères perdus*, or *Elegy for the Lost Brothers*. He dedicated it to the 400,000 French lives lost at Verdun. The sonata was a cry of the heart from a Frenchman forced to watch that destruction from across an ocean. It must have been agonizing for him."

When Ben stops to gather his thoughts he has the distinct impression that the entire audience is leaning forward to listen. There isn't a whisper in the hall.

"As best we know, the sonata is all that survives of Jacques Garnier's genius. Only a few months after the recital, he went down on a steamer in the North Atlantic, torpedoed by a German U-boat. By then he was around fifty, but he'd decided to go home and join the fight. He couldn't stay away. He was a Frenchman through and through." Ben holds the cylinders high. "The sonata was his parting gift. From the moment I heard it I knew it had to be brought to light."

Ben allows himself a deep breath, looking out over the orchestra section and then up to the balconies, embracing the moment. To his right he spots Willa, sitting stolidly with a luminous smile on her face, and sends a silent *Thank you* her way.

"And now, ladies and gentlemen," he says, "it's my great honor to present to you, in its first known public début, Jacques Garnier's 1917 *Élégie pour les frères perdus*."

The audience is on high alert, aware now that something exceptional is afoot. It's just possible that history is being made. With a nod Ben signals Peter Roth and the remaining house lights are dimmed, the stage suffused with violet light. Quickly he slips back into the wings beside Nikki and Robin, leaving the stage to his great-grandfather. "Bravo," Robin mouths silently, while Nikki squeezes his arm.

There is a long interval of silence and then, without warning, the music arrives, flowing through the stupendous sound system to fill the hall. From the crackle of the old recording, lofting up like swallows, rise the airy opening notes of the sonata in wax, then the seven silent tolls of Jacques Garnier's mourning bell.

WHEN IT IS OVER, the closing fanfare fading, a grave silence descends. Ben's uncertain how to read it. But then the applause starts, a crackling from somewhere in the orchestra section that quickly spreads until the whole place is on fire. Assouline himself kicks off the standing ovation, rising from his seat and clapping with hands held high, turning to face the house as seat after seat is emptied. Fifteen hundred music lovers spring to their feet in a categorical homage to Jacques Garnier.

"Bravo!" someone calls out from the balcony, and the cry is echoed immediately and everywhere. On a cold January evening, in the course of fourteen short minutes, the lost virtuoso of Roxbury becomes indispensable.

IN THE WINGS, Ben's eyes have filled with tears. Beside him Robin's crying too, her face washed in the dusky violet of the stage lights. She's never looked lovelier than she does tonight. Nikki stands to her left, scrolling through something on her phone, her eyes bright and sharp.

Ben gazes back out into the shadowy audience and Assouline's gaze finds his. The maestro is shaking his head slowly as he claps, a question written on his face. The sonata he's just heard is the same one Ana Clara Matta played for him in Amsterdam, the same one whose score he studied late into the night, yet somehow between then and now its provenance has changed. He must be wondering, behind his tactful smile, whether he's been played for a fool. Perhaps by Ben Weil; perhaps by Ana Clara Matta, which might surprise him less. Or perhaps the explanation is subtler, less obvious. Surely he's lived long enough to be open to wonder. What he cannot know is that the Garnier sonata is only the beginning of the story.

"JESUS, LOOK AT THIS," Nikki says, handing her phone to Ben as the ovation gets a second wind. "Twitter's blowing up."

Ben hesitates to break the spell, but Nikki insists. "You *have* to look, Ben. This is amazing."

Nikki's right: her feed is boiling over with tweets, all of them about the Garnier sonata. Larry Lourenço, the *Classical Music Digest* critic in the third row, is already hailing the piece as the most important classical music discovery of his career; as Ben watches, the little heart icon throbs like the heart of a hummingbird, the number of likes climbing by threes and then fives and then tens, Twitter barely able to keep up. But within seconds Lourenço's tweet has been pushed off the screen by others, a steady stream of adulation. Distracted by the live audience so close by, Ben catches only certain words: *groundbreaking, exquisite, rewrite the history books* . . . the gist is clear enough. It's a consummate triumph for Jacques Garnier. But Ben can't linger over the phone. His tribute to the composer isn't yet complete.

"This is great," he says, and begins to hand the phone back to Nikki. But just as he's looking away he spots two faces he can't ignore. One belongs to Ana Clara Matta; the other belongs to him.

@ACMaestra has sent out a tweet of her own, attaching an old photo of the two of them posing in front of the Counterpoint Studios lobby sign, Ana Clara clutching her first Grammy in one hand and pointing to Ben with the other.

Can you spot the liar? Let me point him out for you.
#fraud #frenchsonata #benjaminweil

Another tweet follows immediately:

409

For months Ben Weil led me to believe the #frenchsonata was his own work. Now we know BY HIS OWN ADMISSION that it was all a self serving lie. #fraud #benjaminweil

Then another:

But it gets worse. He had to trick Maestro @JAssouline too. Watch the vid. #outrageous #fraud #benjaminweil

Attached to this last tweet is a video clip. With Nikki and Robin at his side and his heart in a vise Ben taps the play button, the three of them huddling to hear the audio over the applause from the auditorium. It's impossible to look away.

The video shows Assouline seated at a restaurant table with a score spread before him, his blue eyeglasses abandoned on the table in favor of an old-fashioned, rectangular magnifying glass through which he peruses the manuscript. From behind the camera Ana Clara conducts a playful interview:

— So, Maestro, here we are in Amsterdam again. What have you got there?

— It's Ben Weil's French Sonata.

— And what do you make of it?

Assouline shakes his head, as if to say that words fail him.

— What can I say? It's utterly original. It's brilliant. I was up half the night just trying to understand it, and I'm still not sure I do. Stellar work.

— Is there anything you'd like to say to the composer?

The maestro looks straight into the camera and says emphatically:

— Ben Weil, it seems to me that you're a genius of the highest order. Mazel tov.

"Fuck this," Nikki says, reaching to take her phone out of Ben's hand. "That's enough." But they all see Ana Clara Matta's final tweet:

Question: When does a liar finally tell the truth?
Answer: When he knows he's about to get caught.
#benjaminweil #frenchsonata #fraud

Just above it, the tweet with the Assouline video gets one like, then another and another.

Nikki takes her phone back and locks it. Ben closes his eyes, the violet stage lights glowing faintly through his eyelids. His heart should be racing, but he actually feels it slowing, as if he's set it adrift to live out its life alone.

"Ben?" Robin says in his ear. "None of that stuff matters. You know that. Forget her—you've done the right thing here. A very good thing. I'm proud of you."

He can feel her breath on his cheek. Her cool hand clasps his. Out in the house the ovation is finally running out of steam, the audience no doubt wondering when the house lights will come up to signal that the evening is over.

But the evening is not over. With deliberate steps Ben leaves the wings and walks back on stage, trying to clear his mind, trying to breathe. The music has only just begun.

QUIETLY Ben SWIVELS ON THE BENCH to face the Steinway's keyboard, closing his eyes, withdrawing into himself as the applause gives way to a murmuring and then a puzzled silence. Peter Roth pushes a fader up and the golden spotlight that illuminated Ana Clara Matta spills down to illuminate him, the violet lights falling back.

On the giant screen, a title appears on a field of black: THE FRENCH SONATA, BY BENJAMIN WEIL.

The concertgoers resume their seats, surprised to find that the revelation of the Garnier sonata was not the grand finale. A few of them snap furtive photos of Ben, perhaps already aware of Ana Clara Matta's online mischief, keen to capture the moment of the liar's undoing. Meanwhile Assouline sits back and knits his fingers before him, even more intrigued than before, the sonata's mystery only deepened by the title projected above the stage. But Ben notices little of it. He is fully within himself now, turned too far inward to perceive much beyond the music beginning to stream from his heart.

All is still, all is quiet. Ben curls over the keyboard and plays his great-grandfather's opening arpeggio, hands relaxed and confident despite all that's come before. Though only the most perceptive listeners would notice it, he's added a hint of syncopation to the notes, an intimation of surprises to come. After letting the first notes ring out through the hush, he thumps the stage seven times with his heel, giving solemn voice to what was voiceless before, the heartbeats of the slaughtered Fleury family pounding through his blood and into the cavernous hall.

Again his fingers touch the keys. Tacking into fair winds now, the sun inside him high and lively, Ben sails unafraid from the safe harbor of his old life. The air sparkles; the sea stretches wide before him. Gathered in their radiant, eternal parlor at Aigremont, his steady-eyed relations wish him godspeed on the journey to come. As he glides through the sonata's first suspended chord and into the opening theme Ben feels their momentum gathering behind him, an energy accumulated over a century's dormancy, the wind of the years squarely at his back. The music is singing through his body tonight just as it sang through Ana Clara Matta's on the night his life changed—a change for the better, he knows now, though it's taken him many months to realize it. With every note the pulse of inspiration quickens, the vibration hums stronger.

After tonight his world can disintegrate if it likes, his reputation and career and his private life right along with them, but not before he and Jacques Garnier have said what they need to say to one another. Ben knows exactly why he's here, on this stage, in this hall, on this slowing planet. He feels his great-grandfather's hands resting lightly atop his, guiding and being guided in turn, the years collapsing into a single, shining point of light. He's never felt less alone.

It's time to set his course for the high seas. With a sweeping turn he departs from Garnier's original melody and is caught by a current of pure jazz. Quietly he slips into a syncopated chord melody that came to him, unbidden, sometime in the midst of last night's riffing. After exploring it for a time he finds a beautiful segue into Lili's descending passage, which he plays exactly as it was written, his heart entwined faithfully with the hearts of the two long-dead composers, Garnier and Boulanger. In and out of the French sonata Ben moves, passing easily between his ancestor's music and his own. The century that separates them is no hindrance at all. Never in his life has he felt so in control of his voice, so open-hearted.

At a certain point he feels the energy in the hall begin to shift. The engineer in him is ever aware of the soundstage, and something has changed. A subtle modulation flutters on the air. But this time it's not a matter of acoustics. A question is feeling its way toward the stage.

His feet light on the brass pedals, Ben Weil smiles broadly, giving his answer with each touch of fingertip on ivory, each strike of hammer on string. He has a higher and better truth to unfold, and now is the moment. With a nudge of the tiller he steers straight into the perilous waters of the Allegro, fearing them no more, the whole wide ocean of music at his command.

coda

PLUM ISLAND
JUNE 4, 1920

OLD FRIEND, OLD FOE: on summer mornings like this one, the sea flows straight from the ruddy horizon into Elisabeth's body and finds its way to the very bottom of her lungs, soaking into her like a tide disappearing into sand. For a few minutes all is well; she absorbs the wave as it seeps down and down, the brine descending gradually, only lightly touched by gravity. For a time she's a sea creature, breathing water rather than air. She lies absolutely still in her bundle of blankets, trying not to move a muscle—because when she does move, as eventually she must, her lungs rise up to eject the brine, her ease with the sea suddenly gone, the struggle for air gripping her once more. The illusion of health evaporates, nothing but a fata morgana shimmering far out over the water.

The coughing is no better despite six months hunkered down at Plum Island. Frail as she's become, she can barely fight it anymore. In her worst moments she thinks it will shiver her bones to dust. But here, at least, there is comfort, there is balm. When the nurses have had enough of her distress they stop by with the silver syringe and send her off on another wander in her sepia wilderness, time dilating oddly, the past tinting the present like tea seeping from a teabag. The struggle to breathe will ease; on her journey she'll forget her panic, her fear of what's coming. For this, if nothing else, she's grateful for Plum Island. Grateful, too, for Rena Sanborn, who's found her a home here.

This is her life now: a blackness of sleep, a raucous cawing of gulls; a soft knock on her door in the cool of morning. The tedious washing-up, and afterward breakfast taken in bed. The practical nurse helping her dress, standing behind her chair to fasten the cameo locket around her neck with delicacy, her mother's face within, her mother with her even now, even here. They've endured such a long journey together. They've lost so much.

Then it's to the seafront porch in her maple wheelchair, the moody Swedish orderly chatty or cross, his ministrations either kind or brusque as he parks her in the usual spot and fills her glass with mineral water. She's always the first to be wheeled out, thankfully. Those few minutes alone on the porch, the sea seeping into her, are the best of the day. Once she's settled in, the Swede will fetch Albert Sharp and then Grace Cooney, both of them rich as Croesus but dying just the same. For hours the three of them will face the ocean like ancient mariners reading the waves, rarely talking, too tired for gossip or the news of the day. But they'll listen to one another closely, waiting for the next eruption of phlegm and blood, the next muttered curse word, the next rush of tears. This is the language they share. In her more lucid moments Elisabeth wonders which of them will outlast the others in the haphazard race to the finish line, which of them will prevail.

THE BREEZE CARRIES IN THE SCENT OF THE WILD ROSES that cling to the dunes just beyond the weathered fence, crimson blossoms studded among thorny canes tough as nails. The plank path down to the water is flanked by them all the way, crowding out the gentler sea plums that give the island its name, exuberant in their ambition. They are the true survivors—of salt, sand, fishermen and bathers, New England winters, everything the harsh world hurls their way.

The afternoon orderly is an Irishman with a splotchy birthmark on his temple, a cheerful disposition and a name she can't make sense of. The name doesn't matter. Whenever he wheels her down to the gazebo, he remembers without fail to snip a blossom with his pocketknife and lay it in her lap, an offering from the seashore. If he spots a sand dollar or a particularly beautiful winkle or jingle or moon shell he'll lay these in her lap too. Such small treasures, as much as any treatment offered by the Plum Island Hygienic Residence, have kept her heart alive.

When she sees Sylvie again she must be sure to bring her a wild rose.

AS SPRING HAS GIVEN WAY TO SUMMER, the place has reminded her more and more of the rugged beaches along the road from Honfleur to Villerville, the wild, sonorous crash of the ocean playing like

Beethoven just beyond the shore grasses, the broad immaculate beaches of Trouville and Deauville and Cabourg far removed from the more primitive coastline to the north. If she closes her eyes she is there again, a girl holding her papa's hand, the crooked boardwalk rough under her bare feet as they make their way down toward the surf, wobbly wooden planks giving way to a wash of warm sand into which she eagerly digs her toes. Mama is not far behind with the picnic basket and her swooping white sunhat, her boot heels making the journey down the planks a perilous one.

The beach is wonderful because it is nearly always deserted. The current is too strong for swimming, the tide too roguish. The sand is strewn with sea-wrack, of little interest to anyone but them. Here her mother feels freer to unlace her boots and hike up her skirts and splash her feet in the water, Papa to laugh and kiss her as they comb for sea glass and shells. The easy mood of these outings is with Elisabeth still, though she'd all but forgotten them until she came to Plum Island.

She can float in the ocean of memory for hours, listing gently as swells of recollection nudge at her, the struggle for air calmed by the nurse's needle. She hears Papa's snoring when he drops off to sleep with a book splayed on his chest, ankles crossed; she sees Mama's businesslike look as she spreads zinc ointment onto her daughter's cheeks. Shorebirds stalk around the three of them, fearless, hoping for scraps of sausage or baguette. Out among the breakers the gulls hover in search of schooling anchovies. The sea plays its symphony. The Norman sky opens wide. She is a girl loved by all who know her. Here on the way to Villerville, the days are long and forgiving.

On Plum Island, meanwhile, sitting by the sea, she's long since lost count of the days. Some of them seem to go on for hundreds of hours, only to be unraveled by stealthy fingers in the night.

"VISITOR, MISS GARNER," says the Swedish orderly with puzzlement. "Against the rules, but they let her in."

Until a few moments ago Elisabeth was dozing, only to be awakened by a commotion to her right: Grace Cooney, who'd coughed so hard as to be thrown from her chair. With dull interest

Elisabeth watched them rush to her, calm her and right her, the old girl bawling in distress, the head nurse berating one of the orderlies in no uncertain terms. A familiar story.

Groggily Elisabeth turns her head toward the orderly.

"What?"

"A lady. A *lady*, in a Packard Twin Six."

It takes a moment for the strangeness of it to register, her head still foggy from the morphine, but then her heart begins to race.

"Does she have a little girl with her?"

"Didn't see one," the Swede says with suspicion. "Why?"

Elisabeth closes her eyes in disappointment. Her lungs are beginning to rumble. A voice in her head tells her to sit up and prepare for her visitor, who is almost certainly Rena Sanborn. The only other lady it might be is Helen—but Helen's put down stakes in Maine now, having sold one of her grandfather's champion Arabians to buy an antiques shop in Belfast. As far as Elisabeth knows she hasn't been down to Boston since the terrible December day when she sped Sylvie off in a hired car, an unlikely angel of mercy in a mink coat and scarab brooch and plumed hat. Since then it's been the occasional letter, always bringing cheerful news of Sylvie's progress but never once a photograph.

The orderly says, "Here or inside?"

Elisabeth looks out at the sea, which turned stone-gray while she slept.

"Here, I think. Here."

With faint curiosity Elisabeth regards the sluggish waves, too weak to muster much interest in her visitor. Rena has come up several times for dutiful visits, always in connection with meetings of the Hygienic board of directors, which she chairs. Their conversations are brief and perfunctory, devoid of useful news about Sylvie. Though Rena is unfailingly kind, she has precious little to report. What Elisabeth knows is that her daughter is still in Maine at the Sanborn horse farm, growing into a happy and healthy little girl who is most likely unaware of her distant, heartbroken mother. Elisabeth's asked for photographs and Rena's promised them, but time after time her benefactor arrives emptyhanded. She has a daughter herself; doesn't she understand a mother's need to see her daughter's face?

Or perhaps there is another reason. Elisabeth hasn't forgotten the little coughs she heard from Ella Montgomery's flat on her final night in Roxbury. In her worst moments she wonders whether her daughter has died, infected by her own mother . . . perhaps this is what Rena won't reveal to her. Where *are* the photographs, if she's well and thriving as Rena claims? If Elisabeth were stronger she might confront her, but these days it's hard enough not to doze off during their visits. To try to wrest the truth from Rena Sanborn is more than she could possibly manage. Perhaps, too, she'd rather not know the truth—better to remember Sylvie as she was, to assume the best for her. A darker truth might kill her.

And so she sits and watches the sea and awaits Rena's arrival with no emotion at all. Her mind is still a blur; nowadays she's more lucid under the needle than in waking life. Despite the blanket a shiver goes through her. She's rarely without some degree of fever, her body wildly out of balance. The sun warms her face but cannot conquer the chill in her bones.

When a hand squeezes her shoulder she doesn't even flinch.

"Liz," a woman says, but it isn't Rena's voice.

Helen Sanborn circles around to face her. At the sight of the broad, flushed face Elisabeth manages a smile. An unexpected development in a place where surprises are rare and almost never good.

"Helen," she says, leaning forward as if to get to her feet then sinking back into the chair. Sometimes she forgets what's possible and what is possible no longer. "I'm glad you've come."

"You look well," her friend lies. "The sea breeze must agree with you." Helen puts her hands on her hips and takes a deep breath of the salt air, surveying the gray waves. "This place certainly has the feel of health about it, doesn't it? All this fresh air."

"But I'm dying, Helen."

Helen drops her arms to her sides and then hugs herself loosely, hazel eyes gazing down at her friend with open sorrow. There is no longer any reason to turn away from the obvious truth.

"I don't like the sound of that, dear heart," Helen says evenly, "but I suppose we've known each other long enough to speak plainly. Haven't we?"

The orderly brings a chair but Helen waves it away. "I've been wanting to come down for some time, you know." A gleam comes to her eye, renewing her. "And so has someone else. Would you terribly mind another visitor?"

And now they're in motion. The Swede appears behind the chair and begins to wheel her back into the building, Helen walking alongside. They pass the director's office and glide into the reception area, then turn into the stuffy parlor with its antique breakfront and casement windows open to the breeze. Elisabeth covers her mother's locket with her hand as if worried it might fly off. Swiveling the chair around smartly, the Swede parks Elisabeth before the window and Helen gives him a nod, sending him out the front door.

Elisabeth's body knows what's coming before her mind does. It's the quickening of her pulse that tells her. She's sitting forward in the chair, trying to catch a breath and arrange her limbs as best she can, when a fine green Packard pulls to a stop directly in front of the window, the Swede at the wheel. Through the rear window she can just make out the face of a woman. The face opens into a broad smile at the sight of her.

"Oh!" Elisabeth says as the Swede rushes around to open the woman's door, pleased to be pressed into chauffeur service with a car so grand. Helen squeezes her friend's shoulder gently. Elisabeth covers her hand. *Thank you!* she says, but the words don't reach her lips.

The woman alights carefully from the car with Sylvie asleep in her arms. Elisabeth's whole body responds to the sight of the smooth, slumbering little face, the perfect little hands, the headful of auburn hair. It's hard to believe how much she's grown. Her little girl is almost too large to be a babe in arms. Elisabeth reaches out her arms hungrily, needing to feel the weight of her, the heft of her presence in the world, and then she's out of the chair and on her feet and stumbling forward, Helen taking a huge step from behind to intercept her fall. Somehow the two friends end up on their knees side by side, the flustered Swede gusting through the door to their aid. To make matters worse, a deep, retching cough overtakes Elisabeth before she can be helped back into the chair. She falls forward onto her hands, crouching on all fours like an animal, the misery in her chest felling her yet again.

Quickly the accident is unwound. The orderly lifts her back into the chair and bundles her in her blanket. Helen dusts herself off, smooths a bunched stocking, straightens her cream-colored dress. When Elisabeth looks back at the window, the woman from the car—she must be the wife of the Sanborn caretaker—is standing just on the other side of the glass with Sylvie asleep in her arms, beautiful Sylvie, the very picture of serenity. . . .

Elisabeth beckons to the woman to invite her inside, but she only gives a sad smile and shakes her head.

"No!" Elisabeth cries out, the shape of things suddenly clear.

"Liz," Helen says from a slight remove. Once again the world draws back, her friend keeping her distance, her daughter behind glass. "We can't. We just can't. For Sylvie's sake. I shouldn't be here myself. But of course I had to come. Wanted to come."

It's torture. There is no other word for it.

"Take me to *her*," Elisabeth pleads, "if she's not allowed inside. *Je t'en prie!*"

With a nervous look the Swede consults the home's director, Mr. Cullen, who's rushed from his office donning a surgeon's mask. Cullen shakes his bald head. "This is how it has to be, Miss Garner," he explains. "I'm very sorry. It's irregular enough for Miss Sanborn to be inside, much less your little girl."

If only Sylvie would awaken. To gaze into her eyes would mean everything. Elisabeth concentrates all her energy into the wish, and almost at once it's granted. With a wriggle her daughter opens her blue eyes and the first thing she sees—Elisabeth is certain of it—is her mother. The caretaker's wife bounces her charge gently until she breaks into a laugh and blows a bubble from her little lips, never taking her eyes from the woman watching so intently from the other side of the glass, the woman whose florid cheeks glisten with tears of joy and sorrow.

Back on the porch overlooking the miserable sea, Helen sits holding her friend's hand as the shot goes in. In a matter of five heartbeats the world is changed. Down through Elisabeth's over-excited limbs spread the warmth, the ease, the blessed raddlement. Though the cough has faded they've decided that this course is best. In the head nurse's judgment, the brief glimpse of Sylvie has left her patient in a state of pernicious hysteria which cannot be allowed to spread to the other residents.

Elisabeth closes her eyes, as much to shut out the sea as to sink into her sepia world. Someone is stroking her hand, fingertips brushing her skin with a woman's touch, then the hand moves to cover her forehead as gently as a fallen leaf. *I remember that beautiful locket,* the woman says, *from the first day I met you.* Elisabeth wants to smile, and perhaps she does. She remembers: the woman beside her is Helen. *It's yours,* Elisabeth replies. *When I go.*

In time Helen speaks to someone else. A male voice responds and in a fleeting quiver of the heart Elisabeth knows it's Charlie Westerlake, but no, now it's Papa, and now the Swede . . . and then it's no one she knows. From the direction of the voice comes the sound of something heavy being settled on a tabletop, adjusted. Then a creak, a hinge in need of oil, and she knows without looking that it's the sound of her father raising the squeaky piano lid in the Paris apartment, a snowstorm blowing hard outside the leaking windows, the scent of cooking and the coal furnace on the air. Her father's hands cover hers which in turn cover the ivory keys, her papa guiding her patiently through the *Clair de lune,* working from Monsieur Debussy's hand copy of the score. She takes the melody part; Papa's big left hand picks out the accompaniment. Together they bring the new music to life.

A seagull caws sharply, far too close for comfort. Elisabeth drifts leftward in a warm tide, lolling away from the harsh noise, and feels the locket with her mother's tiny portrait slide from her throat down to her collarbone, the hair-thin gold chain shifting against her warm skin, her mother forever with her, forever close. With numb fingertips she finds it, touches it, and then a more intimate music arrives, the salt air in her nostrils, the sun on her forehead. Unforgettable: her papa playing his sonata for her by the sea, the sound of his piano made brittle by the years until she cures it in her heart, as only she can do.

Papa, she whispers to the wide world, a smile ghosting her lips.

Papa

END MATTER

Acknowledgments

End Note: Fact and Fiction

Detecting the Sanborns and the Composer

About the Author

Book Club Questions

Acknowledgments

I'm happily indebted to numerous friends, mentors, and colleagues for making this book what it is. Two good and generous souls deserve particular thanks, because their contributions were extraordinary.

The Winchester storyline of *Sonata in Wax* is based in part on family lore and my recollections of certain real-life Sanborns. These dubious sources were tempered by archival research in which I was tirelessly assisted by Dr. Ellen Knight, an authority on all things Winchester. I bent her diligent research to my novelistic purposes in countless ways, which I fear must have pained her as a professional historian. Her forbearance and good humor are truly world-class.

I discovered somewhere along the way that Dr. Knight is also an authority on the violinist Martin Loeffler, Jacques Garnier's best friend in America. She is directly responsible for Loeffler's presence at the feast. To have found a Winchester expert and an expert on the early-twentieth-century Boston music scene united in one human being was as priceless as it was unlikely. In this and so many other ways her contributions are woven deeply into the book.

The other friend I wish to call out for special thanks is Charles Haverty. Charlie and I published our first books together, as recipients of twin Iowa fiction awards. Once the initial writing was done, I asked Charlie to give me his honest feedback, thinking we might have a good long telephone call about the book. Instead I received eight single-spaced pages of the most incisive notes I've ever received on a work of fiction. Later I found out that Charlie had filled an entire notebook with thoughts as he read the manuscript. This was so above and beyond the call of duty that there are no words to do it justice. The book is stronger, in countless ways, for Charlie's unstinting candor and impeccable judgment.

In addition to these two incomparable collaborators, I'd like to acknowledge the varied contributions of many others.

In the pole position is surely my mother, Mary Hamlin, who shared her rich memories of the Sanborns, particularly of Helen— her redoubtable and ever-solicitous mother-in-law. Her recollections are part of the lifeblood of the book.

There were the early readers of the manuscript: Paula Hamlin, Lisa Roberts, Julie Goldstein, James Graff, Elizabeth Anderson, James Filkins, Steve Reinthal, Erin Keogh, Claudia Hinz, Nancy Allen, Kaki Kohnke, William Hawkins, Jesse Eichenbaum, Wendy Gladstein, Phoebe Zerwick, Karen Frankel, Tom Roll, Margaret Strumpf, Brendan Neil Casey, Natalia Kazaryan, Ben Fountain, Dominic Smith, Paul Cohen, Erika Krouse, Steven Schwartz, Rachel Swearingen, and Jane Harper.

Others offered non-literary supports: Jenny and David Rea, for providing the cozy little barn space where the book's first pages were written; Dave and Holly Megay for providing an evacuee a safe space to work during the Calwood Fire; Natalia Kazaryan for keeping Lili Boulanger's music alive; Christophe Eklouh-Molinier, for lending a native speaker's polish to the book's French dialog (not to mention helping the author discover the Garnier sonata's true name); Yanis and Nathalie Sèbe for additional French assistance; Anna Frick, for lending her expertise as both mastering engineer and audio restorer; Isaac Peterson, Jane Hunt, Karen Yost, Paula Hamlin, Mary Hamlin, Adam Dooley, and Amy Campion for collaborating on the jacket design; Marion Kreith, for making me aware of the Jewish diaspora in Havana; and Angela McNaughton, for the incomparable gift of Maestro Assouline's electric blue glasses.

My editor, Joseph Olshan, deserves the sincerest thanks for believing in the book and giving it a loving home, as do Jessica

Hammerman and Isaac Peterson of Green City Books. You have all been wonderful to work with.

My agent, Deborah Schneider, has the stamina of an ultra-marathoner and the flinty honesty of a true friend; I can't thank her enough for her efforts, with this book and others. She is my literary rock.

Finally, it gives me the best sort of pleasure to thank my wife, Paula Hamlin, for her two decades of encouragement and support.

I'd have loved it if my father, Stirling Sanborn Hamlin, had lived to share his memories of his mother Helen and his grandparents Oren and Rena, but it was not to be. Instead I'd like to dedicate this book, in loving gratitude, to his memory.

ENDNOTE:
FACT AND FICTION

SONATA IN WAX IS A WORK OF FICTION—full stop, as Ana Clara Matta would say. But some of its denizens—I mostly mean the Sanborns, of whom I am the last living descendant—were inspired by men and women who once walked the streets of Winchester and Chicago.

For those who want to dig deeper into the historical record, I'd point you to the Winchester Historical Society (winchesterhistoricalsociety.org) and the archives of the Town of Winchester. Aigremont, the Sanborns' home, has been lovingly restored by the Society and may be visited by contacting them. Since Aigremont passed from my family two generations ago, I will be forever grateful to the Historical Society for saving it from the wrecking ball.

It should be said that while the house never served as an overflow ward for the hospital, Rena Sanborn did deliver soup to the hospital during the influenza epidemic and was one of the hospital's founding boardmembers.

Now to the ghosts.

Helen Sanborn was my grandmother; my memories of her are few and vague. I knew her when I was very young and I'm told we were quite fond of one another. She was a confident, resourceful woman who found ways to land on her feet, time and again, as the family fortunes waned.

The Helen Sanborn depicted in *Sonata in Wax*, on the other hand, is entirely my creature, and her youthful foibles are of my own making. She did not marry an H. E. Rollins, for one thing, though the real Helen did marry someone a bit like him. She did not suffer a disastrous miscarriage in a hotel bathroom, nor did she take a bright young Frenchwoman under her wing. Almost none of Helen's adventures in the novel track with the real Helen's.

The through line from the real Oren and Rena Sanborn to their novelistic versions is even more tenuous—necessarily so, as they are further removed in time. They are surely more fictional than real. As for Helen's little brother Caleb, I did know his widow, Edna Hagen, and have wonderful memories of picking wild blueberries with her very elderly mother, Granny Hatch, near the family farm in Belfast, Maine. Well north of ninety, Granny Hatch was still a prodigious puzzle-solver and rat-drowner, stoic as any Maine farmer of her generation.

As a final confession, I've engaged in both heavy pruning and creative grafting with regard to the family tree. The branch occupied by my father, Stirling "Skip" Hamlin, is occupied in the novel by the fictional Willa Blount, because Skip's story deserves a book of its own. Helen did, however, open an antique store in the financially fraught interval between her divorce from my grandfather and her marriage to Edward Merrit Hamlin, my namesake. Since the fictional Willa is childless, I myself am nowhere to be found in this novel—the author's shameless prerogative. QED.

DETECTING THE SANBORNS
AND THE COMPOSER

HISTORIANS ARE DETECTIVES, tracking down clues, discovering facts, and piecing together stories of a life, a family, community, structure, incident, event, movement, or an era. Some mysteries remain unsolved, but there is usually a reward for all the research, including an understanding of how things came to be. History isn't just about facts. It's about lives and everything about life as it was in the past. But it is not just about what is past, over and gone. History is the early chapters of present stories.

The detectives may simply pass on their research. Or, like novelists, they may themselves become the storytellers. Either way, history allows portraits from our past to emerge and take on life again in mind and imagination. So it has been with the Sanborns. Oren was not simply a person who ordered the Sanborn House built. As the son of a businessman, he had a position in his father's company. But after James Solomon Sanborn died, he spent his inheritance as if there were no end to it. He spent it on the latest and fastest automobiles, yachts, and a mansion set on a hill proclaiming his status. He spent it on enjoying life. His friends in Winchester were some of the leading men in the town, whom he joined on fishing trips, invited to his pool parlor, or hosted at his family's horse farm in Maine. Then, he almost disappeared from public view. He and his wife separated. Why? A mystery. Where did he go? For a time he lived with his sister in the family home in Somerville. Following her death, he was supported by his son James who had a trust fund from his grandfather. Then he faded away more obscurely in Rhode Island where he died from cancer.

Rena was the youngest daughter of a farmer in Maine. She moved to Massachusetts to live with a married sister in Reading.

Sisters were then commonly the solution for domestic help in families unable to hire. How did Oren and Rena meet? Unclear. They married when he was twenty and she possibly just 16 (her age is another mystery created by different dates in different documents). A bitter daughter-in-law said Rena had been a servant in the James Solomon Sanborn home. Not impossible, but unsupported by any evidence. Another possibility is that they were introduced by Rena's brother Ellery, who joined the Chase & Sanborn company in 1885, the year before the Sanborns' wedding. But, though there is evidence of a friendship between Ellery and Oren, a definitive answer is still illusive.

What was their married life really like? The two were so unalike. Rena Sanborn was a generous woman, a tireless worker for charities. She marched for women's suffrage and delivered broth to needy families during the Spanish Influenza epidemic. Her favorite cause was Winchester Hospital, built and originally managed by the women of the Visiting Nurse Association. Rena chaired the building committee. She organized annual Pop Concerts in Town Hall to raise money and held annual fund-raising events at her home, Aigremont, ranging from dance spectacles to fashion shows and finally to horse shows. It was she who first made the house part of community life.

Oren kept her in ignorance about their finances. Suddenly, left in debt by his improvidence, he sold their home. Rena had to go to court to appeal for support, where Oren admitted he had spent it all (and more). Rena survived because Helen also had a trust fund and, for most of the rest of Rena's life, was inseparable from her mother. Happy in her second marriage, Helen joined her mother in carrying on charitable work in Boston.

Why did Helen's first marriage fail? Still a mystery. The novelist has manufactured one answer, not quite factual, but historical fiction is, after all, fiction. The story plays out according to the novelist's will and inspiration. But when some of the characters are based on real people, history helps to dress invention in the appropriate style.

The role of an historical advisor may be confined to furnishing and checking facts. In the case of *Sonata in Wax*, it led to the introduction of a new character, Charles Martin Loeffler. It just so happened that the novelist's advisor on Winchester history was also a specialist in Boston music history at the turn of the 20th century, specifically the life of Charles Martin Loeffler. A member of the Boston Symphony Orchestra with a cosmopolitan European background, Loeffler was a Francophile who promoted French music in Boston and was the go-to person for French musicians looking for opportunities in America. The novelist's work of fiction included a French-American pianist. The advisor had written the first (and only) full-length book biography of Loeffler. The novelist purchased a copy. A new character was created who easily fit into the Garnier history, for had Jacques Garnier been real, he surely would have known Loeffler and they might well have become friends. It was a delightful surprise to read the revised draft.

Loeffler was a real man of mystery when I first became acquainted with him. There were some encyclopedia and journal articles, but they were incomplete and they were all wrong about at least one part of his life. Loeffler, who hated the Prussian government, blaming it for his father's death, had bamboozled everyone in America into believing that he had been born in Alsace, suggesting he was part French. He was, in reality, entirely German, born outside Berlin. But the facts excuse the obfuscation. Events of his youth formed his Weltanschauung. But whatever his inner grief, he was outwardly charming (as shown by the novelist), as well as a brilliant violinist. He was strongly attracted to French Decadence, Symbolism, and Impressionism, whose musical forms he introduced to Boston. However, he was interested in all music, even defying Bostonian reserve and going mad over jazz. As a composer, he was innovative. A New York critic, noting that hardly a season went by without a Loeffler composition on BSO programs, wrote that "there is even a mild Loeffler cult in Boston." His professional accomplishments were admired, as was his gentlemanly demeanor with old-world manners. There were, of course, other sides to this complex person. One who knew him said he did not suffer fools gladly. His friendship with Garnier speaks well of Elisabeth's beloved father.

Did Loeffler ever visit the Sanborn House? Not as far as is known, but the fictional concert is completely credible. Rena hosted musical events there. The family owned a baby grand and an upright piano. Arthur Fiedler played their piano in the music room. Rena's niece Charlotte Armstrong was a professional violinist who counted Loeffler among her teachers. He would have been a welcome guest at Aigremont. Fact and fiction blended well here.

Ellen Knight Ph.D.
Independent historian, author of *Charles Martin*
Loeffler: A Life Apart in American Music

ABOUT THE AUTHOR

EDWARD HAMLIN'S STORY COLLECTION *Night in Erg Chebbi and Other Stories* was selected by Pulitzer Prize finalist Karen Russell as winner of the 2015 Iowa Short Fiction Award and went on to win the Colorado Book Award. Over the past few years Edward's work has won the Nelson Algren Award, the Nelligan Prize, the NCW Short Story Prize, and a Top of the Mountain Novel Prize.

Book Club Questions:
Sonata in Wax

1. Much of the plot turns on Ben's lie of omission concerning the provenance of the French Sonata.

   Why is it so important to Ben that he set the record straight?

   Who would be harmed if he didn't?

   Are the potential negative consequences of telling the truth proportional to the harm caused by the lie?

   How does Ben ultimately resolve his guilt over allowing the lie to stand?

2. By the time we reach the end of the story, there are two "French Sonatas"—one composed by Jacques Garnier, the other by Benjamin Weil.

   Do you think Ben realized he was composing a sonata of his own as he delved into Garnier's work?

   Is there a connection between Ben's lie and the creation of the new sonata? What is it?

3. What role(s) does Willa Blount play in Ben's life?

4. The book is mostly fiction, but the Sanborns were a real family.

   How does the author balance historical fact with fiction? Does he succeed?

   Does it add anything to the story to know that the Sanborns were a real family, and that the author is their last living descendant?

   What challenging decisions do you think the author might have faced in writing about his long-dead ancestors?

5. The novel follows two timelines set a century apart. We experience the historical timeline mostly through the eyes of young Elisabeth Garner; we experience the contemporary timeline through Ben Weil.

   Were you drawn to one of the timelines more than the other? Why?

   Did you feel more affinity with Ben or Elisabeth, or were you equally engaged with both of them? If you connected more with Ben or Elisabeth, why?

   Did you find it interesting to see part of the story through eyes of a woman and part through the eyes of a man?

6. The novel contains many descriptions of the power of music to evoke powerful emotion.

   Did the book remind you of moments in your own life when you were deeply moved by music? What was the music?

   Could you "hear" the Garnier sonata in your head? Were some parts easier to "hear" than others?

7. In the course of the novel we learn about two of Ben's lovers, his ex-wife Robin and Ana Clara Matta. Both are superb musicians, but they are very different people. Robin leaves Ben for a café owner, Alan Hurwitz, who is not in the music world at all, and is different from her in nearly every way.

   What does Ben see in Ana? Ana in Ben?

   Why would Robin leave Ben for Alan?

   If you could see past the last page of the book, what do you think will become of Ben and Robin?

8. How would the story have been different without the Nikki character?

9. The origin of the Garnier sonata emerges slowly, through a mosaic of pieced-together information, as does Ben's ancestral connection to it. Did you see any of the key revelations coming before they appeared in the text? Did the author drop any clues along the way?

10. Elisabeth experiences many losses in her life. Which was the most painful for you to experience with her?

www.ingramcontent.com/pod-product-compliance
Lightning Source LLC
Chambersburg PA
CBHW030545020726
47494CB00005B/1486